CONTEMPORARY
ODIA SHORT STORIES
A BLACK EAGLE BOOKS ANTHOLOGY

CONTEMPORARY
ODIA SHORT STORIES

A BLACK EAGLE BOOKS ANTHOLOGY

Edited by
Dr. Manoranjan Mishra

BLACK EAGLE BOOKS
2020

BLACK EAGLE BOOKS

USA address:
7464 Wisdom Lane
Dublin, OH 43016

India address:
E/312, Trident Galaxy, Kalinga Nagar,
Bhubaneswar-751003, Odisha, India

E-mail: info@blackeaglebooks.org
Website: www.blackeaglebooks.org

First International Edition published by
BLACK EAGLE BOOKS, 2020

CONTEMPORARY ODIA SHORT STORIES
A BLACK EAGLE BOOKS ANTHOLOGY
by **Eminent Writers**

Edited by
Dr. Manoranjan Mishra

Cover & Interior Design: Ezy's Publication

ISBN- 978-1-64560-072-5 (Paperback)
Library of Congress Control Number: 2020936746

Printed in United States of America

We are thankful to
Ohio Arts Council
for their generous support
towards this project

To
All writers of the Odia short story
who have kept the tradition alive

Contents

Foreword

Fakir Mohan Senapati laid the foundation of Odia short stories with the publication of 'Rebati' in 1898, about a hundred and twenty two years ago. Ever since, the genre has evolved much. He wrote about twenty short stories between 1898 and 1916. Critics have accepted this phase as the first phase of Odia story writing. Some contemporaries of Fakir Mohan who rose to prominence during that period are Chandra Sekhar Nanda, Dayanidhi Mishra, Dibyasingha Panigrahi and Laxmikanta Mohapatra. The writers raised a voice of protest against the blind beliefs prevalent in the society. Compassion for the poor and the exploited, voice of protest against the exploiters, love and romance in the lives of the common people, real life incidents and the writer's own reaction to those were the subject matters of the stories written during that period.

The period between 1910 and 1947 is known as the second phase in the life of Odia short stories. This was the period when realism, progressive thoughts, Gandhian ideals, Marxism, the freedom struggle etc. had their impacts. The story writers were guided by an instinct to reform the society, serve people and help in promotion of nationalistic feelings. The conflict between the capitalists and the bourgeois class was represented, with the story writers showing compassion for those who suffered. They also raised fingers at social evils and economic disparity. Gadhian thoughts and socialism had their say too. During this period, the writers who made remarkable contributions to the field are Godabarisha Mishra, Godabarisha Mohapatra, Kalandi Charan Panigrahi, Baikunthanath Pattanaik, Bhagabati Charan Panigrahi, Sachidananda Routray etc.

The period between 1947 and 1960 is known as the next phase. The much awaited independence not only impacted the social life but also the economic and political life of the people. The zamindari system was abolished. Education reached the masses. Accumulation of money and power became the two guiding principles of politics. The number of middle class people increased, resulting in large scale unemployment. People flocked cities that were raising their heads but they had to encounter various troubles there. Struggle of the individual gained superiority over the class-struggle. The devastated economy and collapse of morality crippled the nation. Joint family system broke down. Women received education, gained employment, and started demanding equal rights. Morality, spirituality, tradition, conservative attitude—all these went for a toss. As a result, feelings of disappointment and helplessness took over. Existentialism also impacted Odia stories. The stories written during this period reflect all these elements. The writers who contributed immensely during this period are Rajkishore Ray, Rajkishore Patnaik, Pranabandhu Kar, Bama Charan Mitra etc.

After the 1960s, writers started delving deep into the subconscious state of mind and analyzing it minutely. Besides, a period of 'quest' or 'search for knowledge' ensued. The writers were more serious about their quest into life, world, death, sorrow and suffering. This was a phase when the conservative mindset was set aside. This apart, many movements like 'Humanism,' 'Socialism,' 'Existentialism,' 'Symbolism' etc. took the writers into their grips. 'Sex' which was hitherto a concept to be discussed in bedrooms, came to be discussed openly. This gave a serious jolt to the conservative mindset. Imagination came to be replaced by real life experiences. With the world shrinking into a global village, how could Odia short story writers remain unaffected by changes taking place in other parts of the world?

The present anthology has thirty-one Odia stories translated into English. Each story gives a new taste in so far as treatment of the subject matter and style are concerned. We have past masters who have carved a niche for themselves. More than half of our writers have been conferred on either the Odisha Sahitya Akademi award or the Central Sahitya Akademi award or both. We also have new talents who are venturing to touch the sky.

The writers who gained prominence during the period from 1960 to 1980 and whose translated stories have been included here are Achyutananda Pati, Santanu Kumar Acharya, Manoj Das, Binapani Mohanty, Ramachandra Behera, Padmaja Paul, Satya Misra, Yashodhara Mishra, Bibhuti Pattanaik, Debraj Lenka, Banaj Devi, Radha Binod Nayak, and Archana Nayak. The writers who shot to prominence during 1980 to 1990 are Dash Benhur, Tarunkanti Mishra, Prativa Ray, Hrusikesh Panda, Paresh Patnaik, Manoj Panda, and Bibhuti Bhusan Pradhan. Similarly, the writers who reigned the world of Odia stories during 1990 are Gourahari Das, Gayatri Saraf, Dipti Ranjan Patnaik, Supriya Panda, and Paramita Satapathy. The emerging talents whose stories have been included in the anthology are Adyasha Das, Kshetrabasi Naik, Manas Panda, Rabinarayan Dash, Sreekanta Kumar Barik, and Ranjan Pradhan.

This anthology is a product of the laudable efforts of Satya Pattanaik and his Black Eagle Books to propagate Odia literature and present a bouquet of stories in translated from both to the Odia readers residing in different parts of the globe as well as to the global readers interested in Odia literature. It's true that all great writers of the past and all great works have not been given space in this anthology. But, it's also true that we have just made a beginning. We dream of undertaking many such ventures in the days to come. For the dreams to turn into reality, cooperation of writers, copyright holders, as well as translators is highly solicited.

Let's undertake a short journey through the stories we have selected for you.

Achyutananda Pati's Tale of an Ominous Son has an impatient, insistent, and rebellious owl fledgling as the protagonist. Disregarding his mother's advice, 'We must live in darkness. Otherwise, we'll perish,' he dreams of a world where light reigns. He is not ready to accept that he is the member of an ominous species and a curse on the world. He is always ready to challenge the children of light who hang around the realm of light to victimize them. He wages a war against them. Before death he tells his mother never to feel ashamed of his death but rather inform his siblings that he became a 'martyr fighting valiantly to win the kingdom of light.'

Santanu Acharya's The Living God deals with the mysterious disappearance of a five-year-old Miskun, who along with his parents and uncle is on a tour of some heritage sites in Bhubaneswar. After touring through Kedargouri, Mukteswar, Rajarani, Lingaraj temples and the State Archaeological Museum they decide to have lunch at Hotel Kalinga Ashok. It is from here that Miskun suddenly disappears. A frantic search ensues. Seema, Miskun's mother, wails out the names of gods and goddesses to help her trace out her son. This invocation works. Moments later, Miskun is discovered sitting in a lotus posture behind a Buddha sculpture. He is found saying, "I'm not a dead god! No, you can't sell me—you can't sell me!" The entire incident remains shrouded in mystery.

The world might teach us a lesson in 'helplessness' anytime; we should never make fun of others' helplessness. With his characteristic touch of humour, **Manoj Das** in **Night in the Life of the Mayor** describes how Mayor Divyasimha learns the lesson the hard way. The Mayor comes to the riverbank one evening to enjoy the cool and quiet moments of sunset. It is then that he is infused with the desire to 'plunge his bathroom conditioned body into the free transparent flow' of the river. He takes off his clothes except the underwear and dashes into the water. Just when he comes out of the water, under the cover of darkness, he marks an apparition swaying between the water and the embankment. It is a cow, known for its notoriety. It had munched away his shirt and part of the trousers. The mayor remains inside water. On the other hand, his long absence necessitates searches by his colleagues, police and family members. Every time people come close to him, he moves deeper into water, ashamed to expose himself. He floats downstream in the current of water and reaches a boat. The next morning, he is helped by a fisherman and his daughter, who help him with clothes. He returns to the town but not without learning a lesson.

Binapani Mohanty's **Patadei** is a strong slap on the faces of the representatives of the patriarchal society who leave no stones unturned to scandalize women. All fingers are raised on Patadei when she returns from her in-laws house a few months after marriage. Everybody gets an opportunity to cast aspersions on her. When she disappears suddenly on the Dola Purnima night, tongues wag again. When she returns years later, with a child in her arms, how can the villagers lose a God-given opportunity to victimize a woman? The truth is finally revealed. Her husband had left her for another woman only a few days after marriage. On the night of Dola Purnima, she was brutally raped by some young men of the village. Haria Bauri, a villager, bribed by the culprits, had dropped her at Cuttack the next day. The revelation forces her accusers to hang their heads in shame.

'Just as a society has no respect for an honest man if he has no money, a family never ever cares for one who did not earn.' Freedom fighter Naran Das in **Bibhuti Pattanaik**'s **A Pair of Parallel Lines** realizes this towards the fag end of his life. Naran Das and his son Sanatan were like parallel lines; they lived under the same roof but there was hardly anything common between them. A morally upright person, Das, never took advantage of his role in the freedom struggle for materialistic or other gains after independence. On the other hand, his son became a misguided young man with a penchant for easy money. He took to boozing. He wanted to use his father for personal gains. The chasm between Das and his family members increased as he 'had never learned the act of bartering his selfless sacrifice of the past for personal comforts on the present.'

The Music of Life by **Debraj Lenka** is a pathetic account of a father, who loses his only son in a freak accident. The dreams of the poor but hardworking father are shattered. Raghu Pradhan's master owned vast tracts of land. Raghu was in charge of tilling, harvesting, and storing the grain. Besides, he weighed the paddy, carried it to the sellers in the city and collected cash from them. Despite his hard work, he got a pittance. Although the store houses were overflowing with grain, Raghu hardly had enough to feed his family. Only when his son grew up and worked with him, they would have plenty of food to eat. Just when he was lost in such a dream, his son fell off the cart, rolled under it, and was dragged under its wooden wheels. Moments later, he died. In order to avoid harassment by police, he disposed off the body into a river. He had to return home, cursing his fate.

'Your wooden son (Lord Jagannath) is great. If you surrender to him, he doesn't give you prosperity. But, he guards you diligently in the path of love and compassion.' Chandu, a constable, learns this lesson while performing his duty in **Banaj Devi's The Wooden Son**. The heart of Chandu is filled with intense grief and compassion the moment he gets an order to carry out an evacuation. On the eve of the evacuation, he proceeds to the slum intending to convince people to vacate in time and prevent bloodshed. He is misunderstood. He returns on being pushed around by the slum dwellers. However, the condition of some of the slum dwellers moves him a lot. During the evacuation process, when the bulldozers roar on over the helpless shrieks and cries, leaving behind rubble of bricks, torn tarpaulins, and broken bamboo, Chandu drags two women out of their sacks and saves their lives. He also shields a pregnant woman from being lath charged. Chandu is badly bruised in the process; he could even lose his job on charges of non-performance of duty. But, he is found beaming with a strange satisfaction as his wooden son had guided him in the right path.

Bidhan Sir, the protagonist of **Pratibha Ray**'s **Adoration**, worshipped sandals of his uncle, much like Bharat of *The Ramayan*. When many an eyebrow was raised, he explained that he did so not only as a mark of respect and adoration for what his uncle had done for him but also as a penance for having forgotten to buy a pair of sandals for uncle at the right time. As Bidhan's father was very strict, Bidhan grew closer to his uncle. His uncle loved Bidhan more than he loved his own son. During the scholarship examination in class seven, uncle would carry him on his shoulders for about a month, growing blisters on his feet. When Bidhan stayed in the hostel for his higher studies, his uncle would carry rice, ghee, jaggery, coconut from the village. On his deathbed, Bidhan's uncle wished to have a pair of sandals. Bidhan suddenly remembered that he had forgotten to bring him a pair although he had promised him earlier. When he finally bought him a pair, uncle became so elated that he didn't take them off till he died. After his death, Bidhan carried the sandals home as a relic and worshipped them as a fond remembrance.

The Torn Edge of the Saree by **Archana Nayak** is a tale of guilt, remorse and repentance. Surama, a housewife and successful literary personality, goes to attend a felicitation ceremony, leaving behind Bilu, her pet dog on his deathbed. She had brought Bilu home when he was only ten days old. She had faced a great deal of difficulty in taking care of such a small dog. However, with the passage of time, her love for the dog had grown. Even though she was present at the felicitation ceremony, her mind was constantly diverted towards Bilu and his condition. It was as if Bilu was asking him, "Maa, you left me and went away. Didn't you realize that I was not going to live any longer? What was so important that you left me in this condition and went away?" By the time she came back, Bilu had already died. Towards the end, he had been frequently looking for Surama. He died when the domestic help brought a saree and covered him with its ends. Surama is filled with a sense of guilt and regret for having abandoned a dying animal for a mere literary award.

Temporary Address by **Ramachandra Behera** is about a poor, helpless father whose nine year old daughter, Jolly goes suddenly missing and remains untraceable. Jolly, one afternoon, was sent to buy some grocery but disappeared mysteriously. Sambhu brought the matter to knowledge of Shantanu, a local leader, who promised to help. The police officers, on being informed, conducted enquiry but it remained inconclusive. After a few days, the bag and bottles of Jolly are recovered from a bridge about a kilometer away but there is no trace of Jolly. 'The incident that had created a ripple and moments of excitement, was forgotten like other such incidents. The daughter remained mysteriously missing and untraceable.'

The narrator in **Radha Binod Nayak's Village During Winter** had lived peacefully in the city for twenty years, snapping all his ties with his village, where he was born. One evening, a person named Panunath visits him. After prolonged conversation with the narrator, he invites him to visit his village, which he had left after the death of his mother. The next day, the narrator takes a bus and reaches his village in the evening. Panunath informs him many of the former people had passed away. The old patriarch of the Sahu family was counting days. The narrator meets his father and other members of his family after long. Later, he visits the Sahu family. The pathetic condition of the old patriarch moves him deeply.

Giridhari in **Padmaja Paul's Witness** attends a court session as a witness in a murder case. He requests the judge to fix another date for the hearing. He had come to the court for the first time and was feeling nervous in the presence of so many lawyers. Back home, when his wife asks for an explanation for his conduct, he reveals that a couple of days back some hooligans had surrounded him and warned him not to be a witness. They had also warned him of dire consequences if he participated. When Giridhari's wife learns that he had refused to depose owing to fear, she flies into a rage. She accuses him of not thinking about virtue and deserting a person whose son was brutally murdered in broad daylight. She condemns her husband for giving in to fear and wavering from truth. She bangs her hands on the floor, breaking all her bangles. Giridhari is left stunned.

The journey of life is to be completed somehow; it can't be abandoned midway simply because nobody agrees to accompany us further or because the pathway seems too difficult to tread on. Manju in **Tarunkanti Mishra's The Pathway** lives with her ailing grandfather. 'She couldn't possible remember the face of her mother or father; she didn't know whether the paralytic man lying in the next room would be alive tomorrow. There was no knowing if she would continue in her temporary job next month.' Though her life is beset with troubles, she is hardly ready to surrender and succumb. She is ready to put up a fight, face the situation as it comes, undeterred. When her friend Jajati, who visited her at times, informs her that he would not be able to meet her for an indefinite period, she doesn't lose her cool or become nervous. 'She could see how lonely she was and realize how complete she was in her aloneness.'

The Picture Within by **Yashodhara Mishra** presents Amita, the only lady doctor in a small hospital. The people of the small town and the nearby tribal villages who come to the hospital carry their aspects of life, personal problems in addition to their illness. Once a tribal couple visits her for an abortion. The husband claims that he had already undergone an operation and hence he could never father the child. His wife claimed that his operation had probably failed. The husband wanted the pregnancy to be aborted whereas the woman accused him that he wanted to kill her in the name of abortion. Finally, when the woman gets ready for the abortion, the husband pleads the doctor not to go ahead saying, 'Let the child live. Let it be born. I forgive her this time.' The man was proud that he was the master of the house, and hence, he should overlook a few mistakes of the woman once in a while.

The protagonist of **The Avenger** by **Satya Misra** is a female cat, who tries to express the agony of her heart, as a tomcat had devoured all three of her little kittens. All she needed was an audience and some compassion. The owner of the house where she lived and his children do not give her a decent hearing although her heart bleeds with unspoken agony. She wants to narrate her agony to the tomcat thinking that he would understand what villainy he had perpetrated, but he only says 'Oh!' and goes away, pretending as if he is not the culprit. Just then, she finds a cute mouse and starts narrating it her pathetic experience. Slowly, she pierces the soft body of the mouse with her talons, tears it apart, and pulls the innards out just as the tomcat had done with her children. She finally avenges their death.

For Gayatri, the protagonist of **Dash Benhur's Keeping Words Company**, words were troublesome. 'Their constant badgering had turned into a form of persecution'. Life, for Gayatri had been a torment. A textile engineer by qualification, Gayatri falls in love with Sunand, a journalist-poet with an MA degree in Odia. Both of them separate when one day, suddenly Sunand decides to withdraw his hand. With necessary support not coming from Sunand's family, Gayatri returns to her father. She starts a brand of T-shirts christened 'Black One'. Each t-shirt was to be hand woven. The front was to be embroidered—some in Sambalpuri designs and some others in Pipili appliqué work. On the back of each a traditional Odia song or proverb or couplet was to be printed. The lines come to her in dream but those were lines written for her by her poet-husband Sunand. After a chance-meeting with Sunand, Gayatri found "Words had been pursuing her like swarms of insects drawing blood, tugging at her clothes, surrounding her on all sides. Some stroked her lovingly; others pricked her with needles.' Gayatri decided not to consider words her enemies but let them be what they are.

The Story of the Gypsy Fish by **Manoj Panda** is the tale of an old, black fish that wanders aimlessly in a bottomless ocean. It neither bothers to make friends nor to be a member of any school. It bears no grudge against anybody or anything. One day, four dark-brown coloured fish attack him and tie him up. They enquire about his family members. They allege that they had taken a huge advance but hadn't turned up for work. The old fish understands that they were brokers involved in unlawful dispatching of labourers. The old fish got an opportunity to escape after about ten days. After two days of continuous swimming, he reaches an unfamiliar patch in the ocean, a 'beautiful dreamlike place shimmering brightly in the light of dazzling pebbles, like a park resplendent with colourful lights.' The old fish later comes to learn that his family was tortured the most in the hands of the fish-mafia bosses. After finding his dead wife, he lets out a wild wail and speeds away.

Hrusikesh Panda's **Reba** is different from Rebati of Fakir Mohan Senapati. Rebati's desire for education, in Fakir Mohan, was thought to be the cause of all suffering. Panda's Reba is highly educated. She is the first MSC in not only her village but also several villages around. She later goes on to acquire a PhD degree. She even goes to USA to carry out research. She is appointed as a teacher in a university there. The problem with Reba is her feeling of loneliness and helplessness. The village where she spent her childhood days had lost its charm. Lilies didn't bloom anymore, the village cremation ground had been encroached upon, and the community culture hall had been embroiled in many litigation. The feelings haunted her even in America. Despite her busy schedule, she often felt lonesome. It is this deep, cold, and complex feeling that bothers her.

Gayatri Saraf in her story **A Disconcerting Truth** believes "Adversities can change the nature of man". The story is about a class ten student, Leena, who throws into wind the rules, regulations, and norms of discipline of the school and elopes with her boyfriend, who had impregnated her. The strict, disciplinarian headmistress, Aradhana is pained to see the norms set by her shattered like this. Taking the moral responsibility, she informs Leena's father about her elopement. She expects a broken, helpless father standing before her. Contrary to her expectations, Leena's father appears nonchalant. Aradhana takes some time to understand that behind the façade of cruelty and carelessness lurked a father's helplessness. He had not been able to marry his two other daughters off due to various reasons. Aradhana, herself a mother and a lady with a compassionate heart finally wishes, "Leena should marry the young man of his choice and lead a happy life. His boyfriend should not hand her over to a pimp. She should not be abused as a child-bearing-machine. Let her live in peace."

"No Rudrapratap can ever annihilate love and freedom from the surface of the earth. Meghna will be reborn; she will love poetry; she will love plays. The deceitfulness of all Srikants will come to a big nought in comparison to her deep faith." Invincibility of love is the central theme of **Supriya Panda's** story **Backbone**. Meghna, the heroine finds herself madly in love with industrialist Rudrapratap's son, Srikant. Class stands as a barrier between the union of the two. Besides, Srikant fails to undertake the promised revolt against his autocratic father. Finally, Srikant gets married to Tanu, daughter of a friend of his father, an equal in class and status. With the passage of time, Srikant forgets his earlier love. A heart reverberating with the cry "Sky is the Limit" replaces his loving heart. One day, he comes to learn that it was his father's goons who had abducted Meghna and left her bedridden. His father's instructions had led to the removal of Purbi, Meghna's sister, from the theatre group where she was employed. Although driven to penury, Purbi had been struggling to turn her sister from a 'spineless creature' to a 'human being' who could stand erect with the support of her backbone.

Bibhuti Bhusan Pradhan's The Home of the Butterfly presents a growing up girl Maanu's normal day-to-day desires, the non-fulfillment of those in view of the restrictions imposed by a step-mother, the helplessness of a father who unsuccessfully tries to strike a balance, and finally, Maanu's realization of her father's helplessness. Maanu's school hostel closes for vacation. Other students leave one by one but her father doesn't arrive in time. Maanu, though not initially, but at the end realizes that if she reaches home her father would have to encounter problems like "a disconcerting atmosphere, hurling of things, cassation of cooking" caused by her step-mother. Maanu realizes that her father bears all the torture for her sake. She also understands that behind the façade of the calm and cool appearance that her father presented, there lurked an unfathomable grief for not having done her justice. "No matter how unruffled an appearance he tried to maintain, his inner being was tormented by an incessant storm." What is striking is Maanu's way of solving the problem, like a mature person. "The Board Examination is only two months away. I'll not leave for home. Matron Madam has assured to take care of my food." Maanu's actions garner much respect in the minds of the readers for her.

Kanhu in **Kanhu's Home** by **Gourhari Das**, is a sixteen year old boy who comes to the city from Nayagarh in search of work, as his mother finds it difficult to provide for his enormous appetite. The mistress of the house employees him to supervise and guard the newly-constructed house. Smart, diligent, and affectionate, Kanhu not only protects the construction materials but also supervises the works of masons and labourers. He believes in the words of the mistress who says after the construction is completed, he will be given a room and he can bring in his mother to stay with him. However, when he comes back to the city after a visit to his home town, the greatest shock of his life awaits him. The owner of the house had not only let out the house but had also left for Delhi. Kanhu feels cheated.

Abinash, in **Paresh Patnaik's** **Goodbye, God**, receives the greatest jolt of his life when one night he receives a call from 'God'. Thinking it to be a prank by a friend, he disbelieves the caller at first but a series of events over the next few days convinces him. On being incited by God, he asks for boons. These boons are fulfilled, no doubt, but he has to pay a price every time. Finally, he blurts out, "If I ask for a job now, you will inflict on me torture along with the job. If I ask for eternal bliss, it will be accompanied by deep sorrow. They are all blended together like binaries." Abinash wishes not to be enticed by boons any further and bids God a goodbye.

The narrator of **Dipti Ranjan Pattanaik's** **In Search of Ms. Adela Quested** is puzzled to receive an Email from Emma

Gallagher, an internationally acclaimed writer two years after sending one to her. He intended to write a post-colonial version of the novel *A Passage to India* and shared the idea for the first time with her at a workshop on creative writing. Emma invited the writer to come to England and see the women from close quarters before venturing into the writing of the novel. The narrator, while in England, spends two days with Emma. He learnt that Emma, despite being beautiful and middle aged and possessing unimaginable wealth, power and fame was terribly lonely and desperate. The narrator also noticed that all the women whom he met there were struggling for their existence. 'To be desperate for the extrasensory' was something rare there. The narrator is surprised to find Emma and some of her writer friends indulging in 'provocative talks,' 'vulgar queries' and 'furtive smiles'. However, he was happy that he could retain his worth as someone whose behavior didn't abandon his life's philosophy and Emma's respect for someone who represented India remained unaffected.

Like Ranjan Pradhan's The Duma, **Paramita Satapathy**'s **Wild Jasmine** also presents a conflict. Here the conflict is between the traditional ways of thinking of the inhabitants of a remote village and the so-called 'modernity'. Ratan Singh, the supervisor of a road-construction company informs Rina, an Anganwadi worker, that once the huge concrete road is constructed, there would be a great change in the economy of the area. The inhabitants will get gas, electricity, grocery etc. easily. Their place will have schools, colleges, hospitals and doctors. On the other hand, the locals suspect that they are going to blast the mountains and start mining in the area. "Why should they abandon their traditional ways and embrace something modern?" the locals ask. They claim that they feel pleasure and pain the same way; are affected by summer and winter the same as the so-called moderns. The day Rina overhears the conversation between the overseer and his friends, the real character of the 'moderns' is revealed. She sends his brother and his friends to take revenge on Ratan Singh and his people for having tried to cheat them.

Smita in **Adyasha Das**'s **The Road Inwards** is terribly disturbed when she encounters her deceased husband's shadow everywhere in the lonely house at Kasauli. She even 'unmistakably heard footsteps on the stairs' which sounded like the ones that Ambuj made when he was alive. When Ambuj's sudden exit from her life is as lethal as death, she wonders why she is filled with 'such an uncontrollable fear at these signs of his return'. The conflict of wanting Ambuj on one hand yet hesitant to face his formless presence on the other tortures her. Smita remembers the advice of her mother, '...fear was myth, an illusion of the mind...when the mind would be weak, fear would enlarge its size...the longest road is inwards, leading deep within yourself.' This provides a resolution to her mental conflict.

Manas Panda's **Hide and Seek** is a pathetic account of how a simple child's game can often turn disastrous. It was Lulu's turn to count and Kunu's turn to hide. The excitement of the game continues till they both try to befool each other. However, Lulu's feelings of joy turns into concern as the little boy eludes her search and remains out of her reach. She starts suspecting that in his attempt to emerge victorious, he might have run outside the gate. Finally, Kunu's dead body is discovered, in a sitting posture, from inside the fridge. His wide open eyes reflect his victory over his sister but it comes with a great price—his death.

Ranjan Pradhan's **The Duma** presents a clash—the clash between tradition and modernity. The clash arises out of the construction of a dam over river Indrabati. The dam, once completed, was going to submerge large tracts of land and a number of Adivasi villages. The government had announced compensation, constructed a rehabilitation colony, and taken every step for the resettlement of the would-be displaced. But the problem was— how could an adivasi abandon the land of his fathers and forefathers? Displacement meant separation from their Dangar (hill), their Dumakudi (graveyard), their Dumas (spirits), their Baali kudia (place of worship), the seats of Bhima debata, goddess Durnimata etc. Buddu Jani, the oldest member of the community, pooh-poohs the idea of compensation by the government and wonders, "How dare these people obstruct the flow of running water of our rivers, streams and springs? It is the property of water to flow downwards with a murmuring sound. It is a great sin to prevent its flow." The arguments put forth by Robert Domb, a convert Christian in favour of their departure cannot convince Buddu Jani. Robert says, "...the new village to which we will be shifted has electric lights. The school building has been completed and the village has been connected by a pucca road. Two tube wells have been dug up… our children will be admitted into school and shall be civilized through education." For the older adivasis it's a question of abandoning their tradition. The Dumas are scared of electric lights; they would never agree to stay with them. In that case, who would protect them, their village, and their corn fields? Finally Buddu Jani is bodily lifted by some youngsters into the truck carrying them to the rehabilitation village but his soul remains with the salap tree in the erstwhile village.

Kshetrabasi Naik's **Bonded Labour** is the story of Maguni Bariha, a farmer. Maguni's exploitation and torture, first in the hands of a local landlord and subsequently in the hands of the brick-kiln officials in a neighbouring state, are delineated here. Drought, flood and famine for three consecutive years force Maguni to release his oxen and leave for Andhra Pradesh to work in a brick-kiln. Inclement weather, lack of adequate food, unhygienic conditions and slogging from morning till night take their toll on Maguni. Without medicines and proper care, his youngest child dies. There's no escape from the hands of the contractor and his people. When his other son suffers from high fever, Maguni and his wife Kaincha rush to the contractor and plead for some money. The contractor has a condition—"Kaincha would have to share his bed for a night". With her son's fever refusing to subside and all options to obtain money for treatment exhausted unsuccessfully, Kaincha surrenders to the contractor's demands. Devastated Kaincha jumps into the fire of the kiln the next day. Her son succumbs to the fever. Only Maguni is left—alone and devastated.

Rabinarayan Dash's **Mother's Home** is a graphic account of a selfless, hardworking and determined mother who braves all odds to save her family from disintegration. Instead of being per-turbed by the untimely demise of her husband, she pulls herself together and works tirelessly to steady her family-boat and fi-nally, saves it from sinking. When everyone in the neighbourhood feared that "The Tripathy family was going to be obliterated; that the five children had been orphaned" she took to herself the act of restoration. "Everybody feared that she might end her life" but a lady with an undaunted spirit she "surprised everybody by steadying herself" and by readying "herself to bear the burden". Besides, she plays a pivotal role keeping the members together by exercising an astounding control on each of them. "Sometimes Siddharth wondered how mother could keep the snakes and mon-gooses together; where from she had procured the magic-root that mesmerized everyone." It's only when she gets bed-ridden that the same children, whom she had fondly grown at the cost of her sweat and blood, display how selfish they can be. All of them become worried when she simply "refuses to die". They conve-niently forget their responsibilities but are more interested in her gold ornaments that they can share only after her death. The final action of the second son reaffirms our faith in humanity. He says, "The house belongs to her. She will live here till she rots and her body mixes with the soil" and gets ready to take care of her.

The narrator in **Sreekanta Barik**'s **Passionate Tune** is fasci-nated to hear heart-rending and pathetic tunes on a flute on a Pousha evening. Upon enquiry, he discovers a weak and emaci-ated man playing the flute. "The soulful lamentations of a human being expressed through the tune of the flute" attracts him. When acquaintance grows, the man lays bare his heart. Makaru lived a blissful life with his pregnant wife in a slum. One day, on being directed by the government, some officials arrive to vacate the slum. The slum-dwellers visit the collector, ministers and leaders but nobody comes to their rescue. When policemen arrive a few days later, some slum-dwellers charge at them with lathis. A good fight ensues. In order to evade backlash by policemen, Makaru tries to escape with his wife. She falls on the road; her stomach is bumped. She is rushed to hospital where she gives birth to a dead child and dies. The flute, whose tune fascinated Sumati when she was alive, becomes the medium through which Makaru expressed his grief and gets peace.

As the reader traverses from one world to another that these stories portray, one would easily discover that no two characters are the same. The experience that each protagonist goes through in life is also a different one. The protagonists display normal human emotions like pride, helplessness, compassion, love, devotion, remorse, vengeance, betrayal, exploitation, conflict, deceit, feelings of loneliness and many more in the course of life's journey. Besides, life teaches everybody its own lessons.

If the stories fascinate you, kindly don't forget to write to us. If your expectations are betrayed, kindly don't forget to criticize us.

Wish you all a happy reading.

Manoranjan Mishra
manoranjanmishra74@gmail.com

■

"Make up a story... For our sake and yours forget your name in the street; tell us what the world has been to you in the dark places and in the light. Don't tell us what to believe, what to fear. Show us belief's wide skirt and the stitch that unravels fear's caul."

Toni Morrison, *The Nobel Lecture In Literature, 1993*

"Short stories are tiny windows into other worlds and other minds and other dreams. They are journeys you can make to the far side of the universe and still be back in time for dinner."

Neil Gaiman, *Author*

Tale Of An Ominous Son

Achyutananda Pati

Translated by **Supriya Kar**

That day, the owl fledgling opened his eyes for the first time. In the deep hollow of the tree trunk, he saw thick darkness around him. His mother sat covering him with her wings. He dreamt of many things; his soft limbs lay on the pricking bed of twigs.

He could hear some noise from above. His mother's wings fluttered slightly. She puffed up her feathers for a while and then drew him close to her body. He felt cozy. He chirped merrily. His mother rubbed her beak on his tiny beak and whispered to him to be quiet and still. He did not understand why his mother said this. But he grew quiet. The creases of his skin slowly unfurled absorbing warmth from the soft feathers of his mother. He felt buoyant. He thought of standing up. He stretched his limbs in that bed of twigs. His mother too moved a little away from him. She pecked his tiny limbs and straightened them. The fledgling looked up. The darkness seemed less thick. He closed his eyes. Again, he looked at his mother and then looked up. Mother understood his mind. She placed her stub nose on his and said smilingly, "Darling! How soon have you become so sensible? All right, wait for some more time; let feathers grow fully on your wings. I'll teach you how to fly. I'll tell you how to flap your wings. You'll travel across the sky and see new things for yourself. Here you lie in darkness, but when you go out, it will no more be dark out there. The sky will be filled with bright moonbeams. Little stars will fondly wink at you. I'll introduce you to new things when I take you out on a walk. Grow up soon. Let your limbs strengthen."

His mother shoved a bit of guava into his tiny beak, picking it out of the cavity. He swallowed it slowly. Ah, how sweet! He imagined seeing the world for himself. The world must be very sweet.

Some creatures ran under the tree making the familiar *huke-ho* noise. The fledgling felt drowsy lying under the warm feathers of his mother. He dreamt of many things. He dreamt of the world. All around, sweet guavas spread in pieces on the ground. The round moon was descending from heaven. There was no trace of darkness. His beak opened with a smile. The noise from the ground woke him up. There was darkness all around. The fledgling felt upset. He had just seen a light in his dream. His mother ruffled her feathers sitting on the edge of the hollow. He cried out, 'Ma, I'll go to see the world today. I'll go out to play with the moon."

His mother came and drew him beneath her wings. He slipped out of his mother's wings. He did not like darkness at all. His mother told him tenderly, "You've come into this world. Who would prevent you from going about it? You must go out into the world when you're grown up and strong, or else you will be cheated. Have a little patience. It's just a matter of a few more days. I'll take you out myself. Sleep here for a while. You must be hungry. I'll be back soon with new food for you. Don't make any noise."

His mother left him with a fond peck on his beak. The fledgling went into a reverie. With eyes closed, he dreamt of light spread everywhere. The world of light tempted him with a guava. His eyes were heavy with sleep. He found that his wings had now grown thicker than that of his mother. He was flying happily, his wings brushing against the moon. His leg had grown stronger. He was able to stand up on his own. Feathers thickened on his wings. He grew crazy thinking of the world. In his imagination, the world got filled with moonlight and guavas. He grew restless. He pestered his mother. He was grown up now and he must go out to see the world.

That day, the mother-owl brought her son to the edge of the hollow for the first time. She pointed at the moon with her beak. His eyes dazzled. Ah, how lovely! He lay in such a dark hollow. The fledgling tried to fly accompanied by his mother. He hopped from one branch to the other. His wings grew tired. He flew to the topmost branch of the tree at once. He sat there, gazing at the moon. The pain in his wings gradually lessened. The moon sprinkled light. He felt like gulping down drops of moonlight. His mother arrived at that moment. She took him back into the hollow after much persuasion.

One day, the mother-owl had dozed off. The owl fledgling slowly ventured out of the hollow.

Oh, how bright it was outside! The moon looked bigger and shone brighter than on the previous occasion. He kept staring at it. His eyes started burning. My goodness, such blazing light!

Two myna fledglings were hopping on tree branches. They were singing with their mother. The owl fledgling felt sad — perhaps his mother was not as good. She never taught him to sing under such a big moon. He went near the myna fledglings, singing. They were frightened and started yelling. Their mother came and pecked him hard. A cawing crow advanced towards him, hearing his voice. The mother-owl was jolted out of her slumber. She came rushing and hurriedly took her child away into the hollow. The fledgling was very angry with his mother. She had spoilt everything. In a fit of anger, he bit his mother. He tried to go out once again. He screamed at his mother. Why had she not shown him the big moon earlier? While comforting him, his mother told him mournfully, "Keep quiet, my son. That isn't the moon, my love. It's the sun. In our world, there's no sun. We must live in darkness. Otherwise, we'll perish."

The fledgling was annoyed at his mother's words. Why wouldn't he go to the world of the sun? Why would not he stroll in the kingdom of light? Who had made such laws to trouble them? He marched forward angrily. His mother dragged him beneath her wings. He plucked out a few feathers from his mother's abdomen in frustration. His mother simply cried. Outside, a gang of crows cawed endlessly. His mother regretted that she had unnecessarily told her son about the sun.

"We live in the dark. We belong to the ominous species. We're a curse on the world. If we seek light, we'll die. In the realm of light, the children of light hang around to hunt us." His mother broke down saying this.

"Have a little patience, ma." He tried to comfort his mother, "Let me grow up. I'll surely take you to the kingdom of light. I'll destroy all our enemies."

That day, both the owl-mother and her son perched on a mango branch. There was no moon in the sky. The owl fledgling felt bored. Suddenly, a flicker of light came through a chink of the house nearby. The owl fledgling was thrilled. He opened his beak and sang a song. Someone from the house shouted abusively, "Fly away, you wretch! I'll parch your back with a hot frying stick, do you hear me? Get lost, may you succumb to diarrhoea!" The mother-owl kissed her son and asked him to keep quiet. The fledgling felt enraged. How unfair! They would use light as though it was their own property. We would be told off if we rejoiced upon seeing a glimmer of light! No, that wasn't done. He wanted to enter through the window and snatch the light away from them. His mother howled and brought him back home.

After sunset, the fledgling examined his wings carefully before setting out of his hollow. All the feathers had grown on his wings. He stretched his legs and strutted around twice. His limbs felt strong. He struck his beak on the tree trunk. It was quite hard now. He flew away. He would not return home. He would roam freely in the kingdom of the sun. He would conquer light. He would confront his enemies face-to-face.

The dawn broke. From below the horizon emerged a spring of red light. The owl-fledgling had never witnessed the entry of light in the kingdom of the sun. He saw this spectacle of light with his eyes wide open, oblivious of himself. Hundreds of birds flew away singing and flapping their wings to the beat. All these birds would roam around freely in light, savoring the taste of life, and he would rot in the dark and die? No. He felt determined. Slowly, the sun rose up in the sky. The daylight grew intense. In such a big and beautiful world of light, was there not even a little space for him? No, he would make merry to his heart's content today. He would let the world know that he was a son of light, too. He also had a claim on this kingdom.

The fledgling started moving around freely. He looked at everything carefully. Suddenly, he was attacked from the back. He turned around. His mother had marked them as enemy-birds that day. These birds had snatched the light from the cursed owls. He struck the crow back with his beak. While defending itself, the crow cawed loudly for help. Flights of crows came rushing, cawing aggressively. He realized that he was too weak to defend himself against such a large army of foes. He flew swiftly towards the tall building near him, flapping his wings. He slipped into the house through a small hole on the wall. Outside, the crows continued to screech. He sat quietly for some time. His chance would come. His enemies would disperse and he would take his revenge. He would reclaim his due from the kingdom of light. He was not a curse of darkness. He was a child of light. Today, he would enjoy light to his heart's content.

In that building, on a thick mattress, lay the wealthy Dhirumalla. He was having fever and fits of delirium. He groaned in pain and shouted now and then agitatedly.

"Make sure that the mustard oil is eighty percent adulterated. Remember to file a suit against Madana Barik. That scoundrel's sister, Chandrama shows off as a chaste woman. I fondly placed my hands on her, that bitch almost hit me! Can you hear me? Send around twenty goons and harvest the rice crop from Priya Mishra's land. Money won't be a problem. He doesn't care to greet me just because he is a little educated! Come here and listen to me carefully — that Bengali from Calcutta has promised to provide me hundred *bharis* of smuggled opium. Keep an eye on him."

So these were the so-called elite of the kingdom of light! It is for them that the sun offers light every day. The fledgling observed everything with his eyes wide open. All of a sudden, someone sitting near Dhirumalla's bed, a sincere and true servant of the kingdom of light, saw this owl-fledgling.

"Ominous! Inauspicious! Sign of death! An owl has entered the room. Master is ill" The servant cried out impatiently. A long bamboo staff was brought; the fledgling was poked and driven away. Both his wings were injured. He somehow managed to fly to the top of the building and sat there, writhing in pain. Some crows from the nearby tree rushed to attack him again. Annoyed with these noisy crows, a servant came to the terrace and landed a hard blow on the owl-fledgling, the cause of the trouble. The fledgling tumbled down. They burnt a bunch of straw on the terrace and snuffed out the flame with turmeric water. The evil omen would no longer have any effect.

The army of crows pounced on the injured fledgling. Blood streamed down his wings in heavy spurts. He looked skyward. High up in the sky, the sun was still pouring down light. In great pain, he rose and turned homeward. He fell down at the bottom of the tree that was his home. His mother was waiting anxiously for her son. What could she do? How will her son take refuge in this broad daylight? The mother's heart was oppressed by all sorts of anxieties. Hearing her son's call, she rushed to the bottom of the tree. She was speechless at the sight of his blood-soaked body. The fledgling looked up for a moment. The mynas were singing boisterously among the branches.

The sun continued sending beams of light from the sky. The owl-fledgling said with his head resting on his mother's lap, "Don't weep, ma. Tell my siblings, if they're born, that their elder brother became a martyr fighting valiantly to win the kingdom of light."

The owl-fledgling closed his eyes forever. The sun still poured down light in abundance on the earth.

Original Odia: *Ashubha Putrara Kahani*

■

The Living God

Santanu Kumar Acharya

Translated by **Supriya Kar**

W hat kind of a house is this, daddy? The five-
year-old Miskun asked his daddy.

"This isn't a house, my boy, but a place of
worship. God dwells here. We Hindus call it a
temple. This temple was built in the seventh century
AD—very ancient."

How strange, how very novel this
information seemed to Miskun. Though he was only
five, his information base was quite strong. He was
born at Glastonbury in Connecticut, America. Mark
Twain's house-museum was a shout away from his
home. He had visited Mark Twain's place a number
of times with his daddy and mommy. He intimately
knew Mark Twain's character, Huckleberry Finn.
Miskun also knew Henry Thoreau, Emerson, and
other writers. Their house-museums were all
around Boston. However, visiting a temple was
altogether a new experience for Miskun. He was
amazed to see such a structure. Who knew what
thoughts crossed his mind while witnessing that
peculiar kind of a house called 'temple' from inside

the car while his soft, tiny hands clasped his daddy's stretched hands that reached for him from the backseat?

Seema and Bijan Senapati, Miskun's parents, sat in the backseat of the car. Miskun sat in the front seat. His maternal uncle, Sidharth, a high-ranked officer in the Indian Civil Service, drove the car.

Sidharth was very fond of his nephew, Miskun. His only sister, Seema was always dear to him. Sidharth knew Bijan long before he married his sister. Bijan was a brilliant student during his time, but he had a rather naïve worldly point of view. In those days, a number of students chose to study arts after the intermediate level, but Bijan preferred science. He had topped the examination and graduated in physics. Again, instead of going for a Master's degree in physics, he enrolled himself in a bachelor's degree in engineering. In the meantime, Sidharth had completed his Master's degree and sat for the Indian Civil Service examination. His first attempt was a failure, but he got through the second time. Bijan joined as a Junior Engineer at a government office on completing engineering.

The same year, he got married to Seema. Before finalizing the marriage, Sidharth's father had sought his son's opinion: "What do you think of this young man, Sidhu?"

"He's very brilliant, but, on the whole, a dolt." Sidharth had offered his certificate.

"A dolt?" Sidharth's father looked at his son, rather puzzled.

"What else is he if he isn't sharp enough to guess which direction the winds blew in? He should have realized by pursuing a second bachelor's degree, he would lag behind his contemporaries. Take my case—by the time he became an Executive Engineer with all his brilliance, I'd already been in a superior position of Commissioner-cum-Secretary in his department." Sidharth had laughed.

"But, he has been first-class-first throughout his career—a gold medalist in Engineering from the Indian Institute of Technology!" Sidharth's father, Sankar sir, a retired high school headmaster, did not commend his son's vanity. He was rather adamant on forming this matrimonial alliance, so Seema's wedding was fixed with Bijan. Sidharth had no option but to accept it. Though he loved his sister dearly, he looked down upon Bijan. Whenever he met Bijan, he had the same feeling of disdain. Ah, poor Bijan!

However, life changed for Bijan Senapati in no time—he went to America for higher studies. He completed his doctoral degree at the world-renowned Massachusetts Institute of Technology and joined General Motors. That was the year Miskun was born. And this was the first time in five years Seema and Bijan had come to visit India with Miskun. It was Sidharth's responsibility to take them to Puri and Konark on a trip. He had set a travel plan to send them to far-off places with the driver and car provided by his office but chose to drive them to nearby tourist spots in the town first. While taking the car out of his garage, Sidharth asked his sister, "Where would you like to go? Have you ever visited our famous Odisha State Archaeological Museum, here in the capital city of Bhubaneswar?"

In fact, neither Seema nor Bijan ever had an opportunity to visit any of the famous sites of Bhubaneswar, the capital city of their native state Odisha. They knew the city was dotted with marvelous, ancient temples, which were declared as world heritage sites. They often came across a description of these temples in coffee table books on art.

They got into the car and took their seats. Sidharth drove the car out into the street.

"Brother, are there really a hundred thousand temples here in Bhubaneswar?" Seema asked on the way to Old Town, where most of the ancient and famous temples were situated—this part of the city always witnessed a flow of tourists from all over the world round the year.

"Don't you know this is known as the city of temples?" Sidharth laughed. "Come, let me show you the oldest temple in the city."

They passed by the museum and drove towards Kedar Gouri road, which led to a cluster of temples. Sidharth halted the car near Parsurameswar temple: "Look, there," he pointed at the beautifully preserved ancient shrine of Shiva, built in the famed archaeological style of Odisha, and declared, "The glory of Odisha! The Parsurameswar temple—it was built in the seventh century A.D."

At that time, the little boy who was sitting by his uncle's side in the front seat was heard asking his dad, "What kind of a house is this, daddy?

When Miskun heard 'seventh century A.D.' from his daddy's mouth, a similar expression came to his mind: "Mark Twain was born in nineteenth-century A.D., wasn't he, daddy?"

'Yes, yes, Mark Twain was born a hundred years ago. You're right, my boy! But do you know how old this temple is! Thirteen hundred years old, one thousand and three hundred years! Just imagine…!"

"Ho, ho, ho"—Sidharth laughed out loud—he did not quite like the idea of asking a five-year-old to imagine thirteen hundred years. He wanted to change the discussion.

"Bijan! You have got elections this year in the USA? Who do you think will win? Will Bush come to power? How good are the chances of the Republicans?"

"No, no, no," Miskun protested immediately, "Dukakis, Michael Dukakis will win. The Republicans have got a poor chance."

Sidharth was left astounded—he looked at his five-year-old nephew from top to bottom, smiled and turned to his sister.

Seema returned a smile in the manner of the Americans. She looked very charming. She had not looked so attractive when she was in India. Those days, she hardly knew how to smile . The daughter of a high-school teacher, she was not as bright as her brother, Sidharth. Somehow, she plodded through till graduation. Then she got married to Bijan, who hailed from a poor family. He was in a less lucrative job than her brother. At times, Seema would feel upset about it. She would ask her brother in private, "Seriously, brother? How could father decide to tie me with such a blockhead?" Tears streamed down her cheeks. Sidharth would comfort his sister, "You don't know, dear! Bijan was considered a prodigy in our time. We could hardly hold a candle to him. Had he opted for political science, he would have topped the civil service list. Never mind. He's so brilliant."

"Bullshit!" Seema had twisted her face away in anger when this alliance was finalized by her father. Her face usually wore a dry, melancholic look. That was then. Now a smile played at the corner of her lips. She had picked up the typical manner in which the Americans smiled with their thirty-two teeth out on display. It was another matter of surprise for Sidharth that Seema's personality could develop so much in a matter of just a few years.

Unraveling her personae a little more, Seema remarked, "Brother, children are born smart in America. Miskun can operate a computer if you get him one now."

Sidharth was elated to learn about his nephew's talent. After hanging around temples such as Kedar Gouri, Mukteswar, Rajarani and finally the Lingaraj temple, they set out to visit Odisha State Archaeological Museum. While his uncle turned his car towards the huge iron gates of the Museum, Miskun asked, 'Uncle, is it a science museum? In Boston,we have a number of such museums…"

"No, no, my boy! "His dad quipped, "This is an archaeological museum. Old sculptures thousands of years old are preserved here. Come, we'll see."

"Yeah, you'll see very old images of gods and goddesses here in this huge mansion! But alas! All of them have died long back!" said Sidharth, laughing heartily.

"Dead gods!" —Miskun was taken aback as though he had seen a ghost. He simply could not believe what his maternal uncle said. "The gods have died?" He asked in Odia heavy with an American accent, "Is this a cemetery for gods, uncle?"

Sidharth laughed indulgently. Bijan explained to Sidharth in good humor, "In America, being an atheist has connotations with being a Communist. The boy might be shocked suspecting his uncle was a Communist!"

"Yes, yes, I'm a confirmed Communist. If you remember, I

was a member of A.I.S.F during college days. You might have seen me then. I ran in the college union presidency election. I still believe in socialism," Sidharth grew serious on this note.

The museum tour took quite some time. They inspected most of the important archaeological sections where galleries of images of Hindu, Buddhist and Jain deities from classical to Baroque periods were put on display. All along, while introducing the deities to his sister and brother-in-law, Sidharth would remark—"Do you know the real worth of these dead gods in international markets? Billions, if not trillions, in American dollar!"

Their museum visit was coming to an end. Miskun lingered on and continued to ask all sorts of questions—"Daddy, which god was this? Uncle, was this god a very cruel god? How terrible he looks! Mommy, that's a god or a goddess? Were they all alive indeed?" Miskun was given appropriate answers as far as possible. His daddy would say, "This god is known as Abalokiteswar—he's Padmapani—they belonged to the tenth century."

"Look, look here, this god is called Mahakala. He's a ferocious god. He killed and devoured everyone. Oh, how terrifying he looks!" His uncle added.

While gazing at the image of goddess Tara, Miskun's mother mulled over something and remarked: "Ah, how beautiful! Brother, do you know how much such an image would cost? None of these would be less than ten thousand dollars. If you sold this entire museum, say, to Americans, they would pay billions and billions of dollars and lift these images, even all your ancient temples and restore all of them in America."

Sidharth gave a smile. "That would be wonderful! Poverty would get eradicated from India in a day. You do one thing—start an antique business, Seema! I believe the eradication of poverty would remain a dream until these dead gods are not removed from this country. Such foolishness! Millions and millions of rupees lie in the form of stone sculptors, and yet we're poor!" He shared his observation.

Miskun listened to everything attentively.

The museum tour now over, they were supposed to head to

the hotel Kalinga Ashok for lunch. They had been roaming around for a long time and were tired. It was slightly past lunch time. All of them sat in the car. Miskun took his seat as before in the front, but he was no longer his talkative self. Perhaps, he was hungry. He looked drowsy.

The car stopped at the hotel's portico. They got down the car and entered the lounge. Sidharth was a known face at the hotel. The manager received them warmly. A few of Sidharth's acquaintances and friends were present too. In the lobby, Sidharth, Bijan, and Seema sat amidst the gathering of friends. All of them seemed to forgot about Miskun for a while.

As a waiter came and informed Sidharth that the food was ready to be served, everyone rose to their feet. They realized that Miskun was nowhere in sight.

Seema grew restless. Bijan got alarmed and ran around the hotel to check if there was any swimming pool or water body inside its premise. Miskun always ran to the swimming pool whenever they went to a hotel in America. Filled with anxiety, Sidharth shouted at the hotel staff—"Find the boy! I'll get you sacked, all of you…"

A frantic search ensued. The boy was here a moment ago—how did he disappear suddenly? Was it a case of kidnapping? Could this be possible at such a renowned hotel?

Bijan was struck by a memory. He told Seema, "If you recall, a similar incident had happened earlier. While roaming around Mark Twain's house-museum, the boy had gone missing, hadn't he?"

Seema felt flabbergasted. In a choked voice she said—"Yeah, I'm at a loss. Could he, by any chance, go back to the museum? Let's rush there!"

Bijan and Sidharth followed Seema. Only a wide road lay between the premises of Hotel Kalinga Ashok and the museum. Before Seema and Bijan could rush into the museum through the gate, Sidharth's people had jumped off its boundary wall to get inside. They searched desperately all over the museum premises, inside and outside, but there was no sign of Miskun.

Seema could no longer keep herself in check. She started crying loudly like a rustic woman. Last time, events had turned out in a similar manner at Mark Twain's house-museum. The police were informed when Miskun went missing—the police thoroughly searched the three-storeyed building of the Mark Twain museum, but in vain. Helpless in the wake of such a crisis, Seema could no longer control herself and had let out a loud cry which seemed to have shaken the huge mansion of Mark Twain. She had howled uncontrollably—"Oh my God! Mark Twain, please give my child back!"

Strangely, this invocation to Mark Twain seemed to have worked. After a while, the police discovered Miskun at what seemed an improbable place inside the museum. Apparently, the child had fallen asleep on one of the couches inside Mark Twain's library, a book in hand—Tom Sawyer. Perhaps, he had dozed off while reading and the book covered his face. What was astonishing was someone had covered him with an overcoat, perhaps fearing the boy might catch a cold. That overcoat belonged to none other than Mark Twain; that very overcoat, which visitors saw hanging as a museum piece in his wardrobe in another room.

Bijan and Seema had felt overwhelmed discovering Miskun in that state. The police had expressed surprise, too. They had not been able to solve that mystery. How could the overcoat be taken from the wardrobe in another room and placed on the child sleeping peacefully in the library? Was it the job of Mark Twain's ghost?

They had harboured such a suspicion, but no one had asked that unpleasant question directly to the boy.

However, today, in this outlandish environment of an archaeological museum, where the halls were packed with sculptures of gods and goddesses, Seema could take it no more. She began wailing out the names of all gods and goddesses like a village woman beseeching their favor to return her child wherever they might have hidden him. She approached a huge sculpture of Lord Buddha. The information provided underneath said 'Abalokiteswar.' She kneeled herself down before the huge granite sculpture and prayed aloud— "Oh Lord Abalokiteswar! Please give me my child back. Otherwise, I'll end my life here in front of you...Miskun, my child...."

It seemed as though another supernatural incident had occurred in Miskun's life. Miskun was sitting in a lotus posture behind a Buddha sculpture adjacent to a wall. Probably shaken out of his meditative state by his mother's call, he responded nonchalantly, "I'm here, Mommy."

Everyone rushed towards the huge room, from where Miskun's voice was heard . He was still sitting in the lotus position. His eyes were half-closed as though he was awakening from a trance.

Sidharth stretched out his hands at Miskun to hug him, but Miskun pushed them away: "I'm not a dead god! No, you can't sell me—you can't sell me!" He yelled at his father and moved away. What was he saying? Everyone whispered, but no one had a clue. Seema gathered her son into her arms and broke into tears: "No, no, no one would sell you, my child. You're my living God! Oh, Lord Buddha! Lord Abalokiteswar! Mother Tara, bless my child with a million years...." She sobbed through her words like any mother in India.

Original Odia: *Chalanti Thakura*

Night In The Life Of The Mayor

Written and Translated by
Manoj Das

After his most memorable few hours, Divyasimha now felt, somewhere deep within, a hitherto unknown kiss of calm.

Had the sky been always so beautifully blue and the stars so very elegant and yet tranquil? He wondered.

The little boat glided on. Each cell of his body was tickled with the gentle cool breeze. Along with the darkness that was now slowly fading, his anguish and anxiety too were leaving him. The experience was so real, that he thought he could have seen them leaving him were they not immediately swallowed by the departing darkness!

What was the time? He looked at his wrist. He had forgotten that his watch too had gone along with his trousers!

But the contours of the land and the horizon, emerging from darkness, showed that it would soon be morning.

What must his family and friends and the people of Madhuvan be thinking now? He laughed and felt a kind of sweetness, for he was laughing after so much crying.

He had laughed twelve hours ago, at the meeting of the Councilors of the city Corporation. But what a difference between the two laughs! He knew he would no more laugh as of old. Streams of tears had washed away several values and attitudes from his mindset.

Only if this experience had come to him two or three decades ago! He would not perhaps have cared for all those so-called achievements to which he had devoted so many precious years. Perhaps he would not be the Mayor of Madhuvan. But he would surely have lived a more meaningful life.

He had laughed last when his old professor, Sudarshan Roy, now a Councilor, had wept. Of course, he had hidden his laughter behind a large handkerchief with which he pretended to be mopping his face.

Till then he was sure that the old man, when excited, showed signs of eccentricity. Why else would a scholar like him, once well-known for his discourses on logic, be moved to tears while speaking of trivial and funny incidents? It is true that his defeat at the Mayoral election at the hands of Divyasimha had given him a great shock. Maybe that was the real cause of his tears. Divyasimha remembered he had tried to pacify the venerable professor, through a friend, asking him to quote a famous Sanskrit dictum which asserted that it was glorious to be defeated by one's own son or pupil. The professor had shouted at the friend, saying, "Shut up! That maxim applies to a defeat in a contest of learning. To apply that to an election dominated by coercion and corruption is sheer indulgence in intellectual corruption."

The professor's speech at the Corporation meeting had sounded droll. He was narrating the hazards wrought by stray cows and bulls in the life of the peace-loving citizens of Madhuvan. His eerie and hyperbolic tone and style suggested as though the city had come under a siege by the Nazis in the guise of cattle! Then, when he came to narrating the mischief of a particular omnivorous cow who no doubt had lately gained wide notoriety, he could not check his tears.

Professor Roy's dear grand-daughter was appearing for her B.A. examination with Honours in psychology. The poor girl had captured all her learning in two notebooks. In the process of transferring the knowledge into her little head, one afternoon, she had fallen asleep on the verandah of her house. When she woke up, the villainous cow was quietly making her exit. One of the notebooks had clean disappeared. Of the other, only the bare covers could be recovered.

While Professor Roy wept in the course of narrating this crisis in the life of his grand-daughter, Divyasimha had laughed.

Had the old professor observed him laughing? Lest he should feel offended, Divyasimha, in order to explain his conduct, had walked over to him after the meeting and said, "Sir, I'm afraid, you are getting a bit too emotional!"

Prof. Roy stared angrily at him. "What makes you say so?" he asked.

"Sir, a cow, after all, is an animal!" said Divyasimha.

"I do not remember having ever contested that item of general knowledge. My question was whether the Corporation should protect us from such an irrefutable animal or not," retorted the professor.

"Sir, I mean, a cow chewing up a sheaf of papers could not be counted any tragedy of sorts!"

"No?" The professor shouted with deep resentment "In a city with such a jubilant Corporation, a cow would dare to chew up, of all things, psychology, that too in broad daylight and you the Mayor laugh and say that it was no tragedy?" His voice was choked.

Divyasimha laughed again, but in a subdued mode.

"You will not understand, Divyasimha, I am sorry to say, you are not capable of that. The more I think of the tragedy, the more helpless I feel." Prof. Roy sighed and continued, "All the safeguards evolved by the society over the centuries, your government and your law, nothing can help me get over this despair. Even if you were to award me two million rupees as compensation for the loss of the two notebooks, that would fail to console me. How helpless, indeed, man is!"

"Perhaps not so helpless as you think, Sir! Ha!" Divyasimha cut short his laugh with difficulty.

Prof. Roy got hold of his stick and stood up, "No, Mr. Mayor, it is not so easy to appreciate what I say. Let us not argue. Leave me alone with my tragedy." He said remorsefully and left the hall.

But Divyasimha was in one of his occasional high moods. He would have loved to argue and emerge triumphantly. Frustrated, this time he laughed deliberately with some vigor, just to irritate the departing old man a little more.

Tragedy, eh? How obstinate the professor had grown! Divyasimha felt a burning sensation in his heart and he had no difficulty in diagnosing it. It was his own obstinate desire to score a victory over the professor that remained unfulfilled.

Indeed, it could not have been possible for Divyasimha to appreciate the professor's avowal twelve hours ago. Divyasimha had climbed the stair of success in life; making cautious calculations of actions and reactions at every step. Not that he never slipped, but he had made up every slip with a vengeance.

Helplessness? No. He had never known it. He never lacked the powers that matter - of mind, men and money.

Dawn was breaking out. How sweet were the cool and quiet moments of sunrise and sunset! Divyasimha sat erect and breathed deeply.

It was to breathe deeply that he had come down to the riverbank last evening. He wanted to extinguish the burning inside his heart.

He had chosen a lonely spot. Parking his car on the grassy wasteland of the suburb he had descended into the water. He had suddenly felt an irresistible urge to plunge his bathroom-conditioned-body into the free transparent flow.

Nobody came to that part of the riverbank for an evening walk leaving the well-lit long concrete promenade on the other side of the city. There was none near about to notice him. He took off his watch and tucked it into a pocket of his trousers. He stripped himself of his clothes barring the underwear and kept them on a boulder between the car and the water and then made a dash into the flow.

This had once been a familiar river – in his days as a student. There was then a girls' hostel on the opposite bank. He and his friends would sing and shout while swimming. The sound brought only faint echoes back from the walls of the hostel but never any melodious response from beyond the walls.

Divyasimha smiled as he remembered those jolly days.

His thirst for attracting others' attention had long been satiated. The evening he returned home after delivering his maiden speech, his mother had told him, "Better do not speak in public!"

"Why?" the budding orator had challenged.

"Because so many eyes will scan you with envy. That may make you lose weight," explained the shy mother.

"How superstitious of you!" The defiant son had laughed.

How he wished that his mother's fear had come true! But all that had happened was he had grown fatter during the past quarter-century so much so that during the last election his opponents often referred to him as Divyahasti (the divine elephant) instead of Divyasimha (the divine lion).

He suddenly felt a tickling sensation inside his underwear. Something had crept in, maybe a tiny fish. He took off the garment and the sensation was gone. But the small creature slipped out of his hand and drifted away in the steady current. He could have recovered it if he had acted promptly. But he did not care.

He smiled again. It was already dark. It should not be any problem to leave the water and slip into his trousers very fast.

He had the last dip and then he plodded towards the riverbank.

What was that indistinct apparition swaying between the water and the embankment? He hoped it was not a cow! Nevertheless, panic overtook him. In any case, it could not have been the mischievous one that featured so prominently in the meeting, he assured himself.

He hurried towards the boulder on which he had deposited his clothes.

The cow had already stomached his bush-shirt and the undershirt and was busy making short work of the trousers.

Divyasimha screamed at the animal and splashed water at it furiously. The cow retreated, but with the trousers in her mouth.

Still knee-deep in the water, Divyasimha felt he was sweating.

He looked around. Nobody was there.

The naked Mayor rushed to confront the terrible cow. But the cow gave him the slip.

While he stood on the bank, befuddled, two beams of light focused on him – headlights of a jeep. For a second his wet body glowed in its huge bareness. He squatted instantly and, hopping like a frog, plunged into the river.

The jeep came to a halt and three men jumped out of it. From below, Divyasimha heard their voices and recognized them. They were the Executive Engineer of the Corporation and his two assistants.

"What was that strange creature that sprang into the river?" asked a perplexed voice.

"God knows. Looked like a gorilla."

"Gorilla? Since when have gorillas begun to frequent our suburbs?"

"God knows. But what other creature could resemble us so closely?"

"Could be the abominable snowman?"

Surprisingly, none of the suggestions sounded absurd or jocular in that creepy combination of space and time.

They stood in silence for some time. Then one of them asked, "Whose car is that?" Another replied, "God knows. Oh no, I too know. That is boss's of course!"

"How come is it left here, unlocked?" questioned the third, opening its door.

There was silence again. Then the engineer cried out, "Sir, Sir, are you somewhere around, Sir? Will you please respond, Sir?"

There was a long silence.

"Boss is not the kind of person to leave his car in this fashion at a desolate place like this. And what business could he have here at night? Mysterious! Let's hurry to his bungalow."

They jumped into their vehicle. It turned and instantly gathered speed.

Divyasimha was shivering with shame. What should he do? Should he drive home? But by now the engineer must have burst a panic-shell there. The surprised members of the family must have collected at the portico. The watchman would rush forward and open the door with an awful show of reverence. Others too would rush upon him. He shut his eyes visualizing the scene.

The current was slowly pushing him away. That was, in a way, safer, he imagined.

Only if some intimate friend happened to pass by! He could shout at him to stop and then confide his plight to him. The friend could run and fetch some clothes for him!

Or couldn't there be a miracle? Couldn't a few yards of linen come floating by?

No. There was no help. He must tell the engineer everything when he returned. He alone could help him. No alternative to waiting.

Light flashed at some distance. Three vehicles followed the engineer's jeep. They stopped around his car.

The sharp young European lady who jumped out of a car was his younger brother's wife. She was followed by her husband and they joined the engineer's party. Several policemen hopped down from a large van. And last but not the least, Prof. Roy came out with his walking stick from his car, the oldest vintage in the city.

With a mighty effort, Divyasimha suppressed a surge of sobs deep down his throat. Even if he could gather enough courage to expose himself before his European sister-in-law, he could by no means do so before Prof. Roy. It had not been even four hours when he had laughed while the old man had wept.

Divyasimha retreated farther. The leader of the police party focused his torch into the river. The engineer shouted "Sir" several times to elicit a response from him.

And soon came yet another van with more policemen.

It was no longer possible for Divyasimha to suppress his sobs. Must he be hurled into such a predicament? Which were the forces working behind this? And why?

He kept floating for a while and the current led him away gently. He came upon a small boat tied to a tree on the brink of the water. He unfastened the knot and got into it.

The boat smoothly glided downstream.

Now that the search party had been left far behind, he cried boldly and loudly.

When did he cry last? He tried to recollect; it had been ages ago.

A naked babe, he had cried lying on his mother's lap or clinging to his father. Once he had grown up, everybody, near and dear ones included, looked upon him as an institution. He was not expected to cry.

He woke up to his aloneness.

The river had narrowed. At times the drifting boat mildly dashed against the muddy edge; it circled once or twice and then continued on its course.

There were wide fields on both the sides of the river. The sky appeared to have come quite low. He felt in the river his lost mother's lap and in the sky his father's chest: broad and generous.

It would be foolish not to cry.

A thin sleep had crept into his tired eyes and he dreamed of a tiny bird beating its tinier wings against the rolling clouds.

He woke up to see the boat arrested at a bend. He got down, gave it a push and hopped in again.

With this little movement, he felt that his body had become miraculously light. And soon he realized how light his mind too had become.

The boat stopped, touching a submerged bush. There was a hamlet close to the bank. Smoke, filtered through the thatches of the huts, was coiling up towards the sky where birds had just begun to fly. The silhouette of the landscape was growing distinct and charming.

A little girl stood under a small tree, gazing at the river. Divyasimha compressed himself as much as possible inside the boat. "Listen, little one," he said breathing in deeply, "I have no clothes, can you give me something to put on?"

The girl looked impressed, but said, "You will give me back, won't you?"

"Oh yes," answered Divyasimha.

"Here it is. Catch it," the girl took off her tattered soiled frock and threw it at Divyasimha.

Divyasimha kissed the frock and wiped his last drops of tears with it. "Little one, this will not do. I am a big man!" he said.

"Big? Like, father? Wait," she ran away. After five minutes she returned with a handloom towel and threw it at the stranger.

Divyasimha put the towel around his waist. He got down and holding on to the bushes climbed up the bank.

The girl had been followed by her intrigued father.

Divyasimha did not hesitate to introduce himself. He followed the amazed fisherman into his hut and sat down near his oven and drank a cup of heated milk and narrated whatever had happened since the evening. The fisherman nodded understandingly and sympathized with him.

After an hour Divyasimha got into a mofussil bus wearing the best piece of dhoti the fisherman could provide and covering his upper body with the towel.

As soon as the bus entered the city he could see groups of people reading the morning's Madhuvan Voice. The banner headline read: "Mayor Disappears Mysteriously!" The front page carried several speculations like kidnap and suicide. What made the matter complicated was, on one hand, a strange creature double the size of average human jumping into the river and on the other, discovery of the Mayor's leather belt and a portion of his trousers on the wasteland.

Talking to a reporter, the old Prof. Roy had conjectured that the brave Mayor, his former student, after listening to his woes, might have confronted the notorious cow and the cow might have chewed up the Mayor whole.

The Professor had shed tears thereafter and had demanded immediate capture of the man-eating cow. The owner of the animal had meanwhile been interrogated and although the cow was still at large, the police and the employees of the corporation had brought their net quite close on it, expecting to swoop down on it any moment.

The local branch of the All-Faith Society had summoned a prayer meeting to plead for God's intervention in the matter.

Divyasimha was experiencing an irrevocable calm. He did not feel any urge to give explanations to anybody. Anyone but Prof. Roy. He wanted to rush to him and tell him, "I beg to be pardoned, Sir. Now I know what helplessness is; I believe I earned my adulthood last night."

Original Odia: *Madhubanara Mayor*

■

Patadei

Binapani Mohanty

Translated by **Manoranjan Mishra**

No one knew where Patadei had suddenly disappeared from home in the middle of that night. It was the night of Dola Purnima. The full moon shone in the sky, scattering its beams down below on the earth. The idols were taken in processions around the villages, to the beating of drums and cymbals, where they were offered *bhog* before being taken to the congregation ground. A huge crowd assembled there. Small children would take short naps and gather in front of their houses to take a look at the procession, in succession. People were in no mood to lose the opportunity to smear each other with *gulal*. The enjoyments on Holi far surpass the previous day's fun. Such occasions are few and far between; they come once in a year. No attempt to prolong them succeeds; they show up and depart in the twinkling of an eye. However, they reign the minds and hearts of all, including that of those who disfavor them.

Despite life's trials and tribulations, the spirit of celebration persists. Such a spirit lies concealed deep within. Perhaps that's why Patadei presented a smile, even though worries and tensions enveloped her. On such a day, when the moon shone brightly in the sky and the lanes and by-lanes were teeming with people, Patadei emerged from home, wishing to offer the gods *bhog* and watch the theatre performance at the congregation ground. At sundown, she had eaten a bowl of *pakhala* along with fried leaves of the drumstick tree. As she had an upset stomach, she was lazing on a mat spread on the kitchen floor. Her father had gone away, since morning, to a distant village as a carrier, carrying the idols of gods. There was no one left at home with whom she could have struck a conversation. Her neighbor Manibhauja visited her with an invitation to partake in a game of cards but Patadei refused to oblige, citing ill-health. Manibhauja and all the other acquaintances had to go back. While shutting the back door, someone remarked, flashing a smile, "Hmm...She is only lazing around. She is lying like a wooden rice-crusher, pretending ill-health. To hell with her..." All of them burst out into a loud roar. The wild wind carried the laughter, no one knew in which direction. However, Patadei continued lying there, staring at the moon. Neither the crowd out on the streets nor the happy occasion could grip her. No one except her knew in which world she existed or what thoughts clouded her mind that day.

The entire village reverberated with the sounds of *bhajans*, *kirtan*, dhols and cymbals. The villagers had been enjoying themselves, smearing each other with *gulal*. Towards midnight Patadei, without fostering any fear for foxes, dogs, ghosts and fiends locked the front door and went to watch a performance of the opera playing in the village. Nobody had opened the chain on the door after her departure nor had anyone displayed any concern as to where Patadei suddenly disappeared.

Celebrations continued throughout the night. After participating in holi celebrations the following morning as well as at noon, people found themselves dead tired; so they lay down to rest. Who had the time to mind whether someone else had eaten or slept in a hungry stomach, or had died or disappeared! Besides, there was a *pala* competition between the two villages that night. Who had the time to be concerned about Patadei? After having spent the night outside, Jagu Behera reached home in the afternoon the next day. When he found the front door locked, he felt enraged. He shouted the name of Pata many times thinking that she might have gone to someone's house in the neighbourhood. However, his own voice got echoed within himself causing a loud noise. He took rest for some time and then searched for her in every house.

Why wouldn't he roar? He had sold five *gunth*s of land to get Pata married off. The groom resembled a prince. He possessed two acres of landed property, in addition to some homestead land. Even he possessed a considerable amount of mortgaged gold. Even so, his daughter could not stay there for two months. Only she knew what had transpired between them. Debilitating worries darkened her complexion within a month. When one enquired what had happened, she would remain mum but give the person a distressing look as if she came face to face with a human being for the first time and was trying to recognize him. Jagu blamed himself for her lack of ability to deal with unforeseen troubles. She perhaps grew up with much care and affection. Had her mother and brother been there, they would have wrested the truth out of her. What more he could do as a father! Had he been a king or a zamindar, he would have cautioned the in-laws of his daughter to behave with her. However, Jagu always felt distressed and apprehensive for Pata.

The knocker on Jagu Behera's door sounded one night unexpectedly. That day, it was raining incessantly; the rain-bearing clouds spread all over the sky with their limbs outstretched. Frogs croaked on the banks of the ponds. Since it felt cold, Jagu had covered himself with a blanket. He got up when he heard the knocking sound. He asked two times who it was that knocked but received no reply. He changed sides and continued sleeping, thinking that it was some ghost that caused the noise. After some time, the knocking sound was heard again. Jagu felt angry as well as nervous. Uttering the name of God and holding the flag of God, he opened the door. He got startled at what he saw in the dark. After all, blood attracts blood. He hardly took any time to recognize his daughter, even amid darkness. Low moaning sounds emerged from his lips, "Is it you, Pata? How come you are here at this hour of the night?"

Without uttering a word, Pata forced her way into the house and shut the door tightly with a bar. Jagu was worried. He asked, "Hey, what made you leave the in-laws' house in the middle of the night? Did you fight with your husband and leave home without informing anyone?

Pata stood leaning against the wall, facing downwards. Her face wasn't clearly visible. Jagu Behera sat down, worried and apprehensive. The moment Pata headed towards the nearby room, Jagu asked in a feeble voice, "Hey... Pata. Why don't you tell me what has happened? Did your in-laws' beat you? Are you not well?"

Pata left without giving any reply. Jagu thought perhaps the situation had turned awry. With the passage of time, it will be revealed; why should he enquire over and over again in the middle of the night? Had she eaten anything? She had always been headstrong. Jagu got up, found his daughter sitting on the kitchen floor, and asked, "Hey, Pata, are you hungry? Will you eat something? There is some *pakhala* in the bowl." Sitting hunched up, Pata broke into sobs. Such horrendous cry! She hadn't even cried so the day she had left her father's home. Perplexed, Jagu wiped his daughter's tears with a towel and fell silent. He guessed she must have left her in-laws' home feeling troubled over something. Wouldn't the real reason be revealed with the passage of time! A young girl, does she have an idea of responsibilities! When the day broke, he expected, her husband or father-in-law would arrive to take her back. This time Jagu would speak his mind to them. But that didn't happen. Despite passage of months no one came from her in-laws' village to enquire after her. Even Jagu, despite the best of his efforts, found it absolutely impossible to learn why Pata had left her husband's home suddenly in the middle of the night. Whenever he tried to enquire, she would only stare at him. Her eyes would brim with tears; her lips would tremble, but words never emerged from her mouth. Jagu had no satisfactory answers to offer to the curious villagers. When compelled to provide some explanation, he would say that her husband had left for Madras in search of a job; once he landed on one, he would come back and take her. However, no letters came from Pata's husband or her in-laws; no one from their village was sent to ask after her well-being. Jagu Behera, for some mysterious reason, thought it improper to contact her in-laws' family. Even at that old age, he worked to earn wages. The father and daughter duo somehow managed to pull through.

Jagu would feel sad to think that not even once did Pata say openly that she was causing trouble to her old father at this age. How can he get angry with her? Considering the troubles that she was surrounded by, he would remain mum. If he said something, she might commit suicide. She might run away somewhere. Jagu had no one else to live for. No matter what her faults were or how insistent she was, he had to live for and with her... he had to accept praise or blame for her, stoically. Especially for her, the loquacious Jagu Behera put up a lock on his lips.

How contemptuously the villagers spoke after Pata returned from her in-laws! Some said she was driven out as she had quarreled with her in-laws. Some others said she was expelled as her husband took no interest in her. Still some others remarked that as her wanton escapades were discovered, she was kicked out. Jagu would look at Pata's face and think of asking her why she had left her in-laws' place. A look at her weeping, pitiful face would prevent him from taking any such step. He would get up when the crows cawed and leave to earn wages. On his way back in the evening, he would pray Gods to find a solution for her daughter's troubles.

Jagu lost his patience. He was feeling hungry, thirsty, and restless after two days' hard work. He expected her to wait at the door, anxious and concerned, with a bowl of rice-water in her hand, waiting for him to return. No... that was not to be. She was either playing cards somewhere in the village or lost in some mean amusement. How long would Jagu Behera bear with her antics? Was he expected to work so hard till his dead body was carried in a bier to the cremation ground? Why is it that only he should care for others feelings; no one would ever try to understand what went on in his heart!

Jagu Behera hollered, "Pata! Hey...Pata! Where are you? Why aren't you listening? Pata...Hey Pata!" However, it failed to elicit any response. He moved from house to house in the entire village looking for her. He returned at sundown and looked at the front door. He found that the door chain was still intact. The dilapidated wood-panels, biting into each other, grimaced at him. The sun was now set and darkness spread all around his dwelling.

Jagu Behera sat leaning against the wall on the outside verandah, and dozed off. At dawn, he got up to the wake-up call of crows and *kumbhatuas* and cast another glance at the door chain. He found it intact, just as it was on the previous evening.

People of the village as well as the passers-by say that there was no change in the posture of Jagu Behera, who sat leaning against the wall and sat dozing. When elderly people of the village visited him and tried to console him, he would only stare at them. If someone else's daughter or daughter-in-law appeared in front of him with a bowl of *pakhala* and rice-water, his lips would tremble. A stream of tears would flow down but he would hardly say a word. People told each other that words didn't emerge out of the old man's mouth and he turned deaf and dumb as his daughter became an evil adultress. Jagu Behera continued in that state for ten days and dozed off to his final sleep. When the day broke, villagers gathered and called out to him but he didn't respond. However, both of his eyes were fixed on the chain on the closed door. A swarm of flies buzzed around his still face.

Three years elapsed since Patadei had left home and since Jagu Behera had left for his heavenly abode. During these three years, things had passed off as usual. The deities had congregated in the congregation ground as usual; raw mangoes ripened before falling off; the waters of the swirling and swerving river disappeared into the ocean, after dashing onto their banks. Pata's sister-in-law, Manibhauja, had given birth to a son before turning a widow. Pata's friends, after their marriage into different families, had dispersed far and wide. However, Patadei had not returned. No one had the time to ponder why she had left home or where her husband had gone or whether he had got married to someone else. On the other hand, the sun rose up every day as usual; seasons descended upon the earth and played their part. Patadei existed in the minds of the people as an unwanted and unsolved mystery. Neither Pata herself nor anyone else in the world was able to satisfactorily answer the questions raised by the villagers. The chain on Jagu Behera's door had not been removed. The dwelling consisted of one and a half rooms. Inside, there lay a broken mat and worn out shawls. The only tin suitcase inside lay unlocked. The entire village had seen the sight. Nobody was interested to know what the trunk contained. Who would have dared to touch the articles of disrepute individuals? Who wasn't scared of ghosts and spirits? As ill luck would have it, Behera's dwelling was situated at one end of the village. The tacoma tree in Jagu's compound didn't bear any flowers since that day; so the question of plucking a few flowers from there didn't arise. No one had displayed any interest to reach the door on some pretext or remove the chain on the door and scrounge through the articles of Patadei. Deserted for long, the house resembled a haunted place. While passing by that house in semi-darkness, some people reported to have seen the figure of Patadei clad in white clothes; some others reported to have heard the yelling of Jagu Behera at times.

One day, there was a sudden hue and cry. Three years had passed like three eons. The incident had gone out of memory of some. Those who were completely unaware of the past events concocted their own stories. On the other hand, people who had knowledge of everything, sought deliverance. The reason for the sudden stir among villagers was that one fine morning, they discovered Patadei sweeping the front verandah. A two year old boy, with two of his fingers stuck into the mouth, ran after her.

She had accumulated some fat around her waist; her face and tummy appeared a little fleshy. But her eyes appeared to be wilting under frequent sobbing. The news spread all around... Jagu Behera's daughter who had turned a whore had come back to the village. She had brought a child along with her. It must be her own child; otherwise why should she have carried him along? Did she leave her prince-like husband in the middle of the night without purpose? She couldn't even stay longer at her father's place; she fled from there to execute the secret plan with someone. Who could have lived with her and taken care of her food and clothing of a lifetime? Now that her youthful beauty and charm were on the wane, she would have found it difficult to earn a living, selling her body. Finally, she had returned hoping that she would find shelter and protection at her father's place.

One marked heaven and hell difference between Patadei of yesteryears and Patadei of today. She hardly cared for anyone. When elderly people of the village put some questions, she would stand aside, with her *odhni* duly drawn up, without bothering to answer. When daughters and daughters-in-law of the village visited her, she would spread the torn mat, and look at them with distressful eyes, hardly responding to their questioning or fun. At times, she would give a faint smile and at others, she would be found unmindfully drawing pictures on the ground.

Everybody said she was an unchaste, disgraceful woman. "Let her live the way she wishes. Why should anyone be bothered about her?" No one appreciated her pride in being a mother, long after she had abandoned her husband. "What made her so proud and haughty?" they wondered. Ram! Ram! Isn't there anything called *Dharma*? Was Patadei a deity of heaven that she would convert all indiscretions into niceties? Should she dream of leading a normal life justifying the impropriety of her behavior? Fie! Fie! How shameless! Didn't she get a little poison to get rid of herself? Can she live peacefully, maintaining a mum deliberately?

Patadei's education that she had received up to class three didn't provide her any succor. Besides, she had no father and brother who could have provided her the much needed protection.

Finally, the villagers decided that if Patadei wished to remain alive, she had to leave the village forever. Otherwise, the dwelling of Jagu Behera would be burnt into ashes. Patadei had disreputed each daughter and daughter-in-law of the village and stained their faces with ink.

That day, at dusk, the villagers gathered at Patadei's door and demanded an explanation. Placing a corner of her torn saree on her face, she answered, "Yes…yes…I have given birth to this son of mine. Only a day after our marriage, my husband left for Kolkata. My in-laws kept me locked up in a room, without food. They didn't even bother to look in my direction. I was compelled to steal away to my father's place. At the sight of me, he became worried. As long as I stayed with him, you all heaped abuses on him. I was also scandalized. Only for my sake, he had to work hard to earn wages at that old age. However, it was always difficult to make both ends meet."

Patadei swallowed some spittle, drew her *odhni*, and continued, "I didn't have any solution to my problems in sight. I couldn't even embrace death, to release my father from toil and shame. However, the pitiless world sent me back to this place, with a child in my lap." With the *odhni* veiling her face, Patadei couldn't see the elderly person who pushed through the crowd, a towel wrapped around his waist, and came to the front. With his hands resting on his waist, he asked in a shrill voice,

"What did you say? Will you please repeat? Did the world give you a child? Why did it send it here, to this village instead of keeping you somewhere else? *Hey…* how shameless the sinners have become these days! Tell us… whose child is this?"

Pulling the veil further down her face, Patadei sat down, quivering. A flood of tears swept down the child's innocent eyes; he sobbed noiselessly.

Suddenly, someone landed a kick on Patadei's waist. It was the mother-in-law of Manibhauja, a relation aunt of Patadei. Just as Patadei started wailing, the old lady yelled,

"You shameless wretch! Is your mouth stuffed with frogs? How innocent you appeared in your childhood! How come you could not spend a month's time in your in-laws' house? You are to blame for your father's death. How dare you part your lips and say, 'This is my child. The world has given it to me'? Hey....tell us the truth. Who is the father of this child? Otherwise, I will split you into two with this vegetable cutter... Humph..."

By this time, the old lady had placed her legs on Pata's neck. A group of anxious onlookers who surrounded them enjoyed every moment of the fun.

Pata felt a great deal of pain as her neck was twisted and thrust downwards. She felt choked. She visualized fireflies dotting the night sky. No...it was too much... she couldn't endure any longer without protest. For her sake, the earth was not going to split into two; nor were the gods going to descend upon the earth to protect her. She had to get ready either to protect herself or embrace death.

Suddenly, Pata pushed the old lady's legs and got up. A five foot tall mature woman, her face turned violent, reflecting a blend of arrogance and disgust. She cast a cursory glance on the villagers, placed the wailing child on her waist, and said,

"Oh...it seems you are more interested to know who the father of this child is! All his fathers are standing here. Ramu, Bira, Gopi, Maguni, Naria and the three or four standing at the back, are all his fathers. How can I say who exactly is the father? On the night of Dola Purnima, when the *badipala* was being staged, this Ramu lifted me up, gagging my mouth with his towel. He carried me to the ridge near the cremation ground. Near a bush, they all made me the victim of their passion. They tore every bit of my flesh and ate me hungrily. They had gagged my mouth but I could recognize each of their faces in the moonlight. Then I lost consciousness. How can I tell whose child this is? Go and ask Haria Bauri, who on being bribed by them, dropped me at Cuttack. I didn't return so long lest I should disgrace my father. Even after my return, I didn't wish to blame anybody. I remained mum. Now you can ask them...aunt. Let them confess, placing their hands on their hearts, who the father of this child is!

The situation had suddenly taken an unexpected turn. The

old and middle-aged villagers looked at each other's faces. The young men in the crowd gave out faint smiles. No one was found asking anything else. The aunt sat down with a thud on the verandah, as if sapped of strength. Ramu, Bira, Gopi, Maguni all stood with their heads hanging downwards.

Wiping away her tears, Patadei started sweeping the verandah. Suddenly, the small child began weeping bitterly. Patadei dropped the broom, cleaned his snotty nose with the finger on her left hand, picked him up to her waist, kissed him on the face and said, "Why are you crying? Are you afraid of so many people, dear? What is there to be scared of when I am there? Is there a brave young man in this world who would recognize you as his son? Don't wail, my dear, you have your mother to give you company."

The child suddenly stopped crying. His attention was diverted towards the patches of cloud floating in the sky. Pointing at the moon, he burst into laughter. His laughter startled all the villagers who had gathered there. They felt disturbed, turned back, and started walking away, their heads bent downwards.

A couple of tacoma flowers that had adorned the almost bare tree since the last couple of days was swaying in the breeze. The mother-in-law of Manibhauja was found walking away from the spot, supported by her walking stick, deeply perturbed and perplexed.

Patadei looked this way and that and spit on the child's chest. She was found saying, "Ah...my prince...how you have wilted under the jealous eyes of others! Why should we, the mother and the son, be concerned about others? Are others going to take care of us?" She was the heir of her father's property, the queen. Her son was, undoubtedly, the prince.

At that time, as usual, the earth and the sky remained calm, without a flutter. Patadei looked down and looked up in succession and switched between a smile and a bitter wailing.

Original Odia: *Patadei*

A Pair Of Parallel Lines

Bibhuti Pattanaik
Translated by **Rajat Mohapatra**

Naran Das could never bring himself to believe that self-indulgence of an individual paved the way for a nation's prosperity. Even today, he had an unshaken faith in his ideologies. But Sanatan, his son, had nothing to do with his father's ideology. Their lives ran in the fashion of two parallel lines, always at a distance from each other, never meeting.

Naran sir recalled how the stirrings of filial love for Sanatan had once disturbed his strong nationalistic feelings.

Nineteen forty-two: Mahatma Gandhi and many other leaders of the Indian struggle for freedom were arrested and imprisoned. Naran sir, too, went underground. His mission was to foster nationalistic feelings against the British. In disguise, he roved far and wide within Odisha, a price of thousand rupees on his head.

Saudamini, his wife, stayed at home

with their two-year-old son, Sanatan. The police would come, at times, searching for him and question Saudamini. Naran sir managed to sneak into the house once in a while in the midnight hours to spend a few moments with his family. He would encourage Saudamini not to lose her patience in his absence.

It was on one such night when Naran Das stealthily returned home to find a sick Sanatan suffering from a high fever. Saudamini pleaded with moist eyes, "Will you leave me alone with this sick child and go back now? Only after day breaks can I take him to a doctor, but what can I do alone at this awful hour of the night?"

The sky was laden with dark clouds and stony darkness engulfed the eerie night, its silence pierced by a yelping street dog. Naran Das looked at the suffering child in the arms of a helpless mother and suddenly felt as though all his high spirits were sinking. The little Sanatan tugged at him with his tiny fingers. The child's rising temperature mingled with the gentle warmth of parental affection as he chose to forget his plans for the night after the moments of togetherness.

He held Sanatan in his lap and sat up the whole night. The whistling policeman in the morning reminded him of his forgetfulness. But it was already too late. They surrounded him and sent him into the darkness of prison for four long years.

It was at the call of Mahatma Gandhi that he had joined the freedom struggle. He had never imagined he would live to see independence or even get out of prison to lead a normal life with his son, daughter-in-law, and grandchildren. He had a strong conviction that if perchance he perished within the prison like Pahali Maharana, who died due to lack of medical attention, or like Gokuli Bhola, who protested against the prison officials for their misdemeanors by fasting onto death and became a martyr, then his son Sanatan would take over the fight. His life's philosophy would guide his son through his own life. But as with everything else, change was inevitable.

India won independence. After his wife's demise, he took great pains to send Sanatan to a law school in order to train him as an honest and independent citizen, but the boy chose a different path. Sanatan became a misguided man who was willing to do anything to earn easy money; self-aggrandizement was more important for him than the interest of the nation. He turned himself into a counterfeit rebel, a labor leader, who tried to climb to prosperity on the shoulders of working people without ever working too hard himself and by projecting himself as a leader of the masses.

Whereas Naran Das had joined pickets outside the local wine shop and had been imprisoned thrice on that account, his son fell into bad company and took to boozing. Whereas Naran sir dreamt of an indigenous educational system, his grandchildren went to an English medium school. Sanatan's wife abhorred khadi clothes. When her husband's income seemed insufficient, she started looking for a job as a school teacher.

After Gandhiji's assassination, Naran Das was apprehensive at the thought of India's future. Right under his nose, he saw people switching their priorities by making gross materialistic enjoyment the only aim of their lives. Renunciation became only a matter of rhetoric, never practiced by leaders. It was painful for him to even think of such things. He, therefore, abstained from fighting elections; something that gave many freedom fighters the opportunity of experiencing the authority of power. He preferred to engage himself in gardening, spinning cloth, and reading books and newspapers.

One day Sanatan approached him and said, "Father, a leader of our labor union has been on hungerstrike for the last four days. Because of this, he has become very weak but the government is in no mood to come to a settlement. The workers will have no faith in our leadership if the strike is withdrawn before a single demand is fulfilled. We will lose face and they will join the rival union. Will you please tell the minister to kindly agree to any one of our 40 point demands? The leader who is on fast is dying!"

Naran Das had nothing but contempt for those who started a fast and drank orange juice in order to break it. Sanatan's request caused his face to pucker with the same dislike. He blurted, "Why should I? Why should the minister listen to me?"

Sanatan reminded him that the minister was a freedom fighter like him and that once they had been inmates of the same jail. The minister couldn't possibly refuse the request of a person who had spent seven years in prison for the nation.

An outraged Naran Das cried out, "Did I go to jail for this? Do you expect a return for what you do for the country? What about the sacrifice of Gokuli Bhola, who laid down his life in a fast unto death while serving a prison term? Can you ever call any of your friends honest workers or *satyagrahis*? Don't they plan out, in advance, the date when they would end their hunger-strike? Speak, why are you silent?!"

Sanatan managed to keep his cool eventhough he was seething in anger. He felt his father was his worst enemy, an agent of the rival trade union who was out to prove his own son's inefficiency by refusing to ask the minister for a small favor. Quietly, he left the room. In the receding footsteps of his son, Naran Das could feel the distance between them slowly widen.

Nowadays, Naran Das couldn't get along with either his family or his friends. Everyone was busy - ensuring his own selfish comfort. No one had the time to pause and decide between the good and the bad; the moral and the immoral. He was at a loss in the midst of such selfish people. Even his closest allies grew to be strange and unknown. He thought it would have been fortuitous to have died in jail like Gokuli Bhola and Pahali Maharana. Gandhiji, too, died at the hands of an assassin.

Why was he living to suffer death like this?

While inside the jail, Gokuli Bhola had habitually chanted, "Inquilab Zindabad,"after waking up in the morning or before going to sleep in the night. This was his way of singing the glory of mother India and her impending independence. The jail authorities were enraged at this and cut his food supply by half. Gokuli protested against this illegal step and started fasting. After 21 days of fasting, he cried out, "Inquilab Zindabad" and breathed his last. From that day all the freedom fighters – all 451 of them –

shouted in chorus, "Inquilab Zindabad!" It was not known if their voices leaped the high walls of the jail to reach the outside world. But it daunted the jail superintendent, who thought it would be a terrible thing if all the inmates followed Bhola's example and went on a hunger-strike with no fear of death. Soon after Bhola's death, the political prisoners were granted the right to raise slogans, a fact which Gokuli did not live to see.

Following Gokul's sacrifice, Naran Das dreamt of a patriotic death. He felt for the first time the profound satisfaction and the pleasant peace of mind which come to a man who contemplates self-sacrifice for the nation. It is a pity that nowadays people thoughtlessly kill each other for trifles. So many people died in highway accidents and nobody thought of the nation or the country. Brooding thus, his 66-year-old heart was filled with insurmountable remorse.

One day Madhumita, his daughter-in-law asked him, "Baba, I am under orders of transfer to Koraput. Could you please request the minister to cancel the order?"

Naran Das felt a little nonplussed and answered. "If you are ordered to go on transfer, you will have to go. That's the way the system works. Why should I request the minister to cancel this order? I know Koraput is a lovely place."

Madhumita said with explicit anger, "All those who have gone to jail, fighting for the freedom of the country, have been making money in so many different ways. Now, you don't do anything for yourself, nor will you allow us any happiness."

Naran Das was livid with anger. He retorted, "Do you mean to say that because I went to jail for independence, I should now capitalize on it and take undue advantage of my patriotic acts of the past? Do you know that our leader Gandhiji who himself brought us independence, stayed away from power politics? Speak, why are you silent?"

Madhumita answered back, "I cannot go to Koraput, leaving my children behind. Moreover, if I quit my job how will we pay the milkman?"

The milk was for Naran Das because he was a vegetarian

and the doctor had advised him to drink a glass of milk every day. For this, a milkman supplied half a liter of milk every day. She had brought it up knowingly.

Naran Das refused to drink milk from the very next day. The milkman stopped coming. Nobody raised the issue anymore. His bond with his son had weakened earlier and now the warmth of relationship with his daughter-in-law ebbed away. Naran Das became an unwanted person, friendless and uncared for. An alien in his own house.

When he felt sick, he didn't tell anyone anything. He came to realize the importance of money in the world. Just as a society had no respect for an honest man if he had no money, a family never ever cared for the one who did not earn.

For this, he could not blame anyone within the family. They had all seen with their own eyes how people who had contributed in a very small way during the freedom struggle had been capitalizing on that sacrifice so as to gain money and personal benefits. In this regard, he was absolutely irrelevant in the eyes of his own family. But he could not help it. He had never learned the art of bartering his selfless sacrifice of the past for personal comfort in the present.

Why, he had quit his job as a policeman and joined the freedom movement at the call of the Mahatma. Was it for this that he had embraced so much suffering? What had happened to the India of Gandhi's dream? Where was that supreme example of self-sacrifice? Where had that ideal of loving the motherland gone?

Naran Das's eyes filled with tears and his vision blurred. He lost interest in life. The faces of Pahali, Gokuli, Gandhiji and many other martyrs loomed before his hazy eyes, and he grew jealous. He thought to himself, "You lucky men. You left before India sank. You were fortunate not to be here to witness this degradation of India. Your countrymen now have only love and respect for you. But they do not follow your ideals. You do not have to suffer this degradation."

At Koraput, Madhumita came to know of her father-in-law's ailment from a small news item which somehow found its way onto some inconspicuous middle page of a daily. She was alarmed. The very same day she applied for leave and left for Cuttack to see him. She brought fruits and medicine for him, too.

Sanatan was surprised to see her. He told her, "These are busy days. You did not have to come all of a sudden like this."

Madhumita muttered, "I read about father's illness from the newspaper, I realized it must have been serious otherwise why should they publish news like that?" How is he doing?"

Sanatan was indifferent. "His illness is not all that sudden. He has been suffering for quite some time. He cannot get out of bed. He is already too old; it's better he did not suffer any longer like this. He has lived his life. It's better he left the world without much suffering. You did not have to come away from the school just for this."

Madhumita went pale. She shrieked in a frail voice, "What do you mean? He is your father! A freedom fighter, pride of the nation. The central government has granted him a monthly pension of 500 rupees in recognition of his contribution to the freedom struggle and for the seven years he spent in jail." She showed him the official letter confirming this.

Five hundred per month! Sanatan was also struck with sudden disbelief. Long ago he had persuaded his father to apply to the central government for a pension and then had forgotten all about it. He could not imagine the same could have been granted without follow-up action.

Madhumita looked at the official letter. It had arrived just four days ago at her address. The central government had been kind enough to grant Naran Das a monthly pension of 500 rupees as long as he lived.

Two pairs of eyes were fixed at the letter, happy and still. It was as though Sanatan and Madhumita had come to recognize the real Naran Das for the first time. After all, he was a worthy son of Mother India, a true nationalist who had spent seven long years behind bars as a political prisoner.

Madhumita was atoning for her mistakes. She told Sanatan, "Please send for the doctor immediately. We have to keep him alive. He is the pride of the country, the glory of the nation, go, please quick!"

Sanatan stormed out to call the doctor.

With his eyes closed, Naran Das was painfully preparing for death. His entire body was shivering in pain. He was breathless. He felt someone's hands softly stroking his feet and he mumbled, "Who's it? Gokuli?"

"No, Baba, it's me, Mita, I have come from Koraput just to see you."

He could recognize the voice. It was his daughter-in-law. But he could not believe she was rubbing his feet.

While he was locked up in jail, the intimates had to look after each other when they fell ill. When he felt indisposed, it was Gokuli who nursed him, massaged him, and comforted him. Even nowadays when he felt indisposed, he was reminded of Gokuli. He fondly remembered him, his face before he died. That was why he uttered Gokuli's name as soon as he felt a hand touch his feet.

Madhumita said, "Baba, I am here. You will get well soon. We have sent for the doctor. I shall not go until you are in good health again."

Naran Das realized it was no dream. Mita stood there. He beckoned her nearer. With tearful eyes, she looked intently into the face of her father-in-law and reassured him, "The doctor will be here any moment and you will be okay in two days."

Very calmly, Naran Das told her, "No, my daughter, I do not fear death. I am no more required now that the country has achieved independence."

Madhumita could not control herself. She burst out crying. "No, Baba, you must live on for this country. For many more years. The central government has granted you an allowance. A pension of 500 rupees per month. A small reward for your love for the country. I will nurse you. I will take good care of your health."

Listening to these words, Naran Das felt an intense pain and suffocation in his chest. His heart all but stopped beating. A wide smile blossomed on his lips like a spreading wave. He struggled and mumbled, "Dear daughter, like the government pension, your love too, came to me a little late. I cannot live to share the same."

Madhumita saw the color of his face fade. His eyelids dropped. His face resembled the face of a martyr. It was like one of the profiles of the martyrs she had seen only in pictures.

Original Odia: *Dui Samantarala Rekha*

■

The Music Of Life

Debraj Lenka

Translated by **Saroj Mishra**

A bullock cart was trudging along the road in the dark night. The lantern tied to its front was swaying from side to side.

It was a pitch black moonless night. It seemed the darkness had engulfed the entire earth. The bullock cart was going along tearing through it, the light from the lantern, its only guide. It flickered from time to time when the wind blew.

The trees lining the road were in deep slumber. Even the stray stones and laterite pebbles on the road were sleeping. The cart continued its journey unconcerned.

It was loaded with sacks of rice paddy. It had traveled miles by many ponds and streams on the way.

The bullocks were advancing though tired. The axels of the wooden cart were creaking with the burden. The sound tore through the jungle and pierced the entire surrounding. In the quiet dark night, the sound appeared to be tragic.

A bat was humming, perched on a tamarind tree. When the cart came near it, it flew away.

A small boy called out, 'Father?'

'Are you afraid son?' said his father.

'Yes,' replied the son.

'Don't be afraid. It is only a bat. The bullocks are here. Ghosts or spirits cannot come near us.'

'When will the road end?' asked the child, named Baia.

'It will end soon. When that star comes overhead we will reach our destination'.

It was close to midnight. They were feeling lonely but the bullock cart was progressing slowly.

'Why don't you sing a song?'

'Really?'

Yes, that way, weariness of a long journey will diminish.

Baia looked out to the road. He could see nothing in the darkness. The cart continued its journey. He could not even see the face of his father. What if a snake attacked them?

He was saddened. Then an odd song came to his mind. He sang it out.

He stopped as soon as he had started for he had just seen a huge fire burning on the right-hand side of the road. He could hear crackling sound of burning bamboos. Jackals were howling all around.

The fire looked blood red. A foul stench came out from it.

'Why did you stop singing?'

'Look at that fire father!'

'You don't look at that, you just keep on singing.'

'Is it a graveyard?

'It's nothing, you just look ahead'

'I am asking what that fire is? Is a corpse burning?

'No don't you bother about it. It is not a graveyard. You keep singing your song'.

Baia's throat was parched. He could not sing. He lay back on the paddy sacks. He was scared to death. It seemed as if the fire would engulf them from behind. He closed his eyes.

The dark night and the unending road also terrified him. He did not know what to do. His heart beat faster and faster. The cart was climbing uphill. The bullocks were straining under the load. Raghu Pradhan was trying to control and guide them with his whip.

The thorny bushes along the road seemed to be housing ghosts.

'Baia, my son, have you gone to sleep?'

'Will mother be waiting for us?'

'Yes, she never sleeps without feeding you. She must be waiting for you.'

Baia was upset. He knew how hard his mother and father worked. His mother cleaned the cowshed of her master, swept their house, cleaned their utensils, made cow dung cakes, collected firewood and then cooked food for them. She only fed her own son once her work was completed for the day.

His father carried his master's rice paddies twenty miles to sellers. His master had large tracts of land where the rice paddies were grown. The grain stores were always full to the brim. The mice fed on them relentlessly.

Raghu Pradhan has seen his wife Rupei, drying their paddy in front of their house and collecting them carefully at the end of the day. Rice was not only their life but their gold.

There was plenty of water in the sea nearby but not a drop to drink.

There was plenty of paddies around but not enough to feed Raghu Pradhan and his family. He tilled the land, harvested the grain and stored them in the grain stores. He then weighed the paddy, carried them to the sellers and collected the cash. But he would get only a pittance. He was hardly left with any of it for his living.

Baia was his only son. His wife, Rupei, gave birth to him ten years after their marriage after conducting several prayers and pujas. The boy was now seven. Raghu Pradhan and his wife's lives revolved around their son. He was all their wealth.

'Father?'

'Yes son'

'Will the road never end?'

'Why are you so impatient, who asked you to come? You insisted on seeing the villages by the road. Why are you complaining now? You must be sleepy. Go to sleep'.

Baia lay on the sacks of paddy and went to sleep.

The moon was trying to break through the sky. But it was still dark. The cart was slugging along. The bullocks were tired but were still carrying on.

Raghu was getting old. His hair was turning grey. He was becoming weak. One day he was going to leave this world, then what?

The road was not coming to an end. They had already traversed more than ten or fifteen miles. This road was the life of river Baitarani. It was full of strange experiences and painful memories for Raghu. For him, it spelled thorn filled journeys, sadness and want. Still, there was no end in sight. For him, the only flower of hope was his son Baia. He would've made this journey several times for him only.

There was a village approaching. A spike of light could be seen coming out of a house in the extreme darkness. Raghu Pradhan was trying to manage his bullocks driving the cart.

The young boy had taken his last meal in the afternoon. He had not had a morsel of food since then. Raghu had carried some sweets and condiments with him, but was it enough to satisfy his son's hunger? He needed some home cooked rice which his mother could have given. But there was hardly ever any rice. However, there were fruit trees in the backyard.

It didn't matter. It was a question of another three-four years. It would soon pass. Then Baia could find work as a laborer. Both father and son would work together and they would earn enough to meet their wants.

The bullocks were struggling to take the cart uphill. Raghu was sweating profusely. He began to groan with strain. But Baia was sleeping. The cart carried on its journey. Raghu prayed to God that they would reach home safely. But where was God?

Would he ever remove the sorrow of the poor father and son?

The lantern had become dark with black soot – was there enough kerosene left?

Suddenly Baia fell off the cart. Raghu shouted in grief at the mishap. The moment Baia fell off the cart, he rolled under it and was dragged under the wooden wheels. He started wailing in pain. The groans suddenly stopped as Baia breathed his last.

Raghu Pradhan reached the nearby village, grief-stricken and mad. He banged on the door of someone's house calling out in a loud voice.

'What happened?' Raghu Pradhan's shouting had woken up some of the villagers.

'Please help me. My son Baia has left me alone. What am I to do? My life is finished!' The villagers rushed to the spot of the accident. The bullocks were tied to the cart and were standing on the road. The boy was lying on the ground at a distance. He had vomited blood. His face looked grotesque.

Raghu picked up the body of his son and was wailing like a mad man.

One man asked, 'Old man what are you going to do?'

'I don't know. How can I go back home without him? How will I console his mother?'

'His journey is over. No point in breaking your head,' said the man.

'Will you carry the body back home?' Don't do it. The police station is on the way. The policemen will question you and harass you.'

Raghu was silent; words did not come out of his mouth.

'Now that he is dead, what will you achieve taking his body to his mother?'

Raghu banged his head in absolute grief and helplessness.

'You do one thing: Pick up the body and go to the nearby river and immerse it.

'But…'

'Yes, do that. He will never come back. This is your only option.'

Raghu slowly stood up. He was almost lifeless. He picked up the dead body of his son and with deep sorrow started his long walk towards the river. A few villagers accompanied him, showing him the way.

Raghu reflected on his misfortune. How tragic it was losing his only child. He cursed himself. He should not have brought him with him. He cried inconsolably. He thought about his hopeless wife and what her reaction would be when she heard the news. He blamed God for this mishap.

The river was not far away from there. The water looked gray in the pale moonlight. They stopped.

Raghu had stopped crying. His heart was heavy as if laden with a stone. He threw the lifeless body of his son into the river water. The body of his son dipped into water, but the homemade cakes in his pockets drifted up and were floating merrily along. Raghu cursed himself and his misfortune. He broke into tears and started wailing out the names of his son and wife. He tried to enter the river to salvage the body of his son. The villagers standing near him held him back but by that time, his head had hit a stone on the banks. The warm blood coming out of his head mixed in the water and joined his son on his final journey. Raghu ran along the river bed crying out loud and calling his son's name.

Original Odia: *Jibana Sangita*

The Wooden Son

Banaj Devi

Translated by **Sunita Mishra**

As Chandu havildar got ready to go out in civil clothes, Nayani asked him from behind – "You came back from work just now. Where are you off once again?

"Just towards the market. I'll take a stroll and come back. "

"Going to the market, aren't you? There is no fine rice for the *khichidi* offering tomorrow morning. Get me a kilo. Get some cashews and raisins too.

Chandu said "okay" and came out of the house. He daren't tell Nayani the truth – the fact that he had got orders to do a duty that neither he himself nor Nayani would appreciate. He had received orders for tomorrow morning. The slum beside the canal would be demolished. The small temple at the entry of the slum would be demolished too in order to widen the road. Chandu had been posted for the job tomorrow. He could not announce this to Nayani, how could he? She would immediately object to it saying, "People don't destroy the nests of birds . How can you destroy human dwellings? Just because you have to serve the government, will you do this too?" The other day a Sadhu on the TV was saying, 'Let thousands of temples and mosques be demolished, but let not the heart of a single human being be shattered. Let his home not be broken.' And you will destroy the houses of people? Demolish their worlds? Just because you have to keep your job, should you do all this? Arrest them? Beat them? Punish the innocent? Should you commit these sins day and night? My womb is barren today for these sins of yours. This house is empty, this life is empty. Please don't injure me further by lashing out at my emptiness."

It was difficult for him to digest what Nayani said on such occasions. It is easier to wear the uniform, hold a lathi, try to become a duty-bound havildar. His heart, however, was like the soft, wet soil. Such words from Nayani chocked him. The world around him became wet, tearful. The thought of Nayani's barrenness was painful for him. It created an anguishing nothingness around him. So he avoided telling her about his duties. He loved Nayani a lot and hated the thought of causing her pain. He lied if necessary and silently prayed in the night- "Forgive me, Lord, I lied. But I cannot hurt her."

Whenever Chandu's Job became intolerable, he felt like quitting, but he could never muster the courage to do so. His was a government job. There was the security of a salary at the end of the month. There will be a pension too after retirement. Living well is a fundamental right.

When he got married, he had been a salesman in a big shop for two years. His salary was a meager two thousand and five hundred rupees. How would he manage to live in Cuttack in a rented house with this meager sum? A police officer and his wife were regular customers at his shop. They would talk, spend time with him. Sometimes, he would even supply provisions at their place. They were good people. They got to know that Chandu was married for six months but was not bringing Nayani to the city because he was not sure he could afford it; that she was there at the village with his stepmother and not happy about it. Hearing this, the police officer had helped him join the police department and work as a substitute for another person who had gone on leave. He worked as a temporary employee for a year or two and later, made permanent. After that, he was comfortable. But to speak the truth, he never could make capital of his position. He was a simple man with simple needs. Added to this, his wife was simpler still, with an inexorable sense of justice. Unlike other women, she never made demands on him; never asked for jewelry or clothes or made him take her to cinemas. No, she never seemed to have any wants. Never sulked, never threw tantrums. Chandu probably would have liked all that. Her absolute peace, inner plenitude, her contentment and sense of fulfillment made him unhappy. She was different from others but still, he loved her a lot.

Informing Nayani that he was going to the market, Chandu havildar went towards the slum that would be demolished in the morning. Not only the slum, the temple too would be razed. He was upset since he had received the orders this morning. He is just not able to convince himself to do the job. During his service period, many times he has had to punish and beat innocent people. And every time he regretted, repented and reproached himself. Every Monday he went to the temple to worship Shiva, distributed food and money to the needy. Nayani loved these acts of his. But his mind today somehow refused to accept this demolition job. There was footage of a slum demolition on the TV today. The sight of it was difficult to take in. Houses were shattered; the police was on the rampage. Should anyone be dragged, pushed, kicked and thrown out of their homes? Should anyone have to do this job for a living? He was disturbed when he got the order from the officials. But he could not muster the courage to defy. He just could not watch the TV any longer. Nayani would have sensed his disturbed, preoccupied mind and extracted it out of him. So he had come away towards the slum hoping to convince the people to leave. He wanted to request them to collect their belongings, take their children and vacate the place and not oppose the government move. This would prevent bloodshed. Without homes, the people would be on the streets, true. But at least they would be alive and safe.

While passing through the market, Chandu remembered the rice and nuts Nayani wanted him to bring home. He laughed to himself. Nayani offered *Khichidi* prasad to her wooden son, Lord Jagannath, every Thursday. Her son was made of wood. She had fondly brought him along with her from her mother's home at the time of her marriage. This son of hers played pranks– almost like a human child. Nayani was from a poor family. Her father was a peon in the Patamundai block office. Nayani was his fourth child. Once in her childhood, she had gone to a village fair with her father. There, she bought this wooden Jagannath. And this girl, around ten at that time, instead of playing with other girls of her age, built her life around the rituals of Jagannath. She put him on a wooden plank and decorated him with flowers, and leaves. She would even imagine a sandalwood lamp and carry on her favorite make-belief game for hours. Whenever delicacies were cooked at home or cucumbers and guavas were cut, she would bring some, offer those to him saying, "Eat my darling, eat some." All this make belief became real gradually. She wore a saree, brought water from the river and cooked rice, placed Jaga in the puja room and worshipped him there – offered him sugar, jaggery and puffed rice and lit a lamp in the evenings. Every day in the morning she plucked flowers and made a garland for him. She devoted her time and life to Him. When she got married to Chandu and was leaving home, she wanted to take Jaga with her. Her mother was reluctant but her father agreed. And so, Jaga's Nirmalya and black Sindur too got packed and he came along to be placed at her in-law's puja room.

But did his story end with this? His tricks are endless... difficult to comprehend. After joining the police department Chandu brought Nayani over to Cuttack. She wanted to carry Jaga along with her but her mother-in-law refused to relent. "Gods should not be displaced from their place of worship", she said. Nayani had to give in with a heavy heart. She found it painful to be separated from Jaga, in whose cherished company she had grown, whom she had loved and taken care of since her childhood. Eventually, however, she got used to staying at Cuttack without Jaga. But Jaga found it impossible to stay in the village without Nayani. He came in the dreams of both Chandu and Nayani every night, jumped around saying- "Take me, take me." Chandu could no longer ignore his appeals. He decided to go back to the village and bring him along. But what would he tell his mother? If she had allowed them to carry Jaga earlier, he would have come along with them. What should he do now? One day he finally set out to his village and Nayani stayed back at Cuttack.

As fate would have it, there was a terrible cyclone the same day – a cyclone that brought the heavens down. He was stuck in the village. Nayani was left alone, to experience the turbulent wind. The owner of the house left to take shelter in a concrete house nearby. He asked Nayani also to leave the thatched house. But Nayani stayed on. The tiles of her house started shaking, the earth below was rumbling and Nayani, lying on a mat, was thinking of Chandu. She dozed off for a while and when she opened her eyes, she clearly saw a black boy sitting at the door as if guarding her. On that terrible night, many houses broke. Many roofs were blown away. But Nayani remained unscathed. When Chandu reached his village in the morning, he found the Pooja room wrecked and all the Gods buried in the mud. Jaga has been reiterating, "take me away, take me away". When he found him half-buried in the mud he rescued him from there, packed him in a bag and brought him to Cuttack. His color had faded in the rain. Nayani put fresh paint on him, bought him new clothes and a turban with *zari* border. He was consecrated again with Ganga water and *panchamruta*. The rituals were resumed. Every Sri Gundicha day, she celebrated Jaga's birthday. She fed small children. In winter, he was covered in warm clothes. In summer he was smeared with sandalwood paste. And on Prathamastami he was anointed as the eldest child. In so many ways he became a living presence in Nayani's life. Chandu thought, maybe, she never could give birth to a child because this wooden Jaga was unwilling to be replaced. Whenever this thought occurred to him and whenever he saw Nayani taking care of Jaga as her own child, he got wild. He had the impulse to throw away Jaga in the waste pit. Just because she had no child of her own, should Nayani make a child of this wooden doll? And should he become the father of a wooden boy? At times when Nayani was asleep, he had the impulse to dispose of Jaga. But whenever he tried to do it, he found Jaga laughing silently as if telling him, "Would you have thrown me away if I had been a human child? Tell me from your heart, am I only a piece of wood? With time, Chandu too accepted Jaga as his own. He relished his incessant childlike demands. Jaga gave completeness to their fifteen years of married life. They could not have a child of their own but Jaga filled the void – relentlessly.

Lost in thought, Chandu reached the slum. This was the lesser known part of the city, a little away from the highway and the lamppost at the chowk. The light of the lamppost did not reach the slum. It was rather dingy out there. God knows what the *tithi* was—the sky was bright with moonlight, like a pure white nylon sheet and below stood the polythene and cloth wrapped shacks. At the front were a few brick houses. People from the city had built these to rent out to others. In the slum there were hundreds of people going about their lives. Somebody had polished the walls with red mud and somebody had cleaned the front yard with cowdung—or even planted a tulsi for daily worship. There were cinema posters stuck to some of the bamboo sheets along the walls. In these small shacks there were piles and piles of clustered dreams. Soaked in them were the lives of these hardworking people. All of that will be splintered at dawn. Chandu havildar went a little farther into the slum. People had gathered and were talking among themselves. There was suppressed agitation in their voices. The other side of the slum looked relatively isolated. Have some of the people already left?

Chandu went a little closer. He could hear a woman saying— "There is no oil in the lamp. Come, eat here in the moonlight". She placed a bowl in front of the man. "This is fine. I don't need the lamp". The man said and went on eating just the rice and the dried fish.

"Do you know the slum is being demolished tomorrow?"

"I know"

"How can you go on eating like this, then?"

What else can I do? Shall I jump into the river or hang myself? And why do you fear? Do we have a palace full of things to worry about? Just a few clothes and utensils. We can tie them into a bundle and saunter out like kings. We can easily go elsewhere. There is nothing much for us to worry,"the man said with food in his mouth.

The woman quipped — "How selfish can you get? Thinking only about yourself? Have you thought of brother Kartika? His grandma has been ill for the last six months. She is unable to move. Kartika and his wife curse her to death every day. The poor woman is bedridden. Listen, I have heard Kartika saying he will leave her behind to die. I am terrified. Can you imagine what will happen then?"

She choked again, "Do you know about Nakhi bhauja? She is unable to move with her huge stomach. Literally, she is dragging herself around. The doctor has said, she is going to have twins. Today evening Sukuta gave her 20 rupees and asked her to admit herself in the hospital. He said, 'If you stay here will I take care of the things or drag you around?' Tell me is it possible for her to go to the hospital alone in this condition?"

"Oh God! What will happen tomorrow when the bulldozer runs over these houses? What will happen?" Chandu cried out in despair.

The woman was startled at the sound. She shouted, "Who are you? Why have you come here? Are you the people who are coming for demolition tomorrow? "

"Hey! Why do you want to talk to those people?" her husband talked in a threatening voice. "Why don't you say who you are? Why have you come to this slum? I hope you are not one of those Maoists".

Chandu laughed to himself. The world has become smaller

today. Telephones and vehicles have reduced distance. But the distance between people has only increased. Suspicion, jealousy, lack of trust have devastated relationships.

He answered calmly, "No brother, I have no intention of harming. Just came to request you all to leave the place before tomorrow morning. The police will beat you up mercilessly otherwise."

A well-built, strong man charged in from the opposite side. He shoved him aside asking, "Who are you? Why have you come here? We will look after ourselves. Just leave".

Chandu was returning after being pushed around. Sometimes one has to endure all this when one sets out to do good. He could hear an angry voice from behind – "Look, one more politician has arrived. There are some more getting together at the chowk. Rogues, behaving like our saviors.

Chandu saw a gathering on the other side of the lamppost, in front of the few shops there. There was heated discussion going on between some slum dwellers and some small time politicians who were clearly trying to instigate them. The people too were getting agitated. Someone was saying, "This slum has been here since our grandfather's times. This is all ours. We were born here. We will die here. If they try to evacuate us, a river of blood will flow". The man's face was flushed with anger. He was oozing poison like a snake. Chandu stood there for a while with his soft heart melting. He had come with great hopes of persuading these people to leave. But they seem more interested in violence, bloodshed. Does self-respect, dignity, entitlement, necessarily require violence? Does the person seeking violence ever settle for a compromise? Understand sensitivity? He would rather trample and destroy everything in rage. He lovingly looked on at the people – what more could he do? He was helpless, powerless and miserable. What will happen tomorrow morning if Kartika really leaves his mother behind; if Nakhi bhauja cannot drag herself to safety? Everybody will die right in front of him. They will all be squashed. What should he do? In his mind suddenly flashed Jagannath, Nayani's wooden son. He had made him into a living

God with his love, his service. And he, in turn, had kept them safe, secure. He is not in the temple only. He is right there in their house, in Nayani's arms. "Save these people, my dear!" A silent prayer escaped his lips. "I will get *chhenapoda* home for you". He joined his hands in silent obeisance for Nayani's son – "Save me from this moral dilemma Mahabahu". Chandu came back home quite late. Nayani asked, "Didn't you get the rice?" He answered solemnly, "The shopkeeper had closed his shop. He will send it home in the morning?"

The next morning was a decisive one for Chandu – to accept and face himself or escape his conscience. He was lost in his thoughts. He looked at Nayani stealthily. Her face had the glow of calmness like always. She did not accuse him of not getting her the rice. She herself went out to get necessities sometimes. He felt a pang of guilt—he had been lying to a harmless, selfless person like her.

Chandu got ready for his duty around eight. He put on his uniform, tied his belt, put the hat on and held the stick. His uniform was his identity, his livelihood. Yet, it is with this uniform that he has been at loggerheads at times. His mind and heart protest when he wears them on those occasions. He has to convince himself; get over his hesitation. He stood in front of the mirror and told himself – "You have taken up the job of a policeman. You may not eye the perks the job gives but get ready to beat people now. You are the guardian of discipline. Your job is to protect. But get ready to endanger the lives of innocent people now, destroy their living."

Nayani gave him his breakfast – a bowl of mashed flat rice. And like every day he ate it, stood a while near Nayani's son and went out of the house. He turned back to look at their wooden son once more, looked at Nayani and said, "Don't wait for me. Have your lunch".

Chandu walked up to the slum. There preparations were on, creating a war like ambience. The bulldozer was in front, the driver was at his seat smoking and listening to songs on his mobile. The police force had surrounded the slum. There was even an officer standing, wearing stiffly ironed clothes. One of them had a piece of paper—the government order. The death warrant of the dwellers. The pleasant morning sun was spread around. But the slum looked lifeless, spent and nervous. The morning seemed like a terrorist, the bright sun like the shining blade of his knife. Quietly, Chandu was looking on. There was a gathering of women, children and a few old people under the tree. Occasionally, there were also people moving out of houses, carrying their belongings along in bundles. There were children moving around, eating a piece of roti or dry bread.

The police were marching in the slum, whistling and ordering people to vacate their houses quickly. A woman came out, picked up courage and asked them—"Hey! Listen! Are you all childless? Early in the morning, you want us to vacate our houses. Shouldn't we cook something for the children? Should they all starve on the roadside?"

Hearing this, a policeman charged at her angrily. Chandu held him by his hand. He himself went in the front and said, "Aunt, were you all not given the notice three months back? You should have made some arrangements. OK. Now at least finish your work soon. Why do you want to pick up a fight?" Having said this, Chandu looked at his officer stealthily. He knew it was not him but his uniform speaking. The officer too came forward and requested. Don't delay brother, vacate soon. Your petition is with the government. You will all be settled well. But let us do our work now. We have received orders from above.

Around ten strong men charged out of the slum shouting—"Hey, from which above? There is only one man at the top. All the rest are below. They came ready with sticks in their hands, heads turbaned and towels tied around their waist. One of them came up and roared – "The tigers, lions, and bears have already emptied the country. This land is wounded. You can do nothing to them. And now you have come to slay rats like us? Shame on you." Another from among them charged forward saying, "We are poor people. We tolerate the injustice of fate. Tolerate the rage of cyclones, storms, and famines. But we will not tolerate this abuse and discrimination in the hands of humans. This slum is ours. We have been staying here since our grandfather's times. We will die but not budge an inch.

These words sparked fire around. There was the enveloping rage in all directions. The police charged forward and the battle lines were drawn. The victims were seething in anger and humiliation, the victimizers were afire, ready to prove their strength, make a show of their power. In seconds a hurricane blew over. The bulldozer roared on over the helpless shrieks and cries, leaving behind rubble of bricks, torn tarpaulin and broken bamboo – the remains of homes; lives of men and women.

The vehicles on the roads did not stop by. Some bystanders were watching on. And somebody was heard saying—"Brother look! In all this scuffle and commotion that constable has dragged two women out of their shacks and put them below the tree. He has been shielding that pregnant woman from the lathi blows. Maybe, she will deliver any minute now.

These words were lost in the cries and shrieks that rent the air. All around, there were heaps of the remains of razed homes and people were trying to piece back their living from them – pieces of wood and bamboo, household articles, a calendar with Gods photo on it, broken toys — Life was restless to sprout back again.

The officer and the police troop were returning after completing the task. Still, there was a crowd gathered there. And from amidst them gradually emerged Chandu havildar. He could hardly walk. His back was badly hurt. His bones were rattling. But he was happy and light in his mind. He has been beaten but he has hit none. He has saved the police from committing a grave sin. If he hadn't come last night, would he have known about the sick and the old lady or about Nakhi bhauja? Could he have recognized their shacks? This would have been captured in the TV camera, the newspapers. Now in a while, they will turn back and question, "Why did you do this? Was it not non-performance of duty?" Will he be able to reply? Will he stammers while answering? Will he be able to raise his voice in front of the TV camera and say, "Yes I have flouted the orders given. But first I am a human being — then, a havildar.

Chandu limped his way back home. He knew, tonight the events will be aired on the television. It will be in the newspapers tomorrow. And then will follow the suspension order. Yes. It will definitely come. That will be followed by an order to vacate the quarters. If he disobeys, his world too will be shattered like this. He could see it all. OK so be it. A thought occurred — should he go and ask Nakhi bhauja for a child when she has hers? But no! Why does he need another one when he already has Jaga, his wooden son? He had promised to bring *chenapoda* for Jaga today. Yes, he will take some home. He will give it Nayani and say, "Your wooden son is great. If you surrender to him he doesn't give you prosperity. But he guards you diligently in the path of love and compassion. Gives you absolutely no chance to escape". Chandu's eyes welled up saying, "Your softness is as hard as your toughness."

The image of Jaga with his zari bordered turban flashed in his mind yet again.

Original Odia: *Katha Pua*

Adoration

Pratibha Ray

Translated by **Bikram Das**

The Ramayan tells us that when Ram went into exile in the forest, his younger brother Bharat begged him for his sandals, which he placed on the throne and worshipped in token of his devotion. No one has matched Bharat for piety, but Bidhan Sir's devotion to his uncle reminded many of the Ramayan. Some, however, considered it a mere show. Adoration of one's parents one could understand, but an uncle? There was not even a photograph of Bidhan Sir's parents in the house, let alone their sandals, but the uncle's sandals were being worshipped!

When his children questioned him he explained "When my father passed away I was just a boy studying in the ninth class. It was my uncle who brought me up. I can't remember my father ever holding me in his lap when he was alive, he was so strict! So I was closer to my uncle. "

He knew this wasn't a satisfactory

reply to his children's questions, but could he tell them everything? And even if he did, would they be able to understand?

His worship of his uncle's sandals was widely talked about among friends and relations. Not that he wanted to make it public; on the contrary, the sandals had been kept in a corner, on an old piece of red velvet that was spread over the little wooden throne on which the deities were placed. The sandalwood paste that he had smeared over them had dried up. Each year, on his uncle's death anniversary, he worshipped the footwear with sandalwood paste and incense. Being only a nephew and not a son, he was not entitled to make the ritual offering to his uncle's soul. Each day, however, after his bath, he bowed to the images of the gods and the memory of his parents and aunt. And to his uncle's sandals. That was all, but it could not remain a secret. These days, grown-up sons neglected their parents even when they were living; who had heard of a nephew showing so much regard for a dead uncle? It was an example to others, "Go and have a look at Bidhan Sir," friends and relations would tell their children. "How learned he is, how respected! And yet he worships his uncle's sandals! It's his devotion to ancestors that brings him heaven's blessings! Can't you learn from him?"

When someone praised Bidhan Sir to his face he would shrink with humility. Some unknown sorrow raked his heart. He could see his uncle's feeble feet, tired from eighty years of walking. His eyes would grow moist. Why did people take so much interest in the affairs of others? Why open old wounds? Wasn't it one's personal choice whom one would worship? Why should others show so much concern?

When he told his own children about the family set up he had grown up in, they didn't believe him. Or if they did, they didn't approve. More like a herd of cattle. My God! Grandfather, grandmother, father, elder and younger uncles and their wives, visiting uncles and aunts-in-law, cousins; everyone's children. House servants, farm laborers. All eating together. The fire in the hearth never grew cold. How could they all have lived together, keeping their mouths shut, like dumb cattle, with all individual desires, tastes, preferences forgotten?

The children dressed in identical clothes. The women were divided into those whose husbands were living and those whose husbands were dead; all were dressed in the same coarse saris, except the widows who wore white. Of course, the saris which came as gifts from parents could differ – but there was no ban on women borrowing each other's clothes or ornaments. It was more a crowd than a home. The constant chatter. Each person busy, but no one resentful of the work. Someone engaged in cutting up vegetables, another in fetching water. Work was passed happily from one hand to another, like an infant being passed from one lap to the next. If the women had dissensions among themselves, the men never knew. They lived in separate kingdoms. Young Bidhan was acquainted with the events in the men's kingdom, but like his father and uncle, he knew nothing of the other world. His father was stern, hard-working and honest to a fault. Bidhan never ventured near him. Neither did his father ever display any tenderness for his children. Only, when he sometimes went to Cuttack to attend to his duties in the court, he would bring back an earthen pot full of the rasagollas for which Kandharpur was famous, to be shared by all. Bidhan loved rasagollas. In fact, the rapidly growing child loved all good things. Each member of the family would get one, but there were two rasagollas for each child. His father kept count while ordering the sweets! But Bidhan had never seen his own mother or aunt ever eat a *rasagolla*. His mother would force his grandmother to have her share because, after all, old people had to be pampered, like children. Bidhan invariably got his uncle's share as well. His uncle would call him to the backyard and put the *rasagolla* in his mouth. "Eat it up quickly," he would say, "If that swarm of locusts sees you, they will pounce on you." Bidhan would gobble up the sweet quickly, thinking, "My uncle could have given the rasagolla to his own son Biraj! " Bidhan was known for his healthy appetite but that was no reason why a nephew should be treated differently from a son.

His uncle was neither as intelligent nor as hard-working as his father. He had tried his hand at a dozen trades and failed at each. A lot of his father's money was sacrificed in the attempts to set his uncle up. Gradually, he came to be counted among the worthless. He looked after the family's agricultural lands. In a joint family, no one starved because he was out of work. But Bidhan never thought of his uncle as useless. He was probably the most hard-working member of the family. Bidhan's aunt had charge of the family kitchen and spent much of her life there. When everyone had been fed and the vessels washed and put away, it was midnight. His aunt's weak back would have given way by then. She was unable to get up in the morning. He had often seen his uncle massaging her legs or rubbing ointment into her back. Only useless men who were slaves to their wives were supposed to do such things. But Bidhan knew this was not true of his uncle, or else the foundations of that vast family would have been shaken. Who would have looked after his poor aunt if not his uncle? When she had finished all her chores, she would massage the legs of Bidhan's mother. But he had never seen his mother lay a hand on his aunt's aching body. How could she? The aunt was her junior in the family hierarchy! Bidhan's mother did not share the heavy work; being the eldest brother's wife, all she was expected to do was to order people around, with the bunch of keys tied to the end of her sari. The younger brother's wife had to remain in attendance at all times; that was the unwritten rule in a joint family. But the aunt lacked neither food nor clothing. Her children and those of Bidhan's mother were treated exactly alike. The two women ate out of the same bronze dish. As his aunt had some trouble in getting up in the morning, Bidhan's uncle would go to the kitchen and make a potful of tea, which he served to everyone, servants included. Then he prepared breakfast for the children. Milk and sago were boiled and vegetables fried for the women to eat with their *pakhala*. The aunt bathed late in the morning, when the sun was warm overhead, to avoid getting a backache. How could she go to the kitchen before her bath? The uncle might be considered useless, but being a male, he was allowed to go to the kitchen unwashed. He was an expert cook. When there was a marriage in the family, he would prepare an array of pitches and other sweetmeats. Even the aunt was not as skilled in the kitchen as was Bidhan's uncle. While preparing tea for others he would gulp down several cups himself and chew a few mouthfuls of flattened rice; that was his breakfast. Since he ate so little, he was rather sickly. He made sure that all the children in that vast family had their morning bath, were properly dressed and sent off to school; those too young to go to school were carried around in his lap. There were about five women in the family, but their only responsibility was to produce a child each year. Bringing up the child would be no problem.

Bidhan's uncle spent the afternoons overseeing the family lands. In the evenings he would gather the children together and tell them stories so that no child could doze off before the evening meal had been cooked. He also had to look after visiting relatives, manage the family temple, make sure the cattle were fed and the cattle-shed cleaned. No other member of the family went near the cow-shed, though everyone enjoyed a share of the milk, curd, and ghee. When the ponds had to be cleaned or coconuts plucked from the trees, it was the uncle who looked after everything. But none of these chores were supposed to be a man's job. If one didn't earn money from work, of what use was it? It was only the women who worked for nothing! Bidhan's uncle received no credit for all the work that he did. His father was respected by all as the family head, but whether this respect was given because he was the eldest son or because he was in a government job was difficult to tell. The uncle was only a grown-up dependent, whom the family had to shelter! If the family lands were ever partitioned, the produce from the uncle's share would have been greater than that from his father's share – but in the eyes of everyone, the uncle was only the family retainer! But he had no regrets. That too was part of the joint family code.

His uncle loved children. The children swarmed around him like pigeons roosting on the dome of a temple. There were always a couple of them riding on his shoulders. His favorite, however, was Bidhan – the Bidhan Sir of today. That was because Bidhan seemed the only hope in that crowd of idlers.

In the constant hubbub and confusion of a joint family, no one paid any attention to studies – neither the children nor their elders.

Just as a cowherd boy was appointed to keep watch over the cattle, so too was a 'tuition master,' a failed matriculate, appointed to keep watch over the herd of children. He looked after their studies only in name. His real job was to be witness to the endless battles in which they were embroiled. The children had to be stopped from bathing in the pond too long, so there was the master with his stick. When eating, they had to be told not to leave any rice in their plates, so there was the master with his stick. In the summer afternoons they were supposed to sleep indoors and not run around in the heat, so there was the master with his stick; while playing together in the evenings, they had to be prevented from smashing each other's heads, so there was the master with his stick. There was never a piece of chalk in the master's hands, only the stick. Who else but the poor master could control the little monsters? Even the parents would call out to him when their children needed disciplining "Master, come here! Give this rascal a stroke!"

It was, in fact, Bidhan's uncle who managed the children and attended to all their problems, and not once did he so much as raise a finger at them. Perhaps that was why all four of his sons turned vagabonds. But Bidhan was different, from the earliest days. Quiet and well-behaved, he never neglected his studies. The master's stick had never touched him. Always the first boy in the class. And so he was as dear to his uncle as the string of tulsi beads around his neck. It was always "Bidhan, Bidhan!" Bidhan first and his own son Biraj afterwards. If it had been the other way around, people might have accused him of being partial; but since it was always Bidhan first, people said he was like a god. Biraj was always getting scolded while Bidhan was praised. He must have resented it, and that was probably why he turned vagabond.

That year, Bidhan was to appear at the Middle School Examination. He would be awarded a scholarship if he did well. But the examination was being held at the Haripur High School, five miles away. How would he get there? There were no cars or buses then, and his uncle had never learned to ride a bicycle. His father could ride a bicycle, but he had the court work to attend to.

"No problem, " his uncle said. " He can't walk to Haripur, he's far too weak for that, but I'll carry him on my shoulders." It wasn't just on the few days of the examination that he carried Bidhan; it was for a whole month, for he had asked one of the teachers in the school to coach Bidhan for the examination. It was high summer, and the sandy village road was hot enough to blister the feet. The journey must have been painful because Bidhan's uncle never used any footwear, like most people in the village. If anyone had worn footwear, he would have been accused of being a fop! The family could have afforded a pair of sandals for Bidhan's uncle, but no one thought it necessary.

Bidhan rode to school on his uncle's shoulders, his head protected by an umbrella. His uncle tottered slowly across the burning sand. By the time they reached Haripur, he could barely stand. He would sit resting on the school verandah until Bidhan's studies were done; then he would buy some snacks for Bidhan and a tumblerful of tea for himself.

When returning home with Bidhan on his shoulders his uncle would ask, "Are you comfortable, son?"

"Why shouldn't I be? Bidhan would reply, "You are doing all the walking while I ride comfortably on your shoulder!"

"Yes, but you have to study and use your brains, " his uncle said. " That's the most painful thing of all. Don't I see how much strain your father has to suffer? And what is it I do? Just take the occasional walk, eat and sleep! Nothing painful about that at all."

"But your feet must be hurting, Uncle," Bidhan said.

His uncle would grin and say "Well, it's just for a few days. Your exams will be over soon, and then you'll get a scholarship and a seat in the hostel and come to Haripur to study. And one day you'll become a big officer in the government and bring honor to the family."

"But Uncle," Bidhan would say in a tearful voice, "I can't bear to see those blisters on your feet."

"Well, don't let that bother you, silly boy! You'll buy me a pair of sandals when you are in a big job, won't you?"

"If I buy you a pair of sandals will you wear them?" Bidhan asked.

"I'll not only wear them, but I'll also walk all over the village in them and show them to everyone" his uncle replied.

Bidhan had won a scholarship. What a sensation that created in the little village! One day, the barber asked Bidhan's father, while giving him a massage "Sir, we hear your nephew has got a scholarship. You must be very happy."

"What do you mean, nephew?" Bidhan's father shouted, getting up and giving him a hearty slap. "Don't you know Bidhan is my son?"

"We thought he was your nephew because it is the Younger Master (Bidhan's uncle) who always carries him around on his shoulders," the barber said apologetically.

"What difference does that make ?"Bidhan's father said. "Is a nephew different from a son? I don't have the time to carry him around, that's all."

When Bidhan's uncle heard of the incident he had a good laugh. "When Bidhan was born, his mother nearly died," he explained. "Elder brother brought the baby to my wife and said 'I don't think she is going to survive. From this day, you must look after this child as your own." Well, elder sister-in-law did survive, but I have always thought of him as my own son."

Long after the death of Bidhan's father, his uncle still remembered the incident. "Today Bidhan is a big officer, earning thousands of rupees a month, but Elder Brother is not there to see it." Bidhan Sir's father had passed away at the age of 52, which was a critical time for him astrologically. Bidhan Sir was only 12 or 13 then. He had had to stand on his own two feet and depend on his intelligence and determination to take him to the top. But could he say that he owed nothing to his uncle? True, he had been on scholarships throughout his student career, but would that have sufficed to meet all his needs? It was his uncle who carried rice, ghee, jaggery, and coconuts from the village to the hostel where Bidhan Sir lived. Even after he had started working, the supply of provisions from the village had never ceased. Bidhan

Sir's regard for his uncle had never diminished either; he sent sweets from the town and medicines for his uncle's asthma. That was enough to keep his uncle in bliss.

The years had passed and Bidhan Sir had grown old, while his uncle had become an ancient, doddering wreck. He could no longer come to the city. His sons and daughters-in-law did not give him the care that could have been expected. Who needs a helpless old couple in the house? Bidhan Sir too was enmeshed in his own worries; being in service, he was transferred frequently from one place to another. It was difficult enough to move around with his wife and children; how could he have carried the ancient couple with him? His uncle and aunt were unwilling to move from the village to the city. His uncle was an invalid now; his asthma had grown worse. A ripe mango, waiting to drop. Bidhan Sir visited the village sometimes, carrying sweets, but could never spend more than a day or two there. His uncle was sinking fast. Neighbors and relatives came to see him, certain that the end was near. When Bidhan Sir got the news, he too went, with a pot of rasagollas from Kandharpur.

"Is there anything you wish for?" relatives asked the old man. "If there is, tell your nephew. He will get it for you. He's a rich man now; he has come in his own car."

"Nephew? What do you mean, nephew? Bidhan is my son!"

"Very well, he's your son," Bidhan's aunt said. "Tell him if there's anything you wish to have."

"Wish?" the old man said. "Yes, I do have a wish – I've had it for years. I would like to wear a pair of sandals, like the ones Elder Brother wore when he went to court. Bidhan had told me he would get me a pair. That was long ago. He must have forgotten."

When Bidhan Sir heard these words he felt as though his insides were being ripped apart. It wasn't as though he had forgotten about the sandals – how could he? But perhaps he hadn't taken the old man seriously enough, thinking that he had merely been playing children's games with him. If his uncle had really wanted a pair of sandals, why hadn't he been told? There were so many things that his aunt would ask him for when he returned to the village – a woolen shawl, medicines, an umbrella … But who had ever mentioned the sandals? Maybe his uncle had hesitated to ask … after all, Bidhan Sir was only a nephew. It would have been different with a son. Bidhan Sir had, in fact, thought of getting the sandals once or twice. But then he had thought, would his uncle really use them? Where could he go in those sandals? Did Bidhan Sir too think, like the others, that his uncle didn't deserve a pair of sandals since he did not work?

Bidhan Sir returned to the city, a sad man. But that day he bought a pair of sandals for his uncle.

On his next visit, Bidhan Sir slipped the sandals on his uncle's battered feet and was rewarded by a glimmer in the old man's eyes. His grandchildren burst out laughing, saying "Jeje (Grandfather) can walk to the court now … "

Fortunately, the old man had lost his hearing. But some of the women did smile, keeping their lips pressed together. Someone whispered, "The old man wants to pamper himself now when he is at death's door!"

Bidhan Sir was bowed down by remorse. Why had he staged this farce? It was obvious that he had bought the sandals only to rid himself of guilt, not out of concern for his uncle.

Bidhan Sir's uncle departed. The sandals lay close to his feet. Till the moment of death, he kept saying "Leave them on my feet; Bidhan got them for me. I will walk again soon!" The will to live grew stronger as the end drew near, but the pair of sandals was not powerful enough to halt death's chariot.

After his uncle had been cremated, Bidhan Sir carried the pair of sandals home as a relic. His uncle's feet had touched them only once.

Ram had promised to Bharat that he would return after fourteen years of exile. Bidhan Sir's uncle had given him no such promise, but at the height of summer, when the earth turned into a burning griddle, Bidhan Sir could feel the tramp of his uncle's sandal-clad feet across his chest.

Original Odia: *Paduka Puja*

The Torn Edge Of The Saree

Archana Nayak

Translated by **Gopa Nayak**

Surama came down from the first-floor room clad in a silk handloom saree and wearing light makeup. Her husband was calling her out loudly from the gate, where he was waiting. Surama stopped on the last step of the staircase. Inside the room underneath the staircase, Bilu, the pet dog was lying on two pieces of rags. The servant boy Mantu was sitting next to the dog and caressing it. Dr. Tripathy had arranged for saline to be injected into him. The strong body of the huge Alsatian had shrunk into bone and skin within a few days.

Bilu could hear Surama's footsteps. There was no movement in his numb body. But the end of his tail kept moving, indicating that he had sensed her presence. His still eyes were fixed on her.

Surama felt great turmoil in her heart. She did not want to leave Bilu in that condition and go away. But what could she

do? She had to go at any cost. Ashok's voice was heard from outside-
"Oh Mantu, where did mother go? Call her, it is getting late!"

Before Mantu could say anything, the Doctor said, 'Madam, you please go. He will be alright after one bottle of saline. By what time will you be back?'

- 'It could take around three hours. Tripathi Sir, you have been looking after Bilu since the time he was a baby. You please do whatever is necessary. I will only request you to stay here till I am back. Otherwise I can never be sure' Surama said feeling helpless.

- "Yes, Madam, you can leave."

Surama cast a glance at Bilu for one last time before leaving. He kept staring at her without a drop of his eyelids. He was as if pleading with her- 'Maa! don't leave me. I will perhaps not survive this.' Her legs were lying crisscrossed. Again, Ashok's heavy voice could be heard from outside- Oh Mantu, tell mother if she makes further delay, she will have to go alone. I'll not accompany her.' She rushed out of the house and took her seat in the car. Ashok was already inside the car. The driver started the car.

Both of them sat quietly. But Surama experienced a great chaos inside her. She could not understand where she was going and why. Again, and again Bilu's pathetic eyes flashed before her.

After some time, Ashok broke the silence and started conversation. 'Do you think I liked leaving Bilu in that condition? You must be present at that meeting today. You could not afford to be absent there! Moreover, Bilu has been sick for the last fifteen days. We have not been reluctant to spend money on his treatment. Even today the doctor is with him. We will be back within three hours.

It was not clear whether Ashok was talking to himself or to Surama. Surama did not respond. She had to come to this felicitation ceremony. She could not avoid that. For the last thirty years, she had been busy with literary activities. After so many years a renowned literary organization in the capital city was bestowing honors on her for her contribution to novel writing. The ceremony was scheduled for today.

How could she not come there? Her husband was more excited than her at the news of her receiving accolades from lovers of literature in the grand celebration. He was the first reader of each of her writings. Although he found fault in her and got angry with her for that, he never created any kind of impediment when she indulged in writing. Instead, if Surama sat in front of the TV he would remind her "You should not waste your time watching TV. Unlike others who don't have any work and hence can sit in front of the TV, you should not waste whatever time you get after your work in the house. One cannot read and write all the time. The fountain dries up on its own. After that, there is no meaning in having time, even though there may be plenty of it."

His excitement and cooperation provided Surama the inspiration to write. On hearing the news of her felicitation Ashok had been excited like a child. How could she not come?

Anyway, they arrived at the *Surya Mandap* within half an hour. Ashok had imagined that there would be someone to welcome Surama outside the Mandap. However, nobody was seen around. Instead of waiting outside both went inside the Mandap. It was a very small hall. It had started filling up. Surama did not quite understand what to do. She was looking around for a place to sit. Ashok asked her to go to the front and looked for a seat for himself.

As Surama was wading through the crowd she met a person who appeared as a volunteer. She asked very humbly, "Where are the seats for those who are getting the awards today?"

Without bothering to answer her the person said, "Why do you want to know?"

Very hesitantly Surama answered, "I am supposed to get an award today, that's why!"

"Oh! What's your name?"

"Surama Pradhan"

"Under which category will you get the award?

"For Fiction"

"Can you please mention the year for which you have been selected? Here there are people for three years."

Surama could not remember the year for which she was to be awarded. Noticing that she was not sure he told her- "Alright you go through the back door and sit on the dais."

Till that time Surama had not looked at the stage. As she looked, she found that there were many people sitting on the stage. The gorgeous chairs on the front row were lying empty. The guests and volunteers perhaps had not arrived. But what were so many people doing on the stage?

Surama mechanically went up the stage and sat in an empty chair at one corner. The stage was sealed with cloth from all sides. Two fans were placed at both sides of the front row. It was very hot where she was sitting as air didn't reach that place. The silk handloom saree added to her discomfort. She had not got a handkerchief to wipe her face. What could she do now?

She did not recognize anyone sitting around her. About twenty-five people were sitting on the stage. They were all conversing with each other. Surama was an ordinary housewife. Her world was confined to the four walls of her house. She had written many novels. People knew her name as the writer of novels. No one had seen her in any public place, so it was natural that nobody recognized her. She was sitting quietly. There was a lot of chaos inside the hall and on the stage as there was a delay in the arrival of the Minister, who was the guest of honor.

Suddenly Surama lost contact with the outside world. An incident that had happened ten years back flashed before her. Her younger sister Sumitra was living in Rajabagicha. Her daughter had left for America after her marriage. She had returned home from America after two years. Sumitra had invited family members to celebrate the occasion over lunch at her place.

Ashok was out of town that day. Their children had left the town long time back and settled outside. Hence Surama took a rickshaw and set out to her sister's place. When she saw a huge crowd at her sister's gate from a distance, she was sacred. Did anything go wrong? Why were there so many people in front of her house? Surama was impatient. But how fast can the rickshaw move! As she reached the gate she almost jumped from the rickshaw and cut through the crowd and reached the place of the incident.

Surama could not believe her eyes when she found that the huge Alsatian dog Simba belonging to her sister was lying lifeless some distance away from the gate. She found out that Simba had given birth to three puppies ten days back. That day, as many people were coming and going out of the house the gate was left open. A stray bull had entered through the gate. Simba apprehended danger to her puppies from the bull and chased the bull out of the gate. As Simba followed the scared bull onto the road, she was hit by a fast-moving vehicle and died on the spot. Surama heard Sumitra wailing bitterly and brought her inside the house.

Everyone was distraught by the accidental death of Simba. No one was interested in lunch. And the problem was how to deal with Simba's three new-born puppies who had not even opened their eyes. No one was willing to take care of those puppies, so young. Still, Surama carried one of the male puppies and came home. She had brought it but had no idea that she had to undergo so much pain to take care of him. She had never had any experience of pets like cats or dogs in her house. When her children were there at home, they pleaded to have a pet dog, but she had not listened to anyone. She knew if she got a puppy the children would only play with it, but no one would toilet-train it. That was why she never allowed pets in the house. But that day she was so overwhelmed with pity that she did not think of anything else but just got the puppy home. She named him Bilu.

After that, it was all about looking after Bilu. He was fed with milk from a dropper and then from a spoon; he was made a comfortable bed to sleep on and his droppings were cleaned. In addition, Surama had to keep him in her lap throughout the night to make him feel comfortable so that he did not whine on missing his mother and the noise didn't disturb her husband Ashok's sleep. Among other things, for any small ailment, she took a rickshaw from Badambadi to Buxibazar to the veterinary doctor to get the puppy treated. Noticing her preoccupation Ashok would get irritated at times and say, "Did you go to your sister's house for lunch or to get home a botheration? The puppy is demanding more attention than a human child."

Bilu grew up within no time. He followed Ashok although he was annoyed with him. Wherever he sat Bilu would be next to him. As soon as he got up Bilu would follow him. Surama laughed to herself when he saw Bilu doing that. How smart an animal he was! He had understood that there was no need to placate the mother, only the father had to be won over! Ashok used to go for an evening walk and often came back home before seven. If he was late for any reason Bilu would bark and would not let anyone sit in peace. Surama would shout at him but he would keep on barking until Ashok reached home.

Surama was not able to manage the household duties on her own. She got a boy named Mantu from the village to help her. He was from a good family. As soon as he came, he took care of the whole household. Surama felt assured. He made special food for Bilu. He bathed him and took him twice outside and took care of all other duties. She got respite from the entire burden. Bilu grew accustomed to him. He used to listen to him. But if for some reason Surama or Ashok got angry with Mantu and shouted at him, Bilu would run and start barking at Mantu as if threatening him. Mantu couldn't say anything to Surama or Ashok but he would beat Bilu up later. The whole house would get into a commotion over the fight between Mantu and Bilu. Surama would blame herself for getting angry and attempt to make truce between Mantu and Bilu.

Her son and daughter were tired of listening about Bilu from their mother. When they were in the house, they had pleaded with their mother to keep a pet, but she had not listened to them. They had nothing to do with any Bilu or Milu or whoever it was now! Why must they listen to her tales! Surama became conscious of the feelings now. Unless they asked, Surama did not talk about Bilu anymore.

Bilu grew up into its youth. He needed a partner. The responsibility was on Surama to look for a partner for him. She found out about a prospective partner in a friend's home. Arrangements were made to make them meet each other. But as soon as Bilu saw the active young female he was so scared that he went and hid under the bed and started panting so heavily that Surama forgot the idea of a partner for him forever. Bilu remained a bachelor for life. If Mantu went to his village for four days, he would sit in the verandah and shed tears for him. People who came to the house got scared of his huge strong body. However, instead of barking at the strangers Bilu would come and wag his tail in front of whoever came to the house as if he knew them. Bilu would listen to them and pretend to understand what they said.

During the last ten years, he had never bitten anyone. But to hold onto the edge of Surama's saree playfully with his teeth, suddenly appearing from nowhere, was his favorite pastime. He had torn many sarees in the process and had been punished for that.

During the last fifteen days, Bilu suddenly gave up eating and drinking. Surama and Mantu carried him in an auto-rickshaw to Dr. Tripathy, the vet. He had been treating Bilu since his infancy. This time, however, his medicines did not work. Bilu grew weaker and weaker.

Surama's small household was immersed in sorrow. No one was interested in taking food even. Surama prayed for Bilu by lighting a lamp of ghee every morning and evening. She bribed the deities with all kinds of offerings and beseeched them to set Bilu right, yet the apprehensions about Bilu grew deeper and deeper. Everybody in the household realized that his end was drawing nearer.

Suddenly Surama could hear "Maa, you left me and went away. Didn't you realize that I am not going to be live any longer? What was so important that you left me in this condition and went away? I didn't know who my mother was. When I opened my eyes , I saw that I was lying in your lap. I looked at your face and recognized you as my mother. How much patience you had when you gave spoons of milk into my mouth! You kept me alive slogging through day and night. I was under the impression that you were my mother. Do you realize the difficult situation I am in, at this last moment of my life? Would you have left your own child like this? That day because your son Mithu was having a slight fever you were not able to attend your niece's wedding reception. What happened today? Did you just bring me up out of pity? My heart is pining for you; but...."

Surama was choked with emotion and said, "Bilu dear, just wait."

She could again hear, "Mother, does death wait for anyone? Why couldn't you realize this even after reading so many *puranas* and *shastras*?"

Surama's name was being called again and again. Suddenly she got up and went mechanically to the front of the stage. She was handed over a piece of paper. The guest put a shawl on her shoulder. Surama could not stop the flow of tears from her eyes. The onlookers were speculating if the writer was emotional only with the piece of paper and the shawl. Of course, no one knew the truth!

Both husband and wife were quiet on their way back home. What would be Bilu's condition? This thought was playing on their minds . Wish Mantu had called! They didn't have the courage to call him up from their side.

When they reached home, they found that the vet's scooter was not there near the gate. Surama thought maybe he had left because Bilu was alright.

Surama rushed to the room under the staircase. Mantu came out and said, "Maa, Bilu left us almost an hour back. I tried to call you, but your phone was switched off. Towards the end, he lifted his head and was looking for you fervently. He was very sad. Then I got an idea. I brought the saree of yours which he had torn completely. That day you had been very angry with him and thrown the saree at him. I put that saree under his head and covered the edge of the saree on him. After that he became quiet. He went to sleep on that saree and never woke up. The doctor said, "There is nothing else that can be done. He pulled out the saline needle and went away."

Surama was standing like a stone statue in front of the room under the staircase. Bilu's eyes were open as if he was looking at her. She ran inside throwing away the certificate and shawl. She started crying aloud placing Bilu's head on her lap. Incoherent words came out from her lips along with the gasps of emotion "My dear, please forgive me. I condemn myself for I left you in the last minute for this worthless piece of paper."

Ashok did not try to hide his tears. They rolled down.

Mantu bent down and covered Bilu with the torn edge of the saree.

Original Odia: *Chira Panatakani*

■

Temporary Address

Ramachandra Behera

Translated by **Rabindra Kumar Swain**

One could clearly see the highway from the veranda. The road had looked like a ridge, two years ago, when this house was being built. Its black top was not visible, then. The trees planted that year on either side of the road, surrounded by fences had grown chest-high by now. Vehicles plied on this road at all hours. Sometimes an ill-fated vehicle would overturn, leaving behind the smell of burnt petrol or diesel in the air. The cattle grazed on the roadside; the tree dreaming of the future grew fast, nonetheless. Now the road looked like a fence, stretching out to the distant horizon.

A narrow path led from the house to the highway. There was no other house around this one. The surrounding area lay bare. But there was a village on the other side of the highway, and so a few shops had come up on the roadside. This so-called bazaar consisted of a few shops that sold tiffin and tea, paan and cigarettes, and groceries. A cement pandal had been built around a Gulmohur tree; people assembled there for a game of cards, as also to wait for a bus or a truck.

Sambunath wondered how long he would be here as he was coming back to his home. Since his childhood, he had lived at a quarry-site. Those hills were made of iron, no rocks. The trucks queued up there to load and carry iron ore. Such secret wealth lay hidden in that seemingly brittle stuff that the trucks were lining up to beg for it with spread out palms! And it was the people like Sambhunath who helped to fill those palms.

But he did not like the place. He felt sick the day his elder brother was stabbed by a group of drunken people following a heated exchange of words. Quarrels such as these were frequent over there, and his kind of people always divided themselves into groups, in the name of unions. The unions were always at war, trying to win over one or the other to their side, and it led to bloodshed most of the time. The laborers had turned themselves into mere objects, like the iron ore.

Sambhu saw his brother's dead body. His stomach had been ripped open with a knife. He could not believe his eyes. This man, so sprightly just a little while ago, lay motionless and still on a heap of iron ore. The face looked quiet and innocent as if it was ignorant of the worldly affairs. The blood that streamed out of his body had dried up on the iron ore. Could not the knife that killed his brother, he wondered, have been made of the iron ore he had loaded on those trucks? The knife lay stuck into the dead body as if its quest had not yet come to an end. It appeared as if the knife was looking for, with still and silent concentration, something other than the blood and the entrails that had been left behind on the spot.

Sambhu was stunned. His marrow and blood had turned into ice, and he stood there frozen to the core. A police officer arrived on the spot, and asked, 'Are you his brother?'

'Yes.'

'Who, do you think, has killed him?' he asked, not bothering much about his reply.

'I do not know,' replied Sambhu.

'Listen, it will be sent to the hospital for post-mortem. Then only you can get the dead body back. Do you understand?'

The officer looked terribly distressed as if he was supposed to find solutions to all the anarchy and violence going on.

The dead body was sent to the hospital. Sambhu left immediately after that with his wife, a son, and a daughter. He found a job, after some time, as a coolie in the road-repairing works. His prime assets were his strength and agility.

Somehow he built a house near the city, to protect his family from cold and rain. Other people also came to live in that slum. But it was suddenly announced that all the slum dwellers would have to vacate the place. He could not make out why. He only saw that some pajama-kurta and dhoti-kurta clad people were discussing something, excitedly, in small groups. And when people heard them, they shouted that they would rather die than move away, that they were not afraid of bloodshed, and that they would drag the Government to court over the issue. Sambhu now thought it was better to pack up his things and leave.

They had resided in this lonely and isolated place for two years. Yet there had been no trouble so far. He did not have to sit idle. And his wife could also go out for work leaving his three-year old-son in charge of his daughter, about nine years old.

The area surrounding the house was barren and rough. Nevertheless, it was so vast that it put to shame his tiny house, with its straw thatch and mud walls. It looked as if the house stood helplessly watching the surrounding vastness.

Sambhu was on the way home after a day's work. His house was slowly merging into the thickening darkness. Lately, he has been wondering how to make his house more respectable. He could at least build a fence around it, which would provide a little more protection to the family. But he also knew very well that the place did not belong to him. A time would come when he will have to leave this place for another. But there was no need to worry. He could very well live in the present with no plans for the morrow. He was conscious that his handiwork shaped the surface of the earth. Cars moved on the road built by him. The fields where he worked were covered by a mantle of greenery. All these he imagined, were results of his skill as a craftsman, by which he earned his living. Yet he was oblivious of the well-being of the families living in the houses that he built. And where did the crops of the fields go? And whether a fence built by him would be good enough to protect the wealth kept in the house?

In the faint darkness, he could see his wife leaning against the door. The son was lying face down, on her lap. Sambhu had no time to rest during the day, and he badly wanted one.

'Our daughter has not come back yet with the groceries,' she said, in an anxious voice that seemed hard put to hold back tears.

Sambhu sat down on the veranda. If she had gone to fetch groceries, well, she'd come back. What was there to be so worried about? He expressed a little surprise and asked, 'Hasn't she come back yet? Since how long has she gone?'

'It is over an hour,' answered the woman, and added, 'It should not take her that long to fetch the groceries. The shop is only a stone's throw away from here. I asked her to bring rice, oil, and kerosene, and I have been waiting for her all this time.'

'When did you come back from work', asked Sambhu. That day she had gone to the village to clean a house and get it ready for marriage. Sambhu had gone to another place to build a fence around a field.

'A long time back', came the reply. By then the son had got up and was peering at his father in the dark.

'Let me check if she is there at the shop-keeper or if she is on her way back home. But why are you so worried about it? Sambhu said, to cover up his growing anxiety, as he became conscious of a pounding heart, his almost parched throat, and his sweating body.

"Where could such a sensible and obedient girl go?" he wondered. She was not the type of girl who would forget her work and start playing with other children.

Gauranga's grocery shop was hardly ten minutes' walk. Some people were sitting silently on the bench in front of the shop. Gauranga seemed too busy with his calculations in a notebook, by the light of a lantern. So Sambhu addressed him in a tone of alarm, 'Sir!'

Gauranga raised his head, but his mind was elsewhere. 'Has our Jolly gone back with the groceries from your shop?'

Sambhu repeated his question when he realized that the shopkeeper had not answered him yet. 'Are you asking about your daughter?' he replied and after pausing to recollect added, 'Yes, she has gone back with the rice, oil, and kerosene.'

A tremor passed through Sambhu. His throat felt scorched. 'How long?', he asked.

'I don't remember exactly,' said the shopkeeper. 'Anyway it is over an hour, if I remember correctly. Why, what happened?'

'Jolly has not returned home, Sir', Sambhu declared as if to inform the shopkeeper about the mystery of Jolly's delay.

The shopkeeper looked at Sambhu's face for sometime, and then consoled him, 'Look, she must have got back by now. She is a little child and may have stopped somewhere to play with other children. What is there to be so worried about?'

Sambhu could hardly be comforted by his words and asked, 'which other way could she possibly have taken to come home? We should have met each other. Besides, she is not the kind who would be lost in her games. She has never been that late.'

The shopkeeper was again absorbed in his calculations. His words did not apparently reach the shopkeeper anymore.

So he turned away from the shop. He hoped that Jolly might have gone back from the shop. Shouldn't he return? Perhaps, he would find the cold hearth lit up with a pot of fresh white rice placed over it.

But piteous cry welled up within him, a voice so pervasive that it drowned the noise of all the vehicles on the road. Beside himself with fear, he looked searchingly at the row of shops before him and behind them too. He was sure he could notice his daughter, even if it was dark. And then she would run towards him tearing the veil of darkness. Or maybe he would tip-toe up to her, and close her eyes from behind her and ask the most difficult question of all, 'Tell me, who I am?'

No, she was not to be seen anywhere. A girl, nine or ten years old had got lost, it seemed, with her groceries, in a vast, dark world, without a clue. Still, he did not lose hope. Maybe Jolly was back, and explaining to her mother why she was late.

'Hasn't she returned? was his desperate question, as he returned home.

'Where, when did she return? I have been waiting for her since then,' said his wife, as she almost broke down. But Sambhu had not yet given up hope. He ransacked the corners of his one-room house and circled around it. And then he got really scared as the night grew slowly old.

'Where did my daughter go'? The woman came to the front of the house and looked around. A heart-rending cry 'Jolly, oh Jolly! Where are you, my dear, for so long? The cry burst out from the very essence of her being and left her devastated. It spread in all directions like the light from a blast. The unhindered cry was creating ripples on an earth that had grown dark and silent. But the echo did not bounce back to her with a response from anywhere. It seemed that the cry would strike the horizon, tear it asunder, and bring down the sky, like the deserted nest of a bird.

The cry could be heard at the bazaar before Sambhu reached there again. By then it had settled into a loud helpless wailing. Everyone over there had heard it. And so they gathered around him to know what it was all about. But he was in no condition to answer their questions. He went up to the tarred road, and called, 'Jolly, where are you?'

No one had heard such a thunderous voice before. Would there be a landslide? Would the vehicles be rendered noiseless? It appeared as if the combined voice of the husband and wife would cause a cataclysm, and the accompanying howling would hang over the earth until their daughter was found.

A motorbike stopped near Sambhu, who was drowned in tears. The rider asked, 'What happened? Why is such a big man crying like a child?'

The question came from Shantanu, who was the leader not only of that village but of the entire area. He always claimed that he was not a leader of the common sort and that he talked only to the ministers. It could have been so, for he had accumulated enormous wealth within a short span of time. And his belly was also on a matching upward curve. He was always so busy that he had no time to shave or wipe the sweat from his face.

After he was appraised of everything, he looked at his watch and commanded, 'Come, sit behind me, this has to be reported to the police station. Don't you worry at all! Your daughter will come back to you. Or else I shall blow up the police station and all.'

Seeing that Sambhu was in two minds, some of the people present there urged him to go to the police station. It did not take five minutes to cover a distance of two kilometers. It was evident from the respectful way the officer-in-charge listened to Shantanu that he was a man of some importance in the police station. He looked at Sambhu and ordered him to register an FIR. A file was opened. After sometime the officer came to the spot with his motorbike for verification. There was nothing new to be recorded. Only a boy of fifteen or sixteen declared firmly that he had seen Jolly going back to her house with the groceries.

'Was there anyone with her?' asked the officer.

'No, she was going alone, answered the boy.

'You have not seen her going up to her house, have you,' demanded the officer even though he did not need an answer.

'I cannot say whether or not she reached her house. But she was on her way home after she bought the groceries. She had a bag and two bottles with her.'

There was a ring of sincerity in the boy's words. Sambhu hoped this information would help to recover the lost child. The people gathered there were not merely curious. Their hearts melted in sympathy over the miseries that Sambhu experienced.

Shantanu exhorted the crowd thus after the officer had left, 'Today it is the daughter of Sambhu who is missing; tomorrow, it would be somebody else's. Will all of them go on missing like this? What should we do? Sit idly, and leave ourselves to our fate?'

'No, no… that can't be' a chorus of excited voices went up in response.

Raising his left arm, Shantanu quietened them. Everyone kept staring at his face, as if only he knew the misery of the missing girl, and that when he so wished she would be back in her parent's lap. Then he declared, 'There will be a protest march to the police station. If the child is not found out in a day or two, I tell you, the entire police station will be gheraoed. Will you come with me?'

'Yes, everybody, everyone of us,' they all assured him.

Shantanu was satisfied. But he had to make yet another strong statement, 'All my programs are canceled from this moment until our daughter is recovered. All my work is postponed until then. This matter will be taken up to the Chief Minister. We need protection, protection to our lives.'

It was late at night when Sambhu returned home. His wife was waiting for him, her face tear- stained. He sat down beside her, his palms covering the face. Looking at him, she burst into tears once again. It seemed as if her tears had clouded the entire universe in a mist of sorrow. Sambhu had no words of consolation to comfort her with. He could not reach out into the desolate vacuum.

The next day's bazaar began at 9 a.m. He looked wretched after the last night's vigil without food and sleep. No sooner had he reached Gouranga's shop than people asked him anxiously if his daughter had come back. 'You need patience,' they told him. 'Is the world a tiny place, like the area fenced off by you, that it will be easy to find your daughter? The police must try, but there is no magic that would give you results for sure.'

Sambhu was not listening. He had come here because he did not feel like sitting quietly by, in his house. That apart, he wanted to meet Shantanu, his only hope. He might be able to do something. He looked around, and wondered about the numberless times he had traversed this vast earth, and had moved from place to place. Yet he had never known the end of the road. No one had ever told him that the place he was looking at was the end of the world. If the world did not end here, how could his daughter be possibly recovered from the unending vastness? He was a strong man for sure, but not strong enough to uproot the world and bring it with him so that he could retrieve his daughter, just as Hanuman had done with the Gandhamardan mountains in search of life-saving drugs.

Sambhu stood under the veranda of Shantanu's house. He did not know how to call out to him. But Shantanu came out himself, after a while, buttoning his shirt. At first sight, he frowned at Sambhu. Perhaps he could not place him immediately.

'Oh, you…what happened,' asked Shantanu.

But in fact, it was Sambhu who was in need of an answer. He stood there wordless, wiping the sweat from his face. He was unable to comprehend whether the matter was over, once it was reported to the police station, or had something else to be done afterwards. Shantanu sir, he thought, could enlighten him in this matter.

'Are you going to the police station, asked Shantanu.

'Yes,' it slipped from his mouth, though Sambhu had no plans to go there. What could he possibly do there? He could not even speak coherently.

'Now do one thing,' said Shantanu. 'You go ahead. I have some work over there. After an hour or two, I will go that way to the Capital. I will then find out about the progress of the case from the officer. Do you get me?'

Shantanu could not understand a thing. He only knew that he was being asked to go to the police station. Miserable and helpless, he felt unable to take a step forward without somebody's help.

Shantanu was about to go back into the house, but could not turn away seeing Sambhu's piteous look. He consoled him, ' Listen, Sambhu, this kind of task cannot be accomplished so soon. The police will search for the girl. But nobody can say when they will be able to trace her. Sometimes what is lost can be recovered in an hour or two, in some other cases, it may take days.'

As Sambhu left Shantanu's place, he realized that somehow the firmness in Sir's voice had disappeared. In fact, his voice seemed like a sad, lonely house from which a frolicking girl was missing. Sambhu wondered if Shantanu would be of much help if his daughter was not found within a day or two. Lost in these thoughts, he found himself on the highway. He decided to wait for Shantanu who would consult with the officer. But at each step, Sambhu felt the proud earth sinking under him. He was in a state of total despair, crumbling within himself, and unable to imagine how to carry on living with such sorrow and anxiety. The whole world seemed like a huge corpse that lay still, face down, stabbed with a knife. Everything was still, lifeless, cold, and terrifying.

He climbed up to the veranda of the police station, like yesterday. Some people were sitting inside, gossiping and noting down something. They were all similarly dressed, and so looked the same. Among them, he did not spot the man he had met yesterday. How did he expect that any of them could find his daughter for him, without having ever seen her?

'Hey, what brings you here?' one of them asked.

'Is Sir coming?' he spoke hesitatingly.

'Sir?' asked the khaki-clad man. And then recalling he added, 'Oh, Shantanu sir? Let him come. But can anything be done so quickly? We are trying our best.'

He went inside. Sambhu sat against a pillar. The size of his shadow changed, as he kept sitting. It grew longer. But Shantanu Sir did not turn up.

Sambhu returned empty-handed, his mind having gone totally blank. He had no grievance or ill-will against anybody. Disturbing news awaited him when he reached the bazaar at 3 p.m.

'Hey, where had you been till now? We have already sent boys to your house, four to five times. Come, see the things picked up from near the bridge.'

A terrible shudder shot through Sambhu's body. What could have been found near the bridge? See, this bag, he was told. The bag belonging to the family loomed large before his eyes. Jolly had come with this bag to buy rice. How did the lower part get torn? He was made to understand that it was not torn. The read-ants had eaten it away. The bridge was one kilometer away from the place with a thick bush by its side. The bag was lying inside it, and the red-ants were already busy at the rice when it was found by the cowherd. And see this bottle. The oil was in fact still inside it because the cap was tightly fitted. The neck of the other bottle was found broken. It was tied to a thin thread.

Sambhu wished he had not seen these things. He could not take it anymore with the exhaustion of the night-long vigil, hunger, anxiety, and now this pain. He sat down on the road. Not merely tears but fearful sobbing surfaced now. The excited talk of the people surrounding him was faintly audible. Everyone guessed that his daughter had been kidnapped for some unknown reason, and her belongings had been thrown on the roadside. No doubt it was done by means of a vehicle, most probably a truck.

A woman's maddened cry shot through the air that evening, 'Jolly, my dear, where are you, my dear.' not once, but time and again. Maybe the call was directed at the bridge, one kilometer away from the house. The bridge heard it, as did the water below, the river bank, and the bushes on the river bank. They all heard the call but had no answers to offer. The people of the bazaar also heard it. But they went about their business as if nothing had ever happened. The plan to gherao the police station to demand protection to life was postponed again and again and was finally forgotten. Nobody asked Sambhu, as days passed by, about his missing daughter and the progress of the case. None made anxious inquiries at the police station. The motorbike of Shantanu was active as ever. Even when Sambhu passed by the police station, he never felt like asking the officer about his daughter.

The incident that had created a ripple and moments of excitement, was forgotten like other such incidents. The daughter remained mysteriously missing and untraceable.

And something else was gone after a few days. The ordinary little house by the highway was deserted. Its inmates went out in search of another place, where they would feel protected. The house lay in wait for a storm to be reduced to dust.

Original Odia: *Asthayi Thikana*

Village During Winter

Radha Binod Nayak

Translated by **Lipipuspa Nayak**

After living in a city the memories of the village diminish, and the city's impersonal life takes over. Life goes on ever so mechanically. Like at ten dot you find cars, buses, scooters at the traffic post as if in a VIP cavalcade. The scenes of the village get obliterated like how our fathers, their fathers, and the members of the family tree vanish from our mindscape.

Yet village refuses to abdicate – thanks to our leaders and their high decibel speeches at gatherings. Sometimes people from the village attending to court hassles stay back in small towns, check into cheap hotels, their soiled cloth bags containing their *lungi*s and cotton towels of the Khorda mill variety secure in the hands – people with disfigured mugs, pathetic glances in the attempt to drag on caught in the snare of life. They set out the next morning for the fancy drawing rooms in the houses, clad in shirts of cotton prints and skin-hogging pants awkwardly tugged upwards their ankles. They take off their rubber slippers carefully, with trepidation and peek into the room through the cracks of the blinds to read the mood of the *sir* inside: *will you help me with a job sir, please*? Entreaties from voices dwarfed from a cocktail of helplessness, ignominy and vacillation.

At other times people from villages, respected as local leaders, come to the city to meet leaders of political parties who have used them as rungs of a ladder to reach high up. Airs of nobility in clothes sense, speech marked as if of a leader-in-making, yet sad, stubble-filled faces hoping for a favor: a job for the son, filling up of the winding village road with extra earth, and the accompanying enthusiasm of teaching the opposition a lesson.

Thus the bridge connects, ever so meekly, the people from the village to the city.

I have been living in the city for twenty years now. In the village, in my ancestral home lives the character – my father, who as a result of his unrestrained youthful fancy, not only showed me the light of the world, but also to so many of my brothers and sisters by shredding apart my mother's womb. But he is physically fit, tends to his domestic responsibilities well and very carefully avoids my intervention in these matters. Suits me fine, for I am an unyoked bull. I will not get into the sludgy fields with trousers folded up to my thighs, never be bothered about the sun and the rains, and cast a pampering gaze over the vast stretch of swaying crop fields from a ridge separating two square patches. Perhaps like a turtle.

I am fine here. My wife is peaceful. My children like it here. And I look forward to my relatives too, and to my friends. Each one in the shelter of their respective forts. In the evening in the midst of chaos of the city, walking for a while and an impersonal exchange of pleasantries *how are you…* etc. Every night the gates of the forts are closed: this is *my* space. If some disturbance erupts in any house I do not bother – if something goes wrong, it is better to sleep comfortably. In the morning the newspaper will tell you about the happenings in the neighborhood. *Good morning! How are you?*

A kind of life. Entirely mine. My wife is mine, the only one in this world; my children are mine – there are no children in this world. Day in and day out, once the house is empty, after the servant goes into his room after cleaning the kitchen one can indulge in a circus in the bedroom with the wife.

Yet, one winter evening, a character intruded my fort through the entrance door. Somewhat uncivilized, even barbaric. At first I failed to figure out his class; at least he was not like one from among our fort-owners. His uncouth exterior, terse stubble and above all the gratitude writ in his eyes sunken deep into the sockets surprised me for a while – *who is he?* And why at this hour, when I was relaxing with a magazine in my living room. He stood there staring at my face. I was too astounded to say anything and stared back at him. To lighten the atmosphere he asked through his sarcasm-filled voice: 'Don't you recognize me?'

It was not a mere challenge; it pushed me to an extreme bout of helplessness. He bowed down from waist onwards, greeted me with folded hands and asked again: *don't you recognize me?*

Then he came out with the answer: since I have abandoned the village long ago, there was no point rubbing in. Perhaps a regular physical contact would have helped.

He grew optimistic with that observation and continued to talk animatedly. After all he had nabbed me, and my vulnerability – though from my village, I have failed to recognize him. Then he cleared his throat and humbly proffered: 'My name is Panunatha.'

Panunatha! A word of four syllables. The word bore no significance for me a few hours or minutes or moments ago. But now, when the fellow passed it on to me, with the burden of an emotion and a demand, I felt I was suddenly overwhelmed by a huge responsibility. Like a criminal I was trying to recollect the maiden edition of the fellow and my relationship with him.

Amid the overpowering skepticism I offered him a seat. He looked miserable struggling to hide from me his grubby cloth bag as he settled down on the floor. I stopped him and offered him a chair. Now he looked hesitant, even uncomfortable; somehow villager or no villager, it is a great feeling sitting on a floor with stretched-out limbs.

After he settled down I asked him a few questions from here and there concerning the village, absent-minded. He spoke in broken sentences, hesitantly in apprehensive voice.

I was responding with a robotic "yes" every time he said something. At a point I had been propelled to my village: his face faded in, yes, love, belongingness, and gratitude and allegiance despite his advancing years. He had married as an adolescent and that had injected into my mind a curiosity filled experience about his youthful prowess – this man: Panunatha. His manners and temperament endorsed him as the successor of Bhagia, the peasant anti-hero immortalized by Fakir Mohan in his classic novel on exploitation of farmhands by landlords. His stubble-studded face, whisper like words, eyes innocent like a bullock's had wrapped my childhood years in an opaque nostalgia. The scenes kept floating like images in a film: his appearance in choral sessions at the village club to liven up the drab life, and his off-rhythm crooning of the song in praise of Lord Krishna who is fondly called Natabara for His mysterious sports, where he mutilated the words at the dictates of his whim – *Nata... kutia... Natabara... na...aa...gara...he/ paa...da ta...laku tora paa... da talaku to...ra kootie ... juhaara... nata...kutia... na... tabara...*

Perhaps he read the changing expressions on my face and looked a little relaxed. 'Don't you recognize me sir?' he asked again.

An avalanche of emotions and joy came crashing. I wanted to embrace Panunatha and apologize for my behavior and tell him: why won't I recognize you? You had bequeathed my adolescent years a rare dreaminess; with your simple and gentle conduct you had shrouded me with mystery. You are so humble and you made us taste that rare feeling: "togetherness'!

Yet I could not. My self-inflicted airs of nobility and pedigree stood in the way. I suppressed my ego, which I know was faked, and said: 'Under the pressure of circumstances Panuantha – that is how we have been distanced from the village; but I how can we forget the village or you!

I remember everything. What brings you here?'

Relaxed and reassured, Panunatha emptied out his entire reserve of misery driven trysts, as though I have an answer to them with a snap of my fingers. Because I am a city man – a venerable person. It is not his fault; he merely parrots what our leaders blare through mikes – promises – *we will transform villages to cities*. The slogan has been ringing in his ears.

'It is not the village of yore anymore,' he kept on mumbling, 'the village that you had seen. Year after year it is either the flood or the famine to break us. People from the Lanes of fishers, weavers have left in search of work.'

After a brief silence he came to his personal problems: 'I had sent my elder son to Balimela because of Nira sir, God bless him. Your brother-in-law Biswal sir heard about me and found me an engagement at the project site. Younger son was at home, looking after a small patch farmland. I married off my daughter last year. One day I got a letter that my wife was ill; I could not concentrate and we came back.'

I knew that Panunatha was yet to reveal the purpose of his trip. Certainly he has not come to brief me about the village or his household. I waited with patience. And true to my hunch he resumed after a while: 'My wife is bedridden, so I married off my son: someone has to lit the hearth. He has two daughters now. It is so difficult to manage the family. In our days we could get a child after propitiating a hundred deities, but it's a different time now: a year passes by, a child comes by – my elder son now has two daughters. I have come with a lot of expectations, I am too old. Please put him to some job, a peon, or whatever.'

In one breath Panunatha finished his prayer, rubbed his palms in a gesture of entreaty and breathed out heavily.

So, this is why he has come running all the way on a hungry stomach. On sharing it with me he is relaxed. He feels his problem counts nothing for us, the town people. How can I explain to him that I am an ordinary teacher and a solution to his problem is completely beyond me? Rather a *sarpanch*, a people's representative at the village level, may help in some way. But like earlier I could not open up, my ego overtook and I said briefly: 'Ok, I'll see.'

And lo, he looked satisfied with my one-liner, he felt a huge burden slipped off his shoulders and he sat down in the chair with some ease.

Panunatha. Poor man! With his knowledge that he is a mismatch to the ambience, is trying to make up with his measured words and restraint. 'Relax Panunatha,' I wanted to say, 'I am also helpless like you; my students whistle at my back when I am crossing through the college corridor; they take custody of the classroom and boo and ridicule me for nothing.'

But I could not.

Panunatha will not know about all this; he is a country man, though older to me he reveres my position. He belongs to the old school of the Odishi tradition. The Western air has not invaded his body and there is no scope for it either.

He sat quietly. It was dinner time. I asked him to have a wash. Somehow he shrank from the idea; a person who is used to the spurge bushes for a call of nature and a subsequent dip in the Reba river to enter the house dripping all over, will not be comfortable with a bathroom. 'I have finished all that,' he said in an attempt to cover up his awkwardness.

I called my domestic help to serve dinner to him. He shrank again, and agreed with reluctance. When I got up from to retire for the day he expressed his desire to say something. I stood there and asked him. 'You want to say something?'

Like a loyal admirer he said in a polite voice: 'Will you not come to village again?'

I never had any prior experience about the power of a lone sentence: a sentence that could weaken a person to the extent that I was experiencing. Anger was overtaking me. I gazed at his face for a long time; but his face had begun to blur. Ever since he had arrived, it had been a nostalgic ride down the memory lane, but his last question overpowered me completely. A lump of silent tears rushed up my chest to my voice box; *hey who are you! Are you Panunatha or my mother!*

All that happened so long ago! Thirty years or thirty-two years? Is that ber tree still there, under which I had stood clinging to your sari-end, and you trembled through fear as the pall-bearers of Sunisa's wife, who died from Cholera, chanted Hari Bol – "take the name of the Lord"? Then the women in the family made you bathe in consecrated water, but it did not work. Towards the evening you had contracted cholera, you passed stool frequently, vomited, and then your body gave up. Then my forty-five year old father was charting out his future keeping an eye on your morbid body. About midnight you expressed a last wish to see me; I was carried before you on the arms of a kind woman (aha! she is in heaven now). Were your eyes working then, or did you see me through two glass balls? Did I understand anything? I woke up in the last quarter of the night, to the cacophony of shrill lamentations of everyone and I joined them, without understanding anything. They wrapped you in a bed-sheet and a mattress; you were carried away on shoulders of people onto the village street till you dissolved into the misty luminance of a waning moon. You made me forget my home in the village, the village. Now after all these years why are you here, from the grave, and tying me with your sari-end? Why are you caressing me with your loving hands and weakening me?

Panunatha followed the servant for dinner. I took out a pad from the shelf and wrote an application for two-days leave. 'Ask Prof Panda to reach the letter at the Department,' I told Manju, my wife.

The next morning Panunatha was excited, wallowing in the pride that he made me break a vow that I had undertaken from real long.

I wound up all my work in the morning and kept my briefcase ready in the drawing room. I wanted to start off early in the morning so that I reach Bhadrak, the town sixteen kilometers away from my village by noon. I planned to have lunch there and board a bus at two so that I would reach my village by four.

Panunatha hung his cloth bag, with narrow loop-handles, from his shoulder, took my brief case and went to the rickshaw waiting near the gate.

Manju came along with the children. There was surprise in their eyes as if I was leaving for a long pilgrimage. Of course my feelings were the same. Because I will be touching the earth into which my mother has dissolved after a long twenty years.

But the pilgrimage was only for a couple days. I kissed my children and they left for their studies. Manju stood there unmoved. Each time I go out of the town she expects something. She is not a child that I can console her with a fifty paisa coin, or a rupee. I am an out and out Odia. I was tickled to do something, something I have learnt from my Odia neighbors who are simulating westernized ways, I kissed Manju. 'Com'n, children are in the next room,' she said wiping her cheeks with her sari.

I felt relieved and headed towards the rickshaw. Manju went near the gate, closed it after me and as our rickshaw rolled out she waved.

On board the bus, Panunatha reserved the front seat for me and was going to sit at the back when I called him to sit beside me. He sat with a sense of unease. I asked him to sit comfortably, and after the bus started I relapsed to my "bus-manners". I looked around the place through the window for some time, then my eyelids drooped and I fell into a relaxed nap. In case there is an accident, the driver will get beaten up; how am I bothered?

On waking up it was the "home town" bus stand. We alighted. I checked into the familiar book store Vidya Mandir, exchanged pleasantries with known familiar faces and faces vaguely familiar. We had food at an eatery before boarding the bus to the village.

Covering that sixteen-kilometer stretch on a bus owned by a local rich man is like climbing up a mountain. You are lucky if you get a seat. But once the bus starts moving, you will find that you are the unluckiest passenger, compared to those who are standing next to you holding at the bar above. They have more freedom, when it comes to resting their butt on your shoulders, swinging their bags about you, again and again, hitting your head, poking you with the tail pin of their umbrella, and sometimes stretching completely on you to reach the bus window to spit or look outside.

And the torture continues for an hour and a half, at times

two hours till the bus reaches the stop connecting my village. This time the journey was not all that painful, because all along, from the "home town" to the village winter season had captured everywhere in its impact. In comparison the chill in the city was less.

We alighted at our stop and got a rickshaw. He will carry us for the next four kilometers. Panunatha bargained for the rate; the rickshaw puller was a known face. I looked around the place with investigating eyes; a bubbling little town had come up over the place that was restricted to a few thatched shops and wood-and-tin cabins some years ago.

The place has been gaining in weight: a cinema hall with irregular screenings, availability of local and foreign alcoholic beverages at every hour of the day. People no more are seen in Khordha *lungis*, bell-bottomed pants and printed shirts have overtaken. 'The youth are now hooked to ganja; they stuff cannabis into their cigarette rolls and have fun. The village has undergone a complete makeover,' Panunatha informs.

It is winter.

Panunatha waited near the rickshaw. It was past four in the afternoon. The body felt the chill. I had not brought any warm clothes with me. Perhaps to show off. Panunatha – how my mother's soul possessed him and I was overwhelmed. Now I feel a kind of excitement to touch the soil of my village after a gap of two decades. If Panunatha had not arrived suddenly in a winter evening, my memories of my village would have lain hidden somewhere. For decades.

We sat in the rickshaw. Through the sprawling fields of ripe rice stalks ran a country road of red earth and stones, stretched like a line of vermillion on the parting of a graying woman. It was a nice feeling, the cool air and the harvest scene. No one bothered to look at us. Like load-carrying animals they bent down over the stalks, ripping at the stalks with sickles. Standing at intervals to arrange the cut stalks in rows. The smell of ripe paddy melting into the winter chill. Emotions well up: the village is beautiful if you can feel it. Here you can absorb the seasons into your body;

you can't do that in the city. Seasons come and go; the rat race of city life keeps you from taking note.

I had lost myself in my new surroundings when Panunnatha said: 'Many old-world people have passed away already.' Panunatha said. 'The old man of the Sahu household is counting his days. This winter...'

The words trickled down my ears, hit at the eardrum. I was feeling weak at heart. Suddenly I became mad at Panunatha; he should be satisfied that I was travelling with him to the village. 'Don't take advantage of my gesture, with all these stories,' I wanted to scream. 'Or else I will throw you out of the rickshaw with one tight slap.'

But I could not. Because I had been vanquished by him. I could only turn my face away.

The rickshaw reached the river bank. We got down, paid the fellow and walked along the embankment. It was about to get dark. On seeing us a number of half-naked children of the village made a line behind us and I felt as though I was the fabled Pied Piper, who with his flute has mesmerized the innocent children and is luring them inside some dark cavern.

Before reaching home I glanced at the spot in front of the house where a ber tree stood during my childhood. It was not there, perhaps hacked off from long. Still I paused there for a while – the memories of the tree! Panunatha handed me my briefcase as the members of my father's family stood waiting at the entrance. The children following me stood at a distance, thronging, taking me to be a guest or someone returning from Kolkata, who will unpack his suitcase and hand them each a date.

I cast my gaze on the character called "father", who, the burden of his years loaded on his shoulders, had waited for me with his cataract layered eyes. The children left for their homes as it was getting dark. We sat in silence. In that brief session he uttered his lone sentence: 'You came, I feel so relieved!'

My eyes moistened. My lungs choked. Because, between the geriatric before me and myself perhaps stood the shadow of a woman – of thirty or thirty-two years ago. Unnoticed.

After a while I remembered something Panunatha had said: a number of aging people had passed away, and the Sahoo family-head was on the verge of death. It was rather late for the village, yet I wished to see the old man. Panunatha had finished with his wash and reported back. I took him with me for a visit to the house located at the end of the village.

During winter, the houses in the village shut their doors by seven in the evening. Still people sat on their verandahs sparsely, talking. 'So uncommon!' Someone commented on me.

We reached Sahoo's house. Panunatha entered first, while I stood outside. A few minutes later Sahoo's elder son came out with an uncovered wick-lamp in his hand. He greeted me and led me inside the house: 'Please bend down; or else your head will hit the eaves.'

Sahoo leant against the wall on a mat soaked in sooty oil. He looked macabre with his abnormally swollen limbs. He tried to straighten up when his son gave him the news of my arrival. He was helped to sit up. For a while anger blazed in his sunken eyes. 'What brought you here sir,' he said through his quivering voice. 'You come once in five years, win us with your charming words. You say the government is giving free medicine, but look at my legs. What medicine did you give me? And the scalawags who are on your payroll to implement the scheme – they siphoned off the price money for the medicines too. We will die anyway; why do you come here and show your face.'

He will not buy the testimonies of his son and Panunatha: that I was not a politician; I am a son of the village. 'Get lost, you all are the same, the selfsame bunch of traitors,' he screamed. 'You live comfortably in the city and come here to shed crocodile's tears.'

Then he became quiet resolutely and hung his head.

I felt as if I am passing out. I was sure the aged patriarch hung down his face out of his collective anger and arrogance of a lifetime, and he will never look up. Who is he? The man who fought for countless geriatrics, like Sahoo, and their sons throughout the country – a country of villages and counties – and lost to a bullet from Nathuram Godse? Or is he his spirit? Little Odisha after all is a part of Mother India.

I almost darted out of the house, consumed by anxiety and a sense of guilt. I reached home, had a scratchy dinner and slept off; I did not share with anyone any of my experiences.

The next day I left before sun showed up; and whoever I met on the same red road on my way back appeared to me like the old Sahoo – they all had the same pair of comatose eyes and wilted face.

I raced, panting for breath, till I reconnected to my space in my city and vowed: no, I will not let Panunatha enter the space of my drawing ever.

Original Odia: *Seeta Dine Gaan ra Drushy*

Witness

Padmaj Paul

Translated by **Gopa Nayak**

My lord, I promise in the name of Gita, that I will speak only the truth, nothing but the truth. The respected lawyer adjusted his glasses and looked at the person like a snake that had raised its hood. After that, the portion of his body, from the chest to the head just stirred a bit. As if he could understand that the person was crooked and was there to give some false evidence.

Alright, what is your name?

Giridhari Sahu

What do you do?

Nothing, Sir

So, do you roam around in the market all the time?

No Sir, I don't get enough time to do my work. Why should I waste my time in the market for nothing?

Then are you always at home?

No Sir, I work as a laborer in the farms and agricultural fields.

You just said that you don't do anything

Giridhari looked at the lawyer with shock. As if from those helpless looks of his he wanted to say- 'Don't confuse me anymore, please. So many people and so many lawyers. I am scared. My throat is dry. My heart is beating fast. I may fall down. Please let me go.'

'So you were roaming in the market that day.'

'No, Sir.'

'Then you have not seen anything?'

'No, Sir.'

'Then how did your name come up in the list of witnesses?'

'Sir, my wife did not let me live in peace. She kept on nagging me all the time.'

Suddenly the lawyer cut his words and without allowing him to say anything said – 'So you are here because your wife forced you to come and give evidence here. You had not gone to the market that day or seen anything.'

My Lord, May this point be noted. Giridhari Sahu is a false witness. He has come here because his wife forced him to do so.

Giridhari Sahu got confused

'No Sir. I have never been involved with courts and cases. I am really afraid of these places. That is why I was pleading with Nagamani not to get me involved in those things. I won't be able to say anything.'

Now the Judge leaned back in his chair and said in a relaxed voice

'No you don't get scared. Tell us the truth. Your evidence is very important'.

Giridhari Sahu gathered confidence and requested the judge

'Please don't ask me anything else. Please let me go. My limbs are shaking. Please call me another day and ask me whatever you want and I will tell you everything. Today......' Giridhari looked at the judge and the lawyer folding his hands and as if pleading with his eyes.

The Judge looked at the Najar and said- 'This witness will come as the last witness for this case. So please arrange a date for him. Let him go today.'

'Yes, you may go'.

As soon as Giridhari got the orders from the lawyer he folded his hands and paid respect to the court with gratitude. When he lifted his legs and stepped down from the platform and came out he could not even breathe properly. He pushed himself out and sat down on the verandah outside the court.

There were many people both inside and outside the court premises. There was commotion all around. As soon as he caught his breath he struck his head and looked for the only person that was Nagamani. The lawyer who was questioning him was standing at a distance and smoking a cigarette. His junior was standing next to him and asking him something with a smile on his face. The judicial clerk was also standing next to him with a file in his hand. They were all happy. Giridhari turned his face away in disgust. He noticed two policemen standing next to him. They were chatting with an intention to make him hear- 'The rogue is pretending. At home, he shows off as if he can speak eloquently and knows all laws and regulations. This careless chap spent someone else's money to come here, only to dismiss the case.'

Hey didn't you see the murder happening?

Giridhari stood up and said- 'Yes Sir, I had seen.'

The policeman got irritated and said – 'If you had seen, then why did you say, wife said, mother said, father said?'

'Sir, I got confused'.

'Hey, have you pocketed something from the opposite party?' The policeman rubbed his fingers and gave indications.

'Sir, I swear in the name of Lord Jagannath. Virtue prevails in these courts. Those things are not in Giridhari's horoscope.'

Both the policemen left the place without intention to hear Giridhari any longer. Giridhari felt desperate and turned his face to search for Nagamani. He did not have any money to return to the village or even to eat. He did not know what to do. He was suffering from self-remorse and looking for Nagamani.

He could not believe his eyes when he found that Nagamani was standing close to him on the verandah of the court. As he looked at him he felt like a criminal himself. He did not have the courage to go to him. He just moved to and fro in the same place.

After some time Nagamani himself called him in a not so loving voice -'Oh Brother Giria, come and have some food.'

He started walking. Giridhari followed him.

They entered into Hotel Annapurna. They got water from the bucket with a mug, washed their faces and hands and sat down between a long bench and a desk.

-'Nagu Sir, it may be a lie for you but it is true for me. I got confused.' Giridhari made an attempt to explain himself. I am sitting in front of Goddess Laksmi (food is considered Laksmi in Odia culture). If I utter lies I will not get food for the next seven births.'

'What will you eat, fish or vegetarian?' Nagamani asked without heeding to Giridhari's words.

Giridhari did not want to eat after being treated so callously. He said in a tone of sadness and repentance – 'Are you angry with me?'

'I have stopped taking non-vegetarian food after the death of my son.'

'Please give one vegetarian and one non-vegetarian plate of food here.' Nagamani ordered the cook.

Giridhari was almost in tears. In a tone of utter humility, he said- 'Alright Nagu Sir, I have already committed a mistake. No one benefitted from our coming here, neither you nor me. When I reach home I will return the money that you have spent on me.'

Nagamani was about to take a ball of rice into his mouth when he stopped and looked at Giridhari. With a thick and loaded tone, he said- 'Yes, you can return me the money but can you give me back my twenty-two-year-old son?'

Giridhari was mixing rice with dal on his plate with his fingers.

'If you had wished you could have told the court whatever you had seen. And the murderers would have been punished. Why didn't you do it? Do you think I don't know why you didn't say it? I know everything.'

'What do you know?' Giridhari lifted his head and asked.

'Any way eat. The rice is getting cold. I cannot eat. My heart is burning. Whom will I say these things? People who have seen everything, my own people are not opening their mouths to speak the truth. I have to bear this sorrow along with the sorrow of my son's death. How selfish and callous human beings have become nowadays! Truth and justice seem to have disappeared from everywhere. How will one survive in this world? I thought those hooligans cannot escape after killing my son in front of everyone in the middle of the market place. They will be punished. But those people who have seen everything are hesitating to provide evidence. They are saying they have not seen anything. Don't get us into trouble.' Nagamani heaved a deep sigh and moved away from the food. He washed his hands and came and stood next to Giridhari. He told him- 'You eat your food. Don't worry. I will go out and get a *paan*.'

Giridhari was listening to everything silently. He felt like a criminal and could not eat anything even though he was hungry. He even did not want to leave the plate of rice and move away. Anyway, he thrust the rice down his throat and washed his hand. He wiped his hand on the edge of his cloth and took the paan from Nagamani. He felt very forlorn and low about himself. He followed him silently.

By the time they reached their village bus-stop and got off the bus, it was night. Giridhari had to travel some distance in order to reach his home.

'Let me accompany you till you reach your home.' Nagamani said

'No, I can go on my own.'

'It is already dark. You may be afraid.'

Not really, I won't be scared'. Giridhari stopped as he said the words.

'Don't you get scared?' Nagamani asked in a sharp tone.

Giridhari kept quiet. He did not know what to answer. Nagamani was walking ahead of him. Like a spineless being, he was following him, going wherever his legs carried him. Nandi

Apa, Nandi Apa, open the door.' Nagamani went and banged on the door of Giridhari's house.

Suddenly Nandi Apa came out with a portable oil lamp and opened the door.

'So you all are here? Come inside the house.'

'No, I am leaving. I just came to drop my brother because I thought he may be scared.'

Just tell me what happened and then leave.' Nandi Apa was found saying impatiently.

You ask him and find out everything. I am tired.' Nagamani said these words and climbed down the steps.

'Hey, carry the light with you. How will you go in the dark?'

I can go. After my son's death, what do I care? My love for life has all but vanished. You don't worry.'

Nagamani left after saying these words. His voice got Nandi Apa confused. Her compassionate heart was full of sorrow.

They entered the house through the door. Without saying a word Giridhari went to the well to wash his hands and legs. Nandi Apa looked for a towel and got one. She gave it to her husband. He wiped himself and changed into the towel.

What happened? Why aren't you saying anything?

Nandi Apa kept the oil lamp on the floor and sat down.

'What could happen? Giridhari heaved a deep sigh and sat down on the bed.

'Didn't you give evidence?'

'I gave but couldn't say anything.'

'Couldn't you say whatever you had seen?'

'No'

'No, Why?' Nandi asked, quite irritated.

'I was afraid.'

'Of whom?

I haven't told you something because I thought you would worry.'

What haven't you told me?' Nandi looked at her husband sharply.

'Two days back a group of hooligans surrounded me and

asked me- 'Are you going to be a witness in Aju's murder case? 'I was surprised and kept on listening to them. They didn't let me say anything. They kept on saying- 'Listen rascal. Aju is dead and gone. Why would you waste another young man's life for him? Look, if you say anything in the court about what you saw then be prepared for the consequences. Make sure that your wife has taken out the bangles because no one will be able to save you when you come out of the court.'

'You didn't give evidence out of this fear.' There was hatred in Nandi's voice. 'Everyone kept quiet out of fear. They all pretended as if they had not seen anything. As if they didn't know anything about the incident. They call themselves men. Even after the murder, they had sworn that they would do everything to bring the culprit to justice. However, when the murderer's evil father and his friends bribed and threatened them they all kept mum.'

'At last, you also did the same thing.'

'You didn't think of virtue. You didn't look at my brother, Nagu's face. What a simple person he is! His mother had adopted me as her daughter and he treats me like his own biological sister. He has so much respect for you. How did you forget everything out of fear? Real shame on you − − Can't we live in peace in this country, anymore? Wicked people have always been there and will always be there. It does not mean we will be afraid of these unsocial people and waver from telling the truth. Can't we even say the truth that we saw with our own eyes?'

Nandi's eyes appeared to be burning in anger and hatred. You made me appear so lowly just for these bangles? Did you keep the honor of these bangles? What is the point in having them, anyway?'

Nandi banged both her arms on the floor with a lot of force. The glass bangles broke into pieces and lay scattered all around. After that, she cried aloud out of desperation.

Giridhari stood up in shock.

Original Odia: *Sakshi*

■

The Pathway

Tarun Kanti Mishra

Translated by **Bhagaban Jayasingh**

Right in front of the house lay a heap of garbage; a whiff of the stench emanated from the drain and some splinters of darkness spread on the veranda.

All these the young man crossed, one after another before he touched the front door, such meticulously careful hand lest it should butt in one's sleep.

He did not have to knock on the door twice; it opened slowly, like a magic door.

It was dark inside.

From the other end came an indistinct female voice enquiring, 'Who is there?' and saying a little later, 'O you!'

Inside the room, there was no light, no light on the veranda either; in short, the lane was buried in darkness.

Load-shedding. From evening six to eight-thirty.

'Come in.'

The young man handed over a small

paper bag to the girl. Then bending a little, he started unlacing his shoes.

'Grandpa is unwell, again,' said the girl, fixing her eyes on the listless darkness.

'What's the temperature he is running now?'

'I don't know, but his body feels warm.'

The question was pointless. There was a thermometer in the house. For quite some time, perhaps.

'Has he taken any medicine?'

'No, but if the fever persists, I think, I'll have to go to Dr. Das tomorrow.'

The girl lighted a candle, which shone on a pair of tender hands, tired eyes and the blouse with a button unfastened.

'When did you return from office?' the young man asked.

'About an hour ago. Come, tea will be ready in a minute.'

'A lantern burnt feebly in the courtyard. The air seemed trapped under a slice of the sky, dark and moonless.

The girl went towards the kitchen, candle in hand. Before settling on the plank bed, the young man peered into the bedroom. From inside came the sound of long sleepy gasps and the irregular gulps of air from a phlegm-filled chest.

Somewhere far off, there was a noise. Maybe, someone was squabbling with a hawker at the end of the street. Maybe, it was a minor accident, or usual antics of the street urchins.

From a distance, it's all the same: joys or tears, anger or sorrow. The young man gazed at the sky. He could see nothing in that empty expanse. A hand reached out of the darkness, a voice said softly, 'Your tea.'

The girl held in her hand a cup for herself. After a sip, she asked tenderly, 'Why are you so quiet? Aren't you feeling well?'

'No, I'm okay,' the young man answered vaguely.

'O my God, look, so many stars in the sky!' exclaimed the girl, her eyes glittering like a couple of stars.

'Is it Amavasya tonight?'

The young man did not reply. Either he did not know the answer or the question seemed irrelevant.

Suddenly, a bout of coughing interrupted the sleep of the old man in the bedroom. It was followed by a feeble voice calling, 'Manju, where are you?'

Putting the teacup on the plank bed the girl walked towards the bedroom.

A sip of water, a bedpan or help for turning on the side was all that paralytic man needed now.

The young man followed her after he had finished his tea.

The man was lying on the cot smelt the air and asked, 'Who, Jajati!'

'Yes, it's me,' answered the young man.

'Where were you all these days? Have you forgotten us?'

The young man was going to say something in reply but remained quiet. He came almost every evening; it was only yesterday that he could not drop in. For good reasons.

The old man asked, 'Have you brought that?'

'Yes,' said he, 'I have given it to Manju.'

'Then give it to me,' the old man raised his hand.

The girl pleaded, 'No, not now, Grandpa. You can have it a little later. It's so dark now.'

'Dark! My foot!' fumed the old man, 'Can't one munch a handful of puffed rice in the dark!'

The girl had reasons to object. This stuff would upset the stomach of the ailing man.

The old man always craved for just a mouthful of puffed rice mixed with spices. He would get into a foul mood if he could not have this at least thrice a week. And, mind you, homemade stuff would not do; it had to have all the toothsome spices.

'What would you like to have tonight, Grandpa?', asked the girl, 'rice or roti?'

'I'll have ashes!' growled the old man, grinding his teeth. A blob of anger melted as it slid down his phlegm-filled chest.

Of course, he did not always throw tantrums like this. At times he would also be cheerful. He would then talk endlessly about by-gone days. An encounter with a man-eater in Koraput valley, a rain-washed night in Chilka lake. Or he would talk about his discovery of a recipe for baking fish with *saru* leaves.

'Just wait, let me get a little better. I will one day cook you a wonderful dish of fish with saru leaves. It will be so delicious I bet you fellows would lick your fingers all day.'

Grandpa was confident that soon he would regain his former strength. Almost inevitably, he would begin a journey along a reverse pathway through the various stages of old age, youth, childhood and finally to infancy. 'But, first of all, let this winter pass.'

The girl went out of the room, carrying an empty glass and a urine-filled can. The darkness, sticky and invisible like cobwebs, hung over the room now.

The old man's voice sounded more animated than before.

'A little while ago, I was dreaming a very strange dream.'

The young man bent forward to listen what he wanted to say.

'I dreamed I was on the back of a white horse. A robust horse in fine fettle, a Pegasus, as it were. On either side stretched a jungle. Snowflakes fell silently through the air. I did not know where I was heading. But I galloped along for miles and miles....just pull the blanket over my leg, left leg...

'Yes, then, I merged into a big procession. Not knowing what kind of procession it was. At length, I found out it was my marriage procession. And it continued for long till my horse was completely worn out, the white of his body turned peacock blue and the flakes of snow flew about like plumes of roosters in the wind. Then...'

Grandpa paused. Perhaps he took a deep sigh. Maybe, with his left hand, he wiped the saliva that trickled out of his mouth.

...'I can't recollect what happened next. All that I can remember is I spent my honeymoon night right away... 'Dhut!' exclaimed Grandpa, 'What a fool I was then! A real chump!'

A splutter was heard. The old man was chucking to himself.

The sound faded. Perhaps he was raking up old memories. Or he had dozed off.

The young man came out of the room. Sitting on the veranda, the girl was making a dough of flour. A transistor lay on the plank bed.

'This belongs to Mohanty sir, our neighbor,' said the girl, 'Would you check what's wrong with this, he says it does not tune in short wave!'

There was earnestness in her voice as if she wanted to entrust him with the most important task in the world.

The young man picked up the transistor. He twiddled with it for sometime and then gave up.

'It doesn't work at all, not even on the medium band; does it have batteries?'

Today a customer had come to his shop with a radio like this. 'Have a look at this damned thing, will you! Only a week ago I had put a couple of brand new heavy-duty batteries and barely heard the seven o' clock news twice a day. And now this black box is as dead as a coffin!'

After half an hour's close scrutiny, the problem was detected.

'Did you say batteries are down! Then it must be that Kalia, the wretch! He must have gulped down the tablets and slept with Vividh Bharati center on. Thousands of times have I asked that swine, that skunk not to do this!'

The man walked away in a huff without offering a pie. But not without a parting remark, 'Does it take a whole afternoon for a mechanic to discover such a little fault?'

Today came some seven customers in all. Three of them went away telling that they would get things done cheaper elsewhere. Two others returned, saying, 'Let's see tomorrow.'

Today's total earning was a meager twenty-seven rupee and a half. After a deduction of three for the puffed rice, he was left with twenty-four and a half, eleven rupees less than yesterday's proceeds.

Shyama Prasad was not far from the truth when he pronounced: it's no good running a radio repairing shop these days. Who listens to transistors now? It's better to run a pan-shop, or perhaps sell *gupchups*.

'Do you know? Today that rascal vexed me again—on my way to the office,' the girl said while putting vegetable peels into a brass bowl.

'Of course, he couldn't do that for long,' she added, 'He bolted away the moment he saw Mohanty sir's younger son, Tukuna, coming from the opposite end.'

A few days ago, that boy had sent a dirty letter to her. Full of obscenities. Of course, she did not read a line of it. She handed over the letter to Jajati when she saw a stranger's hand. He ran his eyes over the letter, tore it up and flung the pieces to the gutter.

He did not tell her what the letter contained. Nor did she tell him what obscenities the boy mouthed, finding her alone.

The girl returned to the kitchen. The verandah seemed empty, the courtyard lonely.

There was no moon in the sky. Only a panoply of stars.

At a distance, someone sang softly. Perhaps the girl hummed a tune in the kitchen and fell silent. Perhaps some nameless bird flew into the sky calling out its lost companion. It could also be the whispers of the night.

Radio fascinated the young man since childhood. Voices from distance stirred him deeply. Strains of an unknown song, an inaudible voice from a faraway place awakened strange longings in him, haunted him.

What do those distant voices want to say? What are their sorrows? What makes them happy? The young man fixed his gaze at a solitary star in the somber sky. Then he turned to look at the transistor-lying hurt and humiliated on the plank bed in silence.

He picked up the transistor and held it in his lap for a while. He felt as though it was a strange casket, a tangle of unvoiced emotions. In the dark, he opened the transistor and explored the web of its mysterious secrets.

As though by the touch of a magic wand, the dead instrument's soul was stirred. A solitary human voice from a faraway land drifted in and soon trailed off into the empty silence.

The young man tried again. Snatches of music floated in.

He checked the instrument with deft fingers and found it in perfect order, all its bands accessible, all its switches in harmony.

He turned off the transistor.

But strangely, the musical notes went on. As if this is an eternity, this is destiny.

The girl was humming a tune in the kitchen, stumbling sometimes at the loose ends of the scale. Yet, her voice had the freedom of a bird, soaring into the sky. It held the promises of infinity.

What conviction, what realization animated her song? She could not possibly remember the face of her mother or father; she did not know whether the paralytic man lying in the next room would be alive tomorrow. There was no knowing if she would continue in her temporary job next month.

On whom does she rely? What gives her so much confidence? He has made her no promises. He has no commitment to honor.

The young man got up from the plank bed. Slowly, he moved towards the kitchen and stood at the door. The girl was busy boiling milk in an earthen pot. The burning coal of the hearth cast a strange glow on the contours of her firm and tender body.

He called, 'Manju!'

The girl turned to look.

'Manju, I want to tell you something.'

'Tell me.'

The young man said nothing.

The girl moved closer.

'What do you want to say?'

'Manju!'

The young man drew a couple of long and deep breaths as though trying to ease up after running miles.

The girl now came out of the kitchen to the veranda, and asked, 'Aren't you feeling well?'

'Yes, I'm,' mumbled the young man.

Then, as if trying to recall a long-forgotten script, he said, 'I'll not come here tomorrow.'

'Won't come?'

'No.'

'Then—'

A gust of wind began to blow through the courtyard. The leaves of a peepul tree stirred on the other side of the house. Beyond all this were heard fits of coughing in the bedroom. A frail voice called, 'Manju...Manju...'

'I'll not come tomorrow,' said the young man again, 'I cannot say when I'll come next.'

'Manju, Manju...'

The leaves of the peepul tree dropped into the dark and gaping void. The wind was heavy with uneasy breath.

A spectral hand snuffed out the unsteady flame in the lantern and disappeared into an uncertain void. Now darkness reigned. After it was all dark, the girl could see everything clearly. She could see how lonely she was and realize how complete she was in her aloneness.

Original Odia: *Sanchara Patha*

The Picture Within

Yashodhara Mishra
Translated by **Sulagna Mishra**

Amita had hardly added a line to complete last night's half -written letter when again a face appeared at the door. It was the nurse, with a smile that was meant to continue their earlier conversation.

"Is the patient ready?

Amita's curt question made the other's smile break into a wide grin.

"Madam, the woman must agree first. The husband and wife are still fighting. Let the fight get over first."

Amita picked up the pen and went back to her letter, saying, "Then tell me when she is willing and ready."

The nurse went back reluctantly; she seemed to be in the mood for a little chat.

Amita was the only lady doctor in the small hospital, and the only doctor if the other doctor went on leave. It was the only hospital available to the people of the small town and the nearby tribal villages. When they came for treatment, the doctor could expect to face aspects of their life other than their illnesses, at times even their family problems. Therefore the hospital staff, most of them outsiders who had come to the town on postings, would often extract a dose of entertainment from their workplace. Amita herself was no different from them. When she had first come here two-three years back, she could never understand how one could live in such a place with just the hospital and the patients. She had not met Rohit yet. Then she discovered that one could keep one's real life and concerns aside for a while and lead a contented life - quite different and almost self-contained.

Scribbling a half-written sentence, she scratched it off. Must not think about Rohit now. The letter must be written first. It has to go by today's mail. She wrote one letter a week to Pradipta and one to her son. Had to think before writing.

Earlier she said whatever she felt like. "Baby, I miss you all the time. I have kept your photo on my table, the one in which you are playing cricket. Do you wear that new shirt of yours, the one with the pockets? Do you think of mummy, my dear?"

Pradipta would get irritated with her, "Why do you write such depressing letters to the boy? The poor fellow has to stay away from his mother. Can't you write a few lines to cheer him up?"

She would write to Pradipta, "I miss you so much. The evenings are difficult to spend. Have you enquired about the transfer?"

Pradipta used to write warm encouraging letters, asking her to put up with the situation for a few more days. Now the letters had become different. Pradipta's rare letters and the conversations when they met once in a few months did not have the same tone as earlier. Amita now planned her letters carefully so that her sentences did not leave any hidden meanings, nor any scope for questions or accusations.

From the other end of the veranda, one could still hear some noise. It was already eleven in the day. Perhaps the operation would not be possible today. Not an operation, in fact, just an abortion. Yet the man and the woman had been making such a big row over it for the last two days. It was already late for a normal abortion when they came. If they delayed any more, it could be dangerous for the mother. Actually, it was illegal to go for a medical termination after three months of pregnancy. But Amita knew that sometimes for varied reasons, either to keep the peace of the family or to save a girl's life, a conscientious doctor had to break the rules. At times one had to take the responsibility of persuading them or even making the decision on their behalf.

In the beginning, she reported such events in detail to Pradipta. These days she did not. Even if she started to, the letter did not get any further. For now, the story will not reach him. Pradipta will only get some broken pieces of news from her letter, no different from the ones that he must get to read in the newspapers.

Had this been three years ago, she would have written, "You know, there is this interesting case in my hands now. A tribal woman is pregnant for the fourth time. The husband says, 'It's not my child'. The wife refuses to get an abortion done. ..."

Those days she would even try to tell him how the event came with a knock one evening when the servant girl rushed in and said, "Memsaab, those two have come again". The silent house would suddenly be enlivened with the girl's giggles. Amita would even write about the twelve-year-old servant girl, who became moody and gloomy during evenings with the sound of drums and music coming from her nearby village; how she ran away on the first opportunity and had to be brought back next morning by her poor father. But this evening the girl looked all flushed and excited and smothering laughter with her hands. She couldn't wait to tell Amita, "It is the same couple who came in the afternoon, fighting and screaming at each other, didn't I tell you memsaab?" Amita never saw patients so late at night. But she switched off her transistor and went out to welcome the couple.

This was part of a live drama.

The man said that since he had already had the 'operation', where did the child come from? The wife said that it was not her fault if the operation 'failed': it happened all the time. The man then gestured at the woman menacingly, forgetting the doctor's presence, "In our village, so many men had the operation and nobody's failed, you bitch. Just mine did, eh?" Pacifying both of them, Amita said, "Go home now. We will find out later if it is your vasectomy operation that has gone wrong. Come to the hospital tomorrow, we will do the tests."

Amita thought maybe she should write all this to Pradipta. In the early days of her posting here, Pradipta used to write, "I miss you. The bedroom becomes unbearable at night", or "The lemon tree you planted has borne fruit now. Yesterday there was a party at Ghosh sir's place. Everyone was asking about you." Those days when she was near Pradipta, she slipped into that world like a well-fitting dress. But now, during the days, weeks, and months that she spent inside the hospital compound of this remote place, Amita often felt quite lost and left out. When she tried to tell this to Pradipta, he said, "It is just a matter of a few more days, dear. We will get your transfer orders in a while. Why do you have to worry? Aren't we all there with you?"

Yet, despite everything and everyone in her life, someone else came an unexpected guest, Rohit. And he went out of her life again, leaving a divide between Amita and her familiar world. Such a divide that it hardened more and more each day like a lime-and-stone wall. Whether Amita and Pradipta stayed far from each other's sight, or inside the inscrutable darkness of their bedroom, the wall remained there between them. Not even a letter could get through.

The outdoor patients didn't come to the hospital at this hour. The mail would go at twelve. Her duty would also get over at twelve. The peon Kishan brought in the tea. His expression said that he wanted to say something.

Taking the cup from his hands, Amita asked, "What happened? Has anything been decided yet?"

Crinkling a withered face further, Kishan responded, "No madam, they are still fighting. Can't you hear them?"

"Tell them to go back today. Let them finish their quarrel,

resolve the issue, and decide everything before they come back again."

Leaving with great excitement, Kishan was rubbing his hands as though he had got baksheesh.

It had been two days and still, they were unable to decide. The first day itself Amita had told them, "It's not for a doctor to say anything in such a matter. You two must try to sort it out between yourselves. If you insist, we can find out from the tests if the operation has really failed."

But when the man found out that the male doctor Patel had gone on a long leave, he refused to have the tests done. How could a lady doctor conduct such tests on men? He was not going to let himself be fooled. So he decided, "Doctorni maa, please take that baby out of her."

His wife was furious at this and yelled, "I will never get it done!" She had heard that a girl had died during an abortion. Thereafter the long scenes followed. The probing and prodding of the hospital staff fueled further exchange of words, and facts like who the man suspected, why the tests were an eyewash, and from the wife's point of view, why the man wanted to kill her on the pretext of abortion, were revealed. The employees of the hospital and even some patients, unused to TV and cinema, forgot everything else and spent the next two hours engrossed in the affair of the couple, pacifying, rebuking, and evening threatening them.

Finally, Amita went to them and said, "Both of you, will you please get out of here? And come to the hospital only when you know what you want."

The couple stood there, both of them looking apologetic and helpless. Amita had to change her tone, "You come tomorrow. I'll see what I can do".

The man nodded politely but the woman refused to move. Amita looked at her worried face and said, "Don't worry about the abortion. Would any doctor take the risk knowing that there was a risk to the mother's life? Don't I fear for my job? Go home now."

But this morning it was back to square one again. On the one hand, the wife said that the baby had started moving inside her, why would she incur the sin of killing a life deliberately? And then if she died herself in the process, who would look after her children? She knew for certain that all this fuss by her husband was to bring another wife home.

At this, the husband was all ready to hit her, raving and ranting and abusing when people around rushed to hold him down. If she kept the baby he would never keep her in his house, he said. She could not enter his house again; he would axe her into two, on the way back he said. Screaming in return, the woman hurled a string of abuses at him.

At that point, Amita left both of them in the hands of the nurse and the peons and returned to the room. She opened the half-written letter intending to finish it.

Last evening, sitting in the verandah of her small house, she had opened and read all the recent letters from Pradipta, as if she would find in them somewhere a key to his mind. In all those letters, an invisible question hung unasked. Who was Rohit in her life? How close had he come to her? Initially, Pradipta would ask her this, screaming, hitting at the table and the walls. Her protestations and tears of humiliation would only stall the scene for a while. Even the question of their parting ways had come up several times. Finally, the question was not asked anymore and no explanations were offered.

When Amita went home on leave, everything would seem normal during the daytime, amongst friends and family members. When left alone, nothing was there to be said between them. There were moments when Amita, exasperated, opened her mouth to tell him but could not. And what was there to tell him anyway? A few down-to-earth statements, and a few facts that he thought to be the truth. That Amita had spent some time with Rohit. This much time by the clock, with this much closeness. What about all the facts that Pradipta did not know about her? All those afternoons when Amita finished work and stepped onto the dusty footpath leading to her quarters, with the hot wind from the woods blowing dry leaves and mango flowers into the hospital compound. The evenings when Amita finished cooking her meal and sat in her tiny courtyard to watch the patch of sky till it turned black. What about the fact nobody would ever know? That there was this arid land lying inside Amita for ages now.

Kishan came in and kept a fresh towel and soap near the washbasin, with some lame excuse for the delay as usual. Then he arranged the things on the shelves, looking for some excuse to gossip, and started gossiping anyway. "It is the way they live, ma. Their festivals and celebrations are like that. All they need is a chance to booze. And how can one keep one's senses after that? Anything goes during these festivities. But what can they do? Like you sir sahibs, do they have neatly divided rooms in their houses? Or electric lights? Do they have bazaars and markets to cheer themselves up? They live in forests and jungles in their dark huts. And sometimes when they are drunk, such mistakes do happen. No one thinks of it as such a big thing."

Amita could sense that he was trying to explain something to her about his own people. She asked, "Why are they fighting then if such things do happen?"

As though he hadn't heard her, Kishan continued, "Nowadays so many new things have come about. Because of this operation, they do on men, one knows that this man could never father a child. But then if his wife bears a child, who is to be blamed, please tell me?"

The nurse started giggling from behind. Amita laughed too, a little hesitantly. Excited, Kishan continued his lecture, "Had it been my childhood days ma, the man would have straight away pounced on his wife, no argument, if he really had another man in view".

A little disconcerted by the lack of response from his audience, but again mustering courage, he said, "The wife would get a few blows and kicks from her husband, and the neighbors would come to pacify both of them, and the thing would have been settled. But now ma'm, if this woman is carrying, and the husband has had the operation, then however much she may cry and plead, how can the poor fellow listen to her, tell me?"

The nurse was now laughing out loud. Amita tried not to laugh, as she sifted through her papers. Ignoring their laughter, Kishan raised his voice and continued boldly, "Earlier elders used to say that the woman is like earth. Whichever seeds you put into the soil grew into plants. But how could one say that no other plant could ever sprout there? And if it did, did one leave the fields and go away?"

This time the nurse was laughing uncontrollably. On second thoughts, Kishan seemed to see that there was an amusing side to his statement and laughed too. Amita waited till the laughter had died down and said, "Okay, enough. Instead of lecturing us here, why don't you go and explain it to them?"

Kishan shook both his hands to say that now nothing could be done. The nurse said, "Perform the operation madam, and the entire fuss will be over. In fact, they hardly keep track of the time until the baby is born. And you will see, after two months they would have forgotten everything."

Removing the cups and saucers from the table Kishan suggested gravely, "If the woman does not agree at all, or if the time is past now, just say that the man's operation failed, they will believe you. Let Doctor Patel come. Even a false report of a test could be a good idea."

Amita frowned, "What an impossible thing to say! Why should anyone take such a risk of making a false report too?"

Just then, like a new scene in the drama, the woman herself appeared at the door. Behind her, a few others. All were quiet. Wiping her eyes, the woman said that she was ready now. Ready that her abdomen be washed. Her husband stood beside her.

Amidst that suppressed excitement, Amita looked at the watch. Fifteen minutes more to twelve. She asked the nurse softly, "Should we do it today or defer it until tomorrow?" The young nurse did not have her usual cheerful face, "Do it now madam, please! Let the poor things be free from the mess. Who knows what would happen tomorrow?"

Everyone went out with the nurse. Amita waited in her room, for the patient to be readied on the operation table. While picking up the papers, she noticed the bottle of antacid medicine that Kishan had left on the table. Taking out the letter once again from her purse Amita wrote hastily, "I just remembered. Do you still suffer from acidity? I hope you don't take tea on an empty stomach in the mornings."

Outside the operation theater, the man was standing quietly. As Amita got ready to enter, he suddenly came near her with folded hands and asked nervously, "Ma, I had to ask you something".

"Okay, what is it?"

"Ma, you think she could die?"

"What a thing to ask! Why should she die?"

"Supposing she dies? In case she dies? Do you give me your word she won't die?"

"What is this new fuss again? How can I give you my word? Normally no one dies in such a case. But that does not mean I am God."

Gesturing to him to move aside she was about to enter when the man almost blocked her way putting his hand on the door. Surprised, Amita retreated a step, but she saw the man almost begging her, "Ma, just tell me once. Is the child mine?"

"I can't tell you anything about that."

"Tell me ma. Please say something. If you tell me once that the child is mine, there is no need for anything else."

Clenching her teeth, Amita gave him a stern look, "Look that is your problem. Don't bother me now."

On the operation table lay the unconscious woman. Just as she was about to begin, there was loud banging on the door. The nurse said, "Madam, it is her husband."

"Get him out of here. Call the peon."

The banging got even louder. Helplessly, she took off the gloves from her hands and went to the door.

"What do you want?"

"Ma, let her go. Let the poor woman go."

"What do you mean?"

"I pardon her. Just this once."

"I don't understand. You are telling me that she will not have the abortion anymore?"

"Yes, ma. Let the child live. Let it be born. I forgive her this time."

Amita kept staring at him. Then she asked, "You mean if the baby is born, you will keep it, bring it up?"

"The child belongs to God, ma. Whoever has committed the sin will suffer. She has sworn by everything. You have been witness to it."

After some time, passing through the same veranda on her way home, Amita saw the man sitting beside the trolley, waiting for his wife to wake up. The couple would have to walk a few miles to their village then. What would they face afterward, a closer understanding, or a reluctant sacrifice from one and condescending gratitude from the other?

Needlessly overwhelmed, the man folded his hands in front of Amita as though it was she who had solved his problem. Amita asked, " If you were not so sure of it yourself, why were you after the poor thing? Just out of suspicion?"

He looked grim and said, "Don't blame me, ma. Don't think she is that simple. But then I thought, between a couple, the man is the master after all. Shouldn't he overlook a few mistakes of the woman once in a while?" The man's simple rugged face had self-assurance and pride.

Stepping down on to the dusty road it struck Amita that there were not many days left for the hot summer to come. There was the summer wind, mixed with dry leaves and dusty mango flowers have blown from the forest inside the campus. The tips of the bare branches of the naked *mahua* tree had started sprouting into hundreds of earthy brown buds that faced the sky. Last year, it was around this time that Rohit had come. At an hour like this, after she had returned home with tired feet and just as she had bolted the door close, she had heard a knock and had opened it again. Rohit had come to ask for something, was it a book? She didn't remember anymore.

She could recall some things clearly, some others she could not. The things they talked about that day, and days afterward, in the hustle-bustle of the hospital, just the two of them. And again inside the house, bolting the doors to the dusty storms, noise, and chaos outside. She did recall, each taking one step towards the other, and then stepping further still into each other's earth. The unknown rooms inside her had unlocked one after the other. The claustrophobic house where she had got used to breathing had filled with fragrant forest air. She remembered.

Rohit got transferred and left. He too had left his family in the city and come here. Since the day he had come, his father-in-law had been trying to get him out of this God-forsaken place. While leaving, both had fought a desire not to let the other go, an impossible wish to stay tied. Yet when the time came for parting, both were ready.

Both knew that inside each of them space would be there, covered with many pictures. No one else would see it ever.

Now Amita would walk leisurely the two furlongs to her house, watching the newly arisen treasures of the oncoming summer. Then she would open the door of the empty quarters.

Maybe she should take leave and go home, she thought. Or Pradipta might actually get her a transfer order shortly. For now, she must stay like this, in the temporary setup here. But she has all of them waiting for her anyway, her son, husband, a neatly arranged home, and a city full of friends and relatives. The thought came to her that there would still remain a world inside her, vast and unknown. And it was all hers. There she could sleep or stay awake as she pleased. Or when she wanted, she could bring in a whiff of wind from outside to shake the trees and shrubs inside her, call the bird sitting on the windowsill and bid it fly in her sky. Or invite a guest in, maybe a character from the novel left open in her hands.

Original Odia: *Bhitarara Chhabi*

The Avenger

Written and Translated by
Satya Misra

Winter is a very cruel season. Life is not so miserable before or after winter. Trees look gloomy. Skies shed tears all through the night. The cat delivers a litter of kittens and the big tomcat kills them one by one. Next morning drops of blood can be seen scattered all over. Myriad melancholic moments of life join together and hang around the neck like a heavy bundle of sorrow.

A cat was sitting motionless and silent, legs tucked in, absorbing her share of miseries. Her pensive and sad face reflected some deep inner turmoil. The night was getting darker and denser. Darkness, like a palpable substance, was caressing her body on all sides reminding her of the way her cubs were rubbing against her. She compressed her body into a tight mass to mitigate the fierceness of cold and shot a piercing look into the darkness. She always felt helpless and vulnerable in bright light, as though her many secrets, held deep in her heart, got exposed in the light. The frustration of not being able to see anyone and the misery of being seen by everyone tormented her. This didn't happen in darkness. Hence her pleasant companionship with darkness was neither irrational nor accidental.

After a prolonged session of deep meditative contemplation, she sprang into life with the air of someone who had just taken an important decision. With a melancholic posture and deep, subdued purring, she wagged her furry tail once or twice and said to herself, 'This is too much. I cannot just ingest all alone. Must tell others. Let the world know.' An expression of agony and assurance fleetingly passed on her round face. Very cautiously she walked with slow but bold steps. The faint sound of some hurried movement reached her from the left side wall. A familiar sound. A mouse perhaps. The pussy stood alert for a moment, but no; she wasn't hungry at all. It is no good catching the hapless mouse. Let it keep on dancing noisily; who cares?

She entered into the adjacent room where a few humans were eating their dinner. Squatting on the floor with their backs barely touching a wall, they were devouring food. Now and then raising their heads to look straight ahead, they were generally focused on the food served in plates placed on the floor. Such occasions invariably made the pussy salivate and meow loudly to register her claim for a share; but not today. As the men were pushing balls of food into their mouths, their jaws were moving up and down like hinged brackets.

They were not unknown to her. She recognized them mostly from the acts of cruelty they sometimes unleashed on her. The brat sitting on the extreme left was the one who sometimes would grab her by her furry neck and lift her whole body into thin air, paying no heed to her anguished meows. Then he would throw her forcefully on the ground, sometimes with a mischievous laugh. The man at the center got a queer pleasure by tugging her tail. And the man with a moustache – he would kick on her face whenever she came his way. He often failed, however, his kicks making just swish in the air. The pussy can narrate her pathetic story even to humans, but these specimens are cruel. They wouldn't listen. They may even start teasing her and pull her tail again for fun.

But soon the pussy changed her mind. Cruel they may be, but they need to be told the story. Where else will she get a readymade audience now? The pathos of her story will not be lost on these creatures. It will move even rocks to tears; such was the intensity of her agony. All she needed was an audience and some compassion. She forgot the intense cold that sent a shiver down her spine.

Standing meaningfully in front of the men, she delivered a look of intense pain. Then, with a huge sulk, she started haltingly: 'Yesterday, even my youngest cub ...' she was choking but went on, 'my youngest cub was also taken by that devil of a tomcat'.

Nobody seemed to listen. Her weepy meows attracted a few disinterested fleeting glances, but that's all. The eyes promptly went back to dinner plates placed before them. The mustachioed man probably saw a bit of her pain after a while. He placed a small ball of lentil soaked rice on the floor and ordered her gently to eat. Emboldened, the cat decided that time had come to inform the world the cruelty she was subjected to. She cleared her throat, raised her voice and spoke 'My cubs would have grown to tigers'. Bursting with suppressed emotion, she somehow managed to hold herself. Narration should not stop, now that she has got an audience. 'They looked like tiger cubs; all three of them. But alas, they are no more. The tomcat killed all of them '. Her motherhood, though injured, made her proud and vocal. She was about to launch a long tirade when she was suddenly silenced by a kick on her face. The men were at it again. She ran away in fear. These people are dangerously cruel. As cruel as the blinding light of mid-noon. Like this icy cold night. No better than that demonic tomcat. They are not willing to give her a decent hearing even when her heart bleeds with unspoken agony.

By then the darkness outside had condensed into a thick black envelope. The bone-chilling cold outside the house made her shiver, but she didn't care. She didn't feel anything other than the tormenting memory of the three cubs she had mothered. She had no doubt that the kittens would have grown bold and mighty like tigers. One was milky white. The other two had coats with brown and white patches that looked lovely. Soft and warm like velvet. Their eyes had not opened fully but would have opened in a day or two. One had even started walking with wobbly baby steps. All three were fabulous bundles of sheer joy. She felt as though they were still clinging to her, rubbing against her, sucking her milk. Then she remembered the monstrous tomcat, whose cruelty knew no bounds. He is sure to end up in hell, that bloody villain. First, it killed two of her cubs. And yesterday she came back to take away her youngest, the one with a white coat. As tears rolled down the cat's face, she started wagging her tail pitiably as a tiny meow escaped her mouth. All these needed to be announced to the world. The world must know how they looked, what they were saying or rather trying to say, their potential tigerhood and more.

Two glowing eyes approached her. Seeing their fiery glow in the darkness, the cat could immediately identify the stalker. The terrible tomcat. The monster! Killer of her babies! The vile villain of her life! The frightened pussy stepped back, but suddenly stopped on her track. What else can this brute do now? She would narrate her misery to this tomcat. He has killed all her babies. He should now understand her sorrow.As their paths crossed, he stared at her angrily. But this was not the time to cower in terror.

She uttered feebly, 'my three kittens......'

"What about them? 'The big bully asked carelessly, with practiced and pretended ignorance.

'Someone took them away and killed.'

'Oh....' the tomcat said with a blink of his eye.

Although she hated his pretentious behavior, she went on.

"I cannot, just cannot bear such tragedy. I am going to die'. A long pathetic speech would have followed, but the tomcat started walking away. Then looked back, said 'Ah, aha 'in mock sympathy, turned and just walked away.

The cat became very angry. But what could she do? Nobody

wanted to listen and share her grief. But she cannot just leave it there. Her mind was playing tricks on her. She again visualized, as she had done many times earlier, the manner in which the tomcat would have killed her young ones. A scene of unparalleled violence unfolded before her. The tomcat would have turned into a bloodthirsty devil and pierced his sharp claws into those sweet and beautiful bodies. Her lovely tiger cubs. Three heavenly beings, who provided her such divine bliss! Blood would have oozed out from their tiny innocent bodies. Sweet cubs, her own flesh, her soul. Their assassin would have pounced on those bodies to pull their innards out, turning them into meatballs.

This is how the tomcat would have butchered her cubs – brutal and violent.

The vivid imagination of this gory sequence made her shudder.It was nerve-wracking. The vision of this macabre dance of death just didn't leave her mind. And now that very monster, that tomcat, was refusing even to listen to a word from her!

Night had advanced and so had the cold. Icy knives of cold penetrated into her flesh and bones, somewhat like the sharp talons of that rogue butchering cat. As visions of those meatballs were mocking her tormented motherhood, she didn't seek a warm shelter for herself. The silent night engulfed her. The silence of death and desolation, she thought. The humans had finished their dinner and gone to sleep. She was sure she would not be able to live without telling her story and sharing her grief, but there was not a flicker of hope now. She must punish herself by allowing this piercing cold to freeze her into death. The sooner the better.

Suddenly something dropped on her back. Carelessly she tossed it away with her tail. A cockroach perhaps. It flew away. Indifferent to any physical sensation, forgetting about her own existence, she felt like having been dissolved like a granule of sugar in the surrounding ocean of darkness and agony. She muttered something but didn't know what she uttered.

Some creaking sound suddenly made her conscious of her surroundings. A mouse went running in front of her, clinging to the corner of the wall. For some time she kept staring at it as the mouse looked vaguely all around.   A cute grey creature. Rapidly blinking eyes.   The pussy was indifferent at first, but came to her senses with a start. A mouse, live mouse at that and she was not reacting! How could it be? Her own behavior surprised her. How unrecognizably she had changed! The mouse either didn't see her or didn't realize the danger she was in. It had lodged itself in corner of the floor and looked here and there.

The pussy developed a sudden trust in the mouse. What a fabulous kid! So reliable and humble! It will certainly hear out her saga of sorrow.

The cat jumped on the creature in one sudden vault and held it between her jaws. 'You have to listen. I know you will listen. Only you will listen. You are a cute lovely kid. You will obey me.'

In its desperate struggle to escape, the mouse flayed its limbs wildly and cried noisily in fear and pain. The pussy released it from her jaws, placed it on the floor and then pinned it down with her claws. "No, don't imagine you can run away, you poor little mouse kid. Do you know how beautiful my kids were? You don't. Can you imagine how deeply I loved them? Your mother would not have loved you as much for sure. You are bubbly and full of life. So were my cubs.'

The mouse struggled desperately with all her strength, but the pussy was in total control. She again released the mouse but immediately clasped it before it could run away. 'No, you just can't go. Listen to me. Be calm.'

What ensued was a sort of battle between two unequal powers. The pussy went on with her story, clasped the mouse, played with it and even jumped on it. By then the mouse had no power to move, let alone run away. And the narration continued: 'My cutie would have become a tiger. You would have fainted if you ever came face to face with my tiger. You would have collapsed in awe '. The pussy had started teasingly scraping her sharp nails against the tender body of her captive audience, causing random scratches.   She even rubbed her coat against its torn body and caressed it a couple of times. Then she threw the body and again held it. She kissed the body here and there while nibbling away parts of the mouse at random.

The narrator in her made the best of the opportunity by describing her pathetic experience with all gory details and embellishments. After draining all her pent up anguish out, her face glowed with contentment. Solace at last! What if her cubs were alive now? They would have been midway in their journey towards tigerhood. Alas, but what terrible death they had to die! The vision of meatballs again danced before her eyes – blood, flesh, bones, and sinews all amalgamated into lifeless lumps.

By then stirrings of tigerhood had started flowing in her own veins.

She isn't weak. Or meek. She is the proud mother of three tiger cubs. What if they aren't alive now? She is still their mother, a tigress. More ferocious and courageous than that bloody tomcat, the big bully. She announced her new identity repeatedly with loud meows, still playing with the dying mouse 'I know you are cute and bubbly. Your mother loves you very much, doesn't she? I know she does.' Few more hysteric meows followed.

Slowly she started piercing the soft body of the mouse with her talons. Blood gushed out, which excited her. Then the cat tore it apart with a demonic rage even as the dying creature released a feeble sound from her throat. Its last sound. It didn't go unanswered. 'You are lovely. You are nice. I was waiting to meet you '. She pulled the innards out from its torn and motionless body.

Total silence of the mouse didn't deter her from systematically turning it into pulp. She kept talking to it long after it had died. Then she just left the meatball on the floor and walked away. Avenged at last.

Original Odia: *Pashabika*

A Disconcerting Truth

Gayatri Saraf

Translated by **Manoranjan Mishra**

That year, Aradhana was transferred to a small town. Since the day she had been promoted, she had always worked in different schools of the district headquarters town. Consequently, she didn't know what it meant to work in small schools and schools with lesser students. She looked gloomy the moment she received the transfer order. Her husband ran from pillar to post to get the order cancelled but in vain. Finally, he advised her, "Go there for a year; only then we will try for a transfer."

Aradhana agreed to the proposal. She joined at the new place of posting, suppressing her displeasure. A grand government bungalow, neatly done up, waited eagerly for her arrival. Gusts of fresh breeze, continuous chirping of birds, and bunches of sweet-smelling jasmine welcomed her. Aradhana felt comforted at a sight of them. A look at the school and the number of students cut down her feeling of discomfort further.

The Headmaster's room that had been lying unoccupied for the last two years was found beaming. Aradhana responded with a smile. She took some time to acclimatize her. She listened patiently to the grief that the school had suppressed in her heart. She took pity on the lack of discipline that reigned the place. All around, lay heaps of garbage. Why should only the headmistress be concerned about the upkeep of the school? ; was it not the responsibility of the other teachers too? Why should the school lose its luster in the absence of the headmistress? Aradhana felt sad at this sort of mentality. "Every individual associated with a school has some role to play in its integral development," she believed.

She, on the other hand, knew what her role was; what her responsibilities were. She found it absolutely impossible to betray with the school that she was posted at or the responsibilities her post carried. She wished to contribute meaningfully to each student's life. She wished every student to be disciplined; to abide by the rules and regulations framed by the school. She would, therefore, impart moral lessons; she would plant value-saplings in their mind-clay and inspire them to lead speckles, impeccable characters. She would throw light on our glorious culture and traditions. It's true that times had changed, incepting changes in people's thoughts and beliefs. She found it difficult to tolerate those girls, who treaded the path of incivility and vulgarity in the name of modernity. Education and educational institutions should never be clouded by such uncivil thoughts. She would shiver at the thought of colleges and universities being darkened by such clouds of darkness these days.

Aradhana continued with her ways in the new school too. She proceeded further with her philosophy and life's mission in mind. On the very first day, she spoke her mind on strict adherence to rules and regulations. She said that she would lay emphasis on discipline and order. The young girls heeded her; they nodded their heads indicating comprehension. Aradhana had deep faith that they had understood how they were expected to conduct themselves and how they were going to turn themselves into incarnations of discipline and order. They promised to cleanse their minds and purify their thoughts. Of course, it was easily said than done.

It took some time for transformation to be brought about. Aradhana, with timely aid from her assistant teachers, could create a wonderful atmosphere within days. The sky appeared bright and cloudless. The name and fame of the school spread far and wide. Strong feelings of trust and faith took roots in the minds of the parents; some of them rang up Aradhana expressing their gratitude.

The discipline-flag continued to flutter on the school campus. Rules and regulations swung merrily in the breeze. Aradhana was delighted at her success.

However, her happiness came to an abrupt end.

That day, the prayer meeting was organized at the right time. Reading of news from newspapers followed. Aradhana marked that some of her colleagues were not listening to the news mindfully; they were busy whispering things to each other. The behaviour of the teachers angered her. If teachers failed to become models of discipline, what could be expected of students? However, she decided to keep her displeasure under wraps for some time. She returned to her chamber after the newspaper reading was over. She started signing the lesson-notes kept on her table. Lessons began to be imparted when the first period commenced. Suddenly, she found a senior teacher standing near the curtain and asking for her permission to get in. She came in and sat down, on Aradhana's request. She wished to say something but was a little hesitant.

After some time, she said, "Madam, I have come to you with an important message."

Lifting her head from the lesson-notes, Aradhana said, "Yes, please tell me what it is."

"I got the information on the way to school. Only after reaching here, I had to obtain confirmation from some source. Only then, I thought of passing the information to you."

"Oh... I now understand. Perhaps that's why all of you were absent-minded during the reading of the news."

"Yes, madam... only for that," she said shrinking a little.

"Now please tell me what the matter is, that impelled you to break the discipline of the school."

Accepting their mistake, she continued, "Madam, a student of class ten has eloped with someone."

Aradhana was startled. She placed the cap on the pen. She no more signed the lesson-notes. She appeared gloomy and said, "How did it happen? Where? With whom did she elope?"

"Madam, please don't worry about it."

"Do you expect me not to worry? How would not I worry when a student of our school has eloped with someone? This reflects very poorly on the name, fame and discipline of the school."

"She didn't reach school. On the way to school, she eloped with her boy-friend. How can the school authorities be held responsible?

"If she fled on the way to school, how did you come to know about it?" Aradhana asked, anxiety reflected in her voice.

"I was busy arranging classes for the day. A student of class eight came to the common room and delivered the message to me."

"How did she come to know of it?"

The senior-teacher changed her sitting pose and wiped her face with a corner of her saree. She continued,

"Leena, the girl who has fled, usually came to school with that girl. On the way, they would meet a young man with goggles on. Leena would linger a bit. Both of them would talk to each other till they reached the school campus. Then, the young man would leave. On some days, she would go away with him, instead of attending school, only to return home at four pm."

Aradhana lent her ears to what the teacher was saying. She shrank within. How proud she was of her attempts to impart discipline to the girls and taking the school in a new direction! Feeling depressed, she said, "She might return at four o' clock today."

"No...No...madam. She won't return."

She divulged her intentions to Bobby,

"I don't like what's being taught at school. Nor do I like my people at home. Now, I am in another grave trouble…I don't feel like eating anything. I feel like vomiting all the time. You can't understand this now. You can understand everything only when you grow up. Therefore Bobby, I have decided to elope with my boy-friend… he is the only person who can solve my problems… now you can go to school…" said Leena. She left Bobby's hand and went her way.

"She didn't go her way…she decided to follow an evil path," murmured Aradhana on her own. She appeared weighed down. She wanted to slap Leena on both her cheeks. So what if she had not eloped from school! She was, after all, one of the students of her school, where she prided in imparting lessons in self-discipline, values, and building character. Despite the best of her efforts, instead of reading the lessons taught to her, the girl took more interest in physical pleasure. She decided to leave home secretly. What pervert thoughts a student of class ten can have!

The senior teacher got up to go. With Aradhana's permission, she left for the common room.

The ceiling fan was revolving at full speed. Besides, gentle breeze blew in from outside. However, Aradhana was completely soaked in sweat. There was nothing new in lovers eloping with each other; what she found hard to believe was that a class ten student of her school had eloped with her lover after being physically intimate with him. Didn't it leave a question mark on the rules, regulations, and moral teachings imparted by the school? Wasn't it a kind of deceit with the principles of the school?

"Oh… how did the girl conceive of such an idea?"

The bell rang when the first period got over. Aradhana regained consciousness. She started checking the lesson-notes once again and signed in them. When the work was over, she summoned the peon.

She couldn't sit in peace; Leena and her elopement flashed before her eyes again and again.

Ah! What would happen to the parents when they learnt that Leena hadn't reached school, but rather eloped with her boyfriend and that she wouldn't return home anymore? Was her mother aware of her pregnancy? Perhaps, her family members would not be aware of her elopement. With passage of time, her neighbours would learn about it. What blame and insult the family would be subjected to! How would her parents put up with all this? Why do some girls fling so much torture on their parents?

Aradhana felt, at that moment, that it was her responsibility to inform Leena's parents about what had happened. If she did so, a search to rescue her might ensue. At least, the family members would not be blamed for inaction. With the help of the senior teacher, she collected the office address and phone number of Leena's father. She dispatched a faithful peon to pass the message to Leena's father. The peon reached the Tehsil office. He took Leena's father aside, disclosed the news and returned to school.

A sense of discontent troubled Aradhana. She found it difficult to become her natural self. Wouldn't have the father's heart shattered at the news? Wouldn't it have turned heavy? Wouldn't his face have turned pale?

Damn with the girl who harboured no concern for either the school or her parents! She was only concerned about physical pleasure. Temporary joy swayed her. How come such a small girl's mind was infected by so much filth!

The bell rang at the appointed hours. Aradhana felt as if something had gone wrong. If she couldn't cleanse the mind and thoughts of teen-age girls like Leena, how her efforts to infuse discipline could be said to have worked!

The last period was in progress. The school hour was about to be over. The same peon lifted the curtain and said,

"Madam, Leena's father has come. He wants to meet you."

"What? Yes." Aradhana said absentmindedly. "Get him in," she said then.

"Would he have searched out Leena? What mental agony would he have been subjected to in case of his failure to do so! Perhaps he had come to her to give vent to his frustrations. How would she console him," she thought.

The gentleman came in, said 'namaskar', and sat in the chair, without any sign of worry reflected on his face. Aradhana marked that he looked absolutely normal. Nothing in his appearance exhibited that he had just been outsmarted and vanquished by his daughter. He was chewing *paan*. "Had he found out Leena? Had he come to learn that Leena was pregnant?"

"No...I didn't find her out, madam," he said without remorse.

"In that case, did you inform the police? Leena is not eighteen; she is a minor. Please file an F.I.R. They have committed a mistake, especially the boy with whom she has eloped."

He didn't show any sign of worry. He continued chewing the *paan* gently and said,

"I think, the boy is extremely noble."

"Why do you think so?"

"At least, he has not cheated her. He has taken her away with him."

"That's true. But have you not heard that the so-called boy-friends run away with girls and sell them to pimps in far-away lands? The pimps involve the girls in sex-trade. A few days ago, I read in the newspapers that some of these girls were exploited as child-bearing-machines. The children born to them were sold in the market at high prices. Haven't you heard all these?"

"No...I haven't. I don't even wish to know. Leena has fled...let her go. I don't see there is anything to worry."

In a worried voice she said, "You are her father... Leena's father."

This time he explained explicitly,

"My job doesn't fetch me much money. I have three daughters; my wife is an asthma patient. I find it very difficult to manage home with my meager salary."

Time was up; the last bell rang. The happy noise of girls filled the atmosphere. He remained silent for some time. He finished chewing the *paan*, took out his handkerchief from his pocket, and wiped his face. He continued,

"My elder daughter has completed B.A. but she wasn't

found qualified for any course. She wasn't also found suitable for any job. She underwent a training in computers but nothing came of it. I tried my best to get her married off but could not arrange for the dowry demanded by the in-laws. She is thirty years of age now. The second daughter failed in matriculation. She was afraid of copying in the examination. Could I even arrange a husband for her? She is a seamstress and earns some money that way. Whenever she meets a married friend of hers, she sheds tears silently. How I wish they should find husbands for themselves! Poor girls, they have no mastery in that art. Leena is the youngest of the three. At least, she could master the art of finding a husband for herself. He relieved me of a great responsibility. She also helped me save the expenditures. Let her go...now her fate would lead the way. If she ends up with a pimp, what can I do?"

He got up even before completing his sentence.

He got up leaving everything on the girl's fate. Aradhana somehow felt that he was very cruel and hard-hearted as a father. The next moment she realized that behind the façade of cruelty, lurked his helplessness. Since times immemorial, people have been found believing that adversities can change the nature of man.

Aradhana also got up to go.

She was dissatisfied with Leena as she had not submitted herself to the rules, regulations, and standards of behavior framed by her. However, she was not only the head of an institution; she was also a mother and a lady with a feeling heart. She wished, "Leena should marry the young man of her choice and lead a happy life. Her boy-friend should not hand her over to a pimp. She should not be abused as a child-bearing-machine. Let her live in peace. Let all the girls of the world live peacefully; let there be safety for them."

Gentle breeze blew outside her chamber. Some petals of the gulmohar flower lay on the ground, scattered all around. Were the petals, like Aradhana, praying for the safety of girls with bent heads?

Original Odia: *Eka Asahaya Satya*

Keeping Words Company

Dash Benhur
Translated by **Bikram Das**

Gayatri never knew words could be so troublesome. Their constant badgering had turned into a form of persecution. She could never tell when they tiptoed in stealthily and descended on her in a disorderly heap. But how could she think of them as adversaries or persecutors? They were her very own, though each one of them seemed willing to draw blood.

When she thought of words she was reminded of a solitary camel roaming through the desert. (Maybe she had seen him on "Discovery" Channel.) Life must have been a torment for him, yet he limped on, dragging his feet painfully, searching for food. Now and then he would come across a thorny bush. At the tip of some inaccessible branch sprouted a tender green shoot, surrounded by a ring of thorns. He would reach out with his tongue and try to swallow the entire bunch. The thorns pierced his lips and tongue but he continued to munch, unconcerned. Blood flowed.

Were words really so full of thorns?

Sometimes Gayatri felt she was sleeping on a bed of thorns. How thickly they surrounded her!

When had she started writing poetry? At what age?

Surprisingly, she had no recollection. There were authors who could tell you, without batting an eye-lid "I wrote my first poem in year such-and-such when I was a student of class so-and-so." How could they do this? Well, perhaps a poem could be published in a certain year – but who could tell when it was written? Is writing a poem like running a race, where someone gives you the signal to start? Poetry is like the wind – sometimes a gale, at other times only a whisper. Brooding, like the lull before a storm, or wafting fragrances across dense forests. Could anyone really know when a poem alighted on the sheet of paper?

All her poems were like the wind, she felt. The words were clusters of aerial energy. You never knew when they would surround you; lift you off your feet. Emotions hung motionless within the mind until the wind touched them — then they turned into poems and took flight. Call a poem by any name you like but each is primarily a framework of words. Vivify it if you can.

It was through her poems that she had got to know Sunand.

Hearing Bapa's (Father's) voice, Gayatri got up hurriedly.

"Ma," Bapa asked, "is your daughter ready to go to school?" With a brief "yes" she returned to her bedroom. The child was ready. She didn't resemble Gayatri at all; she was a replica of Sunand. The same eyes, the same nose, and the same gait. Sometimes Gayatri would murmur to herself "God, why are you showering all these worries on me? Setting up thorny bushes for me everywhere. Does it do your artistry any credit? Could you not take the thorns away if you so wished?"

There was a multitude of deities in the prayer room and standing tall among them was the wielder of the Sudarshan Chakra, Vishnu. It was to Him that all her complaints were addressed. Each evening, at prayer time, she felt one layer of her being melting and streaming away in the form of tears.

Meanwhile, Bapa picked up his granddaughter's schoolbag and water-bottle. They set off, with the grand-daughter trailing. She was in the second standard. The school was not too far away – hardly a kilometer. That was how it had been this past year, ever since Gayatri had come to live with her father.

How she felt when she looked at him! He had been reduced to a shadow of himself within that year. Ah, Father!

He had started as a clerk in the Secretariat and risen to the rank of Deputy Secretary, retiring the year before. Bou had departed only six months earlier. Rheumatism and a weak heart had brought her down. Bapa had planned to devote more time to her after his retirement – to stay with her every minute of the day. He had found no time for her when he was working. But was it to be? At the slightest jolt, his eyes would fill with tears and he would say "Was it right for her to deceive me and slip away thus?"

Was this a question or an answer? Gayatri would push back the clouds in her own eyes and look at him. Bapa would lower his eyes. But could the tears be checked?

He had admitted to himself that he had been to blame for Bou's death, hence the tears. And now that Gayatri had left Sunand and come to live with him, he had decided that this too was his fault. He had failed to explain things properly to his son-in-law. That was why they had broken up. That was the way Bapa was – holding himself responsible for everything that went wrong. Always bleeding from self-inflicted wounds. Who could explain anything to him? He would never understand. Living in perpetual self-reproach.

One evening she made him sit down beside her and said "Bapa, I am an educated girl. You sent me to the College of Engineering and made me a textile engineer. How many girls in Odisha have degrees in this subject? Isn't that an asset for me? If I can't stand on my own feet after that, who can help me? Bapa, Sunand was never a crutch for me to lean on. I was his fellow-traveler. We started our journey together, hand in hand, shoulder to shoulder. But he withdrew his hand after only a few steps. Why should I be blamed? And why should you blame yourself? God has blessed me with a daughter. I have been blessed with motherhood. I was your daughter, and then I became a wife and then a mother. What more do I require? Trust me, Bapa – I will look after you, after my daughter and myself."

Niranjan Sir heard everything but said nothing, staring silently into emptiness. What does the poor girl know of the storms of this world? How beautifully she could write! And who did she marry – a journalist-poet with an M.A. degree in Odia! Niranjan Sir too had had a weakness for literature. Sunand belonged to a well-to-do family. Niranjan Sir thought: "My daughter will be well-provided-for and she won't be too far away from home. They are in love. They may not be equally - qualified, but I see no problem in their getting married."

Together, Gayatri and Sunand took the decision. His parents behaved rather strangely: they showed neither enthusiasm nor dissent. They were agreeable to everything. At first, Niranjan Sir found everything to his liking, but then he began to see the snags. They had a home in Bhubaneswar but no past to which they could connect. Every member of the family went his own way and the parents were unconcerned. There was neither root nor branch to hold them together.

Niranjan Sir had been apprehensive. Can my daughter be happy here?

His fears came true. One day, out of the blue, Sunand announced to Gayatri "You and I cannot live together. Take the child and go back to your father's home." He picked up a suitcase himself and walked away.

How strange! What sort of a human being is this? Gayatri spoke to everyone in the family but all they said was "Who can make Sunand understand? That's the way he is. You were married of your own wish, weren't you? Solve your problem yourself! Don't involve us in this pointless affair."

Pointless the son had thrust his wife aside entirely without reason; he wasn't prepared even to look at his own daughter. And none of the others would interfere. What sort of thinking was this? Wasn't there a society they were answerable to? Does a family consist only of man and wife?

Seven days later Sunand was back. Gayatri clutched him tightly and wept; the child cried loudly. The other members of the family kept their doors bolted.

Niranjan Sir came rushing to his son-in-law. His *samudhi* offered him a cup of tea and invited him to sit beside him. But he made it clear that he was not going to intervene. Niranjan Sir held his son-in-law's hand and said "My son, who else do I have but you? You two are everything to me. My sick wife is lying in bed at home. If you have any inconvenience here or find it difficult to manage your household come and live with me. It is your home. I'll transfer all my property to you now if you like."

But Sunand only stared blankly at the wall and said "Gayatri and I cannot live together. I have nothing to do with her. Or with you."

Niranjan Sir was shocked, how could this man be so hard-hearted? How could he be called a poet? There wasn't an iota of humanity in him. How could his daughter survive in his company?

Again and again, he asked for the reason, but all Sunand would say was "I am not obliged to answer your questions."

And that very day, Niranjan Sir decided to bring his daughter and grand-daughter home.

But he didn't lose hope. Surely, Sunand would realize his blunder some day and come back. But there wasn't even a phone call. Sunand never came to see his daughter.

His wife passed away without ever leaving her bed. There was only one thought that she had. "You've brought Gayatri home, but how will she live now? What future does she have?"

Had he made a mistake then, Niranjan Sir wondered. Maybe they would have reconciled if they had remained together. Then he thought "What fault has she committed that she should be so humiliated? She will never go back unless Sunand admits his error."

Sunand did not come for his mother-in-law's funeral. No one from his family came either. Niranjan Sir decided that his daughter must get a divorce. He would look for another match. After all, how old was she? Second marriages were common these days.

Sunand had not started divorce proceedings, but Niranjan Sir filed a case now. Gayatri did not object. Let Baba be happy! There's no question of a return anyway.

While Niranjan Sir was engaged in running to the lawyer and getting the divorce papers ready, Gayatri too was busy with her preparations. She was designing a line of garments and assembling a new brand. It was to be called "Black One" – meaning a black buck, which was native to Odisha. She would design unisex T-shirts for girls as well as boys. In a variety of styles and colors. All the garments would be hand-woven. The front would be embroidered. Some in Sambalpuri designs and others in Pipili appliqué work. The back would be totally plain. But on each would be printed a line or two of a traditional Odia song, an Odia proverb or a couplet from a modern lyric.

The very first garment Gayatri designed for herself. Brilliantly colored and wonderfully tailored. Everyone who saw it was tempted. But the problem was: where to source the poem or song that was to be printed on the back?

Gayatri was searching frantically for an appropriate quotation for the rear panel. Then – no one knows why – a line from the Odia Bhagabat by Atibadi Jagannath Das suggested itself.

"In the universe that Brahma created
Each creature found its space."

A unique quotation had to be found for each T-shirt in the "Black One" collection. Each quotation had to be rich in rasa (tenderness and delicacy); each had to be overflowing with the spirit of Odisha. Only then would the brand attract young customers. Literary taste had to blend with the beauty of textile and color.

Lost in her thoughts, Gayatri went to sleep. She had a dream. A couple of lines from some poem came flying in the breeze and wrapped themselves around her like a banner. Now it was visible and now it vanished; now she could read the words and now she couldn't. Words could play all kinds of tricks when they wanted to. They went into a sulk; they played hide-and-seek with feelings. Who knew this better than Gayatri, who had been a poet herself?

But she caught hold of the words at last. The lines were:

"Oh, lotus petal! Hide, if you must, from my touch

But why hide your fragrance?"

Oh, God! These were Sunanda's lines! But why were they appearing now?

She woke up with a start. She felt like weeping. The words had been written by Sunand, but they had belonged to her one day. They had been composed for her. They could neither be lost nor returned. Words are made of *akshara* (letters). It is because they never die that they are *akshara* (indestructible).

Sunand is no longer a loved one now; he has faded away from the horizon of the body, to someplace unknown. But the words have remained.

Some had been on paper, and of these, there was no trace. Gayatri had thrown away the books and the letters he had written.

But what about the words that hover in the ether? It is impossible to know when they choose to arrive.

Garments bearing the "Black One" label began to take shape. The entire ground floor was converted into a garment factory. Niranjan Sir was delighted with his daughter's enthusiasm and diligence. "Black One Garments" was inaugurated with a Manager, a clerk-cum-cashier and four women artisans. The lines printed on the back of the first "Black One" shirt were retained, exactly as Gayatri had seen them.

One evening, Gayatri was turning over the pages of a magazine in the drawing room when her father said "Ma, the lawyer has sent some papers related to the divorce proceedings. You have to sign them. I have left them on your table. When you are through with your work, will you take a look?"

Gayatri said, "Very well, I'll have a look" and got up.

She picked up the sheets of paper on her table. They were all in legal language – must be divorce papers. Was it necessary for her to read them? What do divorce papers contain? She had never thought about it. She was about to pick up her pen and sign the papers when suddenly she found herself surrounded by a swarm of words. Red, blue, purple, yellow; deep green, like leaves of grass or faintly green, like tender banana leaves. Countless words. Some were flowers, others thorns; some were leaves, others fruits. Some glowed like burning embers, while others were like the ends of burnt-out slivers of wood, pointed and sharp as needles.

Gayatri was flustered. She felt like driving them away. But how does one drive words away – whisk them away like flies or kick them away?

She remembered something that had happened a month ago. She had gone for a meeting at the Rabindra Mandap; then, halfway through the meeting, she decided to leave. At the door, she came across Sunand. Neither said a word. To Gayatri, it was like a chance meeting with any other stranger. No feelings; no change in feelings.

But what was this? From that moment, words had been pursuing her like swarms of insects. Drawing blood. Tugging at her clothes. Surrounding her on all sides when she was in bed. Some stroked her lovingly; others pricked her with needles.

Gayatri tried to explain things to herself.

That's how words are! There's no point in making enemies of them.

She picked up her pen again. Maybe it was best she signed.

Just then, a word, vivid pink in color, came and squatted on the table in front of her. Was it a word or a couplet? She couldn't tell.

Next morning, when Niranjan asked her "Ma, have you signed those papers?" she said, "Bapa, I don't think we should pursue the divorce any longer. What's the hurry? I don't have to be a wife again – just let me be a mother!"

And as she said this, a few dozens of the swarming words shattered like glass, in front of her eyes.

Niranjan was unable to understand this sudden change in her decision.

Original Odia: *Sabdamananka Saha*

■

The Story Of The Gipsy Fish

Manoj Kumar Panda
Translated by **Snehaprava Das**

It is the tale of an old black fish that wanders aimlessly in a bottomless ocean, nonstop.

Its eyes are of deep red color and they never blink. It is never seen more than once in one particular patch of the ocean. It keeps on wandering from one place to another as if engaged in an endless quest. The numerous creases on its old face are testimonial of the pain of carrying on its heart the measureless load of sorrow the world suffers. The old fish never cares to go after food. It eats only if a fish or something came within its easy reach. The pair of its large fins keeps flapping constantly, and its tail wiggles perpetually. Doesn't it ever feel tired?

The wandering blackfish neither bothers to make a friend nor to be a member of any flock of fishes. It hardly speaks to anyone. It never seeks shelter in the crevices of the coral ridge. It seems to have no interest in the celebrations the seahorses so eagerly took part in, nor in playing hide and seek with the mermaids. It does not prefer to rest in the ocean bed under the soothing shade of the ocean-creepers. Time and again it soars to a great height, as though in an effort to reach the sky. It continuously practices the exercise of soaring into the air and making a fast swooping dive into the water. Yes, it gets tired at times, gets frightened by its own imagination, and whimpers and howls as if it receives a jolt from some invisible source of fear. No one ever tries to calm its fluttering heart with soothing words of assurance. It craves to listen to things like 'Don't fear, we are there with you,', but nothing like that ever happens. 'He has lost his mental balance', or 'The old, senile fool of a wanderer,' are the only remarks they made.

The old nomad holds no grudge against anyone or anything. It swims and leaps and dives in the vast ocean. Perhaps it feels exhausted at times, and there is always the fear that its fins may not survive the strain of ceaseless flapping and get snapped off its body. But such apprehensions cannot stop the old fish. It swims, and leaps, and dives and flaps its fins—and its eyes never blink.

To blink is a mark of a change in one's sensitivity index. It is an indication of fresh enthusiasm, of a desire to see the world anew. It is a kind of signal to rediscover your own 'self'. To blink is to pronounce the rise of a new hope inside you—to receive new support to sustain life. It is a hell of an existence where the eyes do not blink—a deathlike life in a bleak, hopeless, dismal world of agony.

Yes, hell could just be the other name of a life caught in the grip of an interminable ennui. People in the polar region do not blink for six months in a year, holding dreams of the six sunlit months that would obviously follow the long dark spell of half of the year in their open eyes. The old fish has no such dreams to comfort itself with. It can never close its red eyes. Occasionally it lifts a blank gaze towards the unending stretch of the sky above, and a pale moon that hangs there surrounded by dimly flickering stars. But soon its gaze flits down to the vast expanse of the grey ocean and it takes a plunge down. It has grown quite familiar to the grey of the ocean. It has also, grown accustomed to a life of unending monotony.

Sunsets and sunrises kept following each other as time moved ahead at its regular pace. Then something happened that the old black fish had never expected in his wildest imagination.

On that fateful morning—the nomad blackfish was at its act of swimming, leaping high and taking swooping dives. Suddenly it sensed that it was no longer alone. It turned its unblinking red eyes around and noticed the four large dark-brown colored fish swimming, keeping pace with it. They were closing in menacingly from all four sides. The nomad blackfish stole a look at them— their brown spotted body, thick whiskers, and the awe-inspiring sharp, serrated jaws made them as ferocious as a leopard. The blackfish felt a sudden frisson of fear. Soon the fear gave way to panic— 'I am going to die soon', it thought and stopped still. The other four too stopped swimming. One among the four looked comparatively more intimidating and ruthless. It had bigger and thicker whiskers and sharper jaws. It must be the chief, the blackfish thought. The other three dared not to utter a word in its presence. They waited silently for orders. 'You scoundrel, you have left your regular habitat and are hiding here! We have swum all the way here looking for you,' it shouted. 'Tie him up', it spat orders at the other three. Instantly, with the speed of lightning, they tied the blackfish to a steep rock that emerged from the water. 'Hit him', the chief shouted again. One of the three swooped high up and came hurtling down with the speed of a shooting arrow, hitting the black fish with all the weight of its flying body. Another waggled its stout, whip-like tail with great speed and lashed at the belly and back of the old wanderer. The third one swam swiftly past the blackfish, and reaching a point at its front took an abrupt U-turn and rushed madly at it, its rock-hard snout slamming into the face of the blackfish. It slashed at the gill and the snout of the black fish with its razor-sharp jaws. Blood spurted out of the nomad fish's mouth. It cried out in pain. Its head began to spin. But it had no idea who those fishes were and what made them so mad.

'Tell us now where have you kept your family hidden? Where is your wife? Where are your sons and daughters-in-law?

Where are your daughter and her husband hiding? You know how much advance was paid to them. You are *the* one responsible for their disappearance. Tied to this rock, you will be left to die of hunger unless you tell us where they have escaped. Even after taking the advance amount they have not turned up for work. You have advised them to run away with the amount, haven't you? Answer or die.' They kept on and on, interrogating the old wanderer and hitting and torturing it in every possible way they could till they were exhausted. The old black fish had no answer. 'You obstinate fool,' the chief spouted the venom of frustration. 'Hey, keep a close watch,' he ordered to one of the three. 'See that he doesn't get a morsel of food'. Then the big brown fish swam away with the other two.

The old blackfish could now make a guess what had outraged them so. He remembered how about four months back while it was not home one of the brokers involved in the racket of the unlawful dispatching of laborers had inveigled its family members to accompany him to some distant part of the ocean where, he had assured them, they would get enough good food in exchange of their labor. Later the old fish had learned that its family members along with many others were trafficked from the Bay of Bengal to the Arabian Sea where they were made to toil and slog. The old black fish had no idea when its family would return, or, for that matter, if they would return at all! The news had left it heartbroken. It had wept and pined for them. But it was even more frightened now after the flock of those brown hooligans told it that they had run away and were chased by these heartless monsters. It seemed as if its heart would stop beating and all the vital organs of its body will come apart. A blinding black cloud of fear engulfed it. It felt as if all the water under its body was sucked away by some giant force leaving its fins stiff and paralyzed.

'What would happen to my family members if they fall into the hands of these hideous tyrants?' Cold fear clutched at its heart. 'They would cripple my sons and maul and mangle my wife and my daughter-in-law',' it's withering imagination pictured how the brown fish would pierce the gills of its sons and tear their tails off their body, and left it trembling with apprehension. It could visualize the weal on their sons' whip-blown bodies. 'Why did they commit the blunder of running away, and where would I look for them?' the old wanderer thought desperately. But pain blurred thinking. It just lay there like dead, its body bruised and sore. The chief came twice daily, repeated his questions and demanded an answer. It shouted and swore and ventilated its frustration inflicting more pain on the old blackfish, and left leaving one to keep guard.

This went on for ten long days, and suddenly to its utter surprise and amazement, the old fish sensed that the knot of the rope tied around its tail had gone slack. A tiny flicker of hope sparked in its heart. There is no harm in making a try to put this fish guarding it out of action, the blackfish decided. After a little struggle with the slackening knot, it finally got itself released. The old fish brought down its heavy snout in a stunning blow on the head of the guard-fish with all the strength its battered, old body could muster up and shot off ahead. Before the guard-fish realized what had happened and tried to make a chase, the old wanderer had disappeared from the range of its vision.

The old nomad swam on and on changing directions time and again, and at the end of the second day of its miraculous escape, it reached a strange, unfamiliar patch in the ocean. It was a beautiful, dreamlike place simmering brightly in the light of dazzling pebbles, like a park resplendent with colorful lights. Thousands of shingles lay scattered on the soft golden sand-bed under the water. Coral-dunes stood at places, laced with sea-creepers of vibrant hues. Flocks and flocks of star-fish drifted about in an orange-red glow. There were unicellular sponges, amber-eyed amoebas swinging their flesh-sprigs, and lots and lots of tiny fish in a riot of colors slithering in and out of the mouth of tiny caves. Huge oysters let water jetting out making a picture of small gurgling streams. Small fishes clung to the coral riffs looking like abseiling mountaineers. The old wanderer had never believed a place as this one could exist even in its wildest fancy.

The old wanderer enjoyed the tickle as the baby fishes

gathered around and rubbed their bodies to its. It lay still, relishing the warmth seeping in while they lick-cleaned its wounds, letting the ripples of comfort sweep past over its exhausted body as the tiny amoeba snuggled close to it, recollecting the pain it had gone through in the past ten days, and making plans for the future.

And then it saw them— five huge fish porcelain white skin slowly advancing towards the place where it lay resting. They swam soundlessly; the old wanderer couldn't sense their presence nor could it see them with its perpetually open eyes until they were at almost a touching distance. Its heart skipped a beat and then began to race. It looked around in frantic desperation trying to find a way of escape. It was surprising to find that all other creatures including the tiny fishes were totally unperturbed by the presence of the new arrivals. Their nonchalance and lack of fear, and the innocuous look the five white fish wore helped to restore the confidence of the old fish. It lay still and looked intently at them keenly observing every movement they made. The five white fish, after a brief deliberation, approached the old wanderer and put some food in its front—dead insects, dead leeches, and the shriveled intestines and digestive organs of dead fishes. It took some time for the old wanderer to come out of the cell of fear and shamefulness, and a sense of inferiority it was confined within, and accept their charity. But in the end hunger won over all other instincts, and the old fish began to eat, slowly, haltingly, overwhelmed with absolute humility. The small fishes those licked at its wounds gathered around swallowing the food greedily. The old fish did not grudge their demand. It had had enough to fill its empty stomach, and slowly energy seeped into its tired body. It drifted under the sea-weeds and lay quietly, resting.

One of the huge white fish spoke in a solemn, bass voice— "Don't fear, tell us everything about you in detail. We assure you of a better and worth-living tomorrow.' Before the old blackfish could say anything, another floated in a movie-camera and positioned it in its front, focusing the lens on the old blackfish. It shrank away from the glaring light but got rid of the fear and embarrassment after they explained the technicalities of the operation. Slowly, hesitantly, the old fish told its tale to the camera. It told about its life stricken with unbearable pain and ridden with terror. It spoke about its family that went to some far-off area in the ocean in search of livelihood. It narrated about the irony of their existence, about the desperate effort to change their destiny turning out to be an exercise in futility, the horrid story of getting caught in that destiny's the deadly noose. The old fish fumbled and stammered as it spoke. Hard sobs threatened to stifle its voice. Lumps of suffocating, black misery stuck at its heart, and scalding tears deepened the red in its eyes. Its gill quivered and its tail fluttered frantically. Water bubbles spouted out incessantly of its mouth. Its body expanded and contracted and the intensity of the emotion made it delirious. It howled and whined, and lamented miserably. At times it hurled abuses at itself and others. It hissed out obscenities and cried bitterly. When it failed to articulate its feelings, it whispered something in a strangled voice which no one understood. Time and again it took a pause, nodded a few times, and began speaking. The number of the small, multicolored fishes that gathered around continued to grow. They gaped at the old wanderer silently, smelling the warmth of emotion its words exuded and watching intently the frantic flutter of its tail, its fins, and its gill. But they had no idea what exactly it told and what made it so disturbed. And finally, when the wanderer was drained out, it stopped. All remained still, stunned by the tale of agony. Occasionally a tail wagged a little that sent a slight stir in the oppressive silence.

A gigantic screen of glass was pushed through and placed in front of the old wanderer. They said it was the screen of a television, and asked it to look. The old wanderer looked at itself in the huge glass screen, amazed. It heard its own quivering, whimpering voice and watched the rise and fall of its gill, the flapping of its fins and the spasms that passed through its body as it narrated its tragic tale. It looked closely at its mouth as it opened and closed, and the changing shades of the red in its eyes. A tiny ripple of confidence rustled inside it and slowly began spreading out in all directions. 'My own self is no longer confined inside my body,' it thought elatedly, 'It has escaped the bounds of its limitedness and reached far, making contact with the vast world outside.' The realization made the old wanderer bolder and more confident. 'I am everywhere, I exist both inside and outside of the screen', it said as it watched its own image again and again. 'My soul is outside my body, detached from it which is just an inert thing, a casting mold to give shape to my physical form; I am no longer contained in that mold—I am free, all-pervasive,'—its heart swelled with the joy of discovering itself, it felt like it has come out of a long hibernation and beginning afresh. Now that my soul, my real self is no longer confined within my body I can have my destiny under my control, the great black fish thought. 'I had always been a slave to a hostile destiny, which constantly robbed my hope and my will to live—but now I can have a hold over my destiny, and I can dictate terms to it. I will ask God to keep me like this forever; I will pray Him to grant me the power to blink, to see the world anew every time I do so.'

It began to scream at the top of its voice startling the crowd of sea-creatures that gathered there.

"I have no regrets if I die at this very instant,' it shouted looking around. "Come on, kill me if you want! I am ready to face death!" And then it swam away at an incredible speed. Before anyone could guess what was happening, the blackfish had disappeared out of sight. About fifty fishes followed it, and after swimming a great distance they finally spotted the great blackfish. They saw it shouting at four fishes of dark-brown color and haranguing with them. It threatened the fishes that consequences would be disastrous unless they brought its family members back. They were shocked and surprised at the confidence with which the old blackfish challenged the large tough-looking brown fishes.

The four brown fishes were thoroughly intimidated by the threatening of the old wanderer and the sight of fifty fishes. There was no way to escape—they kept still, and obeyed the directions of the blackfish without offering any resistance. They were brought to the five large white fishes who interviewed them in front of the movie camera. The statement of their chief was recorded.

The four of them were brokers who collected laborers to work in the industries owned by rich and influential fishes in the Arabian Sea, the chief of the group confessed. Their task was to sell the ones from the lower rung of the fish-class in the Bay of Bengal the dreams of a comfortable life, lure them with talks of easy money and dispatch them to the Arabian Sea to work on contractual basis. The family members of the old wanderer too had swallowed the bait of those empty promises and left home for an unknown destination, nurturing dreams of a happy life in their hearts.

Every year we dispatch about fifty thousand such contractual laborers. It is a job that demands tremendous patience and craftiness. After traveling a few miles they would demand to be sent back and we have to keep on coaxing them, serving them good food, deceiving them with false assurances. Not everyone is an expert in the art of deceit. It might be relatively easy to dupe a few of them, but to deceive fifty thousand at one time is a bone-grinding job. So they had to add a moderate dose of fear in the treatment—a few sturdy and fierce looking fish trailed after the exodus to douse even the slightest grouse in case there is any. The flock of fish swam ahead, flapping their fins wanly, alternatively impelled by hope and despair, unaware that they were inside a huge, huge dragnet. Sometimes a few who made a futile effort to get away told about the net to their friends in a hushed voice. But they had to move on, caught in the snare of belief and disbelief. After covering half of the way or so they were no longer given food, and the fishes were dead-beat by the time they entered the alien waters of the Arabian Sea. They were given a little food as they reached and were immediately sent to the worksite where they were made to slave for their masters. The system of wage in lieu of labor did not exist there. It was rather a cunningly worked-out scheme of collective bonded slavery, coercion, and exploitation. Hours and hours of hard labor take its toll on them. Their fins and tails get severed in the process, merciless beating leaves countless weal on their bruised, shrunken bodies. They keep dragging on till all energy gets drained out of them, leaving them almost lifeless, unable to move or speak.

The laborers there toil like machines, indifferent to all emotions, detached from everything, even their own self — crushed under morbid impotence. They have no choice other than a stoic submission to a cruel fate, accepting resignedly the futility of their efforts, the vain hopes, and mortifying loneliness. They neither get food or wages in commiseration with the labor but no one dared to complain or protest for fear of incurring the ill-will of their masters which may lead to, they apprehended, a further deterioration in their condition. The fishes, after the end of the day, are prodded into an airless narrow enclosure, an outrageously unwholesome patch of greasy, foamy water that was like a living hell. The fierce-looking broker-fishes kept constant watch over them. No one was allowed to move out of the enclosure and swim in the clear water, nor was there anyone to take care of the fishes if any of them fell sick. They were barred from keeping proximity or sympathize with one another, they were forbidden to dream, and to plan or act. Not even a faint light of hope ever could filter through the blanket of fear and fatigue they were bundled inside. But, strangely after some days, they were found missing. An organized search to track them in the vicinity yielded no result. It was quite obvious to expect that they would come back to the old black fish in the Bay of Bengal. That was the reason why they kept the old wanderer in chains and tortured it to extract information. Later, the four brokers were convinced that the old wanderer actually had no idea where its family was.

'How could my family escape from such a situation?' The old blackfish wondered. Even as it kept asking the question to itself, again and again, a large flock of long snake-like fishes approached them. To the utter astonishment of the thousands and thousands of fishes who were there with the old wanderer and the four large brown fishes who had tortured it, the wife of the old blackfish, its son and daughter, and daughter-in-law swam in there along with the snake-fishes. They looked deathly pale, totally drained of life — — their eyes held no spark of recognition in them but only a dull blank look - marks of injury all over their body gave them an ugly, distorted look. They had lost all physical reflex, their dreams were long since mutilated, their hopes dead. They looked like toys molded from transparent plastic, pale and inert.

One of the snake-fishes came forward and narrated what an abominable horror had taken their life and freedom in its grip. It narrated how they labored and starved, fell sick and suffered the brutal treatment of the ones who engaged them at work. All listened in shocked silence as if hypnotized by disbelief. The old blackfish listened too, its red unblinking eyes growing wider in terror. Its wife kept nodding its head constantly oblivious of what took place around; the son floated like a dead fish its head lowered and its torn tail rising straight up, its mouth twisted in a fixed ugly grin. The daughter and the daughter-in-law lay side by side, on their backs. No other image except the vast expanse of the brine water and emptiness that threatened to devour them was reflected in their eyes. They were served some food but none of them cared to even cast a glance at the food.

"They lived in that hellhole for four more months," another snake-fish said.

"And then the cyclone hit the sea.

The storm seemed to unleash all its fury to vanquish the grim defiance of the sea. Raging waves rode high up into the air smashing everything that came in the way. The sea water whirled and whirled as if churned by some gigantic, horrendous force and huge pillars of water rose on its surface. Sea-creatures, large and small, birds, boats were hurled up by the gale and went spiraling around the water-pillars and were sent hurtling down from a great height. The debacle destroyed all living and non-living objects that within the range of its reach.

The ships that had anchored in the port sailed at a great speed towards the Bay of Bengal, on receiving the prior information about the approaching storm. Some, in their panic, to get away hit one another and sank. By some miraculous stroke of luck, some of us were pushed into in the rushing, foamy surge spouted off a ship as it shot forward. We kept floating in the direction which the ship moved, prodded on by the current. The wind had blinded us and we had no idea where we were going, our fins were wrenched off one after another by the rushing current. It was like a deadly tryst with a hostile destiny- a faceoff with Death that stared at us." The snake-fish took a pause here. "It took us fourteen days to reach here. The family of the old black fish is the worst sufferer. The brutal torture of the boss for whom they had been working had left them half-dead, and the deadly struggle to survive the storm sucked away the rest of the life-force from them. Their throats are parched, and so they can't speak or eat, they are now unable even to move an inch."

The old blackfish returned its unblinking gaze towards its wife. The wife was no longer nodding its head. It lay its face up, flat and still. The old wanderer flipped its body up and down a few times but discovered no sign of life. It remained still for a moment, then let out a single, wild wail. An enormous chunk of sorrow that stuck at its throat like a flint-stone smothered its voice.

It offered its wife's body to the all-swallowing waves of the sea and without waiting to know what happened to the others who lay there half-crazy and half-dead, sped away no one could guess where to.

It was never seen again.

Original Odia: *Nirantara Jajabara*

Reba

Hrushikesh Panda

Translated by **Lipipuspa Nayak**
(with the author)

I

Since the day Rebati graduated from the High School with high distinction and continued her studies at the nearby college, I and my friends began to envy her, an envy of impossible dimensions. Her father worked as a petty lawyer at the county courts and he owned large areas of farmland in our village. He filed suits at the slightest provocation and hence, forget us, even our fathers and maternal grandfathers did not wish to be on his wrong side. Though we and our fathers and maternal grandfathers thoroughly disapproved of Rebati, in high heels and salwar kameez [instead of wearing sari], who did not marry and instead went off to the college, none of us dared to convey this to her father.

By then I had already failed once in Standard Eight, and I had three more annual examinations to clear before I could graduate from the High School. But Rebati was famous as a brilliant student and continued to secure high grades at the college every year. We often imagined about her, and her classmates and made up stories about them: how the boys and girls of colleges together roamed around for long hours, went to movies, picnicked in forests, and sometimes spent nights in each other's hostels.

When Rebati did not marry even after she acquired her diploma in Bachelor of Science, we concluded unequivocally that she was in love with a guy who was tall and fair though there was considerable difference of opinion among us on his identity. Some of us claimed that he is one of her college teachers. Some averred that he is the son of the richest civil contractor of the government from the nearby town. Some asserted that he is a terribly handsome good-for-nothing fellow who could not get even a High School Diploma; but since love is blind she cannot see the worthlessness of this boyfriend.

Eventually I graduated from the High School and entered the College at the town five kilometers away from our village. I was a student of Humanities. When we [who studied Humanities] peeped into the science laboratories where boys and girls huddled together, sometimes their faces brushing against each other as they peered into a microscope, we concluded that love was inevitable between these boys and girls studying science, and sighed outside the glass windows. Daft though I am I had learnt that Rebati was a student of zoology. My personal conviction, a very strong one at that, was that Rebati's sweetheart was one of her classmates or one of her teachers.

Meanwhile, our speculations about Rebati's affair had traversed new heights. We had arrived at the firm conclusion that this tall and fair sweetheart of Rebati had come to our village during one summer holidays when Rebati was here. One Basu, whose sister was married in our village, often came to our village. Since the day he graduated from High School, he had told his parents to move a proposal for marriage with Rebati. When we flew kites about Rebati's affairs, Basu snipped them apart. His desire to marry Rebati obsessed him for a long time and all his efforts were focused on how to keep pace with Rebati in the College. Basu scraped through his Bachelor of Arts, and then the proposal for marriage was placed before Rebati.

When Rebati heard Basu's name, she jerked her head so violently with disapproval that she got a terrible sprain in her neck which lasted for several weeks. From then on, Basu too joined us actively and salaciously in gossip about Rebati. Rebati did not marry even after she passed Bachelor of Science and left for Bhubaneswar to do her Masters.

Meanwhile, her poems began to appear occasionally in periodicals. Another time, her photograph appeared in a newspaper when she had gone to distribute relief material in a village affected by floods. It was impossible to recognise her from the photograph, but her name was unmistakably printed beneath it. Yet many of us argued that this was not her photograph.

Every time she returned to the village, she brought along several Cups and Trophies, which her mother displayed proudly in the shelves of the drawing room. Her mother proudly showed off these awards and prizes to everyone who came to their house, though she would show the Cup for Chancellor's Debate and say that Rebati had got this Shield for hop-step-n-jump; she just could not remember what each of the Trophies were for.

By the time Rebati joined M.Sc., most of us had changed. Many of us had been married. But because I had been enrolled into a Pre-Degree course in Humanities, my family members had fairly high ambitions about me. The possibility of my marriage had receded.

Rebati was the first Master of Science across several villages and counties around and this made us proud of her. Soon it became a matter of pride to be able to say before boys of other villages that we were from her village.

Rebati finished her M.Sc. and enrolled for Ph. D. During those days she had once come to the village for about three months. One day Rebati's mother summoned me and requested me to go and pick her up from the bus stop. Perhaps somewhere deep inside my mind, I had always desired to be associated with Rebati, because from the moment her mother assigned me the task, I became restless and excited. In the nights, I began to see strange dreams, of them I remember one very clearly:

For a long time I had been waiting at the bus stop. But no bus came. I wandered away. Rebati alighted from a bus when I was some distance away, and she did not find anyone. Rebati went back by the same bus on its return trip.

After I woke up, I learnt this lesson from the dream that I must not leave the bus stop even for a second. I went through a book on occult interpretation of dreams; but the kind of dreams which had been interpreted in this book did not include my dream of Rebati.

Besides, I was in awe of girls like Rebati because she belonged to the upper class of educated young women. My sisters had never studied beyond the seventh standard. In fact, one of them had studied up to the second standard and had by now completely forgotten the alphabets. Secondly, Rebati was far more educated than I was, and on top of it was engaged in research. During the primary school days I had read about a few scientists and knew that there was some vague relationship between research and scientists. So the possibility that sooner or later, Rebati will enter the School Primers as a scientist along with her picture was lurking in my consciousness.

When Rebati alighted from the bus, she looked around and had no difficulty in recognizing me. I was wearing my best trousers and half sleeve shirt. The hand stitches near the fly of the trousers had given away and to hide this, I was covering this area with my left hand and my long shirt. I loaded her luggage on the baskets of the porter, who was my kinship cousin.

Since I had not spoken to her for a long time, I could not decide whether to address her as Reba or elder sister, nor if I would call her *tu, tum,* or *aap.* So I tried my best to communicate with her without addressing her directly. My statements were like 'We go?' 'Trouble while coming?' 'What is there in the trunk?' Without pronouns.

After we had walked for quite a distance in silence, Rebati suddenly bloomed into a mischievous smile and asked: 'You had acted once as a General in the village opera, didn't you?'

I was dying to find out how she knew, but since I could not address her as *tu, tum,* or *aap* and since a question like *'from where such knowledge'* would have been too stupid and archaic, I said nothing.

Rebati recalled and narrated the anecdote. Instead of saying something like 'Stop, do not progress one more step, you wretched traitor', I had said:

'Stop for a while o steam-driven cart

I wish to behold the beautiful Chilika lake which is like a portrait;

My inexperience makes me think that it is not real

Because in this world I have not seen a place more beautiful…

and so on, ten or twelve stanzas from Radhanath Ray's modern poem *Chilika*, about the largest lagoon in India. The audience had not noticed the massive goof-up and had cheered thunderously this non-stop flow of soliloquy. Rebati had giggled then, and when she saw the applause of the audience, had broken into uproarious laughter.

As she narrated this to me now, she again burst into laughter so boisterously that if she had not been walking on the road, she would have perhaps rolled on the ground.

My face went crimson with the ignominy and I thought angrily: 'She is so conceited because she is studying. Why, despite all this hauteur, she can't even find a groom, she has remained a spinster, ha!'

But I did not have the guts to tell her so. Her sharp nose was straight like a sword, she wore glasses and except Rama Mishra, no one had the courage to tell her off to her face. Rama Mishra was the priest in our village temple of Lord Shiva, and had gone loony by smoking too much hemp. Every time he hobbled over to her and blessed her with incorrect Sanskrit hymns, Rebati opened her vanity bag and offered him, instead of a ten paisa coin, a one-rupee note and floored him with surprise.

This time Rebati stayed in the village for nearly three months. She was studying honeybees for her doctoral research and I had located four honeycombs near our village. I used a net attached to a handle like one which was used by Sir Ronald Ross to catch mosquitoes for studying malaria [a sketch of which was there in my Language Reader of Standard Two], and with some chemicals smeared on this net, with rubber gloves, I caught honeybees for Rebati. For every ten bees I got a candy and a smile like a moonlit night. For every twenty bees I was awarded with cakes baked by her and jam and sometimes a pat on my back.

Though, Rebati *was* moody. Sometimes she was so staid and lost that I became scared. She kept the bees in several tiny glass boxes and talked to them as if they were human. Sometimes she explained and demonstrated to me the movements and the moods of the bees. Though angry, cheerful, bored and sleepy bees looked the same to my eyes, I was not prepared to betray my ignorance and pretended that I could discern their different moods. She had given me an ointment for honeybee stings, which I used sparingly and kept with me for a long time, and this possession earned me some importance in the village.

Rebati finished her field work and returned to Bhubaneswar. A few days later I received a packet from her by post. It contained cloth pieces for a pair of trousers and a shirt and a letter written in English conveying her thanks to me.

Around this time a news item with her photograph appeared in some Odia dailies that Rebati has been awarded PhD.

A few days later, with her photograph appearing in a couple of newspapers, she went off to the USA.

II

After three years Rebati was returning from the USA. I was dying to see her. I had stopped participating in gossips about her because I felt that she was somehow very close to me. But younger children had now started to spin stories about her. Some adults believed ardently that she had learnt black magic and transmuted young men to honeybees. For quite a few years, her father had stopped looking for a groom for her, because as far as his farthest and faintest acquaintances and contacts went, there was no one who could have been a suitable match for Rebati. In the meantime, I had acquired the diploma of Bachelor in Arts, had endlessly looked for a job and had failed to find a job, and frustrated and bored had entered into wedlock. I nursed a clandestine hope that with Rebati's help, I will be able to get into some job with regular salary.

In these three years when she had been away, the number of naked, emaciated and dust-coated children had increased in our village.

Rebati appeared to me slightly thinner, far more solemn, and smaller. She did not smile even once on the way and replied to my questions in a disinterested and listless manner: her research in the USA was about roaches. She had decided that in Odisha she will study some marine animals, probably turtles. She had been appointed as a teacher in some University in the USA. She was also the President of the Odisha Chapter of 'The Society to Protect Marine Animals'. The Society had demanded of the state government to stop for a few years fishing of Indian shad from the coastal waters and estuaries where they came to spawn. This information did not make me happy at all because we all relished Indian shad. She will return to the USA in about a year's time.

After we reached their house, she asked me to come the next day and before leaving I did not forget to mention to her about my need for a salaried job. When I reached her house the next morning she was all ready to go out. We walked through the village lanes, and little children scurried away as if she were a witch or some other spook. Though Rebati was thrilled because she thought the children were playing hide-and-seek with her. When a terrified little child loped past her, she pretended to chase it. Rebati was not running fast or anything, but the child howled like no one had howled before as if it was being seized by a spook. The child's mother came out and swore indecipherably at Rebati.

'*Hey*! Where have the lilies gone?' Rebati asked as we came near the pond by the school.

'Some urchins had dropped water hyacinth weed into the pond. Then the pond had been covered with lilies, and lotus, but the next year they all died. Only water hyacinth survived. That time you were in America.'

Rebati stood wonder-struck before our Community Culture Hall. Years ago, on the verandah of this hall, every year on *Kumar Purnima* – the Festival-of-the-Youth – a full-moon night in autumn, girls drew romantic patterns with lily petals, lotus stems, powdered rice, charcoal and bricks and vermillion. Every family offered rice-and-milk pudding before the Moon-god.

In this Culture Hall, throughout the year Rebati and other girls and boys used to sing *champu, Odishi, bhajans* and songs from old Odia films accompanied by harmonium, tabla, mridang, and violin. Now the Culture Hall had crumbled, and litigations were going on over its possession. Two bullocks were tethered to two of its broken pillars, which had once held the roof. Dung-cakes had been spread on the verandah to dry out in the sun. In front of this dilapidated structure, a three or four year old child was defecating with a blank face. He suddenly broke into a loud bawl when he saw us.

We walked towards the river; the river flowed at some distance beyond several plots of farm land. Then Rebati asked: 'Have a *bidi* on you?'

I nodded.

Years ago I used to be scared of her and she had made me give up smoking. But now Rebati looked small and frail before me; besides since my marriage I had looked upon myself as a man. So I could admit before her without fear that I had *bidi* with me.

She asked: 'Started smoking *bidi* again, eh?'

'Sometimes.'

Rebati winked at me and said: 'Let's go and smoke near the thicket.'

'Which thicket?'

'Why, near the cremation ground! How frightening it used to be when I was a child! Come, let us go and find out if there are any spooks there.'

The places around the cremation ground scared me even now. There was another reason why I did not want to go there: there was no demarcated cremation ground anymore. Since long ago, Chakrapani, the village tout, had managed to get this land recorded in his name as agricultural land during the first stage of land settlement.

[Land settlement introduced by the Moguls and the British and continuing today is a highly protracted matter, where the several stages like Filling up the columns of Land Records, Actual Measurement, preparation of Draft Records, Public Display of Records, Final Settlement and Ultimate Correction etcetera generally took years between one stage and another so that a peasant may face only the first stage and by the time he, or more likely, his successors got the final Record-of-Rights, the grandson would be appearing as a witness in the proceedings of the Land Administration courts.]

As I reflected on all this, I suddenly realized that may be at this moment Rebati is not here; she is preoccupied with something far away in space and time, as if suddenly she was not a human being anymore, she was a preternatural witch, and as these thoughts swooped though my mind, my heart missed a few beats.

The place that had been the cremation ground now consisted of an old banyan tree around which green paddy leaves tossed with the wind.

Rebati looked at the sky through the banyan tree. 'Hey! This tree has gone bald! It has become smaller too, and thinner. This is no cremation ground, how can it disappear? Disappear?'

I narrated briefly the episode of the vanishing cremation ground. Rebati suddenly became quiet and thoughtful. Pensive and lost, she walked around the forlorn banyan tree several times. She did not remember that I was around. Till we returned to her house she did not utter another word.

That evening I went to her place. Rebati was sitting alone in her room, the lights switched off. When she saw me, she said: 'Let us play hide-and-seek.'

After two rounds she became bored and asked me to play the flute.

It is true I used to play the flute, like nearly everyone in our village knew how to play at least one musical instrument, or how to sing. Of course, my expertise was absolutely limited to a couple old Hindi film tunes. In my younger days I would have gratefully played these two tunes let alone for Rebati, even for her nincompoop younger brother, and not once but a dozen times. But now I was sure of my incompetence, and declined over and over again. But Rebati pleaded again and again and sulked like a little child, and said: 'How you have changed! Could you have said "no" to your sister Reba three years ago?'

I ran to my house, fetched my flute and played those two tunes. Rebati enquired about my wife, and suddenly wanted to pick up lilies. I was forced to remind her that lilies did not bloom anymore in the pond near the school where water hyacinth had taken over.

That evening Rebati narrated about her life in the USA though I could not comprehend everything. As far as I could understand:

She was an Honorary Executive Secretary of the Indian Society of the USA and often sang *Odishi* songs over there. Out there, a German gentleman had wanted to marry her. Rebati had become scared and maintained distance from this white man. She has been busy, she is either Vice President or Advisor in several units of the University where she teaches and time does not weigh heavy on her. Occasionally, she feels lonesome. This feeling is so deep, cold and complex that she cannot even explain it. When she wanders through strange cities in the world, sometimes she nurtures a sudden premonition that she is going to meet someone whom she had not met in a long time, *someone who had been very close and intimate and had disappeared long ago, and is now suddenly standing there at a turning, or when she alights from a train he will push through the crowd grinning at her in recognition. Or else, just before she enters through the Airport security, he will run in, and call her, and she will cancel the journey;* but she knows that no such man will ever come, there is no such man, how can he come? Yet such a desperate, deep and pining hope keeps haunting her.

Suddenly Rebati stretched herself on the bed, rolled over and began to sob. I could not hear what she said through the cobwebs of her tears. I stretched my hand to caress her hair but withdrew. I could not touch her out of shyness.

I wanted to hold her, fondle her and explain to her. But what could I have explained, I understood nothing! Somehow I inferred vaguely that Rebati should marry.

After she had cried silently for some time, she raised her face, wiped her tears, looked straight at me and smiled brightly like a bulb had been switched on.

I strove to remember something funny so that I could cheer her up. Unfortunately, I was not so witty that some suitable joke or funny anecdote would come to me on summoning. Besides, in our village nothing really funny happened. The few anecdotes over which I and my wife laugh in the night were usually vulgar and obscene and I could not have shared any of those jokes with Rebati.

Through the rest of the evening, Rebati apologized for having broken down before me. Next day she was to return to her college. I went to see her off at the bus stop. 'When is the next return?' I asked her.

'Don't know, let us see,' she replied.

Somehow I concluded that she will not come again. The man she had been looking for definitely did not reside in our village.

Now I had no feeling of jealousy or respect for her. I had a strange feeling of compassion for her. My Reba, who had marched over the village lane on her stilettos, who had said two hoots to time, who had fainted with fear at the cremation ground, who had smoked *bidis* in a secret pact was going away forlorn and helpless.

Reba! Hand over to me your helplessness, your age, your loneliness, your progeria, your chains. I will give you lilies, honeybees, all my happiness, my innocuousness. Come back hopping over the sand on the riverside, come and ride over the surfs in the sea, quiver like a sunflower in the smarting sunshine. Stand up again, wearing ghungurs around your ankles, the moment you run tremulously your toe nails on the ground, your man will be dislodged out of his indifference, he will be swayed, he will stop playing hide-and-seek with you. If you stretch yours arms, the time will stand still, clocks will move anticlockwise. Write your own address on the back of your exhalation; this breath will bring back that fragrance which will quiver forever.

III

A few days later, I learnt from a newspaper that Rebati had gone away to the USA again.

Original Odia: *Rebati*

Backbone

Supriya Panda

Translated by **Manoranjan Mishra**

My world is populated chiefly by three inhabitants—I, my father Rudrapratap, and Meghna. Those others who dwell here are, for me, worthless and insignificant. They are the crowd, the noise, the transportation system, and the highway enveloped in dust and fume. All of them cause irritation to me. They don't allow me to sit in peace and talk to Meghna for hours.

Meghna is a strange creature. She refuses to get into my car. She strongly forbids me from spending anything on her. She believes the car and the money belongs to my father, not me. Consequently, we get to drink coffee only when Meghna has some money with her. Her financial position determines the number of kilometers we can travel. She provides private tuition to a few students, and that is her only source of income.

I don't appreciate all this at all. Under compulsion I roam with her in a state of enforced poverty. But what can I do? This charming, tall, poetry-loving, and theatre-loving lady is profoundly self-conscious. All these characteristics add up to make Meghna. If there is a dearth of any one of these qualities, the result would be terribly different—a character much different from Meghna. She can only be a part of the crowd. Everybody who constitutes the crowd has the same complexion, same appearance and character. Nothing noteworthy differentiates one from the rest. Therefore, I consider them worthless and insignificant, fit only to be despised.

On getting a whiff of my opinion, she would fly into a rage and say, "Srikant, this is your vanity that makes others look insignificant." I flash a smile and retort, "Because I love you, I differentiate myself from the crowd. I think I am an exception; an exclusive product." Meghna would respond, "Srikant, you are wrong. I believe the right backbone differentiates one from the rest."

Besides 'me,' Meghna has another love—French Literature. I have witnessed how she struggled to learn the language initially. The craving to master a foreign language, despite being born in abject poverty, is no less a luxury. Throughout the day, she would move from place to place, providing tuition to students and during nights, she would translate French poetry. She would often read to me the translations of Apollinaire's poetry. I failed to comprehend the grief of a bird that had died in a snowstorm. I would think of my father while the poems were read out to me. Rudrapratap, a truly mighty and influential person, was engaged in expanding the empire of our family business. Some day in the future, I have to occupy the throne vacated by him. That day is not far; only his orders had to come.

Meghna's younger sister would say, "Mr. Srikant, the remote control that directs you is in your father's hands. I wonder at times how you will go ahead with your proposal of marriage to my sister. Had I been in her place I would never have loved you."

In response I would say, "You will find me, one day, rebelling against my father. At the sight of that incarnation not only your sister but also you, will fall in love with me."

Purba worked in the "Star Theatre". She didn't work on stage but off it, as their accountant. Theirs was a permanent theatre where all kinds of new and old plays were staged. The play entitled "Mesa Sabaka" (The Lamb) was staged for a continuous period of one and a half years.

Meghna and I would visit Purba's theatre at times. The place looked completely different during the day. The place where Purba would keep accounts was a part of their costume room. I would feel greatly delighted in the company of a great variety of clothes, armaments, and costumes befitting historical characters. We would, at times, put on these costumes and enjoy sipping tea. I would put on the costume of Sikander at times and Jajati at some other. Meghna would dress herself in the costume of Greek princess Thebes, who once having lost everything in love, waited for the prince to return. However, she didn't realize that the prince had completely forgotten her. Thebes' 'eternal wait and unwavering faith' are the main themes around which the story revolves. The deceitfulness of the prince was the reality. Perhaps Shakuntalas existed in every land, to wait with patience, to encounter forgetful, heartless Dusmantas.

At times, Meghna and I would playfully act on the stage, with Purba playing the lone spectator. I would play the role of Alexander and announce death-sentence on Puru. Although the punishment had been changed in history, I don't oblige to the decision taken then. I am different from Alexander; I am Srikant. Meghna would present the first scene of the film 'The Bible'. She would change the dialogues a bit and say, "Let there be love; let there be freedom." Looking at the imaginary audience she would say, "I am the representative of every freedom-seeking land and human being... I'm Meghna Dixit."

Bringing our light-hearted acts to an abrupt end, Purba would ask solemnly about our probable marriage. "Mr. Srikant, when is your rebellion going to take shape? My sister has been waiting for long." The manner of Purba's arguments would make one wonder whether she was the younger of the two sisters or the elder. Of course, she spoke the truth. Meghna had lost her father; how long could her mother wait for her marriage?"

It was true. Very soon, I had to confront Rudrapratap. I found it hard to comprehend Meghna's poetry, quite true, but it would be great fun to spend the rest of the life with Meghna's hands taken in mine.

I confronted Rudrapratap. It was a powerful experience to confront such a despotic father, even for ten minutes. How meaningful such experiences in life were!

The invitation cards for marriage lay on the table. They were brought from the press only today. How grand and exquisite the cards that father himself chose were! He was careful with all the arrangements for the marriage of his only son. He wanted to ensure that his only son didn't whine, citing lack of proper arrangement.

The telephone rang. When I picked it up, the steely voice of Purba came floating by from the other side. "Is it Srikant Choudhury?" I kept the receiver down. How did Purba come to know about the marriage when even the cards had not been distributed? Oh! News related to the engagement and marriage of industrialist Rudrapratap's son had already dotted the newspaper headlines. My would-be bride's name was Tanuja. His father was a renowned industrialist and an intimate friend of Rudrapratap.

One day, I learnt that Meghna had visited our home, not to meet me but my father. I don't know what transpired between them. The question of asking father didn't arise. In rich and noble families like ours, certain unwritten laws exist. These laws inform one which topics can be deliberated upon and which cannot. These disciplines are acquired with the passage of time, if one has a rich, luxurious, and noble blood flowing through the veins. My marriage to Tanuja was nothing but union of two noble families.

My world has changed completely for me. Now a days, it is inhabited by me, my wife Tanu, my baby-boy Anuj and my father Rudrapratap, who is on the verge of retirement. Anuj will leave for Shimla soon in connection with his education. He will return one day to occupy the throne of my empire, just as I occupy the one vacated by Rudrapratap.

I have never tried to forget Meghna. She doesn't frequent my memory these days either. She used to waste much of my time. Once, I remember, just to determine the differences between the 'real heart' and the 'lover's heart' she had searched through many English and French poems. Oh, what a bore!

Whose worth is more, whether it is the 'real heart' or 'the lover's heart' in the kind of life I live or the successful business empire I rule over? 'Real heart, definitely. Therefore, every month specialists arrive to check the palpitation of the heart. The only slogan that emerges from my heart these days is, "Sky is the limit."

Once, while going somewhere by car, I saw Meghna on the way. She was bending down to arrange her shoes. Perhaps they had worn out. She might or might not have been Meghna. In this town one encounters many such ladies in worn out shoes, who only contribute to the crowd. The thought of bringing the car to a halt to verify whether it was her, crossed my mind. Then I realized it was nothing but my emotion for her that drove me to such thoughts. Even my car didn't stop. My car worth nine lakh knew for whom to stop and whom to avoid.

Another day, I saw Purba on the way. She was peddling lottery tickets at the bus-stop. What had happened to the "Star Theatre" job? Had she grown poorer? Did she find it difficult to manage herself without supplementary income? Irritated, I turned my face away. That day, I felt thankful to father. How would have I introduced them as my relatives, had I married Meghna as per my own decision? Torn shoes! Lottery tickets! Fie...fie. Rudrapratap, at the right time, had saved me from great disgrace.

I didn't have time to ponder over such trifles. A lot of work needed to be done. I had to collect recommendation letter from a minister to admit Anuj in his school. Mr. Osaka was coming from Japan. There was the possibility of acquiring a handsome contract, if he was taken care of well. My business empire would spread afar. Tanuja would simply be bowled over. I will get a diamond necklace for her designed by the world famous Hamiltons'. Just like her gold vase, a proud possession, Hamiltons' exquisite work of art that will adorn her neck, will be another proud possession. A signature of Mr. Osaka was what they needed.

All arrangements had been made for Mr. Osaka's visit. From a five star hotel, he had been shifted to a bungalow on the sea beach. Special arrangements had been made for the night. A lady with classical taste had been selected to entertain him. Mr. Osaka wished to have an early dinner with me. As soon as the dinner was over, Mr. Osaka's 'classical choice' knocked on the door and came in.

The pattern of shade and light in the room appeared absolutely fabulous. The shade near the door was a bit deeper. Who this lady could be! Mr. Osaka looked pleasantly at her, without dropping eyelids. I also watched her. How delicately and exquisitely she had adorned herself, like a damsel of the Mauryan era! On the alta-laced feet, every toe-ring glistened with a hundred thousand diamonds. Her eyes were embellished with the dark collyrium of Vidisha. A girdle of Vidarbha bedecked her well-proportioned, delicate body. Her lips appeared red like the tinge that spread in Pataliputra during sunset. Her long hair came cascading down like a river. Srikant felt as if he had come across the long hair somewhere. He wondered where he had seen it!

Sitting beside us, she saluted Mr. Osaka in a dance pose first. Then she looked at me. Her intoxicating eyes didn't reflect Vidisha anymore but Mohenjo-daro. In an indistinct voice I cried out, "Is it you, Purba?"

She spoke in a reckless manner, "Yes, Mr. Customer". Mr. Osaka had a phone call from Japan. His wife called up to ask about his well-being. He went to the bedroom. Without wasting much time Purba said, "Mr. Customer, I am eager to know who had dispatched the devils who abducted my sister for three days and who have rendered her bed-ridden forever by breaking her backbone. Who was it? You or Rudrapratap? I lost my job because of one instruction from someone. Whose instruction was it? Was it yours or Rudrapratap's?

I tried hurriedly to say something, "Purba... Purba. Just believe me. I don't know anything."

Purba got up, opened the door and spoke in her usual steely

voice, "Mr. Customer, return quickly to your golden cage. Please inform Rudrapratap that he might have rendered Meghna bedridden and turned her a spineless creature, but I am Purba. I have promised to transform her from a spineless creature to a human being. My sister wishes that at least for once, she would get up and stand erect with the support of her backbone so that she can say, "Let there be love… let there be freedom". Please remember Mr. Customer no Rudrapratap can ever annihilate love and freedom from the surface of the earth. Meghna will be reborn; she will love poetry; she will love plays. The deceitfulness of all Srikants will come to a big nut in comparison to her deep faith.

Oh my God! What pain, what agony I experience! Who is there? Please give me a supply of oxygen. I limped. A human being, who was part of the crowd, came and held my hand. It was a warm, humanitarian touch. Holding on to that hand, I reached my car. I wished to be taken to Meghna. I uttered in a faint voice, "Meghna… Me…gh…na." my driver looked at me. His experienced face looked tension-free. I knew he was driving me back home. I would never reach Meghna's home. A great chasm separated a 'real heart' and a 'lover's heart'.

Original Odia: *Merudanda*

The Home Of The Butterfly

Bibhuti Bhusan Pradhan

Translated by **Manoranjan Mishra**

Doesn't a butterfly have a home? Maanu believed that the wings of a butterfly were always restive. She had never seen them sitting still. She wondered why this lonely butterfly sat in a meditative posture, instead of heading home. The thought of carrying it to the hostel garden had crossed her mind many times but her preoccupation with the Text Examination refrained her from doing so.

The Test Examination got over yesterday. The school was closed for the winter vacation. Children, with their bag and baggage packed, waited for their parents to arrive. Those students, whose houses were not far off, had already left since yesterday. This time, Maanu would head home with her father; she hadn't visited it during the Puja holidays.

Her home town was far away from the hostel. So, it would certainly take some time for her father to arrive. She had procured many things including a pencil box, a doll with an umbrella over her head, two comics books, and a bottle of nail-polish for Sanu. She had also prepared a greetings card to present her on New Year. She had already planned that on the occasion of New Year, they would decorate the house with balloons. They would write "Happy New Year" in front of the house. Manu would draw two cartoons, one on either side of the writing. The place would be decorated with string lights. They would decorate the house grandly, just as their school was decorated on the occasion of Annual Function a few days back. Their house would resemble the one drawn on the greetings card.

Maanu had no idea when her father would arrive. But she was certain of one thing. By the time they reached home, it would be too late. Sanu might have fallen asleep by them. She was one who went to bed early. What fun is there if Sanu falls asleep by the time they arrive! She thought of buying a pack of *peda* for her. No matter how deeply she slept, she would get up the moment the name of *peda* was uttered.

She had to pack all her belongings before her father reached the hostel. The bed had to be rolled. Father would be in a great hurry to return. She failed to comprehend why she stood transfixed, looking at the butterfly. She advised, "You…butterfly…go home…go. Don't you know that the school has closed for a holiday starting today? The hostel will be vacated soon. What will you do alone in this huge hostel? Don't you know when the entire hostel is vacated and one is left alone, one feels like crying? Last Dussehra holidays, I was left alone. Go home…go."

The butterfly did not listen to Maanu. Maanu continued, "You aren't listening to me. Okay…let it be so. You will learn a lesson only when you experience the troubles."

She returned to her room. Rubi, Sobha and Kamla had left in the morning, leaving her alone. Their books, clothes, notebooks along with torn papers, empty mixture packets, used toothbrushes, empty incense packets lay scattered everywhere

While packing their belongings, they had discarded these.

The entire room looked unkempt. How would she arrange her belongings unless she tidied up the room first? Even Rubi had left without rolling her bed. If the old matron took a look at the room, she would never permit her to go. She would say, "Tidy up your room first, then you will think of going." If her father had reached early, she would have left without any bother. But now, she had to face all the trouble.

Maanu brought a paper packet lying outside and dumped all rubbish into it. She arranged their books and clothes; she rolled Rubi's bed and kept the packet containing rubbish outside. While she was sweeping the room, the old matron suddenly appeared. Looking at Maanu she said, "Hasn't your father arrived yet? Aren't you going home during these holidays too?"

"Papa will arrive some time later," Maanu said and remained busy sweeping the floor. The matron was heading towards some other room. She stopped abruptly and said, "Tell your father, if you stay back, I won't be able to arrange food for you. It's really a bother for me."

During the Dussehra vacation, Maanu hadn't gone home. Pre-test examination was scheduled to be held after the vacation. Her father had explained to her that time, "You are going to write your Board Examination later this year. What will you do at home? You should rather stay back in the hostel and complete revising all the chapters. Only then, you won't have any fear for the Board Examination. I have requested the matron to arrange your food."

Board Examination was only a plea; Maanu knew the exact reason. Her grandmother must have reached to witness the Dussehra celebrations that were very famous. The old lady usually paid them a visit during the Pujas. She would return after Deepavali. She was never in good terms with Maanu; she would keep a close watch on all her activities. On every given opportunity, she would taunt her with, "Is this what you learn at school? To hell with your education." Maanu didn't appreciate such irritating words, nor did her father. But he could never gather the courage to raise any objections. Even when mother spoke ill of her, he would remain mum.

The lady whom Maanu addressed as 'mother' wasn't her biological mother. Her real mother passed away on the delivery-bed, soon after the birth of Maanu. This was the reason why no one from the maternal uncle's family liked her. The lady she grew up with, and whom she recognized as mother since childhood, was in fact her step-mother. Maanu learnt this much later in life, only when she was in class four or five. At that time she was the student of a Christian missionary school, situated some fifty kilometers away from her hometown. She spent four years there from class four to class seven. Prior to that, the school was situated in her hometown but Maanu's father had lodged her in the hostel. The present school was situated at a distance of around one hundred and fifty kilometers from her hometown.

With each promotion to the next higher class, the distance of her school from her hometown had gone up. Off late, Maanu had started comprehending the real reason. On such comprehension, she had given out a faint smile—a smile laced with grief. Perhaps she had tried her best to drive away grief from her heart. She realized that her father would be giving out such a smile. His smile always appeared withered like a flower stuck to the stalk before being shed. How did her father bear the sting of so much grief? Were all fathers grief-stricken like him? She never found a friend's father so much bent down with grief.

What was her father's mistake? It was as if he bore the burden of a vicious sin. Sanu told her once that when she arrived during the holidays, father would suddenly grow tongue-tied. Otherwise, he would read newspapers, watch TV, tell her jokes, water the flower plants, and murmur songs on his own. Was she the reason of her father's grief? But, she had never done anything that would render her father so sad. She never disobeyed him. Why then father became sad upon her arrival?

Sanu might have told the truth.

Once, when she was the student of the Christian Boarding school, she had to leave for home all of a sudden. Some trouble had cropped up in the town where the school was situated. The headmistress was directed to vacate the hostel at the earliest. She sent her home, accompanied by a peon.

When she reached home, she found her father happy. His eyes and lips reflected his happiness. Maanu had never seen him so happy. It was natural that she felt overwhelmed. He had brought chicken and was happily cutting it into pieces, murmuring a song at the same time. Mother was grinding spices in the kitchen. She had put on a new saree and adorned herself for some occasion. Three or four types of sweets were stacked in the fridge. Sanu said, "It's good that you have reached. Today we are going to the theatre to watch a movie. I don't understand Hindi well but if I ask Mummy the meanings, she gets angry."

It was mother's birthday. Papa had procured a ring for her. Maanu thought of going to market and buying a gift for her. She also thought of presenting her a hand-made card.

Suddenly, something inexplicable happened. Happiness dissolved into thin air. Father turned solemn. Mother took off her new saree. The sweets in the fridge lay untouched. Father had to cook chicken. Visit to the theatre was cancelled. Neither father nor mother ate anything that night. Mother slept on the sofa in the dining space.

Maanu failed to discern why this had happened. Hoarse cries of mother woke her up towards midnight. Father stood beside her with the ring. Mother roared, "Why should I lay the blame on someone else? It's all my ill-luck; otherwise she should not have reached on an auspicious day like this." The reason behind the discord became crystal clear. Father stood there in the manner of confessing his guilt. It was as if he was responsible for the sudden return of Maanu from school. Maanu feigned sleep. After some time, mother unlocked the front door and ran outside. Father ran after her. It wasn't clearly audible as to what father was saying to pacify her. His voice appeared distressed, like the wobbly voice of an agonized student who fails to answer the teacher's questions.

The disconcerting situation prevailed till Maanu returned to hostel. Papa would move about the house silently, like a sinner. Mother avoided speaking to Maanu, even a single word. If Sanu attempted to sneak to Maanu and strike a conversation with her, mother would threaten her in a booming voice, "Sanu, come here or else..."

Why did mother vitiate the atmosphere at home? Why would she suddenly fly into rage, without any apparent provocation? Why did she scold Sanu and deal with father harshly? She would start flinging things all of a sudden. Instead of doing any cooking, she would sleep the entire day on the sofa in the dining space. Father would go out, only to return at night. He would then prepare omlette or upama for Sanu and Maanu. He himself would go to bed in an empty stomach. Those days, father would appear greatly perturbed. He seemed to have lost a dear thing, but what was that? Maanu never understood what it was. At times, she would feel guilty, although she never realized what her crime was. She would wait eagerly for the holidays to get over so that she could return to the hostel.

Hostel could never provide her a refuge. Once there, she would start counting days and waiting for the holidays, harbouring the wish to go home. Maanu knew quite well that no one waited for her at home. The moment she reached home, the tranquil atmosphere would soon turn turbulent. Despite this knowledge the desire to go home crept in like an obstinate butterfly. Waving its colourful wings, it would roam around in her heart, compelling her to miss 'home'.

For whom did she miss home?

Was it for the sake of Sanu's love or father's sorrow?

Sanu loved her dearly. At home, she would always be found keeping a close company with Maanu. She would fetch sweets from the fridge and offer her those, "Take these...gobble up quickly. If mother got a whiff, she would scream." She would get hold of pickles from the kitchen and tell her, "Let's go to the roof and finish these." She would keep chocolates hidden for her in her school bag; she would also keep exquisite bindi packets in her geometry bag. While Maanu left for hostel, she would ask, "Do you need this pen?" She always wanted to eat with her and sleep by her side. Mother, on the other hand, kept a close watch on her.

When she found Sanu talking to Maanu, she would scream, "Have you completed your homework, Sanu? Do you want a thrashing?" Maanu would whisper into Sanu's ears, "Go away...mother is getting angry."

Crestfallen, Sanu would reach her study table. Maanu didn't have any table, bed, or even, any room especially meant for her. When she reached home, a folding bed would be laid in the drawing room. Her books and clothes were kept, under the bed, in the airbag that she had carried from the hostel. After the holidays got over, her belongings would be packed in the same airbag.

After Sanu left, Maanu would feel lonely in the drawing room. What would she do there, alone and abandoned? She would start counting days left for her return to hostel. In the hostel, at least, she had a bed and a cupboard to call her own. She had friends in Rubi, Sobha and Kamla.

Ironically, the feeling of loneliness would return even in the company of Rubi, Sobha and Kamla. Unlike their mothers, her mother would not pack any pickles or eatables for her. She would also not pack any home-made cakes to distribute among friends. Before dropping her at the hostel, father would buy her a packet of mixture and a few packets of biscuits. They lacked the flavor of mother's affection. Rubi would show the new sweater woven by her mother. Sobha would show the frock purchased for her. Kamla would offer the cheese-*manda* cakes that she had brought from home. What would Maanu show or offer them? Nothing! She also wouldn't have any pleasant memories of home to share with them. She felt as if she had just returned from a study tour. It would have been better if she had not gone there at all. At least, she could have revised a few chapters during the holidays. She would promise herself not to go there in the forthcoming holidays, not even if her father requested her to go. But the strength of determination would wane after the passage of only three or four days. The desire to return home would hover around her like a defiant, troublesome butterfly with outstretched, colourful wings. 'Home' and 'Sanu' would flash upon her inward eyes. She would procure erasers, nail-polish, and stickers. Father's crestfallen and solemn face would torment her.

Maanu would wish, "How wonderful it would be if only papa were there at home! She would sleep in the lap of father, with her face stuck into his chest. While telling stories, papa would caress her hair. She would forget the red eyes of teachers issuing threats, the difficulty posed by home-tasks, the secret jealousy of Ruby and Sobha, and the unpleasant experience of having to eat stone-infested rice and watery dal. She would sleep for hours, unmindful of the worries of life. Her father would ask, "Do you want an ice-cream, Maanu?" When she went back home during the holidays, papa would buy her ice-creams frequently. On reaching home, she would tease Sanu, "Papa bought me three milk ice-creams today. Do you know how tasty milk ice-creams are?"

Mother would soon start hurling things. She would stop cooking and sleep on the sofa in the dining space. Smile would be wiped off father's face. He would enter the kitchen without talking much.

Of course, Maanu was growing wiser with experience. No more, on reaching home, she would talk about ice-creams. Mother, however, would cunningly ask, "What did father buy for you in the market?" Maanu would remain silent. She would shift the question to father, "Didn't you buy ice-creams for Maanu today?"

Father would try his best to evade the question; mother would get an opportunity to cause trouble. These days, even when father asked her to eat ice-creams, she would refuse on some pretext. She would say, "My teacher told if one ate ice-creams, his teeth would be infected. Besides, they were not healthy as not-so-clean water was used in their preparation." Father understood the real reason for her refusal. His face would wither. Maanu hated this. She would finally say, "Okay, give me one."

"Aren't you going home this time too?" Nimi asked Maanu on entering her room.

"Papa will reach after some time," Maanu had only this explanation to offer everyone.

"My father will reach within half an hour. He called me up

a moment ago. Thank God, there is no need of eating the mixed-veg curry at the hostel."

Maanu looked at Nimi, who appeared extremely happy. She further said, "As most of the boarders have left, the old matron has asked the cook to prepare a mixed-veg curry with all the leftover stale vegetables. I will take my lunch in a *dhaba* on the way, where roti and egg-*tadka* are available."

When the number of boarders dwindled, the cook would produce a watery dal. Cooking of curry would be postponed. The remaining boarders had to manage with only dal, half-boiled cold rice, and fried *papad*. Maanu, who was well aware of this, was waiting eagerly for her father to arrive.

"How many others are still there?"

"A very few... Neha was getting ready to go. Her father was waiting at the gate. The Devidwar-bound boarders are waiting. Someone's father is bringing a vehicle to fetch all of them together."

"Will I have to eat all of the mix-veg curry, then?" Maanu made fun of herself and smiled.

"When will your father reach? Hasn't he rung up? asked Nimi.

"It will surely be late by the time he arrives here. I don't think he can reach before twelve o clock. Our hometown is about one hundred and fifty kilometers from here." Even though she was answering Nimi's query, it appeared as if she was consoling herself.

Nimi said, "These holidays we have planned to go on a tour of South India. We will visit many places including Kodaikanal, Brundaban garden. I'll procure an idol of lord Ganesh made of sandalwood. Tell me, what should I bring for you?"

"Don't bring anything for me. I don't need anything."

"Why do you talk like this? Are you angry with me?"

Maanu never went on a tour with her parents. Her world was confined to her hostel and home. While going on a tour her parents would take Sanu with them but when her turn came, father would ask her to mind her studies. Even if she didn't have any studies to do, would mother consent to take her with them? She gauged her father's helplessness quite well. So, she would never insist on going. Father would bring a pen or a frock for her but Maanu would deliberately leave those for Sanu. She knew she would never be fortunate to go on a tour with her parents. She would never be able to bring gift-worthy things for Nimi. Why should she receive anything from her, then? How could she discuss all this with Nimi? She just told her, "I have never visited South India. How can I tell you what to bring for me?"

"It's fine... I'll bring some exquisite gifts for you. Bye, bye for the time being. I've to pack my belongings."

"Bye... Have a happy new year," Nimi said while leaving for her room.

Maanu wished she could ask her father to take her on a tour of Puri. Three years ago, after the class seven annual examinations were over, father had taken her on a tour of Puri. When her mother was pregnant, she had made a vow to take her to Puri. Mother passed away before the vow could be fulfilled. Her father had taken her to Puri, directly from the hostel. They journeyed from Cuttack to Puri. Maanu saw a train for the first time in her life; she saw the sea for the first time too.

She spent seven exciting days there. They also went on a tour of Konark. She witnessed the sight of sunrise at Chandrabhaga; she made sand-castles on the beach. While munching masala-mudhi, she would challenge the waves to chase her. When the waves moistened her feet or demolished her sand-castles, she would feel very sad. Some distance away, sitting silently, her father watched her activities. It was as if he had never ever watched her playful activities earlier. Who knew what thoughts enveloped his mind?

They lodged in a hotel on the beach. The roar of the sea heard like the hissing of a cobra. During night it felt as if there was a storm in the sea. Huge waves seemed surpassing the beach and roaring towards the hotel. Fearful, she would tuck her face under her father's chest. While pulling her towards his lap, father asked, "Do you get scared in the hostel, at night?"

Maanu would get scared in the hostel at times. In that Christian Boarding School, when everyone went to sleep, the surrounding area appeared deserted. The clicking of the watchman's boots sounded like nails being hammered into the coffin. From the branches of the dense peepal tree nearby emerged the sound of someone writhing in excruciating pain. Boarders believed that the spirit of Salman Ekka's wife lived in that peepal tree. Wishing to marry another lady, Ekka had poisoned his former wife. Since the amount of poison proved insufficient, she didn't succumb. For three days and three nights, she vomited blood and flesh and writhed in pain like this. After her death, Salman Ekka brought nails, one hand long each, to hammer into the coffin, so that the spirit of his wife would not escape. But after his remarriage, the spirit somehow got an opportunity to wriggle out of the coffin. It would sit on the branch of the peepal tree and cry out in pain. Maanu would press her face into the pillow, in an effort to sleep but sleep eluded her.

She would dream of her mother. Had her mother turned into a spirit? Did she writhe in pain from some branch of a peepal tree? How was mother to look at? There was not even a single photo of mother at home. On numerous occasions, she would try to paint a picture of her mother. No matter how much imagination she put to use and what bright colours she selected from the colour-box, she could never draw a portrait of her mother. She believed that her mother must have been more beautiful than the portrait. She would tear up the portrait and throw it away.

If her mother had turned a spirit, why didn't she appear before her? Didn't she realize that Maanu was staying alone in the hostel? Didn't she realize Maanu missed her? Someone had told her that ghosts and spirits had eyes made of iron. They saw and knew everything. Her tears would moisten the pillow. She would sob into sleep.

Without any responses from Maanu, father spoke out himself, "Little one... you must be getting scared at night."

A deep sigh emerged, producing a quiver in his heart. It lasted longer than the loud roar of the sea. Maanu felt her father's chest was being constricted by that intense sigh. Caressing his chest fondly, she said, "I'm no more getting afraid. Am I a small child anymore?"

Father remained silent.

Maanu was trying to sleep amid the loud roar of the sea. She felt as if her father was crying silently, just like he did the other day. Father was standing with his face towards 'Ratnabedi,' his gaze fixed on lord Jagannath. Maanu was standing next to him. It was the time of aaarati. Looking at Lord Jagannath Maanu was wondering how big His eyes were! How would He, otherwise, take note of joys and sorrows of the world? But who was He looking at, in that meditative posture?

Was He looking at her?

Why should He look at her? Didn't He have anything meaningful to do? Perhaps His gaze was fixed on her father. Just as in the meditation class her teacher would ask the students to concentrate on the black spot in the middle, similarly lord Jagannath had concentrated His gaze on her father. He didn't blink even for once. Maanu could never fix her gaze on something, without blinking. No matter how much she tried, her eyelids would drop. Lord Jagannath must be a great yogi, but how great? When she was lost in such thoughts, two drops of tear landed on her cheek. She raised her head to look at father. Father's eyes appeared to have widened, like that of lord Jagannath or even wider than His. What was father gazing at? Drops of tear rolled down.

Maanu would think, "Does father cry every night like this, secretly? If she had a home of her own, she would ask father to stay with her. She would serve tea or coffee when he returned from office. She would pack her fridge with a variety of sweets. She would cook fish or chicken for him. She cooked well. She bagged the first prize in cooking competition at school.

Maanu didn't own that sort of a home. She didn't have anything worthwhile to call her own, other than the hostel bed. After the final examination got over, she would have to lose possession of even that. Who knew in which hostel of which college she would have to seek refuse?

The cook shouted, "Sister, come and have your lunch. You are the only one left behind to lunch. I have other things to mind."

"Have all others already left?"

"Yes, children belonging to Devidwar were only left behind. They departed a moment ago."

"Has Nimi also left?"

"Yes, she left some time ago. Please come quickly." Saying so, the cook went downstairs.

Maanu knew quite well that everybody else would have departed. Why was she asking such a question foolishly, then? What did she want to hear? What did she desire? She just desired that someone should be left behind, in whose company she could pass the holidays.

Maanu came out of her room. The hostel appeared deserted and abandoned. What would she do now? The old matron would be sleeping or reading or watching TV. Should she go to her? No... if she went there she would ask her once again as to when her father would arrive and if she wasn't leaving the hostel this time too.

She didn't at all feel like eating anything. She mixed dal with rice, made them into balls, and thrust a few lumps down her throat. She didn't even touch the mixed curry. If she didn't eat anything at all, the old matron would take her to task. She intended to go with father and have lunch outside. She craved to eat rotis with chicken curry. Their hostel cook cooked chicken curry once a month. She would get a piece or two in her share.

The cook said, "Sister... why didn't you eat anything? Had I known earlier, I would not have even lighted the hearth. Unnecessarily, everything would have to be thrown away. If the matron came to learn, she would shout like anything."

Without giving him any reply, Maanu went out of the gate. With boarders having left for their homes, the two shops in front of the gate had already downed their shutters. She looked down the road, as far as she could. No...there was no sign of father. Where had father gone for such a long time?

"Didn't he realize that Maanu would be feeling lonely? What if father didn't reach today?"

Maanu couldn't think any further; she returned to her room. On the way, she encountered the same butterfly. It sat still and unruffled, like a sage. If wishes were firm and unwavering like the butterfly! No… they were restless and strange like the wings of the mischievous and adamant butterfly.

What would Maanu do alone in her room? Should she rearrange the contents of her bag? Should she ensure that she had packed all the belongings that she wanted to carry home?

When she was rearranging the contents of the box, she was reminded of the sweater she was knitting. She had prepared the design herself and was knitting it in line with the design. Whoever saw the design, whether it was her teacher or Rubi or Neha, couldn't help appreciating her skill. Her teacher had once advised, "Maanu, send the pattern to 'Sarita' magazine; you will surely bag the first prize." She had forgotten about it completely as she was busy with her preparations for the Test Examination.

Mother usually knitted a variety of sweaters for Sanu. She would procure issues of 'Sarita' magazine throughout the year to get ideas of different designs. Maanu, on the other hand, possessed only one sweater that father had brought three or four years ago. Not only had its colour faded but it also had grown shorter. She found it comfortable no more. She had knitted the new sweater to put on during New Year. The knitting was over; only the buttons needed to be fixed. She had got the buttons too. She was happy as she found some work to do. She stitched all the buttons. She stood in front of the mirror, putting the sweater on. Really it looked exquisite, with a novel pattern. However she found some vacant spaces. How would it appear if she stitched two butterflies there?

Maanu brought the needle and yarn and started knitting the butterflies. Her father hadn't arrived yet; why should she sit idle? The loveliness of the sweater would increase with the butterflies on them. Sanu would become happy. She would pester her to knit two such butterflies for her. She would insist on learning the pattern saying, "I feel shy to put on the sweaters that mother has knitted with old-fashioned patterns on them."

Maanu would feel happy with the accolade; mother's lack

of ingenuity would increase her delight manifold; Sanu's jealousy would be a satiating experience. Was she jealous of Sanu? Might be!

Ever since her childhood, Maanu had always seen mother doing Sanu's hair, adorning it with head-clips, and putting bindis. She would tell father, "Please buy a red frock for Sanu, like the one that Mohapatra sir's daughter puts on. It's better if it has smaller flowers." If father failed to fulfill her desire, she would start a quarrel and start hurling things. Maanu would feel jealous of Sanu's good luck. Tears would appear in her eyes. She would run to the backyard garden to hide her tears. She would sit there for hours and think, "Sanu bears good luck. She has a caring mother. She has an assortment of bindis, frocks and sweaters. She has a loving and caring father too." Maanu had nothing, other than the school uniform and the faded sweater. Her teacher would often say, "Happiness or misery doesn't continue forever. Everything shall pass away." When would grief bid a goodbye? When can father smile to his heart's content? When would he be able to ask her, without any fear of mother, "Maanu, do you want ice-creams? Tell me how many ice-creams can you eat at one go?"

Maanu put on the sweater after sticking the two butterflies on it. Once again, she stood in front of the mirror. The sweater looked charming. If Sanu saw it, she would surely grow jealous and create a scene. She would teach her the butterfly design. Why should one carry a sense of jealousy for a younger sister?

Why didn't father reach till now? Should she ring him up once? The phone booth was situated some distance away. If she went for the permission of the old matron, she would say, "How can I allow you to go to the market alone? What a careless person your father is! He is unnecessarily putting me in trouble. You should wait a little longer. If he doesn't turn up, I shall accompany you."

How long would Maanu wait? She had already arranged her bag, box and room two or three times each. What would she do now? Couldn't have father left for the hostel a little earlier?

Maanu knew mother would have deliberately taken more

time to cook. At the end of the cooking, as if she suddenly remembered, she would have said, "The stock of suji has finished. Please bring me some from the market, otherwise what would I give Sanu in breakfast? Without protest, father would have left for the market. After his return, she would have again said, "I can't carry the folding bed lying on the roof. Bring it here before you go." She would have demanded then, "Drop Sanu at school." She would have asked him to do one work after another, as if he was going out of town for months. There would have been no end to her demands; there would have been no end to his work. Father would be doing things, without protest, just to avoid unnecessary squabble. He would rather be talking in a soft voice. He would be making her feel as if she was not making any unnecessary demands; as if he should have taken care of these things earlier on his own. Finally, he would have taken out his motorcycle and asked for money. He would not be happy with the amount of money that mother would have given him. He would ask for one or two hundred rupees more. Mother would be saying, "What would you do with more money? Leave the motorcycle; go by bus. Is the place too far from here?"

Father would be pleading with her. He would be saying, "The bike needs some immediate repairs. The clutch doesn't work well. The bike is producing more noise. Gear oil needs to be changed."

Mother understood these were only but false pleas to extract more money. She would be saying, "Only last month you had spent seven hundred rupees to repair the bike. Why are demanding more money now?"

Father would be devising some new plan to get money. This would be causing the delay.

Maanu understood everything quite clearly. Everything was as simple as the unitary method used in arithmetic. Going step by step Maanu would reach the conclusion without much bother.

What could she do? Were wishes like this meditating sage-butterfly? Their wings were as restless as they were colourful.

Maanu tried to read the comics book that she had purchased for Sanu but in vain. Turning over the pages, she glanced through the pictures. She had made a mistake by rolling her bed. Otherwise she could have taken a little rest. She didn't feel like putting up the bed once again. What if her father reached without causing any further delay! She would get late in rolling up the bed all over again. She used the airbag as a pillow and continued glancing through the pictures, when unknown to her, the eyelids closed. She got up only when the cook called out to her. Standing outside the room he was found saying, "Your father has already arrived. He is sitting in the matron's room. Come quickly."

When Maanu looked outside, she saw that sunshine had faded. A polythene bag, discarded by someone, flew here and there in the breeze. Father's motorcycle was parked outside the gate. With the airbag on her shoulder, she ran downstairs.

Father was sitting comfortably beside the matron, as if in no great hurry. He was discussing something with the old matron. When he saw her, he asked, "Had you fallen asleep, dear?"

"What else I would have done alone in the hostel? The boarders have already left since morning. Do you know one feels like crying when the hostel is vacated for the vacation?" Maanu couldn't say anything like this. Nothing! She thought father couldn't be blamed for reaching late. Thank God, he had reached before sunset. It wouldn't take long to reach home. They could reach there well before Sanu fell asleep.

"Let's go to market," father told her midway during the conversation with the matron.

"Why to the market?" Maanu suddenly grew scared. Did father start applying his unitary method? The final answer to this was, "When the Board Examination was a few days away, it was better to stay in the hostel and prepare the lessons."

On finding her silent father asked, "Don't you have anything to buy?"

"Won't we buy anything on the way?"

"Have you decided to leave for home?"

Maanu didn't have any answers to this question. She was

conscious; she might burst into tears in front of the old matron. She came out of the room followed by her father.

The old matron was found saying, "Please try to explain to her carefully. If she agrees to stay, there will be no problem in arranging for food. Didn't I take care of that during the Puja holidays?"

For the fifteen day Puja vacation, father had paid five hundred rupees to the old matron. But, she would serve her pakhala with roasted eggplant and a few pieces of pickles to eat. Maanu wasn't worried about that. Father's unitary method confounded her, even though the answer to it was obvious.

Maanu was standing below a tacoma tree. Father was standing beside her, unnecessarily plucking dry leaves from it. Perhaps he was gathering courage to disclose the answer. His face resembled the baked eggplant that the old matron often served her during the vacation. He must have tried to learn the arithmetic sum, applying unitary method, on the way to the hostel.

Father must have grown scared to think what would happen if Maanu didn't agree to his proposal. He would have to encounter the same troubles—a disconcerting atmosphere, hurling of things, cessation of cooking, his standing in the dining hall in a pathetic state. Father's fear must be fiercer than her fear at the Christian Boarding School.

Ah, how pathetic her father's condition was! It was even more pathetic than the condition of the deserted hostel. How long would he have to stand with a bowed head, like a sinner, in the dining space, in front of the old matron, or Maanu? She looked at her father. His eyes seemed to be widening. Maanu grew scared. After sometime, father's eyes would turn focused and unblinking—silent, serene, self-possessed like that of Lord Jagannath. No matter how unruffled an appearance he tried to maintain, his inner being was tormented by an incessant storm. She clutched her father's hand lovingly and announced her answer following application of that unitary method, "The Board Examination is only two months away. I'll not leave for home. Matron Madam has assured to take care of my food."

Suddenly, two big drops of tear landed on her face. This time, too, she raised her head and found her father shedding tear, just as he had done in front of lord Jagannath.

In an attempt to comfort him, she said, "Won't I go home after the examinations are over? What's the need of crying?"

Father didn't speak, in fact he could not speak until he took a few steps. Maanu took out the comics books, pencils, a box, a doll and the sweater. She said, "I have knitted this for Sanu. Please ask her to put this on New Year's Day and decorate the house with balloons, just like the house on the greetings card." She took out the greetings card, her handiwork, and handed it over to father.

Father at once moved towards his motorcycle. Maanu stepped back towards her room, carrying the airbag on her shoulder.

On the way back, she met the sage-butterfly. Maanu told it, "Butterfly…I'm happy. Had I gone back home, you would have felt lonely. I will build a house for you during the New Year."

She was on her way to her room but suddenly stopped as she remembered something. She addressed the butterfly once again, "I'm sorry. I will draw the portrait of your mother for you, first. I will gather my power of imagination, and I'll use the brightest colours of the world to draw a portrait of your mother. Without mother a 'home' is never worth the name."

Original Odia: *Prajapatira Ghara*

Kanhu's Home

Gourahari Das

Translated by **Saroj Mishra**

Enough Kanhu. Why are you shouting? The mistress of the house admonished the boy. Kanhu quietened down but did not stop cursing altogether; he came towards the house, still murmuring, a piece of broken brick in his hand. He vented his anger, threw the brick towards the stack of sand.

He had found two bricks missing and that had fueled his anger. The previous evening he had counted 84 bricks but this morning there were only 82. He did not know who had taken two missing bricks. He stood on the road and abused all who went by, using filthy language.

His master's house was under construction. The master and his family lived in their government-allotted quarters at the center of the city. They usually came every morning and evening to supervise the progress of the construction, allotted work and paid wages to the laborers. Kanhu remained there throughout. He was the caretaker and the manager rolled into one.

When someone called him junior manager, his chest would swell with pride and he would get on with his job with added enthusiasm. He used to say that if he had higher educational qualifications his master would have given him a better job. But, he had studied only up to standard five.

He was a dark, short, pot-bellied boy of about sixteen. His belly protruded out like a pumpkin. His hair was straight like quills of a porcupine. He wore a chain of tulsi beads around his neck, which his mother had given him. He wore shorts and a red sleeveless vest with a hand-made towel wrapped around his waist.

A year ago Kanhu came to the city with Ramesh Tihadi of Nayagarh town to his present master's house in the city. His father, a habitual drunkard had left his mother and married another. His mother, who worked as a maid was having a tough time since, trying to make ends meet and feed the enormous appetite of her son. He was perpetually hungry and wanted to be fed regularly. He used to poach into the neighbor's gardens and eat all fruits and vegetable available. There was a constant hitch between them and his mother who tried to shield her son. But, Kanhu kept repeating his tricks to satiate his hunger. His mother would curse herself and cry.

Tihadi requested the master of the house to feed the boy and give him a job without bothering about wages. The mistress looked at Kanhu and sized him up in a matter of minutes. She realized that he would be fit enough to supervise and guard the construction of their new house. Her husband agreed with her and gave three hundred rupees to Tihadi for Kanhu's mother. Tihadi thanked them and left. Kanhu kept looking at the receding figure till he disappeared around the corner. His break with his carefree life in the village was finished. He felt himself to be a drifting kite. The lady realized Kanhu's discomfiture and called him in. She gave him a bowl of rice flakes and sugar to eat. Kanhu quietly sat on the verandah and ate his food. For the first time, his hunger was satisfied, as he dived into the bowl, polishing off the last morsel of food.

"You must be tired after the bus journey. Take the rest here. Spend your time in the garden. Tomorrow we shall go to the construction site of our house. You will stay there and look after work. On completion of the house, we shall move there and you will stay with us." the lady of the house said.

Then she looked at Kanhu. His eyes were downcast and he was sobbing. He was probably thinking about his mother and missing his village. Whatever it was that he continued to cry was bothering her.

"Are you missing your village?" She asked.

"Yes," he replied, still crying.

"And your mother?"

"Yes".

She came near Kanhu and wiped the tear from the face of the lonely boy.

"OK. Once the house is completed we will bring your mother to stay with us as well. Ramesh Tihadi comes here regularly. If you feel like it, go with him to meet your mother. Now off you go and take rest. In a little while, my son Bubu will return from school and you can play with him. Come on now, don't cry," she consoled the boy.

Kanhu stopped sobbing and went to the backyard which was dotted with a variety of flower plants and mango trees. Kanhu tried to forget his loneliness and caressed the flowers. He had not seen such plants before. They were very different from the trees in his village. He could identify all trees and plants in his village starting from tamarind, neem, mango, jackfruit, banana, papaya etc. But in this garden, the trees were smaller and of several different varieties. There were two mango trees. He looked up and saw that they were full of mangoes. He picked up a pebble and threw it. One mango fell from the tree as he bent down to pick it up he heard a voice and looked around.

He saw a much smaller boy than him. He was dressed smartly with a school bag on his back and was holding a blue water bottle. He was wearing black shoes with white socks.

"Who are you?" He shouted.

Kanhu did not give a reply. The mistress of the house came out and introduced him.

"This is Kanhu. He is from Nayagarh and this is my son Bubu."

Bubu stared at Kanhu who offered the mango to him.

Bubu appreciated the offer and told his mother, "Kanhu seems to be a nice boy? Look he aimed his target and brought down the mango with a single pebble. I am sure he would be fit for the army."

The following morning they left for the site. There was a one-room out-house by the side of the rear boundary. Cement was stored there. The mason also kept in it his construction implements. There was an empty space in the corner where Kanhu would live. They arranged for Kanhu's food in a nearby shanty hotel. He would be provided with kitchen utensils and a heater by means of which he could cook his meals. Kanhu was happy to be given the responsibility and with the faith shown by his master.

About a year passed. A long time indeed! Young Kanhu was very much in demand. On every visit, his master and mistress took stock of the progress from him. Kanhu was smart. He took care to protect all the construction materials like sand, bricks, chips, etc. Even the mason and the laborers were a bit scared of him as he supervised the work as if it was his own. He did not allow them to sit idle for a minute and admonished them, threatening to complain to his master in case of any lapse.

The women laborer used to laugh at Kanhu's demeanor. The mason would curse him. An upset Kanhu would shout back, "This is our house, understand. If you don't believe me, ask my master."

The matter would not rest there as Kanhu would complain to the master and mistress whenever they came. He had a sharp memory and would recount the day's events like a transistor radio, not forgetting the minutest of details.

The mistress would scold the mason for his misdemeanor asking him not to repeat it. Kanhu would smile and make faces at him before walking away to take stock of the sand and the bricks. Then the mason would curse him and his master.

Kanhu had settled into his routine with panache. He woke up early, before sunrise, and finished his morning chores. Then he ran the pump to lift water from the well. He took the plastic pipe and watered the half-constructed house for a couple of hours. Then he took stock of the materials. Next, he would scoop up the scattered sand and chips, count the bricks. Only then he would go to his shack and have his usual breakfast of rice flakes and sugar just before the mason and laborers came to work. This morning he had not had his breakfast because of the two missing bricks which had upset him needlessly.

"Who are you shouting at?" asked the mistress. On hearing Kanhu's explanation, she said, "Just for two bricks? If you shout like this only for two pieces of brick the neighbors would be upset."

His master parked the car and came over. He told his wife, "Let him shout. It is all right, let the people know that he is guarding the house sincerely."

Kanhu's nature was like that. He went hyper when happy or upset. Most of the time he cursed his father. He said he was a drunkard. He would hit his mother daily. He would loiter around the house when she went to work. On her return, he would snatch the money she brought and went away to the local country liquor shop to binge. Even then his mother would tolerate it, hug her son and try to forget the humiliation. Then one day he fell for another woman and left them. Then Kanhu stopped ranting.

He consoled himself, thinking that he would bring his mother from the village once the master's house was completed and then they would stay in this house. She would not have to work in other's house, washing utensils.

Sometimes he went around inspecting the half-constructed house. He would identify the drawing room, bedrooms, toilets, a kitchen, dining space etc. Then he would stop at a small room that did not fit in. This he assumed in his naivety would be his room.

The mistress noticed an empty pack of chewing tobacco near Kanhu's room and asked him angrily if he made use of the substance. Before he could reply to the master of the house took her aside and explained to her that, "it was good if he had this weakness. That way he would need money and ask you for it. That will ensure that he would stay. Rather encourage him so that his needs grow and his dependence on you with it."

She realized the philosophy behind those words. After all, they were married for the past fourteen years and understood each other well. She smiled back at her husband.

The construction of the house was on at a fast pace. Sometimes it would break down due to rains or want of sand or the absence of the mason. But Kanhu never left the place and his master was happy with him and patted him, showing his appreciation.

Kanhu sometimes missed his village and always remembered his mother and felt her absence. When he expressed his feelings his master used to say that if he left the work would stop. He praised Kanhu's dedication and let him feel that he was indispensable. Kanhu smiled with satisfaction and forgot about going to the village.

One day he ventured to ask, "Once the work is over, I will bring my mother here. Can she stay with us?"

The master was worried about the completion of the work, the problems associated with it, realizing that the expenditure was escalating beyond the budget.

He nodded in response to Kanhu's query and said absentmindedly, "yes, yes, she can stay."

By the time the laborers and the mason finished work, it was well past evening. Then they cleaned the implements, put them in the store, washed off their grime. Kanhu would refuse to run the pump and ask them to lift water from the well in the bucket. This irritated the workers and they cursed him. Then they would leave and Kanhu would be all alone.

The laborers had their lunch in the shade of the house. But Kanhu always had his in the small room. He dreamt of the day when the house would be completed and he would stay in that room with his mother.

The casting of the roof was done. Just the finishing was left. He sat in the room late into the evening, counting the days. Rain, storm, lightning, nothing perturbed him. He would sit there and stare at the sky through the open window. He counted the stars and even identified some as his or his master's. He sometimes talked with the wind that usually blew in the evening. Then he would put some chewing tobacco in his mouth and try to whistle. Afterward he would go up to the roof, sit there and stare at the row of buildings that lined the skyline. He used to wonder at the sight. Perhaps there were more buildings in the area than trees in his village, he thought in his youthful innocence.

Then he would remember his mother and his friends. He remembered the large banyan tree near the crossing adjacent to his house. He remembered the red fruits of the banyan tree hanging from its enormous branches and littering the muddy road. He remembered the scene in which the squirrel picked on those tiny fruits and ate them with relish. He missed them all.

He was not scared of anyone in the village except that raging bull and the mad Madhab, who it was rumored, lifted small children and took them away. Kanhu shuddered at the thought.

He realized it was time for his mother to be back from work and wondered how she passed the time in her loneliness. Tears would form at the corner of his eyes. He then reassured himself that the day was not far when he would bring his mother here. They would stay together in this house.

The wind did not understand Kanhu's words, neither did the stars, nor the clouds, or the trees. But, he felt happy. Then he came down and put on the heater and cooked his rice and dal mixed with vegetables. It would take an hour. Then he had his simple dinner and went off to sleep in his room.

Days passed by.

The construction work made progress.

Kanhu kept tabs on the progress of work. Day by day the house began to look beautiful. But, his master and mistress were worried. The budget was overshooting and the money was running out. Marbles and woodwork were very costly. The carpenters were delaying the work. They had to finish constructing the house within a month, as time was running out. This upset both of them to the point of irritation.

Kanhu approached the mistress as if to ask something. She walked away to avoid him and Kanhu remained speechless.

The outhouse was dismantled to accommodate the sewerage tank. Kanhu did not object as he had his own room in the house. He picked up his belongings and went into his room. The carpenter had kept his implements there. This upset him and he commanded the carpenter to remove them, not forgetting to mention that the room was his.

Finally, the day came when the house warming puja was done to make the new house habitable. Kanhu was presented with a new shirt, which he wore on that occasion. The pundit blessed him and the junior manager was very happy. He went around the neighborhood with pride.

Master asked him to open the bamboo raft as the work had been completed.

The mistress called her husband aside and told him that Kanhu had been insisting on bringing his mother here. He looked at the gleaming house and then glanced at the dark and unkempt boy.

"Tomorrow Ramesh Tihadi is coming. We shall see," he informed his wife.

On Tihadi's arrival, Kanhu was summoned to the master's official residence. He served coffee and snacks to Tihadi.

Master called Tihadi aside and handed over three hundred rupees. He said something to him which surprised Tihadi, "Is that so, sir."

Then he came up to Kanhu and said, "Let's go."

The mistress told Kanhu that he had not been to his village in a long while.

"You go to your village now. I have sent sweets for your mother. We shall call you later and you can come with your mother", she said.

Kanhu left with excitement as he had wanted to hear this

since long. He followed Ramesh Tihadi out of the house on their way to the bus stand.

"What a mad boy. He will keep blubbering to Tihadi on the journey," said the master.

Both husband and wife smiled with satisfaction.

Whatever you say, it would not have been possible to build the house without Kanhu's presence," she said.

"No one is indispensable, her husband remarked.

Two weeks passed and Tihadi did not come. That upset Kanhu. After all, he had to go back to the city with his mother.

Meanwhile, his mother refused to go inspite of all persuasions of Kanhu. That upset him even more. He was thinking of all the unfinished work he had left behind. He was anxious to go back, but his mother did not budge.

"They are big people. How can we stay with them?" was her stock query.

Kanhu refused to listen. He remembered the beautiful house and his small room inside it. He felt all the work would have come to a standstill in his absence. One fine morning he left for the city by bus. When the bus conductor asked where he would go, "Bhubaneswar" was his reply.

On reaching the new house he could hardly recognize it. There was a signboard up there. He saw a man dressed in a cream shirt and brown trousers, standing in front of the gate.

As he tried to enter that man stopped him and asked, "Where are you going?"

"I am going to my house" he replied casually.

"Your house?" The man looked at the boy with disdain.

Kanhu hesitated slightly as he felt that the man did not recognize him.

"I am Kanhu, understand? Are the master and the mistress inside?"

"No one is inside," the man said loudly.

"And Bubu."

"Who's he?"

"Master's son".

"Oh! You are asking about Mr. Patnaik?"

"Yes. Are they inside?"

"No. This house has been taken on rent by the Hilton Company for their Guest House."

Kanhu did not believe him. He quickly went past the man and barged in. He was well acquainted with the house. But he was astonished to see his room occupied with costly furnishers, a television set and a carpet on the floor. He looked around bewildered as he caressed the TV set and felt the softness of the carpet under his feet.

The guard burst in and dragged Kanhu out of the house, "bloody thief", he murmured.

Kanhu was consumed with anger.

"Wait till I return from the master's house. I will see you."

"Alright. Go. Mr. Patnaik and his family have left for Delhi. You say you worked for him and you don't even know that he has been relieved from here and joined in Delhi?"

"Relief, what relief," Kanhu asked anxiously.

"Relieved from his post, idiot. They were only waiting for the completion of the house. Or else they would have left much earlier," the guard replied, putting the issue at rest.

Kanhu was flabbergasted. Master and Mistress had left? Where would he go then? And why was this man preventing him from entering his own house? He was destined to live here with his mother.

He pleaded with the guard.

"Listen. I am Kanhu, the Junior Manager of this house. I have supervised the work and I have lived here."

The guard looked at him. He pointed at the stock of bamboo lying in the corner.

"What is that?" he asked.

"Bamboo. It was used for the construction work," he replied innocently.

"Why are they heaped in the corner?

"The work is over. They are not needed anymore."

"You understand that, don't you? Can't you understand

that now your work is completed and you are not needed anymore?"

"But where will I stay."

The guard looked at the foolish boy with disgust and turned his face away and said, "how can I make him understand?

Stung by the deceit of his master, the innocent boy looked around him in desperation. He had lived here and dreamt about his future and now everything lay shattered.

Then he chanced to see the mason, who worked in the house, going past on his moped. Kanhu shouted and called him. He heard and looked back. Then he turned his bike and came back.

He smiled at Kanhu, "where had you been? I have been looking for you."

"Look. This man is not allowing me to go into this house," Kanhu complained.

The Mason looked at the guard and he looked back. Both smiled. The Mason explained to Kanhu that his master and mistress had left, giving the house to a company.

"But where will I stay?" Kanhu asked, his voice breaking.

"Do you want another job? Mr. Sharma is constructing his house in Baramunda. He needed a boy. Do you want to work there?"

That was not the answer to Kanhu's question. He looked back at the house again and again. He could not accept the fact that his master and mistress had lied to him.

The mason asked again, "Tell me. Do you want to go?"

Kanhu could not reply. He stood rooted to the pavement dumbstruck.

Vehicles passed by in front of him as did many people. The mason's moped also disappeared in the crowd.

Kanhu stood there, undecided. How could he leave his home?

Original Odia: *Kanhura Ghara*

Goodbye, God

Paresh Kumar Patnaik

Translated by **Kamala Prasad Mahapatra**

By the time Abinash's phone rang around midnight, his eyes were heavy with sleep. He was heavily drunk in the evening. Although he felt the urge to smoke a cigarette he had no patience even to light a matchstick. The phone disturbed him at that moment. Feeling deeply irritated, and intending to shower vulgar rebukes, he went to pick up the phone.

He asked, "Who is it?"

The reply was very calm and cool.

The caller said, "It's God speaking."

"God ! What God are you?"

"I am God."

"What is your title? God Nayak or God Biswal? Whatever! What God are you?"

"I am God! The almighty, the creator, the benefactor, the lord, you may address me by any name you like."

Abinash felt rattled. He thought to himself, "God! God rings him! But why?

Phone from God! It's incredible! Does it happen? Does it really happen with anybody at any time? Does God need a telephone to communicate?"

He suspected the caller and his intention.

He asked, "Did you drink a lot this evening?"

The reply came, "No! No! I didn't drink. Rather you drank at Indradhanu Bar. You paid a hefty bill for eleven hundred fifteen rupees. Do you remember?

"The man knows, "Abinash thought, "He knows everything." Abinash became a little conscious. The man had kept him under his surveillance. He knew all about his escapades. Who could this man be? Was he drinking with him at Indradhanu Bar? Was he sitting at the counter of Indradhanu Bar? He had paid all his dues. Why was this man referring to the same Eleven hundred fifteen rupees?

He said, "Look, it's already very late. I don't like to listen to jokes at this hour of the night; kindly keep off the phone. He said this and kept the phone off. But the phone rang again. Abinash initially thought of not picking it up. He was feeling nauseated. His head was feeling heavy. A full bout of vomiting might make him feel relaxed. Sprinkling water on his head might also help. "Bloody, bastard! Is it time to disturb someone?"

The ringing sound of the phone appeared jarring. It appeared to be increasing with each passing moment. The loud ringing tingled every chord of the brain. Very disgusting! Finding no other option, he picked the phone up and said, "What do you want this time?"

"Why did you say 'bloody bastard'?"

Abinash was rattled. He looked into every nook and corner of the house. There was no sign of anyone anywhere; who could hear his words? Was someone hiding somewhere nearby? How could he know he had used such words a while ago? Who could this man be?

Then in a manner of consoling himself, he said, "No!No! That's nothing…it could only be a prank."

Then the voice said, "Tell me what you want?"

"I don't want anything. I have never wanted anything at any time."

"Is it possible?"

"Yes! I have wanted! Wanted many things in life. But why are concerned about that?"

"I am God! I know all this."

"You are God!"

"Why? Do you have doubt?"

"Does God make a phone call like this?"

"Why can't I make a phone call?"

"Does God wake up people like this at the middle of the night?"

"Yes! I wake up, but you may not know. I have made a call to you for the first time."

"Tell Me! Why did you ring up?"

"I propose to offer you a boon."

"Boon!"

"Yes! I intend to fulfill one of your wishes."

"But why! I have never asked you for anything?"

"True, you have never asked for anything; but you must have asked for something."

Abinash had not visited any temple for long. He did not find time to visit a temple. He worked in an office. By the time he finished office work, it would be evening. He would take dinner late in the evening. He would then have a drink. He would return home with staggering, unstable feet. Then he would go to bed. He would get up at nine in the morning. He would finish his ablutions quickly before leaving for office. He had lots of work in the office. He hardly got the time to relax, let alone visit a temple or God.

"Yes, I might have asked you for favors in the past. However, those are things of the remote past."

"Yes…yes… in the remote past! You had asked for favors… boons…"

"Those might have happened during my childhood. During my childhood, I used to visit the temple quite often."

"The list of whatever favors you had asked those days is with me."

"List is with you?"

"Yes it is with me."

"But I have forgotten. I don't remember much."

"How can I forget? I am God, you know. God never forgets anything."

"Are you really God?"

"Do you still have doubt about it?"

"If you claim to be God, provide some evidence."

"What evidence?"

"Prove that you are God."

"Should I provide evidence?"

"Yes, you have to or else how shall I know that you are God."

"When you first remembered me, did you look for evidence? Remember correctly. Once you had stolen money from your father's pocket and smoked *bidi* with that. You prayed to me to save you from being caught or punished."

"Do you remember, during the school days you had thrown a letter at a female classmate through a window near her? You prayed to me to ensure that the letter reached the girl, no one else."

"Do you remember, once you had carried some incriminating material to the examination hall? That day, you prayed to me to ensure that the same topic was asked in the examination. You copied the matter and requested me to ensure that you were not exposed."

"Do you remember? The list of such instances is very long."

"Whenever you committed a mistake, whether small or big, you sought my help to protect you. Why do you ask for evidence now? Dangerous! You are a very dangerous man?"

Abinash was thoroughly shaken from within. Who could this be? How did he know so many secrets about him? He wondered if he had ever disclosed all these things to anyone. If he had really disclosed everything, then before whom he had done so? The man had collected all information about him and was narrating everything over phone. He also boasted that he was God! But how did the man know so many things? Who was this mysterious Mr. Know-all? The way he talked, I am afraid, he would make me mad.

"What did you say?"

"No! No! I have not said anything. I am stunned. How do you know so many things about me?"

"I have told once and for all, I am God. God knows everything. At least you know this for certain."

"But I need certain evidence."

"What type of evidence?"

"Perform some miraculous feat that only God can perform."

"It's okay. Go to the office tomorrow. There, you will witness some miracle."

The phone was disconnected after this. Abinash was feeling extremely tired and inebriated. He fell asleep, his phone beside the pillow. When he woke up it was very late in the morning. Of course, there was nothing unusual about it because he was a habitual late-riser. Every day when he got up, he would find the sun high up in the sky, throwing warm glances at lousy people.

Abinash reached office a little late. He didn't notice anything unusual. He wanted to share the last night's experience with some of his colleagues. He also expected some of his colleagues to come and claim, "Abinash Sir, you were totally out of your wits last night! I only made a fool of you."

But nothing of that sort happened. An accident occurred in front of his office in which his colleague Arun's motorcycle was badly damaged. Luckily Arun escaped unhurt. People started telling that this was possible due to God's grace. To escape safely from such a serious accident was well-nigh impossible. For some time, Arun sat traumatized in his office with his heart beating heavily. Afterwards, he laughed and said, "It's good. Very good. My vehicle had become old. Now I will get good money from the insurance company and buy a new vehicle."

BN Agarwal Company's file that was untraceable for long,

was traced. Office peon Pravakar had ransacked all cupboards and almirahs for that file. He had also checked all the drawers. It was Abinash who had hidden the file. Abinash was intolerant of the intimacy of his boss Marut Saxena with BN Agarwal Company. He suspected of an unholy alliance between the two. When the file was traced, Marut Saxena called Abinash and instructed him to release all the pending payments of the company. In fact, Abinash had forgotten where he had kept the file. It was also not known where from peon Pravakar retrieved it.

Typist Rita came to him and asked whether gold price would rise or fall. Rita had a terrible weakness for gold. She would rush to the jewelry shop on the pay-day itself and spend half of her salary at the jeweler's. He had not talked to Rita for many days. He had not been able to meet Rita owing to his busy schedule. He didn't even get an opportunity to speak to her. Now Rita came to him on her own and enquired about the price of gold. Rita considered Abinash some sort of a researcher or prophet of the market price. These days, Abinash hardly found any time to read newspapers. The hawker threw newspapers everyday through the gap in the door. He was also not able to watch Television. The Cable TV boy asked him for the bill at the end of every month. How could Abinash tell whether gold price would rise further or not. "How about presenting a gold necklace to Rita?" This thought had crossed his mind at times. Abinash didn't want to proceed any further as he had so many payments to make. Payments were due in his name in three bars of the city. Whenever he went to a bar, initially he would pay in cash, but as he became a regular customer he would start demanding wine on credit.

That day he watched all the office staff intently. He began suspecting everyone. He suspected that somebody was keeping an eye on him and minutely observing all his activities. But who that man could be?

That evening, he did not pay a visit to Indradhanu Bar. He returned home after dinner in a small nondescript hotel. He switched off the lights and waited anxiously for a call. "When shall the telephone ring? When shall a voice begin to float from the other side? There shall be a guffaw and the voice shall say; what friend! You could not place me! Made a fool of yourself!"

It was midnight.

The phone rang. Abinash picked up the phone calmly. strange! The voice was a prototype of yesterday.

The caller said, "Good Evening."

Abinash said, "Who are you? What do you really want?"

"Yesterday I told you. I am God."

"Please don't intimidate me any further. I was under tension the entire day in my office."

"I have never scared you; rather I want to help you out."

"There are so many people in the world, why do you want to help me?"

"I, in fact, help out everyone."

"I have never heard in my life that God helps people by ringing them up in the middle of the night."

"It is not that I telephone all. I meet people in various ways. In your case, I decided to ring you up."

"But why did you ring me up?"

"I thought of striking a conversation with you. In the past, in between your childhood and adulthood, how many times you have not prayed to me. Maybe you have forgotten all those, but I haven't. For I am God."

"Please don't confound me. Kindly tell me, who you are. How did you know so many things about me?"

"I am God! I know everything. I know everything about everybody."

"I have doubts in my mind still now."

"I told you miraculous incidents would take place today in your office."

"Miraculous incidents? Nothing has happened."

"Are you sure nothing has happened?"

"Yes, nothing miraculous happened in the office. Had something happened I would have had slight trust in you."

"What trust would you have had?"

"That you are speaking the truth and that you are really God."

"Then I am giving evidence… listen!"

"Tell me."

"Didn't Rita talk to you today?"

"Yes, she did. This is a normal practice; what's so miraculous about it?"

"Is it a normal thing?"

"No doubt about it," Abinash asserted.

"Then why didn't she talk to you for so long?"

"Do you want to say you had sent her to me today?"

"You are a drunken irresponsible person. No woman likes such type of people."

"Is it not a miracle that Rita likes you?"

"Abinash remained silent for some time."

Undoubtedly the man is from within the office. He has kept an eye on his activities. He also has an eye on Rita. Who could that man be?

"Is not the tracing of B.N. Agarwal Company's file a miracle?"

Abinash said, "Missing a file and finding it in an office is a very ordinary matter. In the past, so many files have been lost and later, traced."

"No! It's not the same. It has been exposed that you had a hand in the missing of the file. For this, disciplinary proceedings were supposed to be initiated. You had forgotten where you have hidden the file. You were totally inebriated while hiding the file. You would have landed up in trouble if the file was not traced soon."

"So you will certainly tell now that Arun's motorcycle accident was a miracle."

"Certainly a miracle. Today itself seven accidents have occurred in the town. In the entire world, five thousand seven hundred seventy accidents have occurred. In the seven accidents that occurred in your town, three persons have lost their lives."

"Then, you must be held responsible for all these accidents."

"No! No! Accidents are made by people. Their over-dependence on machines contributes to the increasing number of accidents. Their indiscipline conduct leads to accidents. I only attempt to save everybody."

"Why can't you save all those who die?"

"Anybody who takes birth will have to die one day. This is the truth of this world. That cannot be circumvented."

"It's okay; I trust that you are God. Now tell me what do you want from me?"

"I want to offer you a boon."

"What type of boon?"

"Just a wish fulfillment."

"Okay! You present a gold necklace to Rita."

God said, "Amen! So be it!"

Next day Abinash did not bring anyone into the ambit of suspicion. Rather he treated all the incidents as either miracles or the doings of God. He noticed that a flower had begun to bloom on a tree beneath his window. He had marked some days back that the tree had no blossoms. After that, he had completely forgotten about the tree. Someone had informed him that no flower would ever bloom on that tree. Abinash realized that the miraculous feat was performed by God. It may so happen, when his phone comes, this flower tree issue will come into the ambit of discussion.

In the afternoon Rita came to his seat. Abinash considered this arrival a miracle. But all his thoughts were wounded when Rita narrated another strange story. Rita sat in front of him and took out a jewellery box from her vanity bag. She held it open in front of Abinash and said, "Just look at this necklace. Guess what its cost would be?"

"Where did you get this necklace from? Did you buy it?"

"No! someone has presented it."

Abinash said, "I know." At least now he believed that God had given this necklace to her, on his request.

"I know who has presented it to you?"

"Do you know?"

"Yeah! I know! On my request, He has presented it."

"How strange? He has presented on your request? Since when have you turned to be his advisor?"

Abinash began to smile softly.

Rita said, "I was thinking in a different way."

"What were you thinking?"

"He not only presented the necklace but also proposed to me."

This time it was Abinash's turn to get surprised.

"He proposed? Who?"

"Marut Sahib. He has given me this necklace. He has also proposed. When you say that he has done it on your advice then it should be acknowledged and reciprocated."

Rita went away with the necklace. While going away from there, her eyes looked stressed. Abinash could not say anything even though he wanted to.

That night also Abinash received a call from God. At that time, he was impatient, upset and excited.

He said, "This is not fair."

"Why? Rita has already received a goldnecklace."

"But Marut Sahib's giving it to her …. is unacceptable."

"What did you think, I myself would have given it to her?"

"That would have been better."

"But that never happens. God himself never steps in to do any action. Human beings perform those actions by the will of God."

"But why did Marut Sahib have to give it to her? I could have presented it."

"How could you have given? You don't have any money in your account. Even today, you have pending dues in some bars. Where from would you have arranged so much money?"

"In that case, you could have made the present."

"No! No! That is not done. We can't do that. Do you think I would have dropped some nuggets of gold through a hole in your roof as it happens in stories?"

"If that is so, please tell me how you can help me."

"Tell me what do you want now?"

"I need another boon."

"So now you want to be given another boon."

"Yes, I want one more boon. This is very urgent."

"Tell me what you want."

"Saxena needs to be thrashed."

"Which Saxena?"

"Marut Saxena, the Managing Director of our office."

God said, "Amen! So be it."

The phone was disconnected after that. Next day Abinash was feeling greatly perturbed. It seemed as if his blood pressure had shot up. He was getting irritated at everything. Saxena Sahib summoned him. Peon Pravakar escorted him to his Chamber. Saxena sahib plunged onto him just as a lion plunges upon its prey. He heaped lots of blame upon him. He said, "Didn't you hide B N Agarwal Company's file? Abinash said, "Who said I had hidden? This is a lie."

"Pravakar got it from your drawer."

Abinash had ransacked that drawer repeatedly. He had never found that file. Pravakar also had searched it several times. Now, all of a sudden how did he get that file from the same drawer?

Saxena Sahib shouted further, "You demanded money from B N Agarwal Company to do the job, and therefore, you indulged in this offense."

Abinash's head began to reel. His blood pressure shot up further. He trembled as if it were with an unknown excitement. A strange wave of rage ran through his whole body, from toe to head. Now, it was impossible for him to tolerate any longer.

He shouted, "No! No! You can't blame me like that."

Even Abinash himself didn't realize what followed next. He lost all control over himself and burst into a series of slangs. He picked up the paperweight and threw it at Saxena Sahib. Saxena Sahib's head was injured. Then he rushed towards him and landed a few blows on him. Pravakar, the peon, tried to restrain him but was unsuccessful in his endeavour. All such things happened within a moment. Saxena Sahib had to be rushed to the hospital immediately.

By the same evening, Abinash was suspended on charges of misbehaving with seniors. He returned home.

He did not go to the hotel to eat or to the bar to drink or even switch on the lights at home. He sat alone silently amid the darkness. He was lost in thoughts. He sat looking at the telephone. The telephone rang right at 12 O Clock. Groping in the dark, he picked up the phone.

"He said, "Hello!"

"Yes! Is it Abinash?"

"Yes, Speaking."

"Your wish must have been fulfilled. Saxena Sahib must have been beaten."

"Yes he is beaten. But why did you choose me for that job?"

"I cannot do it myself. The job has to be done by a human being."

"But why did you choose me as the medium; the scapegoat?"

"Because for that job, no other person more competent than you was available."

"Was I adjudged competent for that?"

"Yes! Just judge and analyze. You will find you alone are suitable for that or you deserve the present state you have landed up yourself in."

"Thanks! Thanks a lot! God. Now I am sure that you are God. I harbor no more doubts."

"Tell me what do you want now?"

"I want one more boon. I want fulfillment of a few more wishes."

"I knew you would certainly ask for one more boon. Your condition is very pathetic."

"No! No!" Abinash said, "My condition may be pathetic but for that neither do I desire a boon nor do I want liberation from this condition."

"Then what do you want?" God asked.

"I have understood you, God. I have also understood this world a little more. So I have nothing materialistic to beg."

"But everybody in this world always craves for materialistic attainments."

"Yes they ask for, only because they are ignorant. But I have realized the truth. If I ask for a job now, you will inflict on me torture along with the job. If I ask for bounteous wealth, I will get incurable diseases along with it. If I ask for eternal bliss, it will be accompanied by deep sorrow. They all are found blended together like binaries. The package of society is perhaps like this. Nothing is achieved when one remains alienated from it."

"Then what do you want? Tell me."

"I want one thing. Maybe this is my last request to you."

"Tell me. I am waiting eagerly to fulfill your wish."

"Hence forward, never entice me with the offer of your boons. This is my only prayer to you. Never ever call me over telephone. Never dole out boons. Never tempt me with promises of wish fulfillment. This is my request. Whatever I am, I want to be like that."

God said, "Amen, So be it."

Abinash was overwhelmed with joy. He began to laugh loud amid the darkness.

He said, "Goodbye ! God!"

"Farewell! Farewell! Goodbye! Goodbye!"

Original Odia: *Ishwara Kebe Thare*

■

In Search of Ms. Adela Quested

Dipti Ranjan Pattanaik
Translated by **Chinmay Kumar Hota**

The email came after two years' silence. It had just one line, "Have you finished the novel? Yours Emma Gallagher."

The mail left me puzzled for a while. Why did Emma Gallagher think of me after two years? I had mailed her after returning from England. There was no reply. Maybe the renowned writer didn't find time to read my mail, I had thought. When three or four mails remained unanswered I concluded that she must have forgotten me, which was not unusual. She must have come in contact with many like me; how could she maintain a friendship with all?

Her forgetting me had somewhat hurt me initially, but I got used to it later. This happens always. You'd like someone with your heart and mind and they will treat you as a burden. Even if you are obliged to someone you cannot reciprocate at times. For Emma my idea was different. I would not mind remaining obliged to her for life for all the good she had done to me. It was up to her to accept my gratefulness.

But strange are the ways of the human mind. I forgot her after my mails had remained unanswered. I could have deleted her mail this time before reading it. Many spammails with explicit content target my mailbox daily, mails from 'senders' with usual names such as Jane, Emma, Margaret and so on. I had thought today's mail from Emma to be one such mail inviting me to a pornographic site. Fortunately, I had decided to open it in the last minute.

In my struggle for life, I had also forgotten about the novel she had written about in the mail. The fact is I had read EM Forster's *A Passage to India* in my childhood. Forster is a great spokesman on humanity and human relationship. Ideologically he had placed friendship much higher than nation, religion, and race. He had once said, if he had to choose between betrayal to nation and betrayal to a friend, he would rather betray the nation and not the friend. The friendship between an Indian doctor and an English intellectual is the mainstay of the plot of *A Passage to India*. In the end, the novelist has taken the reader to an enigmatic situation. Can a man really cross the walls, created by him, that separate the ruler and the ruled, black and white, and India and Britain? In the novel, the two friends, Dr. Aziz and Mr. Fielding haven't been able to do that, despite their sincere and conscious efforts.

Why Aziz and Fielding alone, the destiny of mankind is like that only: this was my impression when I read the novel in my younger days. In his conscious mind, a man may think something to be good, but the inner person doesn't agree with that view. Man lives with his fragmented self. He speaks the unspeakable, does the undoable at the prodding of his unconscious mind, although his whole self has to suffer the consequences. I understood the novel in the background of this segmentation of the psychological process. I had taken Aziz and Fielding to be the symbols of man's higher consciousness. And Adela Quested represented that negative unconscious forcewhichtieman up in his ignorance and narrow-mindedness. In the novel, the friendship of two good friends is under strain because of Adela. They have become conscious of their inability to cross distances between them. Adela Quested's actions have carried the plot to a doubtful stage and drawn question marks on the heavenly possibilities of a great friendship.

The plot goes like this: Adela Quested, the fiancée of the district collector is on a tour to India. As a friend of Fielding, she has come to know Doctor Aziz. Dr. Aziz takes Adela and elderly Mrs. Moore on a visit to the caves of Marabar. Who knows what happened inside the caves, Adela comes out from there screaming. She brings charges of sexual abuse by Dr. Aziz. If it had happened today Dr. Aziz would have received fifty lashes and would have lost his job too. Praiseworthy indeed are the English people, they have given ample opportunity to Aziz to defend himself despite the charges coming straight from the fiancée of the collector. The court case has started bringing the English community to one side, but Fielding has not abandoned his friend. In the end, Miss Quested has withdrawn her charges and returned to England. But the feeling of brotherhood that Aziz had for English remains has disappeared. There a great change in his attitude towards old pal Fielding, as if the ground for building a lasting relationship has receded far away.

What may be the conclusion of the plot, what thrilled me at my young stage was the darkness of the caves of Marabar. What was inside that dark cave? The way Adela Quested's character and actions have been portrayed, she can't be viewed as a cheap character. There is nothing in her to hint that she harbored any prejudice towards brown Indians, even though his future husband, the collector, had some intolerance towards Indians. Adela was a woman with an open and broad heart. Then why did she bring such a charge against Aziz? Did Aziz really behave indecently? That was also unlikely. The way Aziz's character has been portrayed it is difficult to expect rashness from him. Hence, my teenage mind had held the cave as the villain of the piece.

With age, my teenage impressions also changed. Before

Miss Quested many foreigner women must have gone inside the caves with their Indian friends. No one had brought such charges earlier, so can we cast the whole blame on the caves? As my doubt on the caves diminished, I became more curious about the character of Ms. Quested. My annoyance towards the character for deviously humiliating an Indian doctor was replaced by this inexplicable attraction towards her. I was not aware of what was the source of this attraction; initially, I had thought it to be just infatuation. This happens so often that we revise our strongly held ideas of childhood as we grow in age. Some ordinary events take new meaning and significance, while what we considered as exceptional appear mundane. Adorable characters of our young days appear full of blemishes, whereas some base ones come out with godly elements. The heroic Rama of our childhood becomes the husband abusing his wife and the evil Ravana emerges as genial. Maybe my recent feelings about Adela Quested had something to do with my growing up. I had thought of writing a novel on the subject as it had occupied my mind for long. Sometimes it happens with writers-what their conscious minds fail to comprehend, appears to them in all clarity when they start writing. I had thought of writing a novel with the hope that the process will illuminate for me the dark crevices of Marabar caves or the recesses of Adela's mind. Forester had seen India from the point of view of a ruler, my novel would see the incident from a point of view that was free from years of colonial rule-providing a fresh look at human relationship and prejudices. Such a post-colonial version of Passage to India was in my mind for long.

I had shared this idea for the first time with Emma Gallagher. She was conducting a workshop on creative writing while traveling in India. British Council had invited a few promising young writers to take part in the workshop. Emma explained in the first few days how to write stories and novels, how to structure language and such matters. Then she discussed face to face with each Indian writer on their individual problems. I considered myself fortunate to have got a chance to exchange ideas with a renowned novelist like Emma Gallagher. When my turn came at the end I was highly excited.

There was an ante-room near the hall where she delivered her talk. I rapped on the door. "Please come in'" said Emma. I went inside; the interior of the ante-room was not quite clear to my eyes having just come in from the brightly lit hall. The room was oval shaped, with a huge table occupying more than half of the space. The light of the table lamp fell on a clutch of photocopies of papers.

"Please sit down," said Emma Gallagher. The air-conditioned room was filled with the smell of a strong perfume. I sat down on a chair saying, "Thank you, Madam." My eyes fell on the papers on the table-they were copies of my stories. British Council had asked me for the copies of some of my stories before the start of the workshop. They had chosen participants after evaluating their stories.

"I've been reading your stories," she said.

I bowed down my head smiling. I was feeling quite obliged. Such a great writer has read my stories in order to discuss them. This is indeed professional. What dedication to her work! Probably this sincerity was the reason why once sun did not set in the empire of their race.

"The language of your stories is influenced by Salman Rushdie and Gabriel Garcia Marquez. My writing is quite different," said Emma breaking the brief silence.

"I haven't read Salman Rushdie much. But I have a strong respect for Marquez. I have seen few writers with such conviction about their own art. Of course, the source of my influence is different, long before Marquez; Indian narratives like 'Kathasaritasagara' and many folk tales have used language in this way."

"Please start a tradition. Literature will benefit if you have such resolve. How you will go about it will depend on your decision."

"I am thinking of writing a novel on Adela Quested-an alternative to Passage to India. Forster has not revealed the real mystery of Marabar Hills. I am often disturbed by that mystery, and by the behavior of Adela Quested. She is a unique example of female psychology," I said.

"What a coincidence!" She straightened herself on the chair, her face turning crimson. "Do you know, I was very excited about Forster's novel too in my young days? I planned to visit India long back, but the opportunity didn't come. I have read many articles related to India after reading Passage to India-Jhabvala's Heat and Dust, Hess' Siddhartha, novels of Paul Scott. But I had not thought of the caves in the light that you described. I have been captivated by the diversity and spread of India's culture."

"Human civilization has started from caves only," I said.

"Probably that's why philosophers like Plato and Bacon have used caves as symbols. India's wisdom has often been kindled in these caves. Even today many spiritual seekers are busy in meditation in the caves of Himalayas."

"As far as I remember, critics have compared Forster's caves with the voidness of Hindu philosophy," said Emma.

"Yes, some others have described the cave as a symbol of the prehistoric ovary, Adela's suppressed sexual desire or racial prejudice. But I feel Forster's caves bring man face to face with his ancient self, dismissing all the man-made identities and differences. We try to get away from that real self without realizing that that is the eternal truth, but we cannot accept."

"You've prepared enough about the philosophical aspect of the novel," Emma said smiling. I felt for the first time she had removed the masks from her personality consciously.

"You praise me unnecessarily, I said, "Do you know, I've tried to start writing this novel so many times; year after year. Every time I've failed to write even a word. I have felt as if my words are unable to solve the mystery of not only Adela Quested's experience, what to speak of the mystery of mankind. Whatever language I use, I will deepen the mystery, without reaching at the truth and Brahma through the medium of words," my voice sounded sheepish as I said this. Emma pressed my palm coming closer. She reassured me saying, "Don't worry about that young man. This is a problem with all writers, the problem of our profession. After all, we are writers, not detectives of spirituality."

My coarse fingers had almost melted inside her soft palm. The sense of surrender in her voice and touch had electrified my whole person. Emma suddenly appeared desirable to me-her stature as a renowned writer and speaker, a wealthy person had vanished from my mind. The feeling of a responsive female lurking behind her real identity sprouted myriad buds of desire in me.

I removed my fingers to suppress a sneeze that was coming. "Excuse me," I said for that unintentional sneeze. I had felt earlier that sneezing had some link with libido. I felt guilty as if this response was not personal, but the expression of our culture. Maybe my feeling was a mixed expression of the fear, the curiosity, the desire and the inferiority Indian's had for a white woman.

"Oh", cried out Emma-the room suddenly felt like a cave due to the sudden power cut. Emma went up to the window to draw the Venetian blinds, bringing some light to the room.

"This power cut is disturbing us for the last three days," said Emma.

"Why three days, this is a regular feature," I said.

"I had thought this is happening in India due to my arrival here," joked Emma, "Writers are somewhat megalomaniac, but I find people untroubled."

"We Indians are fatalists. Our karma is behind whatever happens to us. You may say this is a sense of indifference or detachment in us. But this is the unfailing means for facing the cruelty of history." The light had come and the air-conditioner had started humming.

"Thank God, I'd have melted after some time," said Emma, "I am so pleased with our discussion, we could have spent some more time, but I've to see the high commissioner. This is official work.'

"Unfortunately we couldn't talk more about Adela Quested," I said with a tinge of disappointment.

"Let me say something before I forget. There is lessdetailed description in your writing and more of imagination. You do not place enough attention to the picture of reality. Try to place small incidents and related images in your writing. Think of your novel-you want to write about the subtle difference between truth and reality. But you must not forget that Adela Quested is a human being, her identity thrives on a physical and psychological plane. You must train your attention on that plane. That will make your writing easy. Make the area of your experience wider. To understand Adela you must first see England and the English women from close."

"Where is a good opportunity for me? It's not a matter of wish but of means for me to visit a foreign country. I am an amateur writer; I dabble in writing in the break that I get from my profession. It's not possible on my part to write based on the experience I gather from a foreign land."

Emma thought silently for a while. Then she said, "I'm not promising you anything, but I'll see what I can do." She extended her hand towards me saying, "Nice talking to you."

I said while shaking hands, "Many thanks for your affections." She said while coming out of the room, "Best of luck with the novel."

After a month I received an offer from the British Council to attend a Cambridge seminar. I realized that Emma's promise was not a hollow one. I mailed Emma to thank for her recommendations. Emma complimented me in her reply and invited to be her guest there.

The seminar was for ten days, followed by travel. I had to return after a month. I had laid my hands on small research work, for which I had to collect some material. As Roehampton Institute, where I was to collect that material, was closed for two day holiday, I had nothing on hand. I called the number Emma had given me. She asked me to be her guest on those two days. She was waiting for me in front of a place we had decided to meet.

She told me about her busy life while driving to her flat in the suburbs of South London. She receives huge advances from her publishers to write. She kept herself busy in preparing the manuscript in time, correcting the proof, attending sales promotion and book signing events, interviews, radio talks and so on. She had taken two days off from her work just to spend time with me.

The romantic idea I had about the lives of the professional writers had disappeared after hearing about the personal life of Emma. That, a beautiful, middle-aged woman could be so lonely and desperate despite her busy life, wealth and power was beyond my imagination. Her family consisted of her only daughter and a few pet tortoises, which she had to drop with her parents if she had to go out. Her advocate husband was living separately after falling in love with his steno. I remembered the last dialogue of Oedipus, "Don't say he is a lucky man, that he is still alive."

There was nothing amiss in her hospitality. She had invited some young writers and two of her friends for dinner on account of my visit. I was smoking on a garden chair while the dinner was being laid out. The tortoises moved about the courtyard. At the end of a courtyard, there was a small pool, surrounded by many bonsai plants. There were fishes and a small toy boat on the surface of the water.

"My daughter's collection," said Emma. Her grandparents have taken her out to visit a park; she will return tomorrow. She has asked me to keep you in her bedroom. She has pressed me to keep you here until her return."

"How can I leave without meeting my hostess? "I said.

"How was your experience in England? Did you find some material for your novel? What about Adela Quested?"

"I realized in England that an Adela Quested can take birth only in an imperial nation," I said. "All the women I met are struggling for their existence. Exotic. To be desperate for the extrasensory is something rare here. A beautiful and healthy girl asked me for half a pound to buy her lunch. Maybe she wanted money for brown sugar. For food, she must be getting social security coupons."

"Why did you give her money then?"

"What else could I've done? I had just emerged from the subway. She suddenly turned around ahead of me and asked for half a pound. I feared if I didn't give she might raise a complaint of sexual abuse. If the shopkeepers would attack me hearing her outcry? Wouldn't a white woman's complaint be more acceptable in such circumstances, when the accused is a dark-skinned fellow like me? I remembered a case of an Odia researcher having lost his job on such grounds. I dropped a pound in her hand and scooted away from the scene.

Emma laughed out loud hearing my description. She said, "I find you're possessed by the ghost of Adela Quested. Unfortunate fellow."

"I think the difference between races and nations are only artificial. At least after the geographical barriers are demolished by colonialism and with the march of technology, the similarity in the nature of all mankind is apparent-for better or for worse."

Emma agreed with my view. She said, "Yes, going by the fast movement of the capital the external differences between cultures will be demolished very soon."

"I'm thinking of such a time when democracy will emerge with the coming together of all communities breaking all barriers of geography and folks will work for the benefit of others. The ambitions of the suppressed will always try to harm that ideal state. I got a hint of that in London."

Thousands of Tamil refugees with the problems of the so-called third world have swarmed the city Britain has to face the problems of the third world due to its political necessity or its colonial past.

Stubbing the cigarette on the ash-tray, I said, "Do you know, I met a youth on my way from London to Stroud-a British citizen of Pakistani parentage. He talked of Babri Mosque, the partition of India and religious intolerance with such emotion that for a moment I thought as if I was in Lucknow and not London."

The calling bell rang out now. Emma's guests arrived one by one. Their punctuality had amazed me. A young writer was feeling sorry for being late by five minutes. After the introduction, we all sat near the pool. Emma served French wine and cottage cheese. I felt tipsy after taking the wine. I couldn't fully participate in the discussion on British politics, literature and international issues. Only I was answering the questions about India raised by Emma's friend Anne, who had traveled India extensively.

Late in the afternoon, we all moved to the dining table. Emma had arranged quite a few Indian dishes for me. Some had been ordered from the Indian restaurant and others she had prepared with the help of a cookbook. After dinner, all but two female friends of Emma left. We sat around the now cleaned dining table with fresh servings of wine. Probably these women too were also deserted by their husbands. They didn't broach the subjects of family or kids. Emma asked her much-traveled friend, "Anne, have you ever experience this-a handsome man is sitting beside you on a flight?"

"Yes, so many times," said Anne.

"Have you ever slept with one, maybe for a night?"

"Oh, Emma, you're just impossible," Anne said smiling.

Coming out of their veils of civility the three ladies engaged themselves in so many frolics as if I didn't exist there. Probably excess of drinking had made them oblivious of my presence. I was not able to take part of their tomfoolery. I moved near the bonsai plants to smoke a cigarette.

"Excuse me, I've to smoke outside. Nicotine is an hourly necessity" I said smiling.

"Oh, it's really late. We have to leave," said Margaret, Emma's second friend.

"Shall we drop you somewhere?" Anne asked me.

"Oh no, he will stay here tonight. I'll take him to an expert on children's literature. We have an appointment at nine in the morning" said Emma.

The two ladies exchanged smiles hearing Emma. While Emma walked the ladies till the porch, I had already come inside the house. My head was heavy with the warm drink and the cigarette smoke. Emma called me to show my bedroom."

Emma's daughter has left the marks of her personality everywhere in her room. Life-size posters of Bruce Springsteen, Madonna graced the wall while teddy bears lay strewn all over along with some Mills and Boon romance books. It was not difficult to know that the room belonged to someone caught between childhood and youth. Emma left me there and bid a good night. My briefcase containing my dresses had already been kept near the bed. I went to bed after putting on my nightdress and switched the light off.

I couldn't sleep a wink innight. I and a divorced woman were the only ones sleeping in the big house. Darkness pervaded all around; even sound of crickets was not heard. The moonlight entered through the window; maybe part of the sky was free from clouds. I found it hard to dismiss the discussions of the evening from my mind. What could be the reason behind the provocative chat of the female friends? What is behind Emma's vulgar queries? Why did the departing friends exchange furtive smiles while leaving?

I tried to reason that many things happen or expressed which do not have definite meanings. Different meanings can be ascribed to events or expressions later, but they may not have any link with the original purpose. Yet my Indian mind and culture were working hard to discover a common thread to tie up the evening's events. My Indian mind was convinced that every small matter was a symbol and these symbols were parts of some greater being. My visit to England, coming to Emma Gallagher's house, getting thrilled by wine and sensual conversation-are these not intended to open up a new horizon of my life? But is the new horizon one of growth or descent, I had no clue.

In such a delicate mental state I decided to remain a medium for the rest of the night. I will not initiate anything, but shall not resist something from happening. I will not be responsible for any moral or spiritual reaction. I felt a strange power spreading inside me as soon as I took this decision. I waited eagerly for the footsteps that might come near the open door-how long I didn't know. The whole atmosphere was silent as before. As I heard the beats of my heart I fell asleep.

The exciting but eventless night wore on and by the time I woke up, it was eight in the morning. I finished my morning routine. I was feeling light as the influence of alcohol was gone. I also thanked God and my luck for the eventless night. What if the novel couldn't be written, I could at least retain my worth as someone whose behavior didn't abandon his life's philosophy. Emma's respect for me, not simply as an individual but someone representing India, would have remained unaffected. I started for a new day with new enthusiasm.

That day's main work was to meet Stephen Chambers, the expert on children's literature at nine o' clock. He is a friend of Emma, who was to accompany me to his place. We were to take part in BBS Studio while returning from Mr. Chambers. Although it was almost time, Emma was not seen. There was no sound from her bedroom in the upper story. I browsed the newspaper after getting dressed. It was half-past nine while I waited. I felt uneasy because of my conviction about the British sense of punctuality. I was puzzled at the delay by Emma. With the passing of each second, my anxiety also increased. Has some untoward happened last night? Or Emma is unable to wake up? I created some noise to alert her, but nothing happened. When it was ten I couldn't have patience-I climbed the stairs and rapped on her door.

"Yes", the sound came from inside, Thank God, nothing has happened to Emma. I felt relieved. After a couple of seconds, the voice from inside said, "I'm ready".

After hearing this I made a grave mistake unwittingly. I couldn't think that the door wouldn't have been locked from inside-maybe I pressed the door more than I should have, it opened. The inside of the room looked like the dark crevices of an ancient cave. Yet in that darkness, I could see the naked body of Emma Gallagher. She looked at the door standing in front of the mirror. She was holding her inner wears which were distinctly visible despite the darkness.

After a moment's awkwardness, I shut the door saying, "I am sorry."

"It's all right. I'm coming in a minute," Emma said in a raised voice from inside. She came out after half a second after wearing a pair of jeans and a T-shirt.

She said, "Steve has asked us to come at eleven, some work

came up at nine. I didn't want to disturb you. Let's get out; we will have something on the way."

I felt embarrassed for the experience of the morning, but Emma was quite natural. We spent the whole day together, joined different events. When we returned to her place I bade goodbye to her daughter and then checked into a cheap bread and breakfast hotel. We didn't talk about the morning incident when we were together. Was the 'big show' an intentional one by Emma? If it was intentional what was her motive? This thought kept cropping up in my mind until my return from England.

I bade farewell from Emma while leaving for India. She wished me well for my future novel. I thanked her profusely after reaching India. Emma didn't reply to my emails. When she didn't respond to my emails I thought she must be busy in her works. Gradually Emma Gallagher faded from my memory. In the end, my plan to write a novel on Adela Quested was forgotten like many other plans about writing novels. The past events came flashing today after two years as I received Emma's mail. But I couldn't decide how I should reply to her mail. After thinking a lot I decided to delete the mail as I often deleted the titillating spam mails that purportedly came from senders like Eliza, Jane, and Margaret.

Original Odia: *Miss Adela Quested nka Sandhanare*

Wild Jasmine

Paramita Satpathy

Translated by **Snehaprava Das**

Theforest was aflame. It was the second half of May and the temperature hovered around forty-five degrees Celsius. The sky poured out molten heat. Like a thirst-tormented monster, the sun sucked up life from every living cell, in man, animal or plant. There was nothing they could do but surrender meekly to merciless Nature.

The newly constructed road snaked around the mountain; the work was still on at some places. A few villages stretched out along the road-side. Small huts in a row reached into the forest. On their walls, made of dried-up branches and clay, rested low, sloping thatched roofs. A few had tin or asbestos roofs. Halfway down the looping road stood an asbestos-roofed concrete house with four or five rooms, which served as the Anganwadi (play-school) as well as primary school. It was also used sometimes in the evenings for literacy programs for the elderly.

Most children had stopped coming and the primary school was closed for the summer. But where were the children who used to come to the Anganwadi? The heat must be keeping them away, Rina guessed. They should have been there at least for their mid-day meal. The cooking-gas had run out four or five days ago and no refills were available in the village. The supply of electricity, usually erratic, had stopped completely and no one could tell when it would be restored. Cooking over a wood fire in that heat would mean getting oneself roasted. The house turned into a furnace as the heat came streaming down the asbestos roof. There was no respite either inside or outside the house. Rina kept moving in and out, splashing her face from time to time with the water stored in an earthen container.

The sound of a motorbike was heard outside. Who it could be, Rina wondered. Nobody was expected at that hour. It couldn't be her brother Tuku. He had gone out at day-break to attend some meeting, somewhere inside the forest. It was, he had said, an important meeting and workers from all corners of the state would be coming. Tuku would be late: it might be evening or even night by the time he returned. Rina kept the front door open on account of the heat. She walked out of the courtyard and tried to look out through the open door, stretching forward.

A motorcycle with two men astride it had pulled up outside the house. Their eyes strayed across the open door. Should Rina come out and ask them what they wanted? Perhaps they were new here and wanted to ask the name of the village or the place that the road led to, or maybe they wanted to know something about the construction sites. It was not unusual; many people came inquiring. But it was the timing that troubled Rina. Two strangers arriving during the scorching and deserted afternoon was not usual. Rabi Jani, the tribal domestic help at the Anganwadi, had not yet come. She had kept some *pakhala* for him in a bowl and covered it up. Rina waited for the two men to leave. But they did not go; nor did they get off the bike. There was no one in the vicinity she could call in case she needed help. Rina was feeling ill at ease. It might be wiser to shut the door quickly.

"Can we get some water to drink?"

Rina heard one of them speak as she was about to close the door. She stopped abruptly and looked up at the riders. Two young men, in T-shirts and trousers, were looking at her expectantly. Both wore caps. Perhaps they were on their way to attend to some work but the heat and thirst had made them stop, Rina thought. They dismounted and after parking the bike moved a few steps towards her. She was a little frightened; should she slam the door on their faces? But they appeared visibly tormented by thirst and heat. They had probably traveled a long distance. They might be in genuine need of water.

"It is so hot here; our throats are parched. There is no shed nearby where we could take shelter for a while," the man who had been driving the bike said, looking at Rina, and sat down on the verandah without waiting for her to say something. The other man stood on the road, looking ahead. She paused for a moment – the two men were not looking at her. She drew a breath of relief and went inside without a word. She returned in a minute carrying two metal tumblers filled with cool water from the earthen pitcher. The two men almost snatched the tumblers out of her hands and gulped the water down.

"Some more!"

Rina could read the urgency in the man's voice even though neither of them looked at her directly. This time too she went back without answering, taking the empty glasses and came back after filling them with water. But this time, while returning the empty glasses the man who had been riding pillion gave her a plastic bottle.

"Can you please fill this bottle?" he said politely.

Rina could not refuse, but she was worried within. Who are these men? Did they know that she was all alone there? What if they followed her into the house?

But none of her misgivings came true. She filled the bottle and handed it back to the man.

"Many thanks," the man who had been driving the bike said, smiling gratefully at her and started the engine. Rina went inside, closed the door with one quick movement and stood to lean against it. "Many thanks", she muttered to herself and smiled. She was soaked in perspiration. It was nothing unusual to sweat so much in that dry scorching heat.

Rabi Jani's main task was to get firewood and two pitchers of drinking water for the Anganwadi. He also filled the earthen vessel in the courtyard with water for washing and cleaning. Besides, when the school was open and more water was needed for the children, he filled a few plastic buckets for their use. Rina had to humor him to get him to do all these chores. Rabi Jani was given a midday meal at the Anganwadi in return for the work. But that day he had not shown up at all. Rina was left to herself in the lonely, blazing afternoon.

The next day —

It was late afternoon. Rina cycled to the market for some groceries, leaving Rabi Jani in charge of the house. There was no news of Tuku. He had said he would come back by evening, or at night if he was delayed. He had taken Rina's mobile phone with him. Of course, a mobile phone was not of much use in these parts: most of the time the signal was too weak or entirely dead. But Tuku had not returned at night. Rina waited for him until midnight. Night had given way to morning but he did not return. Nor was there any sign of him at noon. Where was he? Rina was worried. Tuku had been wandering over the countryside, God knew where for the last two or three months. He had opened an S.T.D. booth in the market down below but it remained closed on most days. Tuku did not seem to have any interest in the shop. Unmindfully, Rina rolled her bicycle down the winding road. The beep of a motorcycle horn behind her made her swerve to the left. The motorcycle stopped by her side. Rina looked at the rider. It was the man who had come to the Anganwadi yesterday asking for water. But he was alone now, his friend was not with him.

'Those two glasses of water saved our lives yesterday,' he said. 'I'm glad I got another chance to say thank you.'

Rina got off the bicycle and smiled at the man.

'Is it always this hot here?' the man said in a low voice as if speaking to himself. Rina did not reply.

'Do you belong to this village?' he asked again, looking at Rina.

She shook her head. 'I work in the Anganwadi and stay there. My home is in a village near Kesinga,' she said casually.

'I've come here for the first time,' the man said. 'I've been moving from place to place in this heat for the last seven or eight days, supervising the road-construction.'

Rina did not react to this. 'My name is Ratan Singh. I am from Chandikhol. Do you know the place?'

Rina shook her head.

'Were you going somewhere in particular or just roaming around?'

'I was going to the market', she answered.

'I'm going there too' the man said. There was a note of eagerness in his voice.

Rina got on to her bicycle.

'Will I get some water the next time I come to your Anganwadi?' he asked, gazing intently at Rina. She did not say anything but a soft smile flickered across her face.

'Well, thanks again', he said and started the motorbike.

It was dark by the time Rina returned from the market. From a distance, she saw Tuku sitting on the veranda.

'Where've you been? There was no news of you,' Rina said with anxiety in her voice.

'I'll tell you everything, give me something to eat first. Is there any *pakhala* left?'

Rina stood the bicycle against the wall and hurried inside carrying the groceries. She came out soon with a bowl of *pakhala* and a plate of fried potatoes. She put the food before Tuku and sat by him peeling an onion.   'What do these people think? Can they crush us under their feet? Reduce us to dust? They want to build their factories on our land and suck away our blood.' Tuku muttered, looking into the darkness as if thinking aloud. He had forgotten his sister sitting near him. His hand had stopped in the act of raising food to his mouth. His mind seemed to be elsewhere and he appeared to have been gripped by some deep, overwhelming passion.

'Stop blabbering!' Rina said. 'You have been wondering about for the last two days. You have n't even eaten in these two days. Finish your *pakhala* first.'

Her voice broke the spell.

'We shall fight, *didi*. We'll not let them move even a step as long as we live; we will fight to the last drop of blood in our bodies. And after that, you, *didi*, and all the tribal women and girls must take the lead.' Tuku said, still looking into the darkness as if he was making a prophecy.

Rina kept quiet. They sat there in silence for a few minutes. Tuku lifted the rice from the bowl to his mouth absent-mindedly. Rina looked at the bowl and went inside to get some more rice for him.

'What are these boys up to?' she wondered. Tuku did not say anything clearly. He just kept mumbling in broken sentences. They were conducting meetings in unknown villages, somewhere deep inside the forest. He told his sister just that much – nothing more, although she tried to pry more out of him. This time he had stayed away for two days without any information. Rina felt a shudder of fear. She let out a deep breath and came back carrying some more rice in a small bowl.

Rina had hoped that the heat would come down a little in the next two days but instead, the temperature went up. Tuku had gone away somewhere early in the morning. He had been in a great hurry. Rina had mashed some soaked *flattened rice* for him. But despite all her persuasion, Tuku went away without taking any food. The Anganwadi children had not shown up either. Probably no child will come today as well, Rina thought.

The sound of a motorbike was heard outside. Rina came out of the house. It was as if she had been waiting for someone. It was the same young man, Ratan Singh – but he was alone that day.

'I'm really very thirsty today. Can I have two glasses of

that refreshing water?' he said, getting off the bike and moving towards the house.

A smile appeared on Rina's face; she went into the house and came back carrying two glasses of water, one in each hand.

'Do you have electricity here?' Ratan Singh asked as he sat down on the veranda.

'Yes, but we've had no power in the last four days. There is a table fan but it is of no use without electricity.'

'There was no storm or rain recently — then why the power failure?' Ratan Singh asked looking at her.

'Who knows? Perhaps the wires melted in this heat. It's nothing new. The electricity supply is disrupted regularly for ten or fifteen days every month.'

'There is no one here to talk to, not even down there in the market,' Ratan Singh said as Rina picked up the empty glasses. 'Do your parents live here? I think there is a school here as well?'

'No, only my younger brother lives with me. There is a school but it is closed for the summer vacation,' Rina answered.

'Do the children come regularly? Is there a teacher?'

'Only a few come. They used to come in larger numbers when mid-day meals were provided but now they come only when they feel like it. A teacher has been appointed but he's just as irregular as the children."

"What about your brother? What does he do for a living? Is he educated?"

'Not much, he passed Matriculation but we couldn't afford to send him to school after that. He has opened an S.T.D booth in the market and is planning to stock provisions and a few other things." She tried to sound carefree but her voice was gloomy.

"Well, I must leave now. Thank you." Ratan Singh walked back to the motorbike. He looked at Rina, smiled and started the bike. "I shall come tomorrow." Rina could not understand if it was a promise or a proposition. Her face reddened.

Next afternoon, Rina was feeling a bit restless. She walked to and from the frontyard of the house many times expecting Ratan Singh at any moment. Why should he want to come, she asked herself. What would she say to him if he did come? An unidentifiable disquiet had taken possession of her. But Ratan Singh did not come. Noon passed. The sun blazed down. Rina rinsed her face and hands, spread a straw mat on the floor and lay down. Suddenly the sound of the motorcycle reached her ears. She got up hurriedly and rushed out.

"I'm not just thirsty today but hungry too. I could do with some tea," Ratan Singh said softly to Rina and smiled.

A smile touched Rina's lips and lit up her face.

"Isn't your brother home? I thought I could meet him if I came in the late afternoon." Ratan Singh said.

"No, he may be at his booth."

"All right, I'll wait here for the tea." He sat down on the veranda.

"There's no milk," Rina's said, her face flushed with embarrassment.

"Do you have tea leaves and sugar?" Ratan Singh asked. She nodded.

"Black tea will do." He flicked a smile at her and Rina disappeared into the house.

There was no gas. She would have to use dry leaves to start a fire and prepare tea, Rina thought bitterly. But at last, the tea was ready. Rina came out carrying a cup of tea and four biscuits on a plastic plate.

"It took you a long time!" he said.

"There's no gas," Rina smiled awkwardly and turned to go inside. "I'll get a glass of water."

"Come, sit here," Ratan Singh said.

Rina put the glass down near him but did not sit down.

"It won't be like this much longer in this village," he said. "Life will change. You will be able to get gas easily and there won't be power failures. There will be a bigger market and more shops. Better schools may be a college as well, and a hospital and doctors. The look of this place will change totally." Ratan Singh did not look straight at Rina while saying all this although he sat facing her.

Rina stood there silently listening to him.

"Do you know what we are doing here? We are constructing a road that will connect this mountain to the larger one behind – a real wide concrete road on which two large vehicles can move side by side comfortably, not like the narrow one you have now." The note of assurance in his voice had remained unchanged.

"Aren't they going to blast the mountain and dig mines there?" Rina returned accusingly.

"Well, not exactly. But whatever will be done will be for the good of everybody. All the people living in these villages will prosper from the project," he said calmly.

"How will they be better off?"

"They will get jobs. Not just that – they will get cash, good clothes to wear. They will live like real human beings. They will become civilized." Ratan Singh went on.

"What do you mean by 'real human beings?' " Rina asked acidly. "They are as much human as those you call 'civilized'. They feel pleasure and pain just the same way as the others; summer and winter have the same effect on them. The only difference is that they are poor. But they do not feel deprived in any way. Have they ever begged for your charity?" Rina grew excited.

"But you must admit that they have benefited from the government's programs. There are schools for their children, bore-wells to provide drinking water. Electricity has come to many villages. Medicines have become available. Can you deny it?" Ratan Singh asked.

"No, I admit there are some changes, but most of it is just eyewash. The less said about the government schools the better. As for healthcare, there is neither a doctor nor medicines in the village dispensary. The power supply is down more often than not." Rina sounded bitter.

Rabi Jani arrived with buckets full of water hanging at each end of a bamboo pole balanced on his shoulder. He paused a little at the doorstep and glanced first at Ratan Singh and then at Rina. He went inside to keep the buckets and came out. Without saying anything to Rina, he walked away and soon disappeared in the dusk.

"Shall we go for a walk?" Ratan Singh asked Rina in a tender voice. "Will you show me around the village?"

Rina waited for a moment, turned and closed the door from outside and fastened it with a chain. She stepped into her slippers and came down the two steps onto the road. They walked along the track that passed by the left of the Anganwadi centre. There were no other houses in the neighborhood. The huts in these hill-side villages were built one behind another in a row, at a little distance from each other. One village was at least ten or twelve kilometers away from the next.

"Whatever you may say, life is hard for the people here. Don't you think they deserve a few modern comforts?" Ratan's tone was calm.

"But why should they have to give up their traditional ways for the sake of these modern comforts? Would your people be prepared to do it?" Rina's words erupted suddenly, as though they had been kept suppressed somewhere inside her for a long, long time. "Can you claim that the life you live is the best?" Rina went on. "These innocent people mind their own business; they never hurt anyone or try to grab another's share. In what way are they inferior?"

"You are becoming too serious; that was not what I meant," said Ratan. "Whatever the government is doing is for their good. They may not understand this now but they will surely realize it later. I agree that they have been living a life of their own, but trust me, no one intends them any harm." Ratan Singh pleaded.

They were both silent for a few moments. "Perhaps it would be a good idea to wash them clean, dress them up in expensive clothes and put them in cages, like animals in a zoo, so that the rich people from the city could come and gaze at them," Rina retorted sardonically.

"You really care about them, don't you?" Ratan Singh's voice was placating.

"I have been living among them for the last two years, sir.

Believe me, you cannot find such peace anywhere else." Rina's voice was as calm as Ratan's.

'Don't call me sir– my name is Ratan.'

They walked on in silence. The sun had set. A film of darkness was beginning to spread across the sky. A soft cool breeze blew through the trees, relieving the heat.

'What a sweet smell! What is it?' Ratan Singh stopped and looked around to trace the source of the fragrance.

"Look at that tree on your left, it is a wild fig tree. What you are getting is the smell of its ripe fruits." Abruptly, Rina stopped. "Can you recognize this other smell?" She looked at Ratan Singh. "It is the fragrance of wild jasmine." She picked a bunch of soft white flowers from a shrub nearby and handed it to Ratan Singh.

"Wild jasmine". Ratan Singh's hand touched Rina's, holding the bunch of flowers. Neither said a word. The forest was so unusually quiet that even the sound of a leaf being blown away by the wind could have been heard. Rina held her head lowered.

"Why is it that all white flowers bloom only in the night?" she murmured, looking at the ground.

"All white flowers!" Ratan Singh said gently. He cupped her face in his hands and lifted it close to his own. Their lips met.

"I shall come tomorrow at this time. I am building a small two-roomed house for myself a little above the market, two or three kilometers away. The house that I have rented, in the market place, is too far away from the work site. When the new house is built I shall take you there."

They walked back along the path, hand in hand.

*   *   *   *

Rina was surprised to find Ratan Singh in front of her house so early that morning. They usually met in the evenings. Only last evening they had spent quite some time in each other's company in Ratan's newly constructed house. What could have been so urgent as to bring him here early in the morning?

Fortunately, Tuku was away. He had left at about noon yesterday and not returned. She walked up to Ratan Singh. He sat astride his bike. He looked flustered; his hair was disheveled and his eyes were red and swollen. An unknown fear seized her. What could have happened?

'Where is Tuku? Is he at home?' Ratan Singh asked awkwardly.

"I don't know; he could be in his booth in the market," she replied

"When did he go?" His voice sounded distant, as though he was a stranger.

"Early this morning" Rina replied, her voice quivering. "Why? What is the matter?"

"Someone murdered Pradip last night. His dead body was found lying in the market early this morning. He was stabbed in the stomach. The police are searching for the killer; he cannot get away."

Rina stood rooted to the ground. She had seen Pradip for the first time when he came to her house with Ratan Singh on his motorbike, asking for water. Later, she had met him a few more times at Ratan's new house. Who could have killed him?

"I must leave now," Ratan said. "We shall talk later." He started the motorcycle and rode away. Rina stood still on the verandah, leaning against the wall. Her mind was in turmoil. Who could possibly have murdered the man? Where had Tuku gone since yesterday? She had lied to Ratan. Had Tuku been responsible? No, never; her brother could go to any length, but murder... Rina knew how tender his heart was. Last year, the gentlemen who came to inspect the school had wanted to go rabbit-hunting. But Tuku had prevented him: "I don't like any kind of hunting!" he had declared firmly. Rina remembered how stubborn her brother was. Rina was afraid she would be dismissed from her job at the Anganwadi, but fortunately, nothing had happened.

"Why are you meeting that contractor so often?" Tuku had asked her sometime back.

"No, we just see each other occasionally. There's nothing to it," Rina had replied evasively.

"Be careful, *didi*; these are not good people. They have come here from the city with a purpose — to blast the hills and rob the poor tribal people of their land and their homes. We should have nothing to do with them", Tuku said grimly.

Rina had no answer. What could she have said to her younger brother? As it was, he was away most of the time. She could not tell him that she was in love with Ratan Singh that they had decided to get married. She couldn't tell him what she thought of Ratan – that he was not an evil character, as Tuku believed, but a compassionate man, full of sympathy for tribal people. She would talk to her brother one of those days and try to explain things to him, but with this sudden turn of events, all her planning had gone haywire.

It was evening; Tuku did not come back. Rina waited for him with bated breath. Night came and departed. It was another day. There was no sign of Tuku – not that day, nor the next. Four days passed but Tuku did not return. On the fifth night, there was a soft knock on the door. Rina was jolted out of sleep; her body was trembling in fear.

"Didi, open the door." Tuku's voice came from the other side of the door. Rina jerked the door open. Tuku and three or four other boys stood outside.

"Is there something to eat?" he asked urgently.

Rina had not cooked. She was not able to think properly. She rushed into the kitchen, soaked some flattened rice in a bowl of water, strained out the water and, after adding some sugar to it, handed the bowl to Tuku and his friends. Then she slumped on the floor, worn out.

"Listen, *didi,* the police are after us. But we haven't killed that man. You must trust me, *didi,* some others murdered him and are trying to frame us." Tuku was gasping for breath. Rina's gaze traveled to the pistol and knives which they had put down on the floor. She was startled as if she had seen a snake.

"These are nothing didi, just for self-defense. We are wandering here and there, hiding from the police. We are compelled to keep these things, just in case. Do you have some money?' Tuku asked impatiently.

Rina hurried towards her tin box and took out all the money from it, including the small coins. She counted the money – five hundred fifty-six rupees in all — and handed it over to her brother. Tuku snatched the money from her hand. He and the others went out through the backdoor and disappeared into the darkness. Rina felt her legs weakening and sat down at the very place where she had been standing. She sat huddled up through the rest of the night. When it was daylight she got up somehow and attended to the domestic chores with much effort. A few Anganwadi children had turned up; she gave them some singing practice. She thought she would cook for them but she felt so disturbed that she had to abandon the idea. She gave each of them a couple of biscuits and sent them back. Rabi Jani came in the afternoon. "Shall I get water?" he asked Rina.

"Have you seen Ratan Singh?" Rina asked him and he shook his head.

She secured the front door and came out onto the road soon after Rabi Jani left. She began walking in the direction of Ratan Singh's house, hoping that Ratan Singh would come riding his motorbike at any moment. But the road was completely deserted. She trudged on. By the time she reached Ratan Singh's house, about three kilometers away, she was out of breath. It was quite late in the evening. To her disappointment, both the rooms were locked from the outside. She sat down for a while on the verandah to rest her legs. There was not a soul around, nor was there any chance of getting a little water to wet her parched throat. She half ran, half walked back to the Anganwadi centre. She spent a sleepless night, sick with worry. In the morning she decided that she must find Ratan Singh at any cost. If she did not find him in his house, she would go down to the market and look for him in his usual haunts. "I must, by any means, make him meet Tuku, explain everything and remove the suspicion and ill-feeling they have for each other", she kept saying to herself all day, as if reciting a litany.

Rina moved in and out of the house gripped with anxiety, waiting for the sun to set. She did not have the patience to wait for dusk: she took out her bicycle, locked the door and rode away. It would take her some time to reach Ratan Singh's house, riding uphill along that winding road.

At a little distance from the house, Rina hid her bicycle behind some wild bushes by the roadside and soft-footed down the road towards the back door of the house to avoid being seen by any passer-by. The back door was open. Rina could see a big car parked outside the house. Perhaps Ratan Singh had company. She usually came to this house only if Ratan Singh asked her to, because most of the time he was out, or with friends.

Rina hesitated a little. Should she go in? Most probably there were others in the house along with Ratan Singh. It would not be wise to go inside. Maybe she should call him out.

Still undecided, Rina moved towards the house, a step at a time. Instead of entering through the back door she took a turn to the left and stood below the window. Standing on tip-toe she stretched forward a little and tried to peep through the window. The sound of laughter floated out through the room. Rina waited a while hoping to meet the boy who cooked for Ratan.

"These tribal people are so simple that they will never suspect anything, even if someone cuts their feet away under them," Rina heard someone say. It was Ratan Singh's voice.

"But those boys are really smart. It was they who killed Pradip", someone else remarked.

"Don't worry, we'll get them soon. I have managed to trap their leader's sister and we will come to know of their whereabouts from her." It was Ratan Singh again.

Rina could not believe her ears; could this be Ratan Sigh speaking?

"You are an expert at trapping girls!" a voice said admiringly. "Otherwise, life would be boring in a place like this. What is she like?"

"A real masala dish! Wait until you get a taste!" Ratan Singh said. A burst of vulgar, raucous laughter followed.

Rina turned into stone. Her head whirled. She was not able to decide whether she should go in and reveal her presence or return unnoticed.

"But aren't you afraid of AIDS, brother? We need to take precautions."

"Yes, you must be careful. Anyway, the road will be built in a few months and then we can all go home. Why bother?"

"But Pradip's death must be avenged."

Without turning, Rina moved back carefully, step by step. The jungle was so dangerously quiet that the sound of a foot treading on a dry leaf could have been heard.

There was no time to take the bicycle out of the place where she had hidden it. She ran blindly through the forest, trampling the wild bushes and undergrowth, getting bruised and scratched by the spiky creepers that were entangled with one another. She seemed to be running for her life, as though the men in the room were chasing her.

More surprise awaited her at the Anganwadi centre. The front door was open. A friend of Tuku's was pacing about in front of the house; perhaps he kept vigil over the place. He stopped when he saw Rina. Without a word she half walked and half ran into the house. In a corner of the veranda sat Tuku and some of his friends. Rina did not wait to look at them properly, nor did she say anything to Tuku. She ran straight into her room.

The forty-watt bulb in her room gave out a very dim light because of the low voltage. Rina stood before the small mirror hanging on the wall. She was startled at the sight of her reflection.

"Do you know, *didi*? The fellow that murdered that contractor has been caught this afternoon. There is a rumor that the killer belonged to a rival group," Tuku said standing at the door; there were eagerness and relief in his voice.

Rina turned and stood to face her brother. Tuku stopped short. Even in that dim light, he could see the scratches on his sister's face; he could see the thin line of blood that trickled down her cheek. She had not worn a dupatta over her dress. A portion of the left sleeve of her kameez was torn and hung awkwardly. Tuku stood still as a statue for an instant.

'Didi, what happened? Who has done this? Tell me!" The

grimness in Tuku's voice was frightening.

Rina stood woodenly holding her head down. Tears had begun to well up in her eyes.

"Didi, I am asking you something!" Tuku roared. His friends sitting on the veranda heard him and came there. Standing behind him they tried to peep through the door.

"It was he – that contractor sir and his friends", Rina's tone was calm and clear. She fixed her eyes on Tuku's face. She did not blink even once while she said this although tears ran down her eyes.

"Where are they?"

"In his house."

Rina shifted her gaze towards Tuku's friends standing behind him.

Without uttering a word Tuku turned and stormed out of the room. His friends followed him. Moving with the speed of lightning they reached the other end of the veranda and the clash of metal on metal was heard. Rina tried to see – there were knives and other weapons in their hands that glittered in the dim light. Tuku and his six friends leaped away like wild animals and melted in the darkness in an instant.

Rina stood still at the threshold holding the door in both hands and kept looking into the darkness. Tears trickled down her eyes.

Original Odia: *Kurei Phula*

■

The Road Inwards

Written and Translated by
Adyasha Das

Smita had had a great passion to have a career soon after her marriage. Couldn't she have managed a small job after her masters in History? However Ambuj, her husband, was not only hesitant, but also not too enthusiastic about her plans. So Smita knew for certain that she would have a lot of spare time throughout her life. But she could never clearly fathom how such a torrent of work enveloped her.

Time meanders easily, even through hills and valleys. They had been at Kasauli for fifteen years. By the grace of God, their small family lived blissfully. Tuku, their only son, was known all around as a good student. The best thing about staying in a small town was that everyone knew each other. Ambuj was now the Principal of his school. He remained tied up with his work. Smita's dream and entire time was focused on Tuku. Ambuj would pester Tuku with his studies the minute he got back from work, would tire him out with his penchant for hard work. Then they would both get busy talking about the whole world. Smita would wonder if their world was different from that of hers. At times, Smita would feel very lonely and would go into one of her silent spells, especially with Ambuj. But what was the gain? Ambuj had no time to spare when Tuku was around. Even Tuku would get irritated if she smothered him too much with her love and care and would say, "Have you forgotten that I'm growing up?" Smita would reply, "Parents do get old but not all the Tukus!"

It had been two months since Tuku had shifted to Delhi for his engineering course. But Smita could not get out of her old habit. She would get up in the middle of the night to give Tuku his customary glass of milk. The house felt so deserted. Yet Ambuj always reassured her with his presence. They almost went back to the initial days of their marriage. They ventured out to every nook and corner of Kasauli. Smita had once nurtured many romantic dreams — they would go to an unknown destination, forget the world and she would be immersed in discovering Ambuj. She had not imagined this great wave of love cascading over them once again after all these years! After so many years, where did this novelty come from? Ambuj's handsome appearance belied how beautiful he was within. Often Smita had thanked her destiny for a companion like him. Not only his honesty but the desire to help all made him popular with everyone. They went on long walks in the mornings. With his jokes and clever repartees, Ambuj would turn each morning into an enchanting gift for her. While leaving for office, he would give some task, "Read that book. We will discuss after I return."

At times, Smita reminisced her fond dreams of the yester-years, to have a dynamic career, to make a unique contribution to society. She had been famous in her college as a brilliant student. But her parents hurried her into marriage when they found Ambuj as a prospective groom. After that, she had had neither time, nor inclination for a career. She had become completely dependent on Ambuj. In a certain way, Ambuj liked that.

They had begun the construction work of their house in Kasauli sometime back. There was a great piece of history to this house. When Ambuj applied for a bank loan for the plot of land, Smita felt her ties with her homeland Odisha on the verge of being severed forever. She tried her best to persuade Ambuj. "How can we possibly stay in this hilly area when we grow old? Who will be there for us in our time of need?'

Ambuj's easy answer was, "Don't you worry. I'll send you off first. You can't manage without me at all. "The house looked so different from its blue-print on completion. Just like kids never resembled their childhood photos. Ambuj's favourite garden sprawled right in front of the house, laden with a wide variety of fruits and flowers. From the first day of buying the plot, both would collect plants from all over and fill in the garden. By the time the construction work got over, the garden was in full bloom. Every decision regarding the house including choice of fittings and fixtures for each room, colour combination etc. had been made judiciously and after due deliberation. The silhouette of the mountains streamed in through the windows. As though, the Himalayas swung in the house like the curtains.

The house had been a mute witness to so many special events. Tuku's wedding feast had been organized right in front of the house, in the big field. Relatives from home, almost the whole of Kasauli turned up to bless the newly-weds. While they were returning to their place of work, Tuku had gifted his father a car. Ambuj's favourite model- Maruti Zen. Their small boy was now a capable man and thought about his parents comfort. The car had taken them on countless rides on those hilly roads to unknown destinations. It was their excuse to get lost on those anonymous roads. On these solitary rides, Ambuj often drew her close and promised to be her companion for seven lives. Smita was always amused by this adolescent streak in him, as though he had never really grown up.

Ambuj had driven to the nearby town that day for a meeting. After she was done with cooking, Smita was busy in the garden. Being busy always felt good when Ambuj was away.

Ambuj was unusually late that day. In case of delay, he normally called. At that moment, an employee from the school gave her the news- Ambuj had met with an accident on the way back. Smita could not recall the sequence of events after that. But, like a water bubble, Ambuj was gone, forever, beyond the Himalayas. Such an adept driver he had been. How could he have miscalculated at that turning which pushed him with the car into a deep abyss? Smita had become maddened with grief. How could their precious bond of many years get over in a second? Ambuj had been her whole world, her parents, relatives, friends, everyone and everything. Was he gone forever or just away for a brief spell? Tuku and his wife diligently completed the last rites. After consulting with the doctor, they decided to take Smita with them to Delhi for a change of place. Tuku's wife coaxed her, "Ma, come with us for a few days. Once you feel better, you could return." Tuku was irritated. "Where will she return? Now on, we have to look after her," he said firmly. Smita felt disoriented. She had only wanted to be dependent on Ambuj. Not on anyone else.

Before leaving, she locked up each room, closed the doors and windows. When she was covering the sofa, the tears broke her wall of control and submerged her. So many memories, still so alive and warm...so many yearnings still lingering, half-completed dreams...Oh Ambuj!

Through the rear window, Smita kept gazing at the house as the car started. She felt a choking guilt, as if she was deserting Ambuj, leaving him all alone. Though Kasauli and Delhi were in the same country, they felt far apart, separated geographically and mentally. Delhi residents led breathless lives. Tuku and his wife were immersed in their work. But she always felt Ambuj beckoning her to return, sulking at her absence. Who would take care of his needs? Smita convinced the kids and returned home to Kasauli. On her return journey, she felt her palpitation increase at a strange feeling, a muffled whisper, and "Come back to me". Smita's mind hopped back to her train journeys back home during her holidays. What heavenly joy she experienced when she met her parents! It was always like seeing something familiar in an alien landscape. Would Ambuj appear like that between the hills? So many cobweb-smeared memories, yellowed with age…their very first Kasauli trip… all flashed before her.

Such a big world and Smita was so unwanted. She was not indispensable for her kids anymore. They were modern, practical. The only person who would have wanted her, could not have done without her, left so hurriedly- from their house, from her world, from this world! So many moments, endless, like the sand-grains on the sea-shore; how would she spend time all alone? Once she reached the house, Smita was deeply agonized. From the curtains to the furniture, even the tea-cups held some trace of memory, had his typical smell on them. An old watchman still worked for them. Apart from him, Smita only had Ambuj's memories to be with her in the long journey of life.

It was only on the third night that Smita felt something was amiss, like something just was not right. Often when Ambuj would be in a pensive mood and Smita tried to make him laugh, he would ask to be left alone and say, "I'm not in a great mood. I don't know why I am feeling sour." Exactly like that, Smita just was not having a cheerful mood. Wherever she looked in the house, she saw a shadow of restlessness. The shadow had an uncanny resemblance to Ambuj. She mocked at her obsessive mind. But that night, sleep eluded her. As stray thoughts invaded her mind, she suddenly, unmistakably heard footsteps on the stairs. Someone was coming up the stairs. She sat up on the bed with a start. Often Ambuj would go down in the middle of the night to the kitchen and would return with a glass of milk or some light snack. The same sound…rhythm of the footsteps…identical creak of the stairs. Was it Ambuj? Could it really be him?

Smita was swamped by a shower of sweat. Her throat was dry. She could not even call anyone at this unearthly hour. She put on all the lights of the room and sat leaning to the bed. As she closed her eyes, yet again, the sound of the footfalls. Instantly she opened her eyes. Ambuj was looking straight at her, deeply from the framed photo on the wall. Oh Lord, what kind of a trial was this? Ambuj's sudden exit from her life was as lethal as death. Yet why was she filled with such an uncontrollable fear at these signs of his return? Smita kept up her silent vigil like a statue till it was dawn. The thin, gold sunrays of the dawn melted her conflict. She broke down and cried. Perhaps her tears were the only recourse to fathom that her beloved Ambuj was with her, all the while. Yet she found this unacceptable. How strange this mind was!

Smita felt that things had changed. The head of the house had suddenly become a guest, who stealthily crept in without invitation. She became moist with a tender despair. Desperately, she clung to the loneliness all around. Maybe she would touch Ambuj this way. That night she called the watchman's grand-daughter to sleep in the same room. The rickety sixteen year old had the entire night's sleep shutting her eyes from the very first moment. The sleep did not go even with the arrival of morning's sunlight. Smita felt re-assured that if not anything else, at least they were together in the house at night. But despite her being there, Smita continued to feel Ambuj's presence night after night. Sometimes she would be startled in the morning. Who had covered her so tenderly with the quilt? At times, Ambuj entered through the barred windows and teased her cheek with the feather-touch of the breeze.

Kasauli was a sleepy town. The roads were deserted even during the day. Smita became a member of the local ladies club. At least, an excuse to get out of the house. But on her return, Ambuj troubled her even more at night. The water tap would suddenly start running in the nearby bathroom. Every corner of the house had a voice of its own and she was deafened by the cacophony. Smita feared each moment of the day and night in the house. She wanted to keep busy, to ward off the thoughts of Ambuj. But he coursed through her veins. How could she ever forget him?

In that intense solitary confinement, there was a voice reaching out to her. The loneliness spoke to her in Ambuj's voice. But she had no inclination to listen. That muffled voice followed her all around. Smita was not keeping well, had no desire at all to eat. She had no friends. Along with Ambuj, she had lost touch with all of them. Tuku and his wife called regularly. Tuku would sense the desolation in her voice and snap at her, " Why did you go back there? How will you like it all alone?" Smita had toyed with the idea of shifting to Tuku's place in Delhi. But the very next moment she would be soaked with guilt. What about Ambuj? Would she be a dutiful wife if she deserted him? Smita was angry with herself. Why had she ever made Ambuj promise never to leave her, to always be with her?

Her mind was a sea of questions. She had loved Ambuj deeply. Yet why did she resent his presence now? Why was she always so apprehensive? In their own home, Ambuj's quiet presence, his trapped spirit choked her. He had been her sole companion in all the trials and tribulations of life. Yet his intimacy drove her to the edge of sanity now. An intangible presence made her grieve and yearn. Her deserted figure roamed around aimlessly in the deserted garden. The trees were shapeless, not trimmed since ages. The flowers were a poor consolation with their wan smile. It was a dusky evening with a kaleidoscope of light and dark unevenly spread out in the garden. Suddenly Smita felt a jolt and slipped. Had it not been for the old watchman, she would have straight gone down the jagged hill side. She had read somewhere that progress was impossible if one walked looking downwards. Only those who search for their dreams in the limitless horizon move forward in life. But Smita's vision had been fixed on Ambuj.

Oh God! Smita was appalled at the thought taking shape in her mind. This fall that was averted narrowly, was it what Ambuj wanted? Did he want her to go too? Just the same way as him? Smita felt an aversion searing through her at her thoughts. There was a time when she had contemplated death after Ambuj's sudden exit. Yet today, she had such a sea-change in her opinion? Of course Smita knew all about the great selfish love we all had for our own self. But what was Ambuj trying to convey? What was the smoldering language of this faceless, body-less love? Ambuj had been light, colour and music in her life, the beginning of many fond dreams. 'Often Smita saw his faceless, formless presence. She tried to understand his message in the sounds of the house, the trickle of water from the tap. In doing so, her health was failing. Tuku was exasperated. Time and again he had wanted to take her to him. Finally, he gave his verdict, "I'll sell off the house. You will never think of moving otherwise."

Smita was deeply wounded. She revolted firmly. "This house is your father's dream. He had worked so hard to realize it. Why do you need to sell it off?' How could Smita convince her son that Ambuj was continuing to live in that house? How could he sell off his father's formless presence?

The doctor had insisted on regular walk. She did not have much work in the house except dusting and tidying up, an old habit. Smita enjoyed her daily walk through lanes and by-lanes. She had discovered many unknown, unfrequented roads. At times cloudy skies, tender sunshine, or even misty mornings saw her sojourns. She enjoyed the incredible paintings of nature. Unknown landscapes and faces spoke to her.

She would pass by many old houses on her daily route. They smelled of disuse. Smita pondered about the people who had lived in those houses at one time. These houses were the mute witness of so many happy and sad moments. Most houses had someone living in the out-house. They would recount the saga. About a lone widower or a lonely lady staying by herself. The children were always in some other place. At times the house passed on to new owners. But the people who had once lived there were fond characters to be discussed and often became legendary. Many houses were locked and barred. Many stood as sentinels of past aristocracy. But Smita never felt the houses were empty. Beyond the locked and barred doors and windows, in the shadows and dust, in the faint creaks of the house, she spotted the royal characters of the past. She heard their whispered loving consultations just like she heard Ambuj's. The practical kids of the new age would laugh at her. But Smita had been a dreamer all life. How soon this life flows form present to past, House, family, children, social status, how soon they disappear with a gust of wind. She knew someday she too would go, in the road Ambuj had taken. Like her, others would pass by their house and talk about them, "What a unique couple they were".

The nights ushered in apprehension. The conflict of wanting Ambuj yet hesitant to face his formless presence continuously went on. Her mother had often told them in childhood that fear was a myth, an illusion of the mind. Beautiful, ugly, fear, courage all were the handiwork of the mind. When the mind was weak, fear would enlarge in size. Smita remembered one line her mother used as a moral to the story, "The longest road is inwards, leading deep within yourself."

Smita began walking on that road. She opened up Ambuj's home, the doors and windows of the locked house and her locked mind. She faced the reality. There was no return journey for passengers who left this world, renouncing every worldly pleasure and pain. So how could Ambuj ever retrace his steps? It had all been the creation of her mind. Many rishis and poets had fallen in love with the terrific beauty of the Himalayas, had given up their lives in pursuit of salvation. If Ambuj was here, it would be a spiritual reawakening for her.

Early morning the next day she called Tuku, "I am feeling better after a long time. I have just realized that I have not even discovered this place; there's so much to see and know. I have lot of work left here. Of course I will visit you sometime. Your father is here with me. Don't think again about selling off the house. Maybe you could do that after I go."

Not just the vision of the Himalayas, but the whole mountain range was in her house that day. So much beauty, peace and tranquility it had. In her journey inwards, Smita was exploring the legends the Himalayas had to share. So many of them, lost in time. So many of them still to be written in icy letters .By the time it would all end, she would have lost her eyesight. But the divine vision needed to read it would not be there. Not even Tuku would have that. He would be busy poring through his glasses, drawing up the sale amount of the house that had been a legend.

Original Odia: *Bhitaraku Rasta*

Hide and Seek

Written and Translated by
Manas Panda

O ne... Two... Three... Four... Five...
Nine... Ten... Lulu was counting
restlessly without a break.

Ninety...while uttering the number
she suddenly realized that she had been
trying to accomplish the task rather in a
hurry and that she had inadvertently
dropped ten or twelve numbers during the
process. A sense of shame together with
repentance spread through her and choked
her voice.

Ninety-one... she paused a while and
pulled herself together to utter the next.

A loud ninety-two... followed by
another pause.

Ninety-three... followed by a quick but
loud warning... you are hiding or not.

Ninety-four... Ninety-five... and at
last hundred... She uttered the final word as
if she was in no mood to continue the
counting any further. Finally, when she

turned back, removing her fingers from her eyes, a desolate world greeted her.

Here I start the search... she announced in a loud voice, as if talking to nobody in particular and stepped into the bedroom with slow, steady steps. The space underneath the bed and the large almirah, the gap between the book-shelf and the wardrobe... a strange vacuum reigned everywhere.

She carefully stepped into the next bedroom and scanned the spaces beyond the divan, behind the sofa, under the table, the teapoy, and the heap of bed linens. But no... there was no trace of him. Now she checked the bathroom, kitchen, the god's room, store room, and the rest part of the living room. All the available spaces where one could safely hole up had been carefully scanned but there was hardly any trace of Kunu. Had he evaporated like water vapour?

Kunu...come out...don't you hide anymore...I have already marked you. While announcing this usual cunning message to befool him, Lulu felt as if her voice was slightly trembling. She waited for a while with the belief that little Kunu would suddenly emerge from nowhere and start rolling on the ground upon the discovery that he had been befooled and vanquished. But where was he?

A little apprehensive, she glanced beyond the gate through the front door, verandah, and the lawn. Had he crossed the gate and escaped onto the main road in an effort to emerge a winner? Overtaken by the feelings of worry and dread, she clutched the iron-grill and sat down with a thud.

Kunu...hey Kunu...where are you? The pitch of her voice turning gradually indistinct gave way to a faint wailing.

It was evening by the time Anita left her office. As the road outside her office was deserted and lonely, she realized it was difficult to find a rickshaw for her return journey. To her misfortune, the rickshaw puller who used to carry her daily to and from office was absent as his daughter had been admitted in the hospital for child-birth. After dropping her at the office in the morning he said, "Mam, my daughter is admitted in hospital. I have to reach there soon. If possible, give me some money. You may deduct the amount of advance from my fee. I may not turn up in the evening. If I don't reach in time, please don't wait for me."

Well, she wouldn't wait, but how would she get home? Would she fly there? Had it not grown dark, there would have been a chance of hiring a rickshaw or an auto-rickshaw or even asking someone for a lift. But the unending year-end workload in March had dimmed all such possibilities.

Anita stared again at both ends of the road in despair. No hope. The children would be there at home alone. Who knows whether they would have eaten anything or not? While leaving for office, she had cooked parathas and potato curry and asked the children to eat that. Lulu in fact had assured her saying that she would feed her younger brother. Nothing to worry about that.

At times, Anita would feel amazed at the sense of responsibility that Lulu, studying only in class five, displayed. How old she would be! Hardly nine or ten. She was extremely careful about her younger brother and kept a strict vigil on his movements.

On the other hand how naughty that five year old lad was! He would start avoiding a reading of the lessons, on some pretext or another, the moment he sat down to read. There would be no end to his mischief even at the dining table. Every other day, there would be complaints from teachers or friends. Anita would fly into an uncontrollable rage at times; she would then beat him black and blue. After the thrashed child had gone to bed in an empty stomach, the mother and daughter duo would indulge in a spell of wailing and seek repentance. No one knew how they consoled each other. The night's tension and fasting would come to an end only the following morning and normalcy would be restored. Anita would hardly get any time to conduct a postmortem of the night's events as she would remain extremely busy with her daily chores like preparing breakfast and lunch-packets, sending both the children to school, readying herself for office, and a countless other chores of daily life.

Oh…no… it was going to be seven; Anita looked at her watch. There might be a rickshaw at the next crossing. Though a posh and aristocratic one, this part of the city was less crowded. There were wider roads but hardly any traffic. The freshly painted pavements looked deserted in the day time too. But the old town was too noisy, crowded, and congested. Her quarters were situated at the edge of that road. Anita hurried her steps the moment she was reminded of her lonely children.

Walking alone was no more a dreadful and difficult affair for her; it had turned a habit with her. Who knew, Amar, her husband would leave her alone half-way through the life's journey. One day he set out to office in a very pleasant mood but his lifeless body, a lump of flesh, returned home. She had no alternatives, rather than walking the life-path all alone.

A shiver ran down Anita's spine the moment she opened the gate and stepped onto the compound. The front door lay wide open. A ray of light straying outside blended with the darkness outside and created a strange pattern. Lulu sat, on the uppermost step, with her head tucked between her knees, like the ducks on the bank of the pond after a swim.

"What happened, dear? Why haven't you switched on the lights of the verandah? Why are you sitting here like this? Has Kunu gone somewhere?" Anita directed a volley of questions at Lulu, while closing the gate and entering the compound. She was surprised to find Lulu not providing any answers to her questions. She appeared jolted and flabbergasted. Her pale face and quivering lips implied a mystery that Anita couldn't decipher.

"What happened? Have you two fought with each other once again?" Anita bowed down near the face of her daughter and asked. Lulu's sobs, hitherto suppressed, got an opportunity to explode. Anita threw a cursory glance around the house but the naughty lad was nowhere to be seen. Anita felt a little discomforted.

Every moment she expected someone to drop in, suddenly or with careful steps, startle her up with a 'ho' shout, dance at the prospect of having startled her up, jump into her lap disregarding her discomfort and fatigue, pull at her hair for getting so late, demand punishment for Lulu for having teased and beaten him, narrate the incidents at school etc.

But...no... she could only hear an indistinct sobbing noise. There was none other than a small girl looking completely disheveled with her tear, fear and sobs.

Anita was dumbstruck. Tell me... what happened...tell me. Anita picked Lulu up by her shoulders and looked straight into her face.

Tell me...what happened? Anita found her sobs choking her voice. Her own failure to make Lulu stop sobbing and come out with an answer unnerved her.

Lulu raised her head and looked into her mother's face. In a voice reflecting her concern she said,

"I am not finding Kunu...uuu...uu...u. We were playing hide and seek after lunch. It was his turn to hide. I kept counting and he went to hide. By the time I finished counting up to hundred, he had disappeared. I searched for him everywhere but in vain."

Anita felt like bursting out into a laugh. "Why are you crying so much? Don't cry. I thought some evil had befallen. He must have gone to some neighbour's house. He will come back on his own. Let me have a change of clothing. We will search for him in the neighbourhood. He must be watching TV in someone's house."

While consoling her daughter, Anita stepped inside. She changed her saree. After the day's hard work at office and the subsequent worries, she felt benumbed by an excruciating pain. A cup of tea might rejuvenate her. As she entered the washroom, she found Lulu sitting near the dining table with her teary and expectant eyes directed towards the outer room.

She came forward, held the little angel in her arm and wiped out the tear drops. "Don't worry, baby, everything will be okay. Let me come out. You do one thing. Fetch the milk-pot from the refrigerator. We will prepare tea and go together in search of him." Lulu obeyed her and went to the kitchen. While a splash of cold water was wiping the tiredness off Anita, a loud scream left her flabbergasted.

What's the matter with you now? She rushed towards the kitchen while droplets of water were still running down her face. She stood transfixed at the door of the kitchen.

The doors of the refrigerator inside the kitchen were wide open. Little Kunu was hiding there in the lower berth of the large refrigerator—in a sitting posture. A thick layer of ice had covered his body. His wide open jolly eyes were saying that he had been victorious in the game of hide and seek with his sister. His little face sported a smile reflecting that he had vanquished his sister.

The senseless body of Lulu lay on the floor adjacent to the refrigerator. She had been defeated miserably in the game.

Anita felt as if the ground underneath her feet was going to collapse. She sank to the ground and lay there motionless.

Original Odia: *Luchakali*

The Duma

Ranjan Pradhan

Translated by **Pravat Kumar Mallick**

Sarabu Muduli sighed deeply and rested for the last time under the large Salap tree that seemed to have touched the sky.

The large branches of the Salap tree waved in the wind and produced a hissing noise that distracted him.

At the top of the tree was tied an earthen pitcher for collecting Salap juice. A Myna bird sat on a branch nearby. The vast open sky spread above.

Sarabu looked at the Salap tree for a long time. This Salap tree sheltered the Dumas (Holy Spirit) since the time of his father and forefathers. Their Dumas moved around this tree, in the air, and in the sky. Today, they will have to severe their connections with this Salap tree, this earth and this sky and leave for an unknown distant land.

Sarabu Muduli once more sighed deeply. Alas, he had to face this sort of banishment from homeland towards the fag end of the life! A gust of cool breeze made him unmindful.

Not far away from the eyes stood the hill of Budha Raja, which housed Lord Budha Mahapuru. People celebrate his festival in the month of Asadha (rainy season) amidst great pump and show. This hillock of Budha Raja too will be submerged under water. Oh, how painful it was to think of!

Having returned from Khatiguda, Robert Domb announced that towards today's evening or tomorrow's noon the whole village shall be submerged. After hearing this tragic news all the Parojas of the village had lost their sleep.

The moment the news that the whole village shall be submerged reached, the Parojas ran helter skelter in panic.

Oh, watch; *Nisani Munda* (place of tribal worship) is getting washed away, *the Dumas* are leaving, *the Dadibudha* (a village deity) is flowing away, the Salap and Mahua trees are getting submerged, the *Dokari Pokhana* (the divine old stone) is getting submerged in the water of the reservoir. In dread of being affected by this flood, all the Parojas began running here and there.

The construction of the proposed dam shall submerge their *Dangar* (hill); their home and hearth of several generations shall be washed away. *Nisani Munda* shall lose its existence in the whirlpool of several feet high water. Their village, the *Dumakudi* (graveyard), the *Dangar* (hill) and everything dear to them shall be drowned for all time to come in water several fathom deep. The existence of the Dumas will be under threat and they shall abandon the land. All the corn fields producing *jana* (maize), *jandiri* (millet), *alasi* (mustard) shall be inundated by flood water. With such evil thoughts and apprehensions making their heads heavy, all the Parojas finally surrendered themselves before their village deities, Dumas and all the gods and goddesses and sought their merciful intervention in saving the village from the impending danger.

May whatever it be, this is our village. The Duma, the sky, the earth, the jhola (spring), the dangar (hill), the sweet gentle breeze, the tall Salap trees, the cooling shadows of the Mahua trees, the streams, rivers everything belonging to this village are ours. Why should we go elsewhere abandoning everything that is ours?

The holy spirit of our forefathers fly in the sky in form of Duma. They keep a watch on everything and protect us from all sorts of dangers. The worries of Parojas in this way went on increasing.

They shall have to leave their home and hearth of several generations; the land and everything belonging to their forefathers. They shall have to be rehabilitated in areas unknown and unfamiliar to them. They shall have to acquaint themselves with the air, water, sky and earth of the new village, with everything strange and novel to them. To think of living in such a place sent shivers down their spine. Sarabu Muduli, the village headman thought a lot regarding all these problems. He sat silently for a while and thought deeply about the many vicious thoughts that enveloped his mind. The village was going to face a great danger. All the dumas, gods and goddesses have become angry with this village. What steps he should take as the head of village to dispense with the crisis! He thought seriously over this issue and decided to consult with the *disaris* (astrologers), *pujaris* (priests) and *rayats* (villagers).

After a few days waters several fathoms deep would submerge everything. The narrow walking path leading to the *dangar* (hillock) through the *jana field* (maize field) would be washed away. The *dangar, jhola, alasi field, the Salap trees, the Baali kudia* (worshipping place), the seats of Bhima Debata and goddess Darni mata would be lost out of the sight. Waves would dance on the surface of the blue waters of the reservoir. In apprehension of an unknown danger Sarabu Muduli felt helpless.

The dam was nearing completion. After the completion of the embankment on the Deopali side, their village will be submerged under water and they shall have to leave the village. For days together people have been discussing about these problems. A number of government officers and sahibs visited this village to convince the Parojas in favour of evacuating the village.

After hearing the message from Robert Domb, Sarabu Muduli became sure about the impending mishap. From that moment he made his heart as strong as stone. After his conversion into Christianity Robert Domb had become too much intelligent. He had all the latest news of the world with him. He used to visit Nabarangapur, Khatiguda, Bhabanipatna, Jayapur, Bhubaneswar and had contact with senior officers. He got all important news of the world through his missionary organization.

Soon, the residents of the village were found bemoaning. All the weeping *dokaras* (old men) and *dokaris* (old women) were seen rolling under the Salap and Mahua trees near *Nisani Munda* (place of worship). None of them was capable of consoling the other. The enormity of the problem had turned them dumb.

All the Parojas of the village were weeping pitiably. Having lost faith in all, they were now invoking the Dumas, gods and goddesses for help. Throughout the day all the Parojas were roaming around, feeling utterly helpless.

"Our godly Dumas will be lost in the water. Our great Lord Nisani Munda shall be submerged under water. The Dumas moving around the sky over our village shall go far away leaving us forever. Our Mahua tree, Sargi (Sal tree) and Salap tree shall be submerged under the water. Our Dangar (hillock) will be buried under water. Our rich corn field producing Jana, Jandiri and Kandul (Dal) shall be lost forever. This water shall make us orphan. We will become Dumaless. We will become helpless.

An unknown and unforeseen fear haunted all the Parojas. They were seen moving here and there like crazy animals. Some of them were seen wiping tear from their eyes. A few other Parojas having no ways out were still counting upon the mercy of the gods and goddesses.

O Gumani mother!

O Darni mother!

O Mauli maa Brotherrabi!

O Lord Bhima!

O Budha Raja! Please help us. Please save us from this impending danger.

Buddu Jani, the old and senior most Paroja of the village had made himself firm in this situation. He strongly believed that the Dumas or spirit of the forefathers belonging of seven generations moving in the areal world shall come to the rescue of the Parojas. He was not at all worried.

Buddu Jani was determined not to leave this homeland come whatever danger it may. Let water wash away everything, but he shall be here. Buddu Jani took an oath not to go elsewhere under any circumstance. These strong words of Buddu Jani no doubt gave much-needed hope and patience to the Parojas but a fear of the unknown continued to terrify them. The words of Robert Domb was adding fuel to fire.

All of a sudden Buddu Jani lay down prostrating before goddess Gumani just like an uprooted palm tree crashing to the earth in a storm. He started striking his head, hands and legs on the ground. The rib bones started trembling. He moved his head in a circular way. He gradually became motionless and started staring with bulging eyeballs. He exhaled strongly producing hissing sounds through his nostrils.

Whenever the spirit of Duma entered into the body of Buddu Jani, he behaved in this way. All the Parojas got panicked to see Buddu Jani in this form. An unknown fear gripped the entire village.

On the previous day, Rivini Sir (the Revenue officers), Rihabiliti Sir (the officers in charge of rehabilitation), RI Sir (The Revenue Inspector), and the forest officials were here to convince the people. A number of leaders, MLAs and ministers too were present at Khatiguda to sensitise people about the benefits of the dam. The proposed dam shall facilitate the welfare of the Parojas, Kondhs, Gadbas, Bhataras and other tribal. It shall make them civilized and ensure development of the region. The state will be self-sufficient in production of food grains. The entire Paroja society is bound to benefit from the project. They would get compensation for the loss of land. Hence all the leaders of the ruling party were busy in convincing the Parojas to cooperate with the government by evacuating the village.

In the meantime some leaders belonging to opposition party and some NGOs too were active in dissuading the Parojas to leave their land. They had already started an agitation against displacement. The movement against displacement had spread from village to the capital city of Delhi.

Sandwiched between these two parallel movements the poor innocent Parojas were rather getting confused. Most of the Parojas had started realising that there was no other way than leaving the village. Hence right from the early morning the Jhodia Parojas of Jhodiabadiguda were preparing themselves for evacuation.

Robert Domb issued a stern warning to the villagers to evacuate the village latest by afternoon of the day or next morning. Then he left for Khatiguda.

Ever since the construction work began, Robert Domb had gained a lot of importance and hence, he had very little leisure time at his disposal. He had turned a very busy man. Whosoever visited this village, never missed to meet him.

On the other hand, people from villages like Olaguni, Jholaguda, Gurumaiguda, Mandigumma, Aamaguda, Kukudakata, Baariguda, Dandabada, Jatiaguda, Kandhabadiguda, Goudamalatiguda, Tanganikot, Kapsiguda, Hiriguda, Mandra, Gothapadar, Sithikasili, Bendela, Naragan, Chandeipadar, Balighat, Dhepaguda, Haladisila, Angaraguda, Koraguda, Mundiguda, Nuajatiaguda etc. had started shifting. The government had sent heavy vehicles resembling big houses to carry these displaced people to their new destination.

Some people had already left for these new places in truck, tractor and dumpers engaged by the government. A few other Paroja old men and women were ready to be transported by trucks. The entire area was reverberating with their noise. The Parojas of Jhodiabadiguda were unable to take any concrete decision. *Naik* (village headman), *Pujari* (priest), *Chalan* (assistant to village headman), *Rayat* (villagers), Christians, Dombs and Mali (gardener) congregated together. They shall have to take the final decision immediately. Otherwise the situation might go out of the control.

The oldest Paroja, Buddu Jani sat down and took a long deep breath. He became sure that nothing good was going to happen. No one could save these haughty, arrogant, sinful, irreligious people who were bent upon destroying the beautiful creations of God like rivers, springs, hills and forests. How dare these people obstruct the flow of water in our rivers, streams and springs? Since time immemorial, since the time of our ancestors our streams and rivers have been flowing. It is the property of water to flow downwards with a murmuring sound. It is a great sin to prevent its flow. And these devils, antisocials, inhumans and man-eaters dare obstruct their flow by building dams. What shall be the consequence? These people shall all die. Everything will be destroyed. Astounded by the enormity of their sins, Buddu Jani lapsed into silence.

The changing pictures of every moment and the incidents taking place in the village were gradually making Buddu Jani bolder. His muscles were gaining more and more strength. Both his arms were becoming iron-strong, as if he was getting prepared to encounter all the forthcoming adverse situations. Yet an unknown dread was still haunting his heart.

O' Mother Gumani! Mother Mauli! Mother Brotherravi! Lord Bhima! Please come to the rescue of the Parojas. Please help them.

In case these deities get angry, everything will be destroyed. Unseen and unknown disasters might befall. These stupid Parojas do not think of this. Gusts of warm air coupled with thunderous noises escaped through the nostrils of Buddu Jani. It felt as if a furnace was set up in his chest which warmed up the air and pushed it through the nostrils.

Buddu Jani began to tremble helplessly. In fact he was at his wits end. What would happen, in case these Dumas and deities got angry, annoyed? Then who would come to rescue of these Parojas? The whole body of Buddu Jani started quivering in an unknown fear. Few drops of tear rolled down his cheeks onto the earth.

"O, my Paroja brothers, we should not foster the thought of going elsewhere abandoning this village."

Buddu Jani behaved almost like a mad man and uttered these words meant for the villagers loudly.

"O, my Paroja brothers, our Budha Raja, our Darni Mata, Gumani Mata, Mata Brotherrabi and Lord Bhima will protect us. Please have faith in them. Don't go elsewhere leaving your home land. Stick to this land. You will see the water of the dam would vanish. We shall stay here for all times to come." Buddu Jani cried.

Robert Domb did not appreciate these incoherent talks of Buddu Jani. He condemned Buddu Jani's words as utterances of a mad man. Hanging a bag from his shoulders he left for Khatiguda. Before leaving the spot he warned the villagers in the vilest language.

Go, bloody stupid Parojas, you all are wild, barbarian fools. You will rot here in this forest. You would have no ideas about the brighter world outside. The wrong advice of this old mad Paroja will finally lead you to the hell. It's for your good that the government is building a dam on river Indrabati. With the money granted by World Bank, the largest reservoir of Asia will be built by connecting Indrabati with other rivers like Muran, Podagada, Kapur and Chabri. Your lands shall have water for irrigation. Electricity will be produced and plants and factories will be set up. Towns and markets, schools and colleges will come up. You shall have all the amenities of modern life like park, aerodrome, road, railway, cinema hall and everything. Your illiterate children will be educated. They will know what promises the outer world holds for them. But you have all been biased by this foolish old man. Go and get ready for the new village.

Still these enticing words of Robert Domb could not please and move the people as expected. Buddu Jani placed his fingers on his ears and sat silently near the Nisani Munda and screamed at Robert Domb. Other Parojas pledged not to leave the village.

Robert Domb once more tried to coax and cajole the villagers in his attempt to make them follow his words.

"Hey, stupid fools, why don't you understand? Once Indrabati Dam is completed, this village will be over-flooded by water, several men high. Your homestead land, hill will be submerged forever under deep water. The depth of the reservoir shall be equivalent to the height of fifty men. No trace of your village shall remain. No Gumani Mata nor Lord Bhima can save you fool Parojas. It is worthless to believe what Buddu Jani says. You have all gone crazy. Be sensible and get settled at the new place. Don't allow yourself to be fooled by the words of that bloody Buddu Jani. This foolish old man has gone crazy and absurd like a lunatic. Evil thoughts are haunting before his death."

These irreverent and sinful words of Robert Domb made Buddu Jani fly into a rage. That blasphemous Domb boy has lost all his sense after his conversion into Christianity. Exposing his decaying teeth, grown weak from consuming regular tobacco and displaying bulging eyes Buddu ran after Robert Domb to kill him. Other Parojas present on the spot took away Robert Domb elsewhere and pacified Buddu Jani.

The village headman Sarabu Muduli was now convinced that Robert Domb was speaking the truth. Though a Christian Domb boy, he was not telling lies. Robert simply repeated what *Rivini Sir* (Revenue Inspector) and Rihabiliti Sirs were telling yesterday. Sarabu felt restless, unable to decide how to deal with the situation.

While Sarabu was engrossed in thoughts sitting at the foot of the Salap tree, Robert Domb appeared before him. Sarabu came back to his senses. Really, Robert Domb had much information about the outer world. Whatever information he had provided on earlier occasions, had already been proved true. Counting on Robert's warning he decided to convene a meeting of the community that evening.

The meeting was scheduled for the evening. The *Chalan* (assistant to village head man) made announcement about the proposed meeting by beating kettledrum at important public and private places. Just at the scheduled time in the evening, Sarabu Muduli appeared at *Berana Munda* (meeting place). Gradually, the Disari, Pujari and Rayats reached at meeting place one after another. The meeting continued for a long time. It was finalized in the meeting to vacate the village latest by tomorrow evening.

Robert Domb said, "It is being discussed at Khatiguda that latest by tomorrow evening the dam water will reach our village. The dam work is almost over. Countless officers have encamped at Khatiguda to deal with the emerging situations. They have been visiting the affected areas to convince the people."

The proactiveness of Robert Domb made Buddu Jani furious. For reasons not known, his hatred for Robert knew no bounds. He had been displeased with him from the very day he had associated himself with the Christian missionaries. Each and every act of Robert irritated him. That's why, he grumbled to show his irritation.

Robert Domb continued to speak. Arrangements had been made for the rehabilitation of the Dombs, Mali (gardener) and the Paroja in a new village. The rehabilitation colony had been set up near Sasahandi of Kotpad where two tube wells had been dug up. The village had been connected by cement and concrete road with provisions of electrification and telephone service. A school building was under construction. There was a huge playground at one end of the village. A cinema hall had also been set up.

Robert Domb swallowed a little spittle to moisten his throat, paused a little and said, "You beasts, uncivilised jungle Parojas live in the forest. You do not even own a guntha (4 decimal) of land. Still then the government has agreed to pay Rs. 20,000/- as compensation per acre. Can anyone of you tell me how many zeros are there in twenty thousand? If you wish good days to usher in, don't hesitate to go to the new place with the amount of compensation. Your fate will change. Your illiterate children, after receiving education, shall be appointed as officers and magistrates. Only then will you realise the righteousness of this Domb Christian."

After hearing all these words from Robert, Sarabu Muduli, the village headman remained silent for a while. *Disari*, the astrologer predicted that the villagers were going to hurl themselves into great danger by accepting the change. He further warned that the Dumas i.e. the spirits of their ancestors had become excessively aggrieved. Now no one could protect and save the village. After hearing these warnings Sarabu Muduli sat helplessly with his head resting on his hands.

The villagers felt distraught when they learnt that they were going to abandon the land of their ancestors. All the Parojas became anxious about what would happen. Water had already entered villages like Muran and Deopali which were close to the reservoir. Sarabu, the village headman warned that the same water would reach their village the following day. Hence he appealed to all to leave the village by tomorrow. The Village headman further declared at Berana Munda (meeting place) that before leaving the village they would have to appease Lord Bhima, Darni Mata and Dumas of their forefathers.

For this ritual it was decided that each resident of the village should supply a fowl. The village head man on his turn had to supply a tom goat and a sheep. Goddess Gumani, Kaladarni and Lord Bhima were to be worshipped and appeased by sacrificing these animals.

First of all the Dumas i.e. the holy spirits of the ancestor moving in the sky were to be invoked. They were to be satisfied through offering of blood of the sacrified animals. Sarabu Muduli announced the above decision at Berana Munda. All the Parojas agreed unanimously.

Robert Domb did not appreciate these formalities and deserted the meeting place. He proceeded to the newly built church at one end of the village, touched the cross and prayed Lord Jesus. Then he planned to leave for Khatiguda the next day.

He was concerned with the money distributed at Khatiguda. He seriously thought about how to acquire some of this money. Khatiguda was an area without any connectivity and market place even a few days ago. But this forest area had turned into a prosperous town because of the dam. Robert became overwhelmed with joy.

Robert Domb was happy to see big palatial buildings being constructed at Khatiguda. Giant machines had been set up there. Khatiguda had become noisy with the sounds of these machines and crowded with hotels, shopping malls, cinema halls, theatres and everything.

Everything symbolizing aristocracy such as fish, flesh and wine was plentily available at Khatiguda. O Lord Jesus, how great you are! It is because of you Khatiguda has been transformed into a heavenly place. Just a stray visit to Khatiguda either in the morning or evening was enough to fetch a fifty or hundred rupee note. Robert Domb analysed all these developments and became overjoyed.

Bloody indigenous Kondhas and Parojas could now become civilized! They shall now put on trousers and shirts in place of a piece of cloth covering the waist or loin. Robert Domb used some scathing remarks for these rustic Parojas, their mothers, sisters and ancestors. Then he left for Khatiguda. Now it has become his main duty to commute from his village to Khatiguda and vice-versa.

On completion of dam work Khatiguda would be transformed into a big city. Now the number of heavy and light motor vehicles has increased considerably adding more to the noise caused by plants and machines. O, what a mad rush in the restaurants and confectionaries opened by the sweet venders from Cuttack! The place boasts of hotels, cloth stores, jewelries, hospitals etc. All the engineers, contractors, doctors, police officers of Khatiguda are moneyed men. What matters there is, one should learn how to acquire money. Such thoughts were enough to provide a great deal of delight to Robert.

The panicked Parojas of Jhodiabadiguda were anxiously waiting for any information coming from Khatiguda.

The dam authorities were frequently announcing through mikes and loud speakers to vacate the village immediately. The water was expected to reach the reservoir latest by the same night. The construction of the dykes was nearing completion and those of tunnels almost completed. The earthen embankments near Podagada and Kapur had been completed. Some work near Muran was left to be completed. The main embankment over Deopali too was nearing completion. The water level of the reservoir had increased sufficiently to enter into some nearby villages.

Buddu Jani was not ready to accept such stupidity. In his

opinion, the Parojas were offsprings of nature. All these hills, forests, mountains and fountains belonged to them. How could the Parojas head for another destination leaving all these behind? Buddu Jani screamed at the top of his voice to display his anger and frustration.

Disari (the astrologer) had already warned about the dangers the village was going to face. No one had offered worship to Lord Bhima. The Parojas had neglected the worship of goddess Gumani. *Disari* had further studied the various signs and indications and confirmed that great harm was going to happen. This was due to the anger of gods and goddesses like Gumani Mata and Lord Bhima.

The villagers had to vacate the village latest by the following afternoon. No Paroja was able to sleep throughout the night. From early morning of the next day a few Parojas had already started demolishing their huts and collecting wooden beams, bamboo and straws from it. The women, girls and maidens were filling their baggage with clothes, brass utensils and corn flours of *Jana* (maize), *Jandiri* (millets) and *mandia* (ragi).

They would have to leave for a new place where firewood for cooking might not be available. Alien Dumas must be moving in the air. They would be presented with a new earth down below and a new sky above them. First, Nisani Munda is needed to be established there. Old Hundi god was to be installed and consecrated in the new village. Sarabu Muduli, the village headman was lost in thinking and planning. He had to initiate all these things as he was their head.

The sky was overcast with clouds the next morning. The rising sun had concealed his face at the back of the hill. The Parojas were busy with their tasks. As per the decision taken earlier at *Beran Munda* (village meeting place) fowls, goats, boars and male buffaloes were brought to the place of worship. The village priest sacrificed the animals and worshipped Darni mata, Gumani mata and Bhima Debata by offering them their blood.

Pujari (the village priest) had almost bathed in the blood of hundreds of fowls, goats, pigs and sheep. He had almost gone mad. *Shiras* (exorcist priests) were dancing with their matted hair hanging loose.

Now all the Parojas of the village recited in a chorus.

O the Duma, the holy spirit of our deceased forefathers!

O Goddess Gumani Mata!

O Lord Bhima!

O Goddess Darni!

Accept this blood. Drink till you are satisfied. Be pleased and bless all of us.

Your children have spent their days gracefully in the lap of nature for ages together. For generations together, they have lived happily on this earth, under this sky and in the lap of nature. But O dear Dumas what sin these innocent Parojas have committed? Why are you severing your relationship with them? Why are you punishing them with banishment?

Your innocent children, the Parojas, are now going to set up new homes on an alien land under a new sky. They all seek your blessings. O Duma God, punish them for their wrongs, forgive them and accompany them to their new land, new sky and new destination. But where shall you stay in the absence of jungles, hills, hillocks, caves, rivers and streams? You will all move around in the air and protect the Parojas.

The village presented a pathetic look with the Parojas weeping pitiably. Streaming blood of the fowls, goats and sheep had inundated the place of worship. The severed heads of the sacrificed animals were still lying and shivering on the ground. Bulging eyes from some other severed heads were as if gazing at the sky. The severed heads of animals, after shivering for a while, were becoming motionless and still.

The Parojas were weeping incessantly beating their heads on the blood drenched soil. Some other Parojas were smearing their head with the blood drenched soil. A few others were staring at the sky, beating their breasts and tummy, and bewailing the separation from their Dumas. *Dhangadas* (young men) and *Dhangidis* (young women) were behaving like lunatics while the adult women were dashing their heads on the earth.

Some other Parojas were seen running towards the Mahua trees and embracing them. Still some others were moving round and round before collapsing onto the ground. Their last moments with their earth, with their home and hearth that day were not only boisterous but also stained with blood.

At last the ritual and worship ended and the Parojas becalmed. In some, blood was oozing from fractured heads; some others found their eyes swollen. They all had smeared their bodies with the blood-drenched soil. After bewailing for hours the Parojas tried to become cool.

When normalcy was restored, they engaged themselves in arranging their bag and baggage. The administration had engaged heavy vehicles, as big as their homes, to transport the Parojas to their new destinations. The Parojas would go to the rehabilitation colony by these vehicles. However, the warnings issued by the village astrologer constantly rang in their ears. Sarabu Muduli, the village headman was moving here and there in great agitation. He ran here and there.

At this juncture Robert Domb appeared on the spot and said, "Do you know my Paroja brothers, the new village to which we will be shifted has electric lights. The school building has been completed and the village has been connected by a pucca road. Two tube wells have been dug. Like in urban centres, each Paroja family will be provided with a two roomed house. Our children will be admitted in to the school and shall be turned civilised through education.

The information of Robert Domb about the provision of electric light disturbed Buddu Jani mentally. Who could save these displaced landless Parojas from hell! Oh, what bad times! The Parojas living peacefully in the darkness of dense forest now shall live in houses lighted by electric bulbs. Will our Dumas, so dear to us, stay in a lighted area? They will go far away deserting us permanently.

Buddu Jani was unable to comprehend what was happening. He felt puzzled. Let it be so if this is what Gumani Mata desires. Helpless, he sat silently on the ground.

Buddu Jani shuddered at the thought of the disastrous consequences of the evil acts of the Parojas. They had been misled and the path they now trod on, disregarding their past, was a wrong one, he thought. He apologized to the Dumas; begged the village deity to provide them shelter and stared vacantly at the sky with rheum-filled eyes.

Disari, the astrologer too opposed the idea of having electric light in the new village. The Dumas, scared of these electric lights, shall not stay in the said village. He warned the villagers that this was nothing but premonition of a great disaster awaiting them.

If the Dumas deserted us, who would guard our paddy fields? Who would guard our jindiri, klandula, and suan fields? Who would protect us from dangers that befall us? Even the Disari made calculations with rice and announced that great dangers lay lurking if they went ahead with their decision. The village headman Sarabu Muduli shuddered to hear the predictions.

Robert Domb's joys knew no bounds. Today he would leave for the new village that boasted of all amenities like electric light, school building, dispensary and tube well.

The trucks engaged for carrying the villagers were waiting for them at the end of the village. The villagers one by one started loading their bag and baggage, firewood on the truck. Some other Parojas had assembled to see such heavy vehicles.

A Paroja exclaimed. "Oh, the government has sent moving houses for us. It shall of great joy to travel by this mobile van and gather experiences of flying and rolling at the same time.

Some of the Paroja boys assembled there felt happy to touch the wheels of the truck, press them or hold the steering of the truck out of curiosity. Sometimes the driver of the truck, with flowing moustache and beard, would press the horn to terrify the children. The buzzing sound of the horn prompted the boys to hop around.

All the villagers including the Parojas, Doms, Rayats, Naik and Chalan boarded the vehicle. Even after long persuasion, Buddu Jani declined to leave the village and sat silently on the Nisani Munda. Finally some Paroja young men forcibly lifted him and placed him on the truck. The truck proceeded towards its destination.

The plight of leaving the village, the pang of losing his home and hearth was agitating his heart. The ribs of Buddu Jani shivered fiercely. Buddu Jani felt as if his tired, exhausted and dying body was travelling in the truck. His heart had remained attached to the Salap tree of the village.

The trucks were moving from Jhodiabadiguda village towards resettlement colony at Sashahandi of Kotpad via Tentulikhunti, Nabarangapur and Borigumma.

The vehicles were running smoothly on the black top road leading from the village to town. The Parojas moving in these vehicles were feeling like proceeding towards a distant fairy land. Such an adventurous trip was giving immense pleasure to the Parojas. A few Parojas, while feeling thrilled, were also feeling frightened in anticipation of unforeseen troubles. While the Parojas were lost deeply in such thoughts, the vehicles carrying them reached the rehabilitation colony.

By the time they all reached the rehabilitation colony, the sun had already set. The entire village had been sprinkled with a blood-red hue.

In the night, the Parojas were busy enjoying delightful scenes of a movie on a mobile screen. Suddenly, a voice rose from somewhere, "Buddu Jani is no more. He has become a Duma."

Buddu Jani became the first Duma of the new village, the first Duma of the new sky, their Duma Debata.

Original Odia: *Duma*

■

Bonded Labour

Kshetrabasi Naik

Translated by **Sabahat Tabriz**

Two new members were added to Maguni
Bariha's small family. A pair of sturdy
oxen. They were as old as his son. Maguni was
extremely happy the day they were born. His
father was of the opinion that a female calf
would have continued the line of a milch cow.
Maguni had retorted "Bua, for you my wife
giving birth to a female child is ominous, but
you wish the cow to deliver a female calf?"
That had angered and irritated his father. But
had he been alive, he would have been no less
happy seeing these robust oxen. The milch
cow is no longer there, but its offspring! Oh
my God! They can work real hard, are able to
finish two days work in one day. You cannot
manage them on a plough unless you are very
strong. Maguni's land had never remained
unploughed. He looked after the oxen well,
kept the cowshed as clean as his home. Any
Lapses in the care of the oxen would infuriate
him. He would then shower abuses on his

wife, Kaincha. Kaincha, too, would acquiesce as if the neglect were indeed a sin. Then in a moment everything would be sorted out. Maguni believed that he owed the smooth running of his household to this pair of oxen. He used to worship his cattle along with the gods and goddesses on the day of the Harvest Festival. Thus, the oxen participated in all the ceremonies of Maguni's family.

Once, the village landlord's farmhand mercilessly beat Maguni's oxen. Maguni was out somewhere but as he came back, he saw his stout oxen writhing in pain. This made his hackles rise. He wanted to know who had made his oxen bleed. On his way home, the landlord's scunning farmhand gave Maguni a thorough dressing down. "Your two mammoth-like oxen are eating crops from the fields of others", he alleged. He cautioned Maguni to see to it that such incidents were not repeated in future. Before listening to what Maguni had to say about it, he asserted the justification of his act and threatened Maguni that next time if such a thing happened he would kill the oxen. Maguni could not stand his animals to be hurt by somebody. This was too much for him. Seeing blood oozing from the bruises of his oxen, tears kept streaming down his eyes. Kaincha came and tried to pacify him. She consoled him saying that they would get some medicine from the local medicine man. Maguni knew that Kaincha was talking sense but again he was livid with rage and wished to break those hands that had hurt his dearest oxen. He did not have a wink of sleep that night and felt as if he himself had been flogged. The next evening a lantern was lit at the centre of the village. The village headman (Panch) sat to hear Maguni's case. Maguni pleaded against the torture inflicted on his oxen. But not a word against the landlord escaped the lips of the Panch. Had it been somebody else, the verdict would have been loud and clear. With nobody willing to earn his disfavour, the landlord sought to turn the situation in his favour. He instead claimed compensation from Maguni for the damage caused to his crops by Maguni's oxen. Though Maguni helplessly begged the forgiveness of the villagers, he nevertheless stammered in an angry tone that he wouldn't mind any thrashing or abuses himself, but any harm done to the oxen would be difficult on his part to digest. The landlord boiled with rage at Maguni's impertinence.

Agriculture is the lifeline of a farmer. A good harvest brings joy in his life; if the yield is not enough to sustain his family, he is destined to suffer for the whole year. There were droughts, floods and famines for the last three years. In the first year there was no rain. In the second year it rained so much that all his crops got washed away. This time the yield was less than what he had expected. The rice stock had already been exhausted; Maguni was at his wit's end. In the bellows of his oxen, he could sense the pangs of hunger. The children had to go to school, but there was not even a handful of watered rice for them to eat. Kaincha had always been a source of strength and support for Maguni. Now she too was helpless. All the poor of the region were in the same boat. The sole source of income was working as daily labourers for the rich. How long could such construction work or laying of roads sustain them? At sunset both Maguni and Kaincha sat on the veranda and reflected of the present state of affairs. Maguni often broke down while wiping tears from Kaincha's eyes. He hugged Kaincha and assured her that he would work hard as a daily labourer to provide for the comforts of his children. He would keep Kaincha as a queen. Troubled by strange apprehensions every now and then, he lost his sleep.

Hundreds of people were leaving the village in search of employment opportunities in states like Andhra Pradesh and Gujarat. There was very little to do locally; even if you got to work, there was very little money for it. In these states there was no dearth of employment. There was less work and more money for the labourers. They paid a good deal of money in advance. It was not possible to calculate how much one would get there, but the village landlord's son was preparing a list of people willing to work there. The sooner you left this village the better.

Kaincha and Maguni were helplessly staring at each other. Their eyes spoke volumes although none of them uttered a single word. They were very well aware of the inevitability of the

Hyderabad option. Before Maguni could express the thoughts lurking in his mind, Kaincha blurted out, "Samaru, Kaenru and others are leaving for Hyderabad tomorrow. We are also going with them, aren't we?" Maguni's whole body shivered in trepidation. His hands were petrified. It felt as if the loving earth beneath his feet was slipping. The sight of his two tiny kids and his oxen in tearful eyes flashed before his eyes. There was no time left to think over and find alternatives. Without thinking much they decided to leave home the next morning. The schooling of his children would be taken care of there, but what to do with the oxen? Who to leave them with? Will they ever look after these animals well? They couldn't be taken along. Kaincha suggested selling them to the village landlord. How Maguni cursed himself for having been responsible for a situation where Kaincha was compelled to suggest such a thing! "Yes, you are right, we are going to leave this village, how will they survive after us? We are left with no option other than to sell them, if we are to sell them, who else but the landlord, will be able to afford to buy them?" It was the same landlord whose farmhand had once flogged them mercilessly. Maguni burst into tears. He ran to the cow-shed. He daren't look in their direction. It felt as if they were also crying though they were animals. They were able to fathom Maguni's agony. Come what may, he decided not to sell them. He will set them free. He untied the tether, stroked their ears and said, "Go, eat whatever is available on the way. Both of you also leave this area and go away."

At midnight Maguni and Kaincha got up and packed their luggage. They would have to reach the station at daybreak. Fifty of them would leave that day. Separation from his oxen pained him more than the thought of deserting the village. As after getting ready they proceeded towards the station along with the children, Maguni felt like having last look at the oxen. He found them there, wide awake. Maguni's heart sank. He felt utterly helpless. Gently patting them on the back, he picked up the luggage and proceeded towards the station.

There were many waiting for the train. Maguni was very

perturbed. Kaincha carried the youngest boy while the elder one was holding Maguni's hand. They were standing beside heaps of bales, bags and a pile of wood. Somebody asked them to remain alert before the train arrived. He instructed them to acquire their seats in different bogies. Many such instructions were given beforehand. Kaincha had never travelled in a train, nor had she seen one properly. Their children, too, were amazed at the sight. Kaincha and Maguni made the children sit and they stood close to each other. Kaincha was holding Maguni tightly to stop him from falling over. Though this physical proximity was thrilling, they were more apprehensive about the days to come in an alien land. Kaincha whispered into Maguni's ears, "Don't you feel awkward; I am feeling so ill ease with the whole thing." Although Maguni shared Kanchan's feelings, he could think of no way out.

After two day's continuous journey first by a train, and subsequently by a bus and a taxi, they reached their destination. Maguni's family was provided with a hut made of unplastered raw bricks with a thin polythene sheet for the roof. There was a straw mat and four brick moulds. One did not need any training for bricklaying, watching it being laid a couple of times was enough. Maguni's job was to dig the soil and prepare the mud by adding water to it. Then his wife and children would pour the mud into the moulds, unmold and put them to dry. One was bound to lay one thousand bricks a day.

Maguni looked rundown from the hard labour of digging the soil. One had to keep working despite extreme weather conditions and lack of food. The younger son was running a high temperature for the last three days. Kaincha felt disconsolate. Maguni found it difficult to remain steady on his feet. His turban kept falling from his head. He missed his oxen badly while picking it up from the mud. Had they been there, they would have helped him in his toil.

At first they used to get two square meals a day as they had some extra money. Now there was not a single penny left. It was hard to take the child to a doctor, harder even to arrange half a loaf of bread for him. The landlord's son had disappeared from the scene soon after pocketing his commission. Neither the kiln owner, nor the manager bothered to listen to their problems. Drunk all the while, they were there just to get their work done. In the meanwhile another batch of hundred people reached there. Maguni would enquire after his oxen from them. He came to know that they were in the landlord's custody and he made them toil day in and day out without adequate food and care. The farmhand behaved cruelly with them as if he was exacting revenge. Agonized, Maguni kept staring at the open sky. He even grew oblivious of his food. It was as if his own children had been abducted by someone. He felt desperate as if his oxen, who were like his backbone, were tormented by someone. The moonlight that was visible through the torn clothing of his dearest wife, showed the feelings that stirred the innermost recesses of Kaincha's heart. Kaincha locked the children in an embrace to protect them from the cold winter. Maguni came closer too. The four of them made a circle and lay there speechless, surrounded by a mountain of unbaked bricks, the artificial warmth of the burning kiln and of the listless breathing of starved bodies. Nobody uttered a word. Suddenly the body temperature of the younger one fell, his tender body turned cold. His innocent cries became quiet forever. The pain of keeping the baby in her womb for ten months seemed so futile to Kaincha. She hadn't grieved the poverty and starvation at her own village that made them learn the lessons of survival the hard way. But today she lost the most precious possession of her life, the purpose of her living. How would Maguni console Kaincha, in what words? He himself was dumbstruck, and didn't find the means to relieve his pain. "No it wouldn't be possible to continue here anymore", he said. They decided to leave for home with the body of the deceased at that very instant. Before the golden rays of the sun could illuminate that darkling plane, they put their belongings in bales and started off. But they could not escape the Accountant's hounding gaze. Another six months of labour would justify the advance they had taken. The contractors forced them to return. The funeral rites were unnecessary for a child, they opined. Maguni wrested the dead body from the drunkard Accountant while the latter was trying to fling it at the kiln. He dug a hole and buried the flower which was yet to bloom. In its own soil a child plays, eats, breathes and grows. How would the parasites in a strange land let him grow? Tears kept streaming down the eyes of Maguni and Kaincha. A helpless father, a labourer, somebody unable to stand erect was Maguni. A mother, who had buried a dear son and was hopelessly uncertain about the future of the other, was Kaincha. The ever-smiling face of the elder son had turned lusterless. Bewildered, he kept staring at his parent's faces.

Maguni's priceless possession was his oxen. They had been reduced to skin and bones from tilling the vast stretches of the landlord's fields. They were no more able to withstand the farmhand's flogging. Their bellowing lacked vigour. They used to eat a few bundles of tender grass, fistfuls of Mahuli (Madhuca longifolia), a kilo oil cake, a couple of kilos fodder – all at one go. Maguni would feed them even if he himself was hungry, be it just with a little gruel. Now they even didn't get enough potable water to drink. If they slowed down a bit, they were thrashed with a seasoned kendu-stick. Blood oozed from their gashes. They were dumb animals, no doubt, but for Maguni they were humane and sensible friends. Now they were rotting in the muddy dilapidated cowshed of the landlord. They no longer were yoked to a plough. Nobody came to them, the tether had been undone. The farmhand came to drive them away. They didn't get up. They stayed put. Livid with rage, he picked up the kendu-stick that was lying there and hit them hard with it. Still they didn't budge from there. He kept showering slangs and blows. So fearlessly they had gone to sleep that they did not rise from their slumber, no matter how hard the farmhand hit them. He became hopelessly desperate when he realized that leaning their heads on the ground, the oxen had gone to sleep forever.

Maguni's eldest son was eight years old. He was in standard two when they had left the village. He would have been in class three by now. Maguni would teach him all that he knew. Kaincha is a blockhead. Maguni married Kaincha for her rustic beauty and also to honour the wish of his grandfather. Maguni's strong physique and amicable behavior meant the world to Kaincha. Maguni was explaining to his son what a tractor was, what the different parts of a plough like the handle, the yoke etc. meant. Just then the thought of his oxen flashed in his mind and rendered him speechless. He could not explain anything to his son. Maguni had read in the books that "Happy is the man, who gets to till his land". He had asked his teacher why his father being a farmer wanted him to study well and become an officer. His teacher had explained to him that the extreme weather notwithstanding, a farmer toiled in his land to feed the world. That made him happy. He experienced a soul-felt joy from it. If he failed to grow crops, he was pained. The land remaining fallow brought tears to his eyes. Maguni could not continue his studies. In spite of his sincere wishes, his father could not let him continue in school. The fundamental principles that governed the world were that those who were already distressed would continuously wallow in filth; the already oppressed would be oppressed further. In order to help his son escape his fate, Maguni's father wanted him to study more and get a government job. In those days paddy, wheat and vegetables were available in plenty. Maguni was in the minor school when their land was acquired for the construction of a reservoir. Only a tiny patch was left. The government took away everything, gave nothing as compensation. Maguni's wishes, his father's dreams- all were dashed into the void. All these thoughts kept troubling him.

For the last eight days the only son was not keeping in good health. Though his parents dissuaded him from assisting them in laying bricks, he did not pay any heed to them. He would put mud dough into the mould – though young in years, he was able to understand his parent's plight. Maguni came running when he saw his son. He held him in his arms. He could not touch his body. So hot was his body with fever that his mother could hardly bear to touch him. They had already lost a son to a fever like this, now the other one was suffering. They were at their wits' end. Ask for money and both the Kiln Owner and the Accountant would go berserk with rage. Maguni and Kaincha were prepared to stake their lives for the sake of their child, but how would they go about it? They took the ailing child to the Kiln Owner and pleaded for help. "If the child is cured, we will work as long as we are asked to; will be there at your beck and call", they entreated. But the Owner turned a deaf ear to their appeal. He tried to dismiss them saying that a common fever like that would soon abate. He harshly asked them to complete laying ten thousand bricks in ten days. Maguni looked back, he saw the pale face of his son and the tearful eyes of his wife, they weighed heavy on him. He fell at the owner's feet. So did Kaincha. The Owner looked around and then nodded his head. But he made a condition- Kaincha would have to share his bed for a night. No... No... Maguni wailed. How can he see her tainted? He asked Kaincha to leave the place at that instant. "We will borrow money from somebody and take the boy to a doctor", he said. But that option had already been explored. Kaincha had asked the neighbours, but they also were an equally impoverished lot. Only a few had essential food items like rice and wheat flour, that too in meager quantity. Some of them were in a similar situation – their children were suffering from various diseases and they too had no one to turn to. Kaincha put her foot down, with folded hands she tried to convince Maguni that her body would not wear out if for the sake of her child she spent one night with the Kiln Owner and made him happy. She asked "I have dedicated this body of flesh and bones to you, my heart is all yours, can't you make this small sacrifice for our child?" Maguni was numb, but at the same time he could not but adore Kaincha's magnanimity, her willingness to make such a sacrifice for her son. He felt as if somebody had set his body on fire. He asked himself, "Will any man on earth ever let his wife spend a night with another man?" But here the life of his child was in question. At this crucial moment he did not know how to save Kaincha from such an awkward position. Maguni was yet to take a decision when the door was locked from inside with the hapless Kaincha offering herself to be devoured. Maguni was shown the door with a few bucks in his hand. The Kiln Owner had set his eyes on

Kaincha since long. Now that she was served on a platter, he wanted to make the best use of this opportunity. Her ragged clothing had covered her chastity. Taking it off there she stood – defenseless in her nudity. Still she tried to resist the advances of the brute with all her might, which only fired the man's lust for her. The night came to an end... so did the game of flesh. Kaincha could not just forget the bestiality of that man. In the twilight before daybreak she freed herself from the Owner's embrace.

In the hospital Maguni attended his son all through the night. How Kaincha might be facing that beast of a person, how troubled her soul would be, these thoughts raked him. Then there was the issue of his son's life. He was diagnosed with a serious case of brain malaria. He fell at the doctor's feet, begged him to cure his son; he prayed to God, but all in vain. The son did not survive. Carrying the dead body of his son, the deranged Maguni proceeded towards his polythene shack. He wasn't crying anymore. His eyes had gone dry since long. The day was about to break. He shouted to Kaincha to come and see her son for one last time. But what he saw there was something that really drove him mad. From inside the burning Kiln Kaincha was saying "My loving son, go back to our village with your father, don't stay here anymore. For Heaven's sake leave now, go away." Maguni rushed into the fire with his dead son, he wished to join Kaincha, to be reduced to ashes with her, to be wiped out from the face of the earth forever. The labourers who had come for the day's work in the nearby kiln, came running and held him back. All the dreams of Maguni Bariha ended there. He wondered as to who sent him into such an exile.

Original Odia: *Dadana*

Mother's Home

Rabinarayan Dash

Translated by **Tarun Kumar Sahoo**

O h, she should have confessed by now what sins she had committed. Whom did she exploit during her lifetime? Whose curse fell on her? Even Death didn't cast a look in her direction. Perhaps, she could explain if she opened her mouth. She didn't open her mouth, only a loud gurgle emerged through her throat. After so much of fervent prayer, her 'life' did not desert her. All the members of the family were upset.

Is death of a person awaited in such a way? Do all the near and dear ones eagerly wait for the death of their loved ones?

Everybody waited eagerly for mother to die. If any strange sound emerged from her room, everyone would rush inside. Did mother pass away? After checking with fingers on the nostrils, they would soon realize that she was still alive. Everybody would return, disappointment writ large on their faces.

The youngest son was upset because his leaves were getting exhausted. He had applied for leave three times, stating mother's illness as reason each time. His firm would not agree to grant him anymore leave. The two daughters wished if mother died during the summer vacation they could participate in the rituals without any hassles. The studies of their children wouldn't suffer much. Both the sons-in-law worked as lecturers in colleges, hence things would be easier for them. Besides, her death would present an opportunity to discuss what mother had actually promised to give them. The eldest and the second daughter-in-law were also getting upset. They were tired of living in the village and taking care of her. They would get the much-needed respite the moment she died. The eldest son was taciturn so it was not possible to know what he really wanted. All said and done, it was necessary for everyone that mother should die soon. After her death, everyone would be free to move on his or her way.

However, although mother was confined to the death-bed for a long time, she was hardly ready to die.

Mother had been ill for the last six years. Initially, her condition was somewhat manageable. With a little assistance, she was able to sit and stand. She was also able to take her food herself. She would use the washroom herself, with assistance though. But, over the last one year her condition had deteriorated. Bed-ridden as she had been, bed-sores had appeared on her body. With the loss of bowel and bladder control, she would defecate and urinate in the bed. Everybody had started feeling disgusted.

But, mother was hardly ready to embrace death.

There was a time when the idea of home without mother was inconceivable. Like a queen she reigned over the entire family. Her three sons and their wives as well as two daughters and their husbands submitted to her dictates without any hesitation or complaint. Everybody eagerly waited for her commands. Nobody had crowned her a queen; she made herself worthy of that stature by sheer hard work. When everybody in the neighbourhood thought that the Tripathy family was going to be obliterated; that the five children had been orphaned, at that time invincible mother gave them the necessary support. She took to herself the act of restoration of the family. When father died, no one even dreamt in their wildest dreams that a lonely woman could manage a family of five children, rear them properly, and manage the home and hearth efficiently. But mother succeeded in all her ventures.

Father who had served as an Amin died of heart attack. At that time the youngest son was only five years old. The eldest sister was studying in a High School. In between, there were two brothers and a sister. Mother felt helpless with five children to take care of. The maternal uncle's family was also not a well-to-do one. Their Grandpa could not do anything other than shedding tears. The relations, instead of lending a helping hand, tried to grab their landed property. As the papers were not in order father's pension was being delayed. The Tripathy Family owned a few acres of arable land, a house with four well-built rooms, an orchard of coconut, mango and jack-fruit trees. Widowhood, so early in life and so untimely, crushed mother's dreams. Everybody feared at that time that she might end her life. But mother, who had not stepped out of her house till then and who had not removed her veil even for once, surprised everybody by steadying herself and preparing herself to bear the burden of the world. With the help of labourers she ploughed her land. She grew vegetable in her backyard. She reared a couple of milch cows. She sold coconuts, jack-fruits and mangoes grown in her orchard. She worked hard, day in and day out. She never bent down before the pressures of children's studies, worries related to daughter's marriage and before the conspiracy of the relations. She employed labourers to mould bricks and built a two-roomed pucca house. She never neglected her children's education. Though not much educated, she knew exactly what was best for whom. The eldest son became a school teacher in a school near their village. The youngest served as an engineer in Bangalore. The two daughters studied well and got married in good families. She accomplished everything smoothly. Without allowing troubles to bend her down, she helped each one achieve what they wished.

The most remarkable thing was that she exerted astounding control over the three daughters-in-law and two sons-in-law. Sometimes Siddharth wondered how mother could keep the snakes and mongooses together; where from she had procured the magic-root that mesmerized everyone.

It was only Siddharth who was disobedient to mother. During his childhood, when father was alive, mother used to tease him by saying 'The eldest belongs to father, the youngest to the mother, and the middle one belongs to none.' Mother would explain to him in detail, 'The eldest brother and sister belong to your father; the two younger ones Subha and Anu belong to me but you belong to none.' Siddharth used to feel desperate. Holding on to mother tightly he would say, 'You are mine.' Mother would laugh and say 'you will be mine only if you study sincerely and mindfully.' However, Siddharth was not much interested in his studies. He could not know whether he belonged to mother or not, because mother was never worried about him as she was about the other four. On his part, he didn't display his love for her by unnecessarily worrying about her. No one knew what invisible bond bound them together.

Before mother became ill and emaciated, the entire world had moved around her. Everything happened just as she had planned. Her eldest son Priyadutta was appointed as a school teacher in a High School, some twenty kilometers away from the village. The youngest son Subhadutta was posted as an Engineer in Bangalore. His wife was also an Engineer there. The two Sisters were married to two lecturers. One lived at Bhadrak whereas the other lived at Rourkela. Only Siddharth was jobless. From childhood he harboured great fear for studies. He loved to wander with friends. For that he was often beaten black and blue by mother. But he didn't mend his ways. Mother often threatened him, "Both of your brothers will become officers soon. If you don't study, you will be left in the village to serve them". Siddharth would feel hurt at his mother's words. He would concentrate on his studies for a few days. But he hardly remembered what he read. His studies came to a premature end when he failed in the matriculation examination. Initially he engaged himself in small business ventures, but later on he set up a rice-mill in the village and settled there. He started earning well. The entire responsibility of the village home and landed property rested on the shoulders of Siddharth. But, whatever Siddharth did he did as per the instruction of his mother. Mother discharged her responsibilities throughout her life, one after another. She took care of the sons and daughters, married them off, took care of the post-marriage ritualistic expenses including the thread ceremony of her grandson. Mother could delve deep into what transpired in someone's mind and made arrangements accordingly. No one ever got the opportunity to complain. Siddharth knew that it was because of their mother, everything was going off smoothly. Otherwise the family would have fallen apart. The youngest brother had purchased a house in Bangalore without informing anyone. The ever reticent eldest brother danced to the tune of his in-laws. He also had purchased a plot of land in Cuttack secretly. Both the sisters eyed the gold ornaments of mother. The cunning youngest daughter–in-law visited the house intermittently and created rift between the other two. She exercised strange control over the eldest daughter-in-law and the middle one by spending some money on them. Relationship among them had started turning sour. Siddarth's wife had started accusing him and taunting him more often for his inability to rise higher in life. Siddharth knew everything. He also knew that mother also had an inkling of what was going on. His otherwise cheerful mother sometimes looked solemn and crestfallen. She would often caress Siddharth's hair affectionately these days while heaving a deep sigh.

Mother's age had advanced, but her responsibilities never diminished. It was as if she had taken charge of all worries of the household. She laboured for the family day in and day out unmindful of everything else. It was as if she was under some spell or father, from his heavenly abode, directed her to take up one task after another. Despite being the owner of a pucca house with four rooms, she lived in the room with a thatched roof. She would often wipe its floors clean with cow dung. Some betel nut trees grew in the backyard; coconut trees were planted on the edges of the land they owned; on the backyard were grown saga and vegetables. In the cowshed, she would rear milch cows. She spent most of her time in their company.

Siddharth reprimanded her at times, "You have grown old; why don't you take rest now? How long will you slog? Instead of taking rest, mother would scold him, "Will you take care of me? Do you have any Jobs to bank on? Do you earn a monthly salary? I care a fig for any one's help. As long as I am active, I shall work and earn my bread, after that you people may take care of me, or shun me. I don't care.

This wish of hers was also granted by almighty. As long as she was active, mother worked; but suddenly, everything got topsy-turvy. Throughout life she never suffered from illness, but this time when she fell ill she didn't recover. In the meantime six years have elapsed. Mother came to this house after marriage when she was only fourteen. She served the family for sixty years; sustained it with her sweat and blood. But in six years everything was spoiled. All the members of the family were worried about one thing. Why wasn't she dying?' She had become a cause of concern for everyone.

Both the daughters-in-law seriously wanted a close to the chapter. The most qualified youngest daughter-in-law worsened the situation with her tricks. The youngest son whom she had raised by cutting down on her expenses, was waiting for an opportunity to run away disowning any duty towards her. The reticent eldest brother did not utter a single word, but silently kept himself away from any responsibility. Both the daughters appeared very worried, but the moment any question of taking up responsibility came, they would find out a way to wriggle out.

But mother simply refused to die.

Both mother and her family went on losing their glitter gradually. Mother lay like a heap of filth in her kutcha-house. During the last six years the otherwise clean house had turned a playground for rats. The boxes from which smell of camphor emerged earlier, produced a stale odour now. The leaves of the betel-nut trees in the backyard had turned yellow without water. Wild shrubs covered the patch of land where she once grew sag. The entire house had lost its essence. Siddharth took one look at mother and then at the house. Like in the case of human beings, such deterioration on the part of the house was perhaps destined. If it was in her destiny to suffer like this, why did she labour so hard? Why was she attached so much to the house?

When mother went through such hellish pain many spoke ill of her. The daughters-in-law discussed what they had heard outside. Like outsiders, they believed that mother was suffering because of some sins.

What wrong had mother done? Maggots had infested her body. The hostile relations added fuel to fire and discussed how she became a widow when she was young? Did she ever fast? Did she ever observe the other rituals associated with widowhood? She had defied the restraints that widowhood imposed. She might have consumed non-veg food or indulged in adultery... That's why she was suffering.

Siddharth didn't want to hear all this. He wondered why people wagged their vicious tongues and spoke ill of her when she was lying helpless on the death bed?

The two daughters and the daughters-in-law wondered where the mother's gold-ornaments were! Where was the money that the mother earned from trees, cows and paddy fields over the years? The eldest daughter suggested – "Let's open the chest."

Everyone suspected the others. Once mother died, the box would be opened and they would be able to know what mother had kept for each of them in secret. They spoke about what she had promised to present each but had failed to deliver on her promise.

They could scrounge through the contents of the box only when she died; but she wasn't ready to die.

Everybody was worried why mother was not breathing her last. The youngest son suggested – "Let us offer some puja to cleanse her soul or send for doctor for consultation".

Others echoed his voice-"Yes, Yes, we have to do something".

Siddharth lost his cool and shouted, "What will you do? Go and strangulate her. At one stroke everything will be over. You depended on her for everything and now you want her do die. From today onwards nobody is required to attend on her. I, the middle son, do not belong to anyone. I have never given her anything, nor do I expect anything from her. Mother had raised this home. She will live here till she rots and her body mixes with its soil. All of you get out..."

A loud 'thud' emerged from the room in which mother was lying. Everybody ran towards it.

Original Odia: *Boura Ghara*

Passionate Tune

Sreekanta Kumar Barik

Translated by **Manoranjan Mishra**

I met him during a cold evening of *Pousa*. I was late to return home that day as I had to attend a seminar in the college. I was well acquainted with the road; so, no matter how late I was, I found nothing to worry. I was riding slow, humming the tune of an old Hindi film song. Something distracted me near the backyard of Mr. Pradhani of Bharat Bahal. I felt as if someone was playing a flute. Applying brakes, I came to a halt. I was always fascinated by the tune of flutes. I lent my ears to find out exactly where the sound emerged from. I realized that the sound emanated from the backyard of Pradhani. I locked the cycle and went towards the source from where the sound came floating by.

Of course, I didn't have any knowledge of musical notes or measures; I simply appreciated the tune. The tune that emanated from there was not an ordinary one but rather sounded heart-rending and pathetic. It shook my very inner being. I moved forward and stopped at a very surprising sight. Sitting on a dry log some distance away, a weak and emaciated man was playing that tune. He was bearded; his long hair ran onto his shoulders. I could not guess his exact age in that darkness. When he saw me, he stopped. He looked at me confusedly. I felt scared. After some time, he motioned me to come near him. I approached him, fearfully. In a choked voice, he asked,

"Are you looking for someone, Sir?"

I said, "No."

After a moment's silence he asked, "Why have you come here then?"

I said, "I was fascinated by the tune of your flute. So I stopped here to listen."

He looked downwards and smiled.

I was taken by surprise. After some time, I asked, "Do you play the flute like this every evening?"

Sighing deeply he said, "No... sir. Whenever I feel like playing the flute, I do so."

He left the place in a huff saying, "It's already late. I have a lot of pending work to do."

I had grown unaware of time. It was late evening. Of course, I didn't feel much cold. I reached home at seven thirty. My mother was restless. She was sitting helplessly on a chair after the long wait. Mother would become anxious whenever I got late. I had to cook stories to pacify her that day.

That day onwards, whenever I came by that village road, I would stop a little. Every day, I would find him sitting on the dry log and giving tune to the pathetic tale of his life. When I reached, he would welcome me with a dreary smile. I realized very soon, he was only feigning a smile. Life was always like that; some smile in sorrow whereas some others smile to express happiness. We would equate each smile as we could never delve into the inner recesses of others.

I would sit by him. When he played the flute, the sky and the earth would shudder. Even breeze would stop blowing, sympathizing with his suffering perhaps. He would continue playing his distressing tune. His eyes would be flooded with tears. For the first time in my life, I could experience the soulful lamentations of a human being expressed through the tune of the flute.

Reaching home after a meeting with him, I would sit thoughtfully. I would feel sick. Why did the man wail when he played the flute? Why did he remain mum most of the time? Many such questions would cloud my mind. Not that I never tried to seek an explanation from him; on most of those occasions, he would fall silent. The inhabitants of the village would say, "He is insane. We hardly have any information on where he goes and what he does." My friends would make fun of me. "You will one day turn mad if you spend more time in the company of that insane person," they would say. When I enquired a shopkeeper about him a few days back, he also retorted angrily, "Hello, sir. Why are you worried about that crazy fellow? He suddenly appeared here one day and started living at the backyard of Pradhani. He would work in his fields, herd the cows etc. Go...go...go, sir... you must be getting late for college."

After hearing the arguments I would ponder why men wore masks of insanity. In this materialistic world, when one was always busy in evaluating one's own gains and losses, where was the time or desire to be concerned about others?

That evening we sat together. I was determined to ask the question that lurked in my mind. Today, I would allow him no respite. Thinking thus, I asked, "Brother, you have never bothered to answer any question that I have asked you till today. You are not willing to tell me your name. You are trying to avoid me with a dreary smile. If my presence is intolerable to you, then I will think of not coming anymore."

The man suddenly got up and looked at the western sky. There was still some time for the sun to set. He sighed deeply and sat back on the dry log. That breath of him was laced with intense pain. After a moment of silence he said, "Sir, I am an unwanted person. The whole world calls me mad; you can also call me by that name. Everybody starting from a child to their parents is scared of me. Nobody wishes to come close. That's why I prefer to live alone. However, this living alone doesn't distress me because I have found a friend in this flute. Whenever I feel listless, I sit down to enjoy its company. It comforts me."

I was not satisfied with his answer. I asked, "Why do you wear the mask of an insane person?"

"What else could I do? This world has designated me crazy. Besides, if people feel delighted at calling me mad, what can I do to prevent them? Said the man with a faint smile on his lips. It was noticeable that behind the faint smile of him a fatal fire razed his soul.

I felt sympathetic. I was confused whether I should proceed with my questioning. The desire to know him thoroughly forced me to go ahead. After some time I asked, "Brother, who else do you have in the family? Why are you living alone and aloof like this?"

Suddenly, his face turned red. He fixed his gaze on the distant horizon. The look reflected his utter helplessness.

"Why aren't you telling anything?"

"What should I tell? This is a land where a common man has lost all rights of living a peaceful life; where the adjudicating judges have been rendered impotent; and where the demand for leading a just life renders a person liable to be declared insane. Therefore, I have deliberately put on this façade."

I felt he wasn't a common human being; a rebel lay lurking within him.

He continued, "Nobody cares for me, sir. Everybody despises me, taunts me by calling me crazy. Everybody in this world is busy with gratification of selfish motives; who would care for me? Today, when you are taking interest in an unwanted person like me, how can I avoid you?"

The man continued without a break.

"I also had a small family. It consisted of Sumati, my wife and me. Piety of several births would fetch one such a wife. At the sight of her face, I would forget all my cares and anxieties.

She was the support on which my life sustained. About two hundred metres on the eastern side of the Sambalpur city station, we lived in a slum. We were not alone there. Many others lived in shanties there. They were amicable, innocent. Whenever a family faced some trouble, they all gathered to help them out. Despite being neck-deep in poverty I felt the bliss of heaven. Sir, can one have golden days forever? One day disastrous thunders landed on our happy families."

"One evening we all had gathered to have a talk. Suddenly, people in two vehicles arrived there. One of the vehicles belonged to the police. Four people got off the other vehicle. One of them held a bundle of papers in his hand. He said, 'We have been instructed to get the slum vacated as soon as possible. Plans have been made that a bypass road would be constructed from the station through this slum. We are here to request you to vacate the slum within a week, without causing any trouble. Please lend a helping hand in successful implementation of the government decision.'

"Just as a traveler shudders at a sudden burst of thunder, similarly we all shuddered at the words of that officer. They all left. We were all anxious. Where would we go? What would we do? The next day we went to the collector, ministers, and leaders. They all assured us that the road would be constructed after we had been rehabilitated. Seven days passed. No alternative arrangements were made. Exactly after seven days, some officers arrived with two JCBs and three truck-full of police personnel to vacate the slum. Announcements were made on the mike instructing us to vacate the place soon. The slum dwellers were seething in anger by then. They came out with lathis in hand and fought with the police personnel. Police lathi-charged. Sir, in the melee, my Sumati..."

He stopped. His voice cracked. I asked, "What happened to your wife?"

"People ran helter-skelter when the police personnel retaliated. My only concern was how to carry Sumati to a place of safety. I was running towards the other side of the road with her. Three or four police personnel were chasing us. Suddenly, she slipped. She fell with a thud on the uneven road where the stones protruded. Her stomach bumped into the sharp stone. She writhed in pain and wailed horrendously. How pitiful her cries were! She was six months pregnant then. The slum-dwellers gathered. She was carried to hospital where she gave birth to a dead child and passed away. It was as if I lost half of my life. News of her death spread far and wide. There was much commotion. Road blockades were organized but to no avail. We were cheated by those who were in charge of justice and administration. My family as well as dreams of a peaceful life was shattered."

Tears welled up in Makaru's eyes. His throat felt parched. His chest heaved. I was completely grief-stricken by then. Keeping my emotions under check, I asked, "Where did all the slum-dwellers go, Makaru brother? He looked at me, wiped his tears, and continued, "Where else would they go? Some of them turned mad like me; some others took shelter in the station or near the godowns; still some others went to work as *dadans* in alien lands. Driven by the whirlpool of time I have reached this place. People identify me as a mad fellow. Pradhani uncle saw something behind my craziness; he has allowed me some space to live here."

Makaru sat silently, with his head bent downwards. I was looking at the evening sky that had turned red at sunset. Patches of cloud floated about. The small patches of cloud resembled hapless Makaru, who ran hither thither to save life, whereas the big patch of cloud hissed like the seven-hooded cobra.

"The stolid wings of heartless hawks of this materialistic world have wounded me. This flute is the fountain of life. This flute strengthened the bond of love between me and Sumati once. When I play this I feel as if Sumati is sitting by me, just as she did in the erstwhile Sulia slum." He once again took a deep sigh and played the flute. How passionate that tune was!

While listening to his tale I found myself lost in a country where thousands of Makarus, in search of a decent life, were rendered hapless. I took some time to return to my senses. I had not marked when the sun had set. Makaru got up and said, "Sir, it's already evening. You will get late. Go home."

I didn't have words to console Makaru. He flashed another wry smile and entered the cowshed. With a heavy heart, I returned home.

Original Odia: *Karuna Raga*

Glossary

Babu:	A Hindu gentleman; A Hindu title of address equivalent to sir, Mr.
Bhai:	Brother
Bhajan:	A devotional song
Bhog:	Food offered to a deity and subsequently eaten by people
Chhenapoda:	Roasted cheese dessert from Odisha
Chuda:	Flattened rice used as snacks
Didi:	Elder sister
Dola Purnima:	Full moon day in the month of Phalguna, the eleven the month of a Hindu calendar
Gulal:	Colours used on the occasion of Holi
Gunth:	Approximately 1089 square feet
Khadi:	Coarse cotton cloth
Khichidi:	Indian food prepared using fragrant rice, ghee, raisins, cashews, black cardamom, and cinnamon
Kirtan:	A devotional song; typically about the life of Lord Krishna
Konark:	Ancient temple dedicated to the Sun God
Kumbhatua:	Greater Coucal or Crow Pheasant

Lungi:	A garment wrapped around the waist and extending to the ankles, worn in countries of South East Asia
Mahabahu:	A form of address to the Lord
Odhni:	A veil used by women to cover their heads
Paan:	Betel cones
Pakhala:	Indian food consisting of cooked rice washed or a little fermented in water
Pala:	A performing art from the Indian state of Odisha
Panchamruta:	A holy concoction made from five ingredients and used in Hindu rituals
Puranas:	Hindu religious text part of the Vedas
Puri:	One of the four major places of pilgrimage for Hindus; famous for Lord Jagannath
Rasogolla:	Indian syrupy dessert made from ball shaped dumplings of cheese
Sarapanch:	The head of a panchayat; a decision maker elected by the people
Shastras:	A work of Sanskrit scripture
Satyagrahis:	Those who participate in protests marked by lack of violence

Authors bio

Achyutananda Pati (b 1926): Odisha Sahitya Akademi award winner for his short story collection *Snayu O Sanyasi*. Also has been awarded with The Atibadi Jagannath Das award, the highest literary award of the Odisha Sahitya Akademi. Started his literary career in 1952. However, he established himself in the late 60s. *Asubha Putrara Kahani* (1973), *Ugrasen Ubacha* (1976) and *Nia Jaluchhi* (1976) are among his best collection of stories. His compassion for the poor and the downtrodden get reflected in his stories.

Santanu Kumar Acharya (b 1933): Central Sahitya Akademi award winning writer. Won the award in 1993 for his short story collection *Chalanti Thakura*. Awarded the Odisha Sahitya Akademi award for his novel *Nara Kinnar* too. Honoured with the Atibadi Jagannath Das award, the highest literary award of the Odisha Sahitya Akademi. Real life experiences, weal and woes of the people, immoral practices prevalent in the society get an apt treatment in his stories. Often takes characters from the Vedas, the Upanishads, the Puranas and the Gita and uses them as symbols. Often drives his protagonists from narrowness of thought towards a greater world-view. *Mana Marmara* (1962), *Durbar* (1965), *Ei Sesha Padati* (1972) among the most significant works.

Manoj Das (b 1934): Internationally acclaimed bilingual writer writing in Odia and English. Won Central Sahitya Akademi award in 1972 for his story collection *Manojdasanka Katha O Kahani*. Received the Odisha Sahitya Akademi award for his Essay-

Criticism titled *Kete Diganta*. Also honoured with the Atibadi Jagannath Das award, the highest literary award of the Odisha Sahitya Akademi. Started his career during the post-independence period. Humane attitude, novelty in selection and treatment of subject matter, blending of intellect and satire, and keen observation of social relationships lent newness to his stories. Kings, emperors, zamindars, and nobles are often the characters in his stories. Collections like *Samudra Kshudha* (1950), *Jibanara Swada* (1950), *Bisakanyara Kahani* (1955), *Manoj Dasanka Katha O Kahani* (1971) have immortalized him.

Binapani Mohanty (b 1936): Central Sahitya Akademi award winning writer. Was awarded in 1990 for her work *Patadei*. Received the Odisha Sahitya Akademi award for her short story collection *Kasturi Mruga O Sabuja Aranya*. Also awarded with the Atibadi Jagannath Das award, the highest literary award of Odisha Sahitya Akademi. She is well-known for the large number of stories written on feminine psychology. Torture of women, the staggering position of women in the family, the various problems women encounter in their day-to-day life find place in her stories. The stories are full of pathos and sorrow. Most of her characters are rebels who refuse to accept things lying down. *Nabataranga* (1963), *Kasturimriga O Sabuja Aranya* (1967), *Kalantara* (1977), *Arohan* (1978) are among her best collections.

Bibhuti Pattanaik (b 1937): Winner of The Atibadi Jagannath Das award, the highest award of the Odisha Sahitya Akademi. Has won more acclaim as a novelist than a short story writer. Wrote about love, romance and other social issues in his short stories. *Anya Keun Bharatbarsha, Upanagarira Rupakatha, Rajakanya O Krushna Sharpa Katha* are among his best collection of stories. Won the Central Sahitya Akademi award in 2015 for his work *Mahisashura Muhan*. Also awarded with the Odisha Sahitya Akademi award for his novel *Aswamedhar Ghoda*.

Debraj Lenka (b 1939): Writes stories on love, romance and modern society. Use of language and style differentiates him from others. He puts more thrust on the use of language than on the subject matter. His prominent works include *Debraj Orchestra, Gotie Baksha Galpa, Gan Aha*. Honoured with the Odisha Sahitya Akademi award in 1993.

Banaj Devi (b 1941): Born in Puri, her stories are expressions of feminine psychology and a social consciousness. She has also written many stories on family life. Her collection of short stories is *Ketoti Sabujapatra*. Recipient of the Odisha Sahitya Akademi award in 2001 and Sarala Puraskar in 2017.

Pratibha Ray (b 1944): Winner of the Bharatiya Jnanapitha award, Ray is the only female Moortidevi Award winner.She has immensely enriched modern Odia literature by her pioneering short stories and novels. Awarded with the Central Sahitya Akademi Award for her collection of stories *Ullanghana*, her notable collection of stories include *Ketakibana, Pratibha Katha Kalpa, Radha ra Bansi, Sailasayini, Hatabaksa* etc. Her stories reflect the spirit of the times, the nuances of feminine psychology, desire for social reforms, compassion for fellow beings, propagation of Odishan culture etc. Her works not only reflect the urban milieu but also delve deeply into tribal life and customs. She is the recipient of prestigious awards like Padma Shri , Odisha Sahitya Akademi , Amrita Keerti Puraskar etc.

Archana Nayak (b 1945): Her stories are artistic transformations of day to day problems and opportunities, joys and sorrows. A comprehensive analysis of human mind, realities associated with feminine existence, conflicts in the society are some of the topics on which she writes. *Anya Nayika, Aranya Abhisara, Bhul Thikanara Chithi, Swapna Godhuli* are the works which have immortalized her.

Ramachandra Behera (b 1945): A compassionate writer, he writes about the present world and the 'other' world. On one hand, he has the life of man which is ridden with troubles and poverty. Man finds himself helpless and aloof. On the other hand, there is his mind and the spiritual world whose workings are not known. Both life and the world are incomplete. The only truth is death. *Dwitiya Smasan, Achinha Pruthibi, Abasista Ayusha* are his famous collections. Won the Central Sahitya Akademi award in 2005 for his work *Gopapura*.

Radha Binod Nayak (b 1945): Shot to prominence in the late 70s. Known for his experiments in subject matter, language and style. In his stories, one always finds an attempt to know man and expose his uniqueness. Man, for him, is an enigmatic entity. He was compassionate towards those who were victims of social discrimination and oppression. Was often satiric about the prevalent system in the society. *Purana Pitula Kanduchi, Anucharita, Apekshara Dinarati* are his notable contributions.

Padmaja Paul (b 1947): Won the Odisha Sahitya Akademi award for his novel *Durg Patanara Bela*. Wrote about the contemporary society. Propriety and impropriety, vice and virtues, right and wrong are certain themes on which he wrote. Gave voice to the oppressed and suppressed. Was a socialist and social reformist. In his stories he is compassionate towards those who find it bothersome to arrange two square meals a day and are exploited by the rich. *Nisiddha Aranya, Apeksha Kara Mu Pheruchhi, Eegalra Nakhadanta* are some notable collections.

Tarun Kanti Mishra (b 1950): Central Sahitya Akademi award winner-2019 for his work *Bhaswati*. Basically an existentialist, his stories were based on family life and the feeling of detachment. Most stories paint the picture of an alienated protagonist. In his stories, he delves deep into the fathomless sea of life and brings to fore its secrets. *Komala Gandhara, Nisangatara Swara, Bahubrihi* are some notable works.

Yashodhara Mishra (b 1951): Awarded with the Odisha Sahitya Akademi award for her short stories *Jahnarati*. Among the few women writers who examined male psychology along with feminine psychology. Most of her stories reflected the helplessness of women, their feeling of aloofness, and their economic problems. Her protagonists are often from higher middle class families. Renowned for the simplicity of their language, one hardly finds any exaggeration in them. *Dwipa and Other Stories*, *Jahnarati*, *Dekhanahari*, *Rekhachitra* are some of her notable contributions.

Satya Misra (b. 1952) shot to fame in early seventies of last century as a pioneer of new wave fiction in Odia. His first volume of short stories 'Bahubachan' was published in 1973 after which he disappeared from the literary scene which intrigued his readers . After a prolonged hibernation, he resurrected himself in 2013 and recaptured the slot vacated by him earlier. His second volume of stories 'Michha Raastara Sata' was published in December 2019. While most of his stories are psychoanalytical , undercurrent of macabre and violence also define some of his popular short stories.

Gayatri Saraf (b 1952): Central Sahitya Akademi Award winner for 2017 for her collection of stories *Itabhatira Silpi*. Has so far authored more than thirteen collections of short stories. Through her stories, she deals with the hopes, aspirations, emotions and experiences of the youth. Her language is intensely poetic. Her stories derive mileage from her deft descriptive ability. Writes stories on the social problems as well as problems that one confronts in the family. *Alokita Andhara, Ainara Janha, Nijaswa Basanta, Bapa Bhala Achhanti* have brought her immense name and fame. She has worked as the Vice-President of Odisha Sahitya Akademi.

Dash Benhur (b 1953): Das Benhur alias Jitendra Narayan Das is a prominent story writer of the 1980s. Most of his stories delineate the relationship between Father-Mother, Husband-Wife, Brothers-Sisters living in a family. Use of common man's language and common everyday experiences dealt with a deft touch make him popular. He mostly writes about the workings an ordinary family, the love and affection that binds the members together and incidents related to common life. *Navi Samudra, Samaya Samparka, Kuhudira Ghara* are some of his notable works.

Manoj Kumar panda (b 1954): In terms of approach and style, Manoj Panda's stories are an exception. Touch of philosophy and fearless experimentation gives readers a unique taste. Absurdity of life, alienation of man, man's existential compulsions and struggles, magic realism, psycho-analysis of characters are his forte. *Hadabagicha, Barnabagicha,* and *Mayabagicha* are the collection of his stories.

Hrusikesh Panda (b 1955): An Indian Administrative Officer, he writes about the sense of vacuum that envelops the modern man. A philosophical approach to life is clearly discernible from his writing. *Rajaputra, Rebati, Bahare Chhidahoithiba Lokatie* are the collections that shot him to immense fame. Recipient of the Odisha Sahitya Akademi award in 1995 and Sarala Puraskar in 2012.

Supriya Panda (b 1957): Her stories are based on life and its experiences. In her stories, she presents a psychological analysis of its characters. Most of her characters are found looking within or inwards. Her stories are expressions of the uniqueness of her thoughts. Most of them look like symbols or sketches. *Nirbana* and *Mugdha Nadi* brought her name and fame.

Bibhuti Bhusan Pradhan (b 1957): *Daha, Prajapatira Ghara* are the well-known story collections. His stories are based on real life experiences. Scenes and sights of the village, his intense desire to stick to the roots, interest in the lives of the destitutes and the downtrodden and a deft touch of pathos add beauty to his works.

Gourahari Das (b 1960): A Central Sahitya Akademi and Odisha Sahitya Akademi award winning writer. He is a novelist, short story writer, dramatist, columnist, journalist, editor, translator all blended into one. The experience that he deals with in his stories is never outlandish. The characters are all very common and can be found everywhere. Every normal human being can relate to his stories. *Akhadaghara, Bharatvarsha, Matikandhei, Ghara* are some of his works that shot up his fame.

Paresh Patnaik (b 1960): A prominent story writer of the late 80s. Selection of subject matter and a startling presentation endear him to the readers. His protagonists live for love and dreams. The heroes are remarkable for their sportive approach to life. At times, they take life as a challenge. *Chhayapurusa, Kathathila* are his remarkable contributions. Received the Odisha Sahitya Akademi award in 2006.

Dipti Ranjan Pattanaik (b 1961): His stories present a blending of tradition and modernity. Society and its norms get adequate treatment in his stories. Often, his keen observation blended with humour differentiates his stories from that of others. *Jane Brahmarakshasara Atmakahani, Koti Brahmanda Sundari, Irsaru Sneha Paryanta* are some of his notable story collections. Received the Odisha Sahitya Akademi award in 2013.

Paramita Satapathy (b 1965): Won the Central Sahitya Akademi award in 2016 for her work *Prapti*. A promising writer of the 90s. Her stories have characters drawn from rich families. Most often, the mentality of the higher middle class and their love and romance are adequately treated in her stories. *Bibidha Aswapna, Bhasakshara, Birala Rupaka* are her notable contributions.

Adyasha Das (b 1969): is the Amazon India bestselling author of the *Chausathi Yoginisof Hirapur: From Tantra to Tourism*. She is best known for her insightful and colourful portrayals of life. Her stories have a rare psychological insight and at the same time, reflective, sensuous and elegant in their observations. She is the author of the short story collection *Bhitaraku Rasta*, poetry collections *Anuchharita* (Odia), *Nemesis and BrassFlowers* (English) apart from academic and non-fiction books.

Manas Panda (b 1972): A young journalist who has carved a niche in the fields of reporting and column writing. Written more than twenty stories. These have been published in magazines of repute. His first short story collection *Bharee Manepade* is awaiting release. The story *Luchakali* translated as Hide and Seek was published in 2002.

Ranjan Pradhan (b 1979): A creative writer and journalist. He is endowed with the ability to fascinate the readers with his unique story telling manner. He has special interest in tribal lifestyle and culture. His campaigns to save River, Hill and Jungle are noteworthy. He has been awarded with the "Yuva Puraskar" of Bharatiya Bhasa Parishad, Kolkatta in 2017.

Kshetrabasi Naik (b 1980): Sub-Editor with a reputed media house. Has been awarded with the Central Sahitya Akademi's "Yuva Puraskar" for the year 2013. Short story collections Dadan and *Sababahaka* are his notable contributions. He has also received Utkalmani Prativa Samman-2016, Kishori Charan Puraskar-2019 besides others.

Rabinarayan Dash (b 1980): A journalist by profession. Works as Assistant General Manager with a reputed media house. Has two short story collections named *Drushyantara* and *Nijaloka*; a novel titled *Dirty Picture*, and two prose collections titled *Kathare Kichhi Achhi* and *Pichhila Tarikha*. He has been awarded with the Katha Nabaprativa award-1998, Kishori Charan Puraskar, Paschima Novel Award, and Odisha Youth Award.

Sreekanta Kumar Barik (b 1990): A young but promising talent. Works as a lecturer in Government Autonomous College, Angul, Odisha. Has already three books to his credit titled *Kabyamancha: Spandita Samaya, Ekabinsha Shatabdira Odia Sahitya,* and *Ramyarachana* (Edited). He has been awarded with the Katha Nabaprativa Puraskar-2014, Sabda Samman-2017, and Prabashi Bhasa Samman (Youth) - 2019.

Translators bio

Bikram Das was formerly Professor of Applied Linguistics at the Central Institute of English and Foreign Languages, Hyderabad. He is well known for his English translations of literary works in Odia, including Gopinath Mohanty's *Paraja* for which he received the Central Sahitya Academy Translation Prize in 1989. He lives in Bhubaneswar.

Snehaprava Das is an eminent poet and translator. She has translated Odia classics including Umesh Chandra Sarkar's *Padmamali*, Ramshankar Ray's *Bibasini* and Pandit Gopabandhu Das's *Kara Kabita* and *Bandira Atmakatha* in English. She has also translated Manoj Kumar Panda's short story collection *Refrigerator re hajaredina* and Central Sahitya Academy winning novella *Prapti* of Paramita Satpathy in English.

Chinmay Kumar Hota has a master's in English Literature from the University of Delhi. He has translated both fiction and non-fiction from Odia to English. His articles and reviews have been published in all major newspapers and magezines in India. He is the author of a book of vignettes *Hits and Misses*.

Bhagaban Jayasingh, a Professor of English, is currently working as Dean, Communication and Digital Media, ASBM University, in the temple city of Bhubaneswar, Odisha. He has produced seven volumes of poetry in Odia and several in English translation. He has translated and edited *Footprints of Fire – The Black Eagle Book of Modern Odia Poetry*. He now lives with his wife Indira at Puri on the eastern coast of India.

Supriya Kar, an Editor and translator, has the rich experience of working as an Editor at Cambridge University Press, India. Currently, she edits the online literary journal *Indian Literature Today*. She translates Odia classics into English and writes fiction and non-fiction both in English and Odia. She received the Charles Wallace Trust Translation Fellowship in 2008. She has edited the works of a number of women writers. Some of the anthologies that she has collaborated on are *One Step towards the Sun* (Rupanter, 2010), *Sparks of Light* (Athabasca University Press, 2016), *Burning Mountains* (Dhauli Books, 2018) and *Contours of Salvation* (Timepass, 2019).

Pravat Kumar Mallick is an academician, research scholar, litterateur and orator. He has retired as Associate Professor of History. He has authored five books for undergraduate students and two reference books for research scholars. Currently, works as Guest Professor at Rourkela Autonomous College, Rourkela.

Kamala Prasad Mahapatra is a writer, critic and translator. He has published short story collections in Odia, poetry collections in English, two edited books of translation from Odia to English. Besides, he has also published three edited text books. He is a former Professor of English and lives in Bhubaneswar, Odisha.

Rajat Mohapatra was an Odisha Education Service officer. He worked as a professor of English in various government colleges of the state of Odisha. He was a renowned short story writer and translator.

Saroj Mishra, a chemical engineer by profession, has published five books so far—one in Odia titled *Sagar Trushna* and four in English titled *Eternal thirst, Castle of dreams, Day of reconing, Australian*

Spring. Besides, he has translated three books titled *Kanhu and Other Stories*, *My Sai My World*, and *Koraput and Other Stories*.

Sunita Mishra is a Professor in the Centre for English Language Studies, University of Hyderabad. She works and publishes in the area of English Language Education, Politics, and History of English in India. Presently she is looking at the History of English Education in Odisha and also working in the area of critical pedagogy. She occasionally translates short stories from Odia to English.

Sulagna Mishra has a PhD degree in French and Francophone Literature from Purdue University, USA. At present, she teaches at the Dept. of Modern and Classical Languages and Literatures, Virginia Tech University, Blacksburg, Virginia, USA.

Gopa Nayak is a bilingual poet, author and translator. Her first collection of poems in English was published in 2011 under the title *Dissension*. Her poems have found place in anthologies of English poetry such as the *Dance of the Peacock* published by Hidden Books Press, Canada (2013) and *Suvarnarekha* (An anthology of women poets in Indian English poetry) published by the Poetry Society of India. "Fire Sermon" is her latest book on feminism with translated stories from eminent Odia writers into English. She has a D.Phil from the University of Oxford. She is serving as the Director of English Language Centre at O.P.Jindal Global University.

Lipipuspa Nayak is an academic, translator, critic of Comparative Indian Literatures and freelancer based in Bhubaneswar, Odisha, India. Specializes in translation of Odia classics (to English), she has fifteen published works. She has been awarded the Government of India National Culture Fellowship (2003-05) for her project "Post-80s Odia Fiction".

Tarun Kumar Sahoo worked as Principal, Subhadra Mahatab College, Cuttack. He has authored seven short story collections in

Odia and one short story collection in English. His translated book *Jainendra Narayananka Kahani* was published by National Book Trust, India. He has rich experience of working as the Editor of Jhankar, a popular literary magazine.

Rabindra Kumar Swain has authored four collections of poetry. He also has three books of translation from Odia titled *Dear Jester and Other Stories, Bahubreehi,* and *The Cemetery Flower and other stories.* He has authored two books of criticism titled *The Poetry of Jayanta Mahapatra: A Critical Study* and *Silent Tongues: Writings in Contemporary Indian Poetry.* His poems have appeared in many international journals.

Sabahat Tabriz joined Odisha Education Service in 1999 and is currently deployed to Ramadevi Women's University as an Assistant Professor of English. She did her PhD from Utkal University, Odisha in translation. Her areas of interest are translation and poetry. She believes that every man is a Curate's egg and prefers to see the pristine side of him.

■